Her brow, milky white beneath the gold, creased in annoyance. "Dash it. I'm not very good at hairdressing."

"Dear me, Juliana. There seem to be a number of things you aren't very good at. Cooking, hairdressing. What else, I wonder?" He leaned back in his chair and folded his arms, pleasurably awaiting her response.

"I'd rather talk about the things I am good at," she said softly.

By God, he did believe she was flirting with him.

"I am all ears."

She struck a pose and her figure curved nicely, despite its unpromising casing of bombazine, then her eyes met his with an expression both come-hither and uncertain.

Definitely flirting, but not very good at it. Did she know what she was starting? He couldn't believe her goal was to bed him, but she played a dangerous game with a master of the sport. He could have her naked beneath him in minutes, and there'd be no turning back. She wouldn't *want* to turn back.

By Miranda Neville

THE WILD MARQUIS
NEVER RESIST TEMPTATION

Coming Soon

THE DANGEROUS VISCOUNT

MIRANDA
NEVILLE

The
Wild Marquis

AVON
An Imprint of HarperCollinsPublishers

This is a work of fiction. Names, characters, places, and incidents are products of the author's imagination or are used fictitiously and are not to be construed as real. Any resemblance to actual events, locales, organizations, or persons, living or dead, is entirely coincidental.

AVON BOOKS
An Imprint of HarperCollins*Publishers*
10 East 53rd Street
New York, New York 10022-5299

Copyright © 2010 by Miranda Neville
ISBN 978-0-06-180870-8
www.avonromance.com

First Avon Books paperback printing: March 2010

Avon Trademark Reg. U.S. Pat. Off. and in Other Countries, Marca Registrada, Hecho en U.S.A.
HarperCollins® is a registered trademark of HarperCollins Publishers.

Printed in the U.S.A.

10 9 8 7 6 5 4 3 2 1

The
Wild Marquis

Prologue

Salisbury
April 1818

The second pint might have been a mistake.

Joseph Merton considered the stairs, which swayed a little. Yet it wasn't every day a man discovered a fortune and the occasion demanded a celebration. He couldn't wait to tell his wife.

A good woman, his wife. He'd thought himself lucky to get her. A humble bookseller's assistant wouldn't normally aspire to a pretty girl with a fine education and a knowledge of his trade. And then there had been the matter of her one thousand pounds. Enough to set him up in London. Certainly he had never expected any more.

Over dinner in the noisy tavern he raised a silent toast to Juliana, with a fondness undiluted by consideration of her more annoying traits. Her tendency to develop contrary opinions was forgotten in the prospect of a greater fortune coming his way.

Not even three flights of stairs could disturb his good mood, though he might have taken a more expensive room on a lower floor had he known what he'd learn today.

Such indulgence would be hasty, he reminded himself. He still needed to lay his hands on the proof. He trusted the old woman was right when she said the vital document would be found among her books. That he wouldn't be transporting several hampers of worthless volumes to London for nothing.

He stumbled on the top step, almost fell into the narrow passage, and crashed against a door, fortunately that of his own room. To his surprise it opened. The books he'd left in neat piles were strewn about the room. He had a visitor.

Joseph knew the man by sight and he knew what he wanted. Cheerful tipsiness faded to chill sobriety.

"Where is it?" the man asked.

Though not physically strong, Joseph was no coward and he tried to fight for his life. He never had a chance. His assailant wielded his knife with ungentlemanlike efficiency.

As his life drained away, Joseph's last thought was for Juliana. He hoped she would be able to manage without him. And wondered if she'd ever learn why he died.

Chapter 1

❧

The Library of the late Sir Thomas Tarleton of Wiltshire, to be sold by order of the Trustees beginning 24 March 1819, at eleven o'clock, by Mr. Sotheby, Auctioneer, Waterloo Bridge Street, Strand.

It was the most beautiful illuminated manuscript ever created. At least that's what Mr. Sotheby's catalogue said. The catalogue also opined that the Burgundy Book of Hours was the most precious object in Sir Thomas Tarleton's vast and storied collection.

The Marquis of Chase found this surprising. He had no argument with the aesthetical judgment, but he was under the impression the manuscript belonged to him.

Cain recalled the last and only time he'd seen it, the family's greatest treasure and, in his father's eyes, its greatest shame. Back then, before he knew better, Cain had regarded the late marquis with a mixture of respect and awe. He'd felt nothing but pride when summoned to the locked muniment room to learn the family secret. Eleven years old and unusually innocent, even for his age, Cain had been enthralled by the beauty of the illustrations, so much at odds with the austerity of Markley Chase Abbey under his father's puritanical rule.

The ladies wore elaborate winged headdresses adorned with gauzy veils that fluttered in the wind and against the shoulders of flowing gowns in glowing green and lapis blue. Even within the constraints of the vellum pages, no larger than a foot tall, the artist managed to convey the textures of the gowns, tempting the viewer to touch, to stroke the costly figured cloth trimmed with rich fur. Cain had been admonished to keep his hands behind his back.

Thumbs caught in the pockets of his waistcoat, the former callow schoolboy and present marquis tipped back in his chair at Sotheby's auction rooms. He stared at the open book from the perspective of an extra dozen or so years, and what felt like a weary century of experience. The volume was a book of hours, a devotional work. The sentiments it aroused in the adult Cain were far from religious. He surveyed the women's bodies revealed by the painted fabrics: small high breasts and swelling bellies.

A combination not often found in nature, he mused, except among the slightly pregnant. It must represent the ideal of feminine loveliness in early fifteenth-century France. Fashion was interesting that way. To look at the portraits from Restoration England, for example, one would think every lady of that era suffered from protruding eyes. Nowadays, Sir Thomas Lawrence, society painter par excellence, portrayed haughty, elegant beauties with eyes that would freeze the bollocks off any man who tried to bed them.

Fortunately fashion lied. Cain knew firsthand that several of Lawrence's subjects were far from cold. Though the ladies of the *ton* might eschew his presence in their drawing rooms, some of their number were more than willing to welcome a marquis, however disreputable, into the bedchamber. Lady or actress, wife or whore, they were all women beneath their garments. And Cain knew the truth that eluded many men. That what made a woman beddable had little to do with the particulars of her appearance and everything to do with what went on in her head.

"*Les Très Jolies Heures.*" A courtly voice interrupted his thoughts. Late in the day, he'd had the dusty book room almost to himself, save for a house porter waiting patiently for him to finish perusing the Limbourg Brothers' last masterpiece, created for a Duke of Burgundy. He righted the chair and stood to greet Lord Hugo Hartley with a curt bow.

"Beautiful, Chase, isn't it?" Lord Hugo was not numbered among Cain's intimates who used his nickname. Few members of the *ton* were. And very few had held an unchallenged position among the elite longer than this octogenarian son of a duke. Cain was surprised Hartley even acknowledged his existence.

"Exquisite," Cain agreed. "Are you interested?"

"Too rich for my purse," said the elderly connoisseur, his voice tinged with regret. "The most important manuscript I've ever seen offered, and all the more desirable since it disappeared three hundred years ago. How extraordinary that Tarleton owned it and no one knew."

Lord Hugo had no idea how extraordinary.

"Where did he find it?" Cain asked carelessly.

"That's what every collector in England would like to know."

"I thought you knew everything."

"The reports of my omniscience have been greatly exaggerated." Lord Hugo's face was as straight as his back but he regarded Cain with a glint of interest. "And you, Chase? I'm surprised to find you in this setting."

"I just wandered in off the street."

Which was true in a way. It would never have occurred to him to set foot in a book auctioneer's premises had the handbill with the name of Tarleton not caught his eye.

"Are you looking for something to read, perhaps?"

Cain gestured at the manuscript that lay open on the table. "Lovely illustrations but the story lacks drama." He thought for a moment, wondering if Lord Hugo might have any useful information. "Markley Chase Abbey boasts a famous collection of devotional works."

"How appropriate for the family of the Saintly Marquis!" Maybe he imagined it, but Cain heard just a hint of derision in Lord Hugo's mellow tone when he referred to Cain's late lamented father, whom most regarded with an admiration bordering on reverence.

"Perhaps I'll buy this one in memory of him."

"I had no idea you possessed such filial piety." Lord Hugo now made no effort to disguise his amusement, justified given the common knowledge that Cain's father had thrown him out of the house at the age of sixteen.

"Just a whim," Cain said. "Besides, the ladies are lovely, and that's very much in my line. It amuses me to think of some French prince slavering over those pretty titties as he prayed."

He spoke with deliberate vulgarity, his reflex when confronted by his social peers. Lord Hugo didn't seem shocked. He looked down at Cain from his six-inch advantage in height, his posture proudly erect despite his years.

"For some reason," he said, "I don't believe you're as completely worthless as you like to appear."

Cain met the keenly observant eyes. "Of course I am," he said flippantly. "Pray don't dismiss my only accomplishment."

He inwardly flinched at a fleeting expression that might have been pity. Hartley said nothing for a while, and when he spoke his voice was matter-of-fact.

"Do you know why Tarleton's collection is to be sold?"

"I imagine it's because he's dead."

"Tarleton suffered from the affliction known as bibliomania, the insatiable hunger for books. The disease, for which no physician has yet found a cure, depleted his estate, and that of many others I could list."

"I think I can buy a volume or two with impunity." Cain grinned. "I'm quite adept at avoiding disease."

"If you intend to begin your book-collecting career

at the most eagerly awaited auction in years," Lord Hugo continued sternly, "you'll need advice."

"Advice? Don't I just turn up on the day and bid?"

"Wiser men than you have contracted auction fever and ended up ruined." Lord Hugo's tone suggested that he wouldn't have to look far to find a wiser man than the marquis.

Instead of dismissing the comment with a laugh, his usual reaction to a hint of disapproval, Cain nodded. "I'd like to know more about the manuscript, and I find myself curious about this fellow Tarleton." He glanced around at the thousands of books lined up on shelves, displayed in glass cases, or merely piled on tables. "He seems to have acquired quite a lot."

"If ever a collector deserved to be described as omnivorous, it was Tarleton. His ability to track down rarities and persuade their owners to sell was legendary."

"How could I learn more? And, of course, protect against catching a ruinous fever."

"Engage a knowledgeable bookseller to consult and act for you."

"Where would I find such a valuable fellow?"

"I'd recommend you call on J. C. Merton of St. Martin's Lane. You'll find all the knowledge you need there."

Knowledge. That was exactly what Cain required, though not in the way Lord Hugo meant. He needed to know why Sir Thomas Tarleton had called on his father at Markley Chase Abbey shortly before Cain's own exile from home.

Was that when Tarleton had acquired the Hours? And if so, how had he managed it? The thought of the Saintly Marquis parting with the book did not fit with what Cain knew of his father's intense family pride. Did the disappearance of the Hours have anything to do with the deterioration of his father's temper? Always a rigid and irascible man, his father had seemed very nearly unhinged in the weeks after Tarleton's visit—weeks culminating in Cain's expulsion from the family. Since then he'd barely spoken with his mother and hadn't set eyes on his younger sister.

Restoring the Burgundy Hours to his family merely required money. By discovering why Tarleton owned it, Cain might win back his family, and his reputation.

Juliana Merton sat in the back room of her bookshop and counted out the coins for the third time. However often she did it, her conclusion remained the same. She wouldn't have enough money to buy the Fitterbourne Shakespeares.

Books that should have been hers had ended up in the library of the loathsome Sir Thomas Tarleton. To prevent them being sold to other undeserving collectors, she needed to earn more in the next month than she'd managed in the entire year since Joseph's death. Customers were scarce at J. C. Merton, Purveyor of Fine and Rare Books.

She reached for the Tarleton catalogue and leafed through it for the hundredth time, torturing herself with contemplation of the rarities Tarleton had acquired by fair means or, more often, foul. Finally she could stand it no longer and drifted off into fantasy.

I intend to make substantial purchases at the Tarleton sale. I'd like you to represent me, Mrs. Merton. For the usual commission, of course.

I'd be honored, Lord Spencer, Juliana replied.

You know my tastes very well. I shall gladly follow your counsel as to the condition and value of the books.

Why, Juliana, wondered, were conversations she imagined so much more satisfactory than any she enjoyed in real life? Sadly Lord Spencer, England's premier book collector, was not in her shop and never had been. And no one had engaged her to act for him at the Tarleton sale.

With no more lucrative prospect in sight, she might as well tackle the long postponed task of cleaning the shop windows, untouched since she'd had to dismiss her servant. Closing the catalogue with a snap she stood up, knocking over the sad little pile of coins. Still clutching the volume, she chased a precious golden guinea as it fell to the floor and rolled out into the main room of the shop.

"Confound it," she muttered. The coin wedged itself between a bookcase and the floor. She had to get down on her knees and use both hands to pry it loose. As luck would have it, she was almost prostrate when the door creaked open to admit her first customer of the day.

The first thing she learned about her visitor was that he possessed a fine pair of boots.

Then he offered a hand. Disconcerted, she accepted the help without thought. As she rose she had an immediate impression of youth and elegance. Not that all book buyers were old and unkempt. Bibliophilia gripped gentlemen of all stripes. But Juliana knew most of the serious book buyers in London by sight, and not one of them sported such effortless masculine grace.

The impression made by his figure withered when she met a pair of crystal blue eyes, scanning her from head to foot with alarming intensity. His scrutiny raised a flush in her pale skin and made her grateful for her high-necked black gown and close-fitting cap.

In the past, when alone in the shop, a man had occasionally made an amorous advance. So Juliana dressed herself in enveloping gowns of a particularly beastly cloth, which managed to be both shiny and ineffably drab. Add the sensible linen cap tied under the chin and covering every strand of hair, and the problem had disappeared. She resembled, she knew, a diminutive nun of more than common virtue, or a small black beetle. Her forbidding appearance was supposed to make book buyers see her as a well-informed bookseller and forget she wasn't a man.

With this visitor it wasn't working. His gaze told her he saw through her disguise and knew she was young, blond, and female. Lord, she wouldn't be surprised if he saw through her garments. She'd never encountered a man who exuded such raw seductive potency.

With little knowledge of the species, she had no difficulty recognizing a member of it. This was a rake.

For no reason at all, she was a little breathless. She dropped her eyes and realized her hand was still in his. Even through a glove his grasp gave her a jolt. She almost snatched away her hand and stepped back a pace or two.

"Good afternoon." His low-pitched voice made the ordinary greeting a caress.

Giving herself a moment to recover her composure, she stooped to retrieve the catalogue from the floor.

"Welcome to J .C. Merton," she said. "Can I help you?"

"I don't know. Can you?"

"Why don't you tell me what you want and I'll see what I can do?"

"How can I resist such an offer?"

His smile sent shivers through her. He was flirting with her, and she was alarmed by her instinct to reciprocate. She wasn't sure she hadn't already. He seemed to have found her last answer provocative.

"Are you looking for a book?" she asked, trying to sound stern.

"I'm looking for Mr. Merton. Is he available?"

"I'm the only one here," she answered, her usual cautious response.

"Are you sure you don't have someone hidden away in the back?"

"As I said, I'm the only one here." Then, since discouraging an obviously prosperous customer was hardly in her interest, she indicated her shelves. "I'd be happy to help you find your way about the stock. Are you looking for something in particular?"

"I am looking for Mr. Merton. J. C. Merton," he said with a twinkle of blue. "Are you J. C. Merton?"

"I am Mrs. Merton," Juliana owned.

"Ah, but are you J. C. Merton?"

Usually Juliana managed to engage a new patron for a while before revealing herself as the owner of the shop. By that time a buyer might be impressed enough with her knowledge to forgive her sex. "Yes, I am J. C. Merton, the proprietor of this establishment," she said with a ghost of a sigh.

"Why on earth didn't you say so at once?" demanded the stranger with a touch of exasperation. "I apologize for my obtuseness but I was expecting you to be a man."

"They always do."

"Do they?" he asked. "And what do 'they' do when they find out that J. C. Merton is a female?"

"Often they leave."

"Very foolish of them. I am distressed. I have descended to the banality of 'them' and I try never to be commonplace. And now I think of it, Lord Hugo didn't use a pronoun when he recommended I come here."

"Lord Hugo Hartley sent you?"

"He did. I assume that Lord Hugo knows that J. C. Merton is a woman."

"Of course. He was always one of our best customers and has remained so since my husband's death."

The stranger picked up on the chagrin in her statement. "But not everyone has been so loyal?"

Juliana gritted her teeth. "Loyalty doesn't enter into

it. Lord Hugo is wise enough to realize that my stock is superior and my taste impeccable."

"I infer that others are not as sensible."

"There are some gentlemen," she said grimly, her grip tightening on the buff boards of the volume she still held, "who don't believe a woman can know enough about rare books to serve their needs."

"That looks like the Tarleton catalogue you are holding."

"Yes."

The stranger's eyes glinted like polished sapphires. Juliana felt a little dizzy.

"I understand there are some fine books in that collection. Many fine books."

"Sir Thomas Tarleton," Juliana said, "was adept at acquiring the best."

"Did you know him?" he asked.

"My late husband started as a bookseller in Salisbury, so naturally Sir Thomas was a customer. I grew up a few miles away."

"But did you know him yourself?"

"I can safely say that I am intimately acquainted with Tarleton's methods as a collector," she said, trying not to let her bitterness show.

"Good. You're engaged."

"Engaged? Engaged for what?"

"To represent me at the Tarleton auction."

"Really?" she asked. The day had taken a turn for the better.

The change in Mrs. Merton's attitude was comical. She had been buzzing with irritation, like a wasp emerging from an inkpot. Now she smiled and looked pretty. Cain wasn't surprised. He'd noticed at once that she wasn't a bad-looking woman. Under her monstrous mourning gown lay a slight but trim figure. A strand of fair hair had escaped the hideous cap, and the unrelieved black set off a fine complexion, marred or enhanced by only a sprinkling of fine freckles across the nose.

He shouldn't have tried to flirt with her, he supposed. His initial examination had alarmed the little woman, respectable merchant that she was. But now she regarded him as though he were the answer to a maiden's dream. He was used to that look. Though usually from those who weren't exactly maidens in the technical sense.

For a moment he considered finding out whether he'd been right about the promise of that body disguised by a forbidding exterior and dry-as-dust occupation. He estimated how long it would take him to persuade her out of the abominable bombazine.

"I'd be happy to give you the benefit of my experience," she said. "For the usual commission, of course."

He burst out laughing. "I was about to offer the same thing to you, madam. And my usual commission is nothing."

Mrs. Merton frowned and returned to wasp mode, glaring up at him with a mixture of indignation and puzzlement. With hands on her hips cinching in the voluminous gown he could see that she was, as suspected, petite but nicely curved.

"No commission? I may be a female but surely the laborer is worthy of her hire? You won't get better advice anywhere in London and you certainly won't get it without paying for it."

"Very well, the usual commission," he agreed. "And what do I get for it?"

"Is there something particular you wish to buy?" she asked with a frown of concentration. "If it's outside my area of knowledge I'll tell you."

"A manuscript. A book of hours."

"The Burgundy Hours? *Les Très Jolies Heures*?"

"Those are the ones. The Very Pretty Hours."

"Do you realize, sir, how much it is worth? I wouldn't be surprised to see it sell for two thousand pounds, or even more."

"I think you're tactfully asking whether I'm good for the blunt. The answer is yes. Allow me to introduce myself, madam. I am the Marquis of Chase."

Mrs. Merton seemed unabashed by the revelation that she was alone with London's most disreputable peer. Perhaps she'd never heard of him. Or maybe she was too excited at the thought of his intended purchase. The anticipation in her eyes recalled a pointer spotting a pheasant.

"My lord," she said triumphantly. "You need me."

"I do," he agreed, "though I'm not sure why I can't just march into the auction, stick my hand in the air, and buy the thing."

"Do you play cards?" she asked.

He nodded.

"And do you reveal your hand to your opponent?"

"Of course not."

"Think of the auction as a game of whist. You just

showed me all your cards. I pray you won't do so to anyone else."

For once Cain had a goal more important than his own pleasure. He'd ignore—or perhaps postpone—the pursuit of a woman and take her advice. He'd play his cards very close to his chest.

Chapter 2

"**C**hase!" Arthur Nutley's tone was deep with disapproval. "My dear Juliana, you cannot be serious."

"Oh, but I am," replied Juliana, refilling his teacup. "*He* may not be serious. Indeed I doubt that he is a serious man. But he's all I have if I intend to maintain a presence at the Tarleton sale. No one else appears willing to retain my services and I don't have the resources to bid on my own account."

Arthur was in as close to a state of agitation as the dignified tradesman ever reached. She winced as he waved his cup around. They were seated at the table in the rear of her shop, surrounded by bookcases. One splash and a valuable volume could be ruined.

"Chase is not a reputable man. He is notorious for his wretched morals and never received in respectable houses."

"And do you turn down the custom of those whose morals don't live up to your standards?" Juliana asked.

"That's quite different. I am not a lady."

"Neither am I, Arthur, in the sense that I engage in trade."

"You are a lady in every sense of the word!"

Arthur was fascinated by the gentry to whom he sold visiting cards, expensive hot-pressed writing paper, and engraved invitations on heavy stock. He imitated their accents in his speech—not very successfully—while pretending to decry their morals. Juliana wondered if he'd be quite so anxious to marry her if he knew the whole truth about her birth.

"Since I prefer not to starve, I must take my customers in whatever guise they present themselves."

Arthur put down his cup. Her relief at the loss of danger to her books was muted when he reached for her hand instead. His was fleshy and slightly damp. "Your year of mourning is almost completed and then, as you know, it is my deepest hope that you will allow me to take care of you."

She pulled away. Not that she wasn't, in a way, fond of Arthur. He came once a week to help her with bookkeeping, and their teas afterward were almost her only purely social interactions. But his heavy hints about his intentions were becoming impossible to ignore.

If she had any sense she'd have him, and unless things improved she might have to. His business was vastly more prosperous than hers, and his wife would, as he'd made clear on numerous occasions, want for nothing. Except privacy, independence, and an interesting life. He'd never allow her to continue in her own trade, seeing it as an affront to his abilities as a provider. Instead she'd be helping him sell stationery in the Strand and producing a crop of little Arthurs to follow in his footsteps.

The thought of sharing a bed with Arthur made her queasy. Joseph's demands in that area had been moderate, if dull. He wasn't interested in much aside from books.

The look in Arthur's eye when he delivered his clumsy wooing suggested he might be demanding in the bedroom. On occasion, during her marriage and since, she'd wondered if there was more to that side of things than she'd discovered with Joseph. Surely there must, else what were the poets writing about? She'd never woken in her husband's bed feeling like Juliet on her wedding night, desperate to deny the arrival of dawn.

She glanced at Arthur's wet mouth and shuddered.

"I can take care of myself," she said firmly. "You need not fear any danger from Lord Chase."

A fleeting vision of flashing blue eyes was hastily repressed. Her relations with Chase would be strictly business and conducted standing on her feet.

Arthur wouldn't leave the subject alone. "To be seen in the man's company is to court gossip and disgrace."

"You exaggerate," Juliana replied. "When I accompany him to the auction rooms people will view our association precisely as it is. I am a bookseller and he is a collector. He will employ me for the advice I can offer and no other reason."

"Chase a collector! Actresses, singers, and lightskirts are the only things he has ever collected."

"Great booksellers make great collectors. Under my guidance that is what the Marquis of Chase will become."

It wasn't a bad idea, Juliana thought. The commission on the Burgundy Hours would be large, enough to let her buy at least some of the Shakespeares. But if Chase could be persuaded to wider purchases, she could earn enough to make acquisitions for stock at the Tarleton sale. That would place the world of London booksellers and buyers on notice that the widow Merton, her sex notwithstanding, was a force to be reckoned with.

And she wouldn't have to even think about marrying Arthur.

She drifted into an agreeable fantasy of her shop thronged with well-to-do cognoscenti. She really must get those windows cleaned.

"Juliana?"

"I beg your pardon, Arthur. My mind was wandering."

"I am worried about you."

"There's no need."

"The Marquis of Chase is reputed to be irresistible to females."

"Oh really, Arthur," she scoffed. "He's nothing out of the ordinary. I can't even remember exactly what he looks like." And truly, she couldn't now recall his features or his height or the color of his hair.

Just a vision of piercing blue eyes stripping her naked.

"I am in no danger of succumbing to the advances of such a rake," she said, shaking off the last image

and fixing her thoughts on that commission. What did
blue eyes matter in comparison to a really important
manuscript? "I may assist Lord Chase in forming his
collection, but I have no intention of becoming part
of it."

Juliana turned the corner into Waterloo Bridge
Street, grateful for the slight relief from the cold east
wind whistling down the Strand, and looked for her
new patron. Two gentlemen stood in conversation outside Sotheby's premises, both too tall to be the marquis. She felt a twinge of anxiety; Lord Chase hadn't
given her an impression of excessive reliability.

Unease mingled with irritation as she drew near
enough to identify the pair.

God in heaven! Mr. Iverley of all people! Tarquin
Compton she could stand. He'd been polite on the
occasions he'd visited her shop, even bought a few
volumes of seventeenth-century poetry. He now
acknowledged her with a bow. Sebastian Iverley
was a different matter. He peered at her through
gold-rimmed spectacles and apparently hadn't yet
recognized her. If he deigned to acknowledge her
presence at all, it would be with snide astonishment
that she ventured within three streets of the Tarleton
collection.

The proof of her supposition was postponed by the
express approach of a town coach painted brilliant
red. The matched pair of blacks drew to an exact halt
at the entrance to the auction rooms. A footman in
red and black livery was perched behind, but the door
opened without the servant's help. Juliana glimpsed

a padded interior of what looked like black velvet as Lord Chase, disdaining the step, sprang to the ground with the grace of a large cat.

"Mrs. Merton. I trust I haven't kept you waiting. It's devilish cold. I should have thought to pick you up." It came back to her how the foggy timbre of his voice imbued a commonplace courtesy with sensuality.

"I've just arrived," Juliana murmured, nodding in approximation of a masculine bow. She never curtsied to her customers. She wasn't attending a ball.

The marquis smiled at her, and Juliana noticed his mouth. The lower lip was fuller than its partner. And not at all wet. Really, she ought to look away. She'd given herself a strict lecture on the importance of seeing Lord Chase as a book buyer and only as a book buyer.

On the other hand she'd had trouble recalling his features to mind. It was very important to be able to recognize a customer. Essential. She should memorize his face.

Mr. Compton regarded the marquis's coach with disfavor. "God's breath, Chase," he said. "What is that? I've never seen anything so vulgar."

Chase's grin carved twin slashes on either side of his face, throwing his cheekbones into relief. Just looking at him gave her a shivery feeling in the pit of her stomach.

"You don't like my new coach, Compton? Never mind. It isn't you I'm trying to impress. The ladies love it." He pinpointed Juliana with a flash of blue. "What do you think, Mrs. Merton?"

"It's beautiful," she said. "The coach."

"You see?"

Mr. Compton raised an eyebrow. "Why a coach? Why not a curricle? If you must make a spectacle of yourself, at least let it be with a sporting vehicle."

"I don't care for that kind of sport. I prefer a closed carriage. An open one is so . . . limiting. And I don't like to drive myself. I prefer to have my hands free for other activities." He seemed thoroughly pleased with himself, and it struck Juliana that his aim was to shock as he stood laughing, his greatcoat blown open by the wind to reveal his beautiful tailoring.

Not that anyone appeared well dressed standing next to Mr. Compton. But while the latter's garments seemed sculpted to his tall form in exquisite understatement, Chase, a good six inches shorter than the dandy, wore his with an air that bespoke careless enjoyment and a desire to please himself and anyone else who happened to observe him.

"What are you doing here, Chase?" Compton asked. "Not your usual milieu I should have thought. Precious few"—he glanced at Juliana and changed whatever word he'd been about to use—"ladies to be found at a book auction."

Iverley, who had been staring into space, oblivious to the presence of either marquis or carriage, grunted something that sounded like "A good thing too."

"I've come to buy a book, of course," Cain said.

That got Iverley's attention. "What book?"

Juliana stepped in before her client could say anything indiscreet. "Lord Chase wants to see the Tarleton Caxtons."

Iverley ignored her, of course, but regarded Chase

with a glimmer of interest. Or perhaps it was his spectacles catching the light. "I don't believe we've met."

Compton intervened. "Chase, let me introduce Sebastian Iverley. Iverley, this is Chase. And you must already know Mrs. Merton. I daresay you've been in her shop."

Iverley grunted again. "I have," he admitted. "She still has some decent books left from before her husband's death."

Then and there Juliana swore to herself she'd never sell a book to Iverley, not if he crawled the length of St. Martin's Lane and his money was the only thing between her and the workhouse.

"I can't wait to see the indecent books she has acquired since," Chase said, then paused, smiling at Iverley with a look of pure innocence. "Mrs. Merton has kindly agreed to guide me through the Tarleton collection and help me decide which book to buy."

Instead of being shocked or insulted by the indecent books remark, Juliana had the oddest desire to laugh. And he hadn't mentioned the Burgundy Hours. Maybe the man could be taught.

"I wouldn't have thought you were interested in books, Chase." Compton spoke with his habitual languor, but Juliana thought she detected an edge in his tone.

"I may have been untimely ripped from the bosom of Eton, but I can read, and I do so on occasion. I like to read in bed, when I have nothing better to do there."

"I should think you must get through one, maybe two whole books a year."

"Did I mention that I like to read aloud?"

Compton raised his aquiline nose and dark eyes to the leaden sky. "It's useless to expect a serious answer from you, Chase. You apparently can't move beyond one topic. Shall we go in, Sebastian?"

Juliana watched the two men disappear into the auction house, presenting a comical contrast between the elegant Compton and Iverley's scarecrow figure.

"An odd couple," Chase remarked. "Iverley doesn't seem to be one of your admirers."

"Mr. Iverley has no time for women."

"What a fool! And Compton?"

"Mr. Compton is always polite. As one would expect of Lord Hugo Hartley's great-nephew."

"I didn't know of their relationship."

Which was, Juliana thought, strange. From her scant acquaintance with the small world of the nobility, everyone knew each other and who was related to whom. Indeed, most of them *were* related to each other. Chase, it appeared, existed outside the circles to which he was born.

Messrs. Iverley and Compton might come from the highest families, yet one thing they shared with her. They were dedicated and knowledgeable bibliophiles. The challenge presented by her own client seemed greater than ever.

Fortunately she had a plan.

"Well, Mrs. Merton," Chase said. "Shall we go and look at that manuscript? I promise to listen to everything you have to tell me about it."

"We won't look at the Burgundy Hours today."

"Why not?"

"Because we don't want other bidders to know it's

the only thing you're interested in. We'll view a variety of other books. The most important books are saved for the last day of the sale. The big collectors must plan their earlier purchases so they have enough for the items they want at the end. I trust your assertion that you are a wealthy man?"

Chase nodded. "Without wishing to boast I'd say I can match most of your 'big collectors.'"

"And no doubt everyone is aware of it. If they know you are after one thing, others can husband their resources to bid against you. We need to keep them guessing so they don't know how to plan their strategy."

"This is fun." He thought about it for a moment. "Once I bid, or you bid on my behalf, they'll know it's me."

"True, and if we think it necessary we can set up a secret signal with the auctioneer."

"A secret signal?" He glanced down the street and his voice dropped. "What kind of signal?"

"Well," Juliana suggested, "you could remove your snuffbox from your pocket when you wish to bid, and take a pinch of snuff when you're ready to stop."

"Oh dear," he said despondently. "That won't work. I never take snuff."

"We can think of a different signal," she assured him, then she saw he was making fun of her. His eyes flashed an azure glow while his smile, broader than she'd yet seen, revealed straight white teeth and reintroduced those devastating creases at the cheeks. It struck Juliana forcefully that Chase's reputation as a rake was likely neither exaggerated nor undeserved.

A woman would find it hard to resist his attentions. She experienced some difficulty herself and he wasn't even out to impress her in that way. Why would he be? She was a shabby little black beetle of a tradeswoman and hardly counted as a female.

And that was a good thing, she told herself sternly. The Marquis of Chase was her ticket to acclaim as a powerful and respected bookseller. Being distracted by his undoubted physical appeal was a waste of time.

"Let's go and look at something expensive," she said.

Cain had heard those words before, and from women, but he doubted Mrs. Merton's idea of a luxurious bauble had much sparkle to it. Fifteen minutes later he found himself seated on a hard chair in front of a green baize-covered table, staring at three ugly volumes.

"And what is so marvelous about these?" he asked.

She cast him a furious look. "Keep your voice down," she muttered. "We don't want everyone to hear."

Since the room was packed, their chairs jammed against each other's and their neighbors', he couldn't see how their conversation could be private. But every man appeared absorbed in the examination of books. Not reading, merely looking at them. Some leafed through volumes a page at a time in a measured rhythm, too fast to take in even a word or two from each page.

It all seemed very strange to Cain, who'd spent much of the past half-dozen years backstage in London's theaters. The studious solemnity of these book buyers couldn't have presented a greater contrast to the bright costumes and cosmetics, the gaudy make-believe of thespian life. Oddest of all was the lack of females. His companion was the only woman in the whole place.

The book in front of them was bound in dirty brown leather. With a reverent air Mrs. Merton opened the dull brass clasp that held the covers closed and turned to the first page, careful not to crack the spine.

"What is this?" he asked.

"*The Chronicles of England,* printed in 1480 by William Caxton, the first English printer." From the veneration in her voice he was supposed to be impressed.

"I can't read it. It's in gothic type."

"You're not supposed to read it." She looked at him with droll astonishment.

"It's a book. Books are meant to be read."

She raised a hand as though to shield it from his impertinent gaze. "It's far too precious to read." Surprise turned to disbelief. "You do know who Caxton was?"

As it happened he did, but he preferred to tease her. "I do now. A very important man who printed very ugly books."

"Perhaps Caxtons aren't for you. You are more interested in literature than pure historical significance. What kind of book do you like to read?"

"I may only have time for one or two a year, but I do enjoy the theater. What about Shakespeare?"

"Are you sure? Tarleton's collection features many less common playwrights."

"Less common because less good, I imagine. Why not stick with the best?"

"Of course." It might be his imagination but he didn't think so. The enthusiasm dropped from her voice. She held up a hand to summon a porter. "Please bring us the folios."

Up to that moment Cain had played along with Mrs. Merton's game of deceiving spies about his true goal at the auction. He was also amused by her efforts to persuade him to other purchases. But the name Shakespeare affected her and he was curious to know why. If he had to spend the day in this dreary place, he might as well have a little mystery to solve.

She seemed calm enough while she explained that the four large volumes bound in red leather were the first collected editions of Shakespeare's plays, the earliest printed in 1623, only a few years after the bard's death.

"They belonged to Sir John Vanbrugh and disappeared after his death. Tarleton managed to track them down."

"How did he do that?" A prickle of excitement crept up Cain's spine.

"He was clever that way." Her pretty Cupid's bow mouth compressed into a pout. Mrs. Merton wasn't telling him everything she knew. He needed to pursue this line of inquiry, though perhaps not in the middle of a crowded room.

He picked up the First Folio. A spasmodic flutter of her hands suggested she was terrified he'd drop the precious object. Just to provoke a reaction he jounced it up and down in one hand. "It's heavy, rather too big for reading in bed. And the print is small. I'd have to hold a candle to assist my poor eyesight and I might spill wax on it."

He thought she'd snatch the book away but she managed to restrain the impulse. Mrs. Merton wouldn't make a good cardplayer. Though she tried to look inscrutable, her emotions were written on her face and she appeared to undergo an internal struggle. Then her eyes, which he'd dismissed as hazel but now noticed were an attractive moss green, gleamed with enthusiasm.

"Would you consider buying the folios?" Eagerly calculating that commission, no doubt.

"I might. But if I'm not allowed to read them, could you explain why I want them?"

"The First Folio is the first edition of many of Shakespeare's plays. Scholars find it important because they are used to establish the correct text."

Launched into her subject, she fairly quivered with eagerness, incidentally rubbing her thigh against his in an enjoyable manner.

"Poor old Shakespeare," he said, ousting an enticing vision of what might be so thoroughly hidden beneath the yards of black material. "So his works weren't published during his life?"

She hesitated before answering. "Less than two dozen of the thirty-eight. They were printed in individual volumes known as quartos." Her voice had changed again. It seemed almost deliberately flat, in marked contrast to the fervor with which she'd described other books.

"Do you have any of these quartos?" he asked the hovering porter.

A few minutes later a pile of squarish, slim volumes, perhaps a dozen in all, were deposited in front of them. And there was no mistaking Mrs. Merton's displeasure.

Juliana cursed silently. Resisting her efforts to steer him in a more convenient direction, Lord Chase had, just like a man, unerringly settled on the books she wanted for herself. She did her best to point out their undesirable features.

"Many of them were copied from promptbooks, or even taken down by members of the audience. It means the texts are often inaccurate." She selected a volume from the center of the pile. "This is a bad quarto of *Hamlet*."

Chase growled, drawing curious glances from their neighbors. "Bad Quarto. Down, sir," he said.

She frowned at him.

"Sorry," he said, "but it sounds like a name for a dog. What's so bad about it, anyway?"

"Did you ever hear the line 'To be, or not to be, I there's the point'?"

"Intriguing. Are there any good ones? What about . . . that one?" he asked.

The man had the eye of a magpie, for he'd honed in on the volume in the brightest binding. She'd always loved the soft green calf that covered her very favorite book.

Her hands shook a little as, for the first time in years, she opened the front cover to reveal a penciled signature. "Cassandra Fitterbourne, 1793." The sight of it had never failed to make her heart leap. Without thinking she traced her forefinger under the name.

"Who was Cassandra Fitterbourne?" Chase asked. The alert tone of his voice told her she'd roused his curiosity. Her client wasn't as foolish as he liked to pretend.

"A former owner, I suppose," she replied, striving for nonchalance.

He gave her a look that suggested he wasn't entirely satisfied with her answer, then turned back to the book.

"What does that mean?" He indicated the annotation beneath the signature: "xx/je/t."

"It's a price. Booksellers and collectors often use a code to record what they paid for a book."

"How much?"

"I don't know the code." That at least was true.

"What play is it?" Chase picked up the book and flipped through the binder's blanks to the title page. "*An excellent conceited Tragedie of Romeo and Iuliet*," he read. "I think I'll buy it."

Juliana couldn't stand it. She snatched away the volume and clasped it to her breast. "Don't you dare!" She realized she'd raised her voice, and reduced it again to a furious whisper. "You shouldn't be allowed to buy books if you don't treat them well. These are important and precious volumes. Can't you take anything seriously?"

The marquis didn't respond at once. A certain hardening about his mouth, bleak eyes scanning the room, told her he was displeased. This was no way to treat an important customer. Joseph would never have been so foolish. Carelessly she'd let her disdain show and annoyed him.

"My lord," she said, touching his sleeve to reclaim his attention. "I apologize . . ."

He looked back at her, and in a mercurial switch his eyes seemed to laugh.

"No apology needed," he assured her. "I don't pretend to be a serious man but I would like to hear what you have to say about Shakespeare. I find myself intrigued by the previous owners of the books. Do you suppose Cassandra Fitterbourne owned the *Romeo and Juliet* because she was herself a 'star-cross'd' lover'?"

"An agreeable speculation," she replied with as much composure as she could muster. Not only had her client shown a surprising knowledge of Shakespeare, he'd also asked the question about Cassandra Fitterbourne that Juliana would like to have answered for herself.

She feared she hadn't succeeded in deflecting Chase's attention from the Shakespeares. Well, he couldn't have them. They were hers by every moral right. He could have the folios, but she wasn't going to let him get his careless hands on the quartos, especially Cassandra's *Romeo and Juliet*.

Juliana considered what she knew of Lord Chase's tastes. He had a showy red carriage with velvet seats; a scorn for important books in dull bindings; and a reputation as a rakehell. She had his measure and knew just the book for him: a French edition of Aretino's *Dialogues*. Bound in red morocco gilt. With illustrations. Let him get one look at that bawdy classic and he'd forget all about her humble quartos.

"I've thought of another book that will interest you, my lord." She looked around for a porter and found none available. "Please wait while I fetch it."

Left alone at the table, Cain pondered Mrs. Merton's reluctance to let him buy the Shakespeares. He examined each volume, looking for Cassandra Fitterbourne's signature. Several of the volumes were inscribed with the initials "G.F." but apparently only *Romeo and Juliet* had belonged to the lovely Cassandra.

Lovely? She was most likely a prim spinster of a literary bent.

Sebastian Iverley took the next seat and muttered a distracted, though civil greeting. Either the bespectacled bookworm was unaware of Cain's unsavory reputation, or he didn't care. Cain subjected him to a rapid assessment. Iverley might dislike women, but Cain wasn't receiving any of the signals occasionally sent him by men of different tastes.

"Tell me, Iverley," he asked. "Do you know of a book collector named Fitterbourne? Cassandra Fitterbourne?"

Iverley frowned. "Not Cassandra. George. From Wiltshire. Died three or four years ago. Tarleton bought his collection."

"Could Cassandra have been his wife? Or perhaps a daughter?"

"I never heard of any wife or daughter," Iverley replied with a note of approval, as though any man should be congratulated on the lack of female appendages. "And women don't make good book collectors."

Iverley was a fool. Cain knew women's brains worked just as well as men's, merely in a different manner, one he understood and appreciated. During the past hour he'd seen enough of Mrs. Merton to judge that she knew her subject well.

She certainly knew a good deal about Sir Thomas Tarleton, which was after all the whole point of his presence here. He would enjoy getting the information out of her, since she was quite lovely herself and, he was beginning to suspect, far from prim.

He relaxed in his seat and watched her thrust her way with single-minded determination through the crowd of men, to whom she was, apparently, invisible. Were they all blind? Speaking for himself, he found the view of her excessively well-formed derrière, swaying with unintended lure, most enjoyable. And appreciated the irony that he had managed to engage the only female bookseller in London.

Chapter 3

Juliana was headed for a red morocco binding behind the doors of a glass-fronted bookcase when a soberly dressed gentleman impeded her approach.

"Mrs. Merton?"

"Mr. Gilbert," Juliana replied with a nod. She'd never exchanged more than a few words with him, an occasional browser in her shop. But she had the deepest respect for his reputation. Only in his thirties, Matthew Gilbert was perhaps the premier rare bookseller in London. Although *bookseller* was too humdrum a word to define Gilbert's position as adviser and confidant to the book-collecting nobility.

"I'm glad to meet you," he said. "You had some interesting volumes of ecclesiastical history on your shelves. Nothing I wanted, but I wondered if you had any others."

"I have a few other volumes from the same source in my back room. If you'd care to visit the shop I'd be glad to bring them out."

"I have a customer who might be interested."

Juliana was somewhat surprised. The books he'd

mentioned were among the last Joseph had acquired, on the fatal trip when he'd met his death. She'd almost given up hope of finding a suitable clergyman on whom to unload them.

Maybe one of Gilbert's clients was a bishop.

"I shall call on you soon," he said with a polite nod.

"It might be best to send word when you wish to see me. I shall spend much of the next few weeks in these rooms."

"Of course. Where else would any successful bookseller be?"

Being so described by *Matthew Gilbert* put a smile on her face. But her good mood at rubbing shoulders with a major figure in her trade shattered when she asked the porter for the Aretino.

"I'm sorry, madam," he said stiffly. "Ladies are not permitted to view the contents of this cabinet."

"Why not?"

"It contains volumes of an unsuitable nature."

She drew herself up to her full height of five feet, one inch and glared at him.

"I am not a lady. I am a bookseller. And I wish to see Aretino's *Dialogues*."

She spoke louder than intended. Every eye in the room rose from its bibliographic perusal and fixed on her.

Wonderful. Most of the London book world, the men she was so anxious to impress, including Mr. Gilbert, had heard her demand a notorious work of erotic literature. She blushed to the roots of her hair.

Uncertain whether to retreat or stand her ground,

she rested for a moment, trying to summon the courage to argue her case, when she felt a light touch on her arm and a smoky voice in her ear.

"Why don't you let me see to this, Mrs. Merton."

The marquis had come to her rescue. She returned to her seat in mingled gratitude and resentment, with a touch of wry amusement at her own expense. For all her lectures she could hardly now accuse *him* of indiscretion.

Poor girl, Cain thought as he waited for the now amenable porter to unlock the cabinet. He'd been watching, curious about what Mrs. Merton was up to, and felt a shadow of annoyance at seeing her smiling and curtsying to a man who looked as though he had a stick up his respectable arse. Irrationally, perhaps, he felt possessive of the little bookseller. She was supposed to be working for *him*. Then he heard her scandalous request echo around the almost silent room. He'd never been able to resist the urge to assist a woman in distress.

Tarquin Compton stood beside the same bookcase. Cain often encountered him in the haunts of the demimonde: green rooms, masquerades, entertainments hosted by fashionable courtesans. Unlike Chase, Compton was also welcome in every haunt of the beau monde, a darling of the ladies who craved his opinion in matters of taste and lauded his wit.

Cain had no reason to dislike Compton more than any other member of the *ton* that rejected him. Why should he care that the dandy exercised his wit at Cain's expense, coining a series of stupid names for him? The Sinful Marquis (too obvious), the Unchaste

Marquis (a bad pun), the Meretricious Marquis (lamentable alliteration). Most recently Compton had reportedly called Cain the Feral Marquis, suggesting he'd been raised by wolves.

All these soubriquets referred, in apposition, to that of his saintly father. As usual Cain's stomach roiled with acid at the mere thought of his sire.

"Interesting choice of book," Compton said.

Seeking the hidden barb in Compton's mild tone, Cain raised his head to meet the taller man squarely in the eye. "Then I'll step aside and leave it to you, Compton. Let me recommend the thirty-five postures. You could use some lessons in performance, I suspect. I seem to recall Maria Johnson was under your protection until she found she preferred me."

"I doubt it was my skills she found inferior. Rather the size of my purse."

"And Belinda Beauchamp—not her real name, I fancy—left you after a week. Mm." Cain put forefinger to his mouth in a mockery of concentrated thought. "Oh, yes, I believe she came to me. Without anything very flattering to say about her most recent lover. And I don't believe she was referring to the size of his *purse*."

"I defer to your knowledge of the ladies of the night, Chase, since you were all but born in a brothel." Compton's tone matched the disdain on his perfectly shaven hawkish face.

Cain adjusted his balance into a fighter's stance. He could see the other man's muscles tighten in preparation.

Compton looked down his nose in silence.

"You're nothing but a hypocrite, Compton," Cain said with a provocative grin. "But forgive me if I'm wrong and you sought these virtuous ladies only for the pleasure of their conversation."

Peace hung in the balance as Compton hesitated, clearly less willing than Cain to cause a scandal. Cain tossed another stick on the fire. "And speaking of hypocrisy, what are you doing next to a cabinet full of 'unsuitable books'?"

Cain prepared to dodge a punch but instead, to his great surprise, he was the recipient of a sheepish grin.

"You have a point," Compton said. "It so happens that I collect, among other things, the kind of books found in this bookcase. But only those," he added with a hint of mock piety on otherwise expressionless features, "of outstanding artistic merit. I can highly recommend the one you're about to look at."

The moment when every man in the room had raised his eyes at the sound of her voice had to number among the worst of Juliana's life. Almost as infuriating was the fact that, as a woman, she was not permitted to show a valuable book to a client.

The marquis experienced no difficulty having it brought out for examination. He returned to their table with the red volume tucked under his arm and took his seat at her side.

She found his proximity disconcerting. Accustomed as she was to crowded viewing rooms and cramped seating, the presence of her fellow bookmen never bothered her. Her attention, like theirs, was engaged by the assessment of fine bindings, the condition of engravings and fore edges, the steady rhythm of collating pages.

Even the odor of the occasional unwashed dealer dissipated in the familiar scent of book dust and old leather. But not Chase's. An indefinable bouquet—cleanliness, a hint of tobacco mixed with some kind of pricey masculine unguent—assailed her nostrils. When his thigh, accidentally or not, rubbed against her own, she found it hard to concentrate.

It had been bad enough when the object of their examination was something as untitillating as a Caxton. But the Aretino. Good Lord, what a book!

She'd never actually seen an edition, merely knew of its repute—or ill repute. He placed the volume between them and opened the volume to the title page.

The Dialogues and Thirty-Five Postures, after Aretino, she translated silently. Innocent enough, it appeared, until she discovered exactly what was meant by "postures." She had no idea men and women could do such things.

She felt her cheeks grow hot. Was that rather plump and almost naked woman actually about to . . . ?

She looked at the caption. *La femme embrasse le Dieu Priape ailé.* That meant embrace or kiss. She glanced back at the picture. Kiss in this case, definitely kiss. And the meaning of "the winged God Priapus" was all too obvious.

"It's a nice large copy," she remarked, trying to project dispassionate judgment.

"So I see." Lord Chase's voice was completely bland.

Hurriedly she turned a page. This time the man was doing the "kissing" and in an equally shocking place.

"Notice the freshness of the engraving," she said. "A fine impression."

"Yes indeed," he murmured. "I can see he's making a very fine impression."

She shot him a look. His face showed nothing but perfect gravity, and she didn't believe it for a minute.

She babbled on about the quality of the drawing, the rarity of the edition, the splendor of the binding, with little idea if she made sense. Every minute the book lay open before them she was aware of Chase, not as a book buyer but as a man. Every nerve prickled and the room seemed stifling.

Visions of herself doing some of those . . . things . . . with Lord Chase flashed through her mind. Heat bloomed in areas she never thought about and her breasts felt tight. She glanced down to make sure the hardening of her nipples wasn't apparent through the fabric of her gown. The heavy mourning concealed her excitement but it also exacerbated her fever. She'd never been more relieved than when she reached the last page and closed the book.

"Thank you, Mrs. Merton. That was very educational."

She muttered something, fairly sure that in this case the education had been all hers.

"If there's nothing else you'd like to show me today," he continued, "let me take you home."

"Thank you, but I have a couple of errands to perform on the way. I shall walk."

"It's a cold day," he coaxed.

Dear Lord, she hoped it was snowing. Then she would have a chance of cooling off.

Chapter 4

It should have been the footman's job, but Chase wasn't surprised when his housekeeper limped in with a pot of coffee. He wondered what had kept her so long.

"You're up early. And you've been home early three nights in a row. Did your cock fall off?"

She filled his cup, curving her arm with a trace of elegance that had rendered her successful early in her career. Unfortunately Mrs. Melisande Duchamp's gentility was as spurious as her French name and had never extended to her speech, which was as earthy as her former profession.

"I don't believe the state of my private parts lies within the purview of your responsibilities as my housekeeper," he said.

She emitted a crack of laughter. "Purview! That's a good one. Especially since it was me what taught you how to keep 'em in good order. Lusty little bastard you were. And is it *within my purview* to know why you're upsetting the household by calling for your breakfast at nine in the morning?"

"I'm told the agencies that furnish the gentry with

their staff open early. I've decided to replace the lot of you with respectable servants."

"Like any of them would come and work for *you*," she replied, unconcerned.

"Oh sit down, Mel, and have some coffee. Tell me the news."

"Certainly not. It wouldn't be proper." It was absurd, but Mel insisted on clinging to the notion that she knew her place. Yet Cain had been as close to her as any person since the day she and her friend Bet had found him bleeding in the gutter and given him shelter at Mrs. Rafferty's bordello.

She might refuse to sit in his presence but she had no scruples about speaking her mind. "I've got your paper and mail here. You can read the news yourself. Why don't *you* tell *me* what's going on."

"Nancy and I have parted company by mutual agreement. She has decided to devote more time to her vocal efforts."

"From what I hear she's sparing a minute or two for the efforts of Sir 'erbert Litchfield."

Chase wondered how long it had taken for the news that his mistress had found a new protector to reach the ears of every servant in the West End of London. About an hour, he guessed.

"Gave you the boot, did she?"

"As it happens she did initiate the severance of our arrangement."

"Smart lass, that one. Coming up to six months with you. She knew it wouldn't last. But what I don't get is why you ain't out there finding another one. It ain't like you, Cain."

"Haven't you heard? I've decided to devote my attentions to literature. I'm going to buy a book. Or, if Mrs. Merton has anything to say in the matter, many expensive books."

"Hah! I knew there had to be a woman. Why d'you want to buy books? Don't you have enough of them?"

"Mrs. Merton tried to interest me in a famous Italian work on the lives of prostitutes and pimps."

"Not much point in that. You know all about them already."

"As it happens, I had read the book."

"Is it good?"

Cain shrugged. "Signor Aretino's work is, at least, blessedly free of the moralizing that some commentators seem to feel a necessary accompaniment to titillation."

"Why'd this mort want you to buy it then?"

"I believe she thought it the kind of book that would appeal to me." He smiled. "I punished her a little for her presumption. I made her examine the book with me."

He felt guilty about causing his little bookseller embarrassment but hadn't been able to resist. She'd blushed quite charmingly, speaking with earnest enthusiasm about the quality of the engravings. All the while trying to ignore the fact said engravings depicted acts that were, he was quite sure, foreign to her experience. His own mind, predictably enough, had toyed with the notion of giving her a practical demonstration.

In the end he'd got what he deserved for his teasing. She'd fled Sotheby's with flustered haste, refusing his offer of a ride home. He never had the chance to interrogate her about Sir Thomas Tarleton's unorthodox methods of acquisition.

Mel's gray eyes glinted, revealing a flash of the beauty she'd once possessed before hardship and injury had dulled it. She'd been past her peak already when Cain had met her, eight years earlier. No longer a prime article with her own rooms, she'd descended to the level of brothel fodder.

"Are you going to make her an offer?" she asked.

"Mrs. Merton is a respectable shopkeeper and much too good to be associating with someone like me."

"Is she a looker? Young?"

"I don't know. Not very old. And I'll thank you not to gossip about her. I'm not in the habit of ruining tradeswomen."

Mel snorted. "Only those what are already ruined." She raised an arm at his mutter of protest. "I'll keep my mouth shut. I've got better things to do than stand around and palaver with you. That new maid needs watching every minute, silly little drab."

Alone once more, Cain shuffled through the post: bills; a missive from the steward of his estate; the usual selection of requests for his charity or patronage. He left all this to his man of business. Robinson, a canny and tough old fellow, had even stood up to his father, convincing the Saintly Marquis that his heir should be granted a meager allowance rather than continue the scandal of living in a brothel.

Which left one letter in a feminine hand.

He held it for a full minute, both reluctant and

eager to open his mother's monthly genuflection to duty, then tore off the seal.

It was the usual rant, full of exhortations to renounce his wicked path and surrender to the will of the Lord, embellished with plentiful quotations from the Reverend Josiah Ditchfield, the pompous blowhard of a clergyman who had once been his tutor. After their last face-to-face conversation, following his father's funeral, he never knew why she bothered to write at all. Yet he thanked her sense of duty, because of the brief letter enclosed within her own.

In the eight years that had passed since he had been cast out, frightened and almost penniless, to face London alone, the only times Cain felt like weeping were when he received his sister's notes, the slight, unsatisfactory contact that was all his surviving parent permitted.

"Dear Brother," she wrote.

"I trust I find you in good health and obedient to the will of Our Lord and Savior. My studies progress. I have learned to play three new hymns on the pianoforte and have made a copy in watercolors of the Italian painting of the *Martyrdom of Saint Sebastian* acquired by our late Respected Grandfather. Mr. Ditchfield says it is very like. Mr. Ditchfield is also good enough to supervise my studies of the Bible. This month I am reading the Book of Ruth.

"Your affectionate sister, Esther Godfrey."

Did she mean these pious platitudes? Did she enjoy her education, devoid, as far as he could tell, of any kind of frivolity? She never wrote of anything personal: a new gown, a pet, a thought that couldn't have been placed in her head by their mother. Perhaps she was like their mother. He had no idea. He hadn't seen her since she was his adored, adorable eight-year-old Esty, all eyes and curls and sweet laughter.

A postscript at the foot of the page caught his eye. "Ruth 1:20."

He hurried to his library, the letter clutched in his hand. There had to be a Bible somewhere. Thanks to his father and the Reverend Josiah, he'd once been an assiduous if unenthusiastic student of the Good Book. Now, when he tracked it down among a group of reference works, he half expected it to go up in smoke at the touch of his hand. He riffled the pages in search of the Book of Ruth.

And she said unto them, Call me not Naomi, call me Mara: for the Almighty hath dealt very bitterly with me.

Was the verse a message? His first instinct was to take horse for Markley Chase and discover what had made his sister unhappy. But likely it was nothing serious. A broken trinket, a scolding for a poor lesson. Better to imagine nothing more grave, or to see it merely as a recommendation for biblical study of the kind his mother occasionally made and he always ignored. Because if Esther was in trouble, there was nothing in the world he could do that wouldn't make things worse.

As usual his sister's letter depressed his spirits. For a couple of days now he'd lived with the hope that

solving the mystery of the Burgundy Hours would
provide him with something, some piece of information he could use to understand his late father's behavior and make his obdurate mother relent and let him
see Esther. In the cold morning light the idea seemed
absurd. Why waste time pursuing a chimera?

For eight years he'd been without family, thanks to
his father's accusations and banishment, virtually es-
tranged from his social peers. He'd managed without
them and survived to inherit his title and fortune. He
hoped his hedonistic existence caused the late marquis considerable anguish in whatever section of the
afterlife he inhabited.

He thrust aside the momentary gloom engendered
by word from home. What was the point? He had a
reputation to live up to, and nothing better to do with
his time and wealth than enjoy himself.

Yet the present day stretched ahead of him, empty
of engagements, one of the problems with going to
bed early and alone and rising at this hour. Had he
been a real gentleman of the *ton* he would have sought
the company of his peers at Tattersall's, or one of the
other haunts of the sporting-minded. But horses interested him solely as means of transportation. He was
adept at both boxing and fencing but maintained his
skills only as a means of exercise. So much did he
avoid interaction with his fellow men, he didn't even
belong to a club.

Which left the ladies. After breaking with his mistress he should be in eager pursuit of new companionship, haunting the theaters and the promenade in

Hyde Park to assess the fashionable impure. Or venturing into the few drawing rooms where he was received in search of more refined bedfellows.

But today he found his mind dwelling on Mrs. Merton.

He might harbor fantasies about stripping her naked and unleashing the passion he was convinced lingered under her forbidding exterior, but she wasn't a woman who deserved to be trifled with by a worthless rake. Still, she was amusing to tease. And she knew more about Tarleton than she'd admitted.

Perhaps, after all, he ought to find out what.

Juliana blushed whenever she thought of the Aretino affair.

Back in the shop she convinced herself that this was a perfectly natural consequence of examining erotic images in the presence of an attractive male. Yet again she found herself in need of a self-administered reprimand on the folly of thinking of Lord Chase as anything but a customer with deep pockets. With his reputation for debauchery it would be something of a miracle if she could manage to retain his attention.

His attention to books and nothing else. Of course.

Luckily she had just the task to help achieve the laudable goal of forgetting the sexual urges and images he'd aroused: finding those dreary volumes Mr. Gilbert had mentioned.

Joseph was never shy about soliciting book owners to sell their collections. In this case a Miss Combe, resident of a substantial house in the Salisbury Close, had responded to his letter of inquiry with an invitation to look at her library. Although any purchases were financed by Juliana's modest fortune, he refused to take her with him on the trip to Salisbury. As usual, he traveled alone, leaving her to mind the store while he made the important decisions.

In this case his business acumen had been inexplicably poor. She'd have suspected he'd bought Miss Combe's collection out of pity for an elderly lady, except that it was so unlike Joseph.

A few volumes had been found in the room when his body, stripped of his purse and watch, had been discovered. The local magistrate had concluded that robbery was the motive for Joseph's killing. The thief had left the books, which were now shelved in the shop. The rest of the collection, a couple of hundred volumes, had been delivered by carrier a few weeks later. Still reeling from the shock of her husband's murder and the challenge of running the business alone, Juliana had given them a cursory glance, enough to see they weren't going to make her fortune. From that day to this they sat disregarded in the back room.

Now her eye ran over the spines with practiced ease. Mr. Gregory's *History of the Christian Church*. Very dull. *The Church History of England* by Hugh Tootell. Excellent bedtime reading, for an insomniac. And many more in the same vein. Perhaps Mr. Gilbert would be interested, but she wasn't optimistic. She pulled a shabby folio volume from the bottom of a pile. The calf binding had once been fine, with traces of a distinctive gilt tooling on the spine and along the

inner dentelles and a coat of arms on the front cover.
But the hinges were cracked and the leather badly
scratched. Gingerly removing the loose front cover
she discovered a collection of manuscripts.

Hoping for a buried treasure, she carried the folio
upstairs to look at after dinner. It turned out the contents of the volume were more soporific than precious, and it wasn't long before she gave up and went
to bed.

She awoke from a heated dream in which she knelt
naked before an almost fully clothed man. A particular man. Her half-sleeping mind shied away from
what she'd been doing to him, but she knew. It wasn't
something she'd ever have imagined before looking
at that shocking book. The act should have disgusted
her but instead she found it exciting.

On the occasions when her husband felt amorous
he'd give a little cough before they retired for the night
and suggest she "prepare herself." Then he merely
rolled over in bed on top of her and did his business.
She hadn't exactly disliked it, but it bored her. Her
role was passive and his exertions never varied. In
her dream she was an active partner in lovemaking
and she enjoyed the sense of power. She awoke with
a frustrated ache between her thighs, not wanting the
dream to end.

The inky darkness and silence told her that the city
outside had called it a day and predawn deliveries to
the busy commercial street hadn't commenced. Yet
something had woken her. She listened nervously.
Was that scratching she heard on the floor below?
Rats? She shuddered with distaste. The alternative

was even more unwelcome. She'd told herself over and over again that Joseph's death was the result of an unfortunate mischance, the attack of a random thief turned murderous. For weeks she'd suffered night terrors, but they'd subsided when nothing threatening occurred. Nevertheless, the idea of an intruder in the shop was horrifying. She huddled under the covers, pulling a blanket up over her head.

An hour later, when she heard nothing further, she convinced herself she'd imagined the noise. But sleep eluded her almost until dawn, and she awoke unrefreshed, with a sense of foreboding. Steeling herself for disaster, she descended the narrow wooden stairs and entered the shop through the door from the passage. The door was locked, as it should be, and she could tell at a glance that nothing had been disturbed. The same appeared true in the back office. Her money was still in place, and she was sure no one had disturbed the papers on the desk. She stared hard at the corner where the Combe collection was lodged. It looked different. But she'd moved some of the volumes the previous day and couldn't recall how she'd replaced them.

Obviously she'd been imagining things. Just looking at the books had no doubt brought back thoughts of Joseph's murder and her own fears.

She was late opening, not that the bell had rung. With most of London's bookmen attending the first day of the Tarleton sale, she expected an even quieter day than usual. How she wished she was there too. She tried not to feel sorry for herself.

She returned to the front room to unbolt the street

door and immediately it opened, almost knocking her off her feet.

Lord Chase seized her arm. Recalling her midnight fantasies she blushed deeply.

"Just opening?" he said. "I'd have thought a hard-working merchant like you would have been up and busy for hours."

She was ridiculously pleased to see him. He really meant to be a serious customer. Her pleasure certainly had nothing to do with the way he seemed to bring light and excitement into her drab premises, with his air of careless elegance and the mischief in his blue eyes. She stared at him stupidly and smiled, eliciting a responsive curve of his sensuous lips.

"Are you ready to go?" he asked.

"Go?"

"To the auction."

"You want to go to the auction?"

"Of course. I'm going to buy some books."

"But it's the first day."

"So?"

Juliana gave her head a little shake to restore her brain to a sensible level of performance.

"There isn't anything good being sold today. Just minor works and books in poor condition."

"I don't care. Surely you want to see the action?"

She did, indeed she did. How strange that a neo-phyte like Lord Chase could understand the appeal of seeing even the dross from a fine collection go under the hammer.

"Of course you do," he coaxed. "Let's go."

"I shouldn't leave my shop unattended for the third

day in a row." As though she'd be losing money by her absence. If only it were true! But she didn't want Chase to think she was ready to accede to his every wish.

She peered past him at his waiting carriage, shining scarlet in the gloomy drizzle. A footman held the door open. The interior looked warm and inviting. And she'd love to know if the seats really were upholstered in velvet.

"I suppose I can spare you an hour or two," she said. "Let me fetch my bonnet."

At first Cain found Mrs. Merton's response as entertaining as the auction itself. She seemed fascinated by the dynamics of the sale, giving little jogs of excitement when something significant happened. She maintained a sotto voce commentary about the various players in the room, imbuing apparently dull men with character and creating drama out of the monotonous progress of the lots, punctuated by the rhythmic cadence of the auctioneer calling the bids.

Most of all she was astonished by the prices. On the face of it they seemed low enough, most books selling for a few shillings, some for a pound or two. She bid on a few items herself but never won any.

"The prices are outrageous," she complained after losing a very dull-sounding volume to another dealer. "It's one thing to see great copies and exceptional rarities go high, but these are very ordinary books."

"Why did you bid on that one?" he asked.

"I have a customer who will buy it from me, but not for a ridiculous price. I warn you, my lord. If you intend to buy at this sale, expect to pay a lot."

"I've been duly warned. In fact I think I'd like to buy this book."

He pointed to an item in the catalogue, two lots ahead. He had the urge to enter the lists.

"It's rare," she said with a frown, "but it must be in terrible condition, and very likely incomplete, to be sold today."

"I don't care. I want to read it. I like Herrick's poetry." The title appealed to him too: *Hesperides, or The Works Both Humane and Divine.* He didn't know about the divine side of things, but recalled that the poet had quite a fondness for women.

"I've spoken to you before about reading these books." Her admonishment was without bite. In fact, he suspected that she teased him after his own manner. He could tell she was as anxious as he to get into the fray.

"I won't go too high," she said firmly.

"You'll bid until I tell you to stop, or I'll do it myself and Mr. Sotheby's ceiling will collapse with shock."

A porter held up the Herrick and he could see, even from his seat halfway down the room, that it wasn't a pretty sight. The volume was knocked down to him at five pounds against two determined gentlemen, Mrs. Merton grumbling with every bid that he was paying too much.

Since coming into his inheritance, Cain had been able to buy anything he wanted, hence his color-coordinated carriages and liveries, his wardrobe, and the lavish style in which he maintained a succession of mistresses. He couldn't remember an acquisition giving him such a rush of pleasure as a shabby edition of poetry by a country parson. This book-buying thing could become a habit. He began to scan the catalogue in earnest.

"That's a good book, and damn rare." Tarquin Compton came up as he waited for Mrs. Merton to collect the Herrick at the end of a long day. Compton had been sitting in the back of the room with Lord Hugo and Sebastian Iverley.

"You didn't bid on it yourself."

"I already own a copy. A beautiful one in contemporary polished calf."

"Mine looks as though it were bound in ancient distressed weasel."

Compton laughed. "You can have it rebound. But it's complete. I collated it myself. The auctioneers made a mistake selling it today with the rubbish."

How about that? He couldn't wait to tell Mrs. Merton.

"Would you like to dine with Iverley and myself next week?" Compton asked. It was the first time Cain could recall a male member of the *ton* seeking his company that didn't involve a visit to a den of vice. This was Tarquin Compton of all people, addressing him with a degree of respect.

Just because he'd bought a rare book.

Chapter 5

L ord Chase offered to take Juliana home. Since it was raining hard it didn't take much persuasion before she succumbed to the allure of the carriage, with its heated bricks kept in a compartment in the floor.

"You must be hungry," he said. "Do you have someone to serve you a meal?"

"I cook for myself."

"You've been working all day. It isn't right."

"That's why people have wives," she remarked wryly.

"No, that's why people have cooks."

Juliana climbed the stairs wearily to her tiny rooms over the shop, sorry to leave the luxurious velvet upholstery and delicious warmth. It had been a long day. Collapsing in a chair, she swathed herself in a heavy wool shawl and contemplated the state of her larder. Some bread and cheese was all it contained, stale and staler.

She also felt apprehensive. The memory of that noise in the night, forgotten in the excitement of the auction, returned in a rush and made her jittery. For the first time in months she missed Joseph. He had never been the most scintillating company, and she hated cooking dinner, but she would have enjoyed thrashing out the events of the day with him.

Surprisingly, she would also have enjoyed discussing them with Chase. His ribald comments had added an extra element to the personalities of the auction room.

During one heated exchange of bids between two collectors, she'd whispered that one of them liked to run up the prices against his longtime rival, who was unable to resist the challenge. The baited gentleman often found himself hanging out to dry in possession of an inferior book at an inflated price.

"Not the only thing Featherstone has had hanging out. The poor fellow was once compelled to depart the home of the lovely Lola Garcia through the window with his breeches unbuttoned."

Juliana looked at the stout baronet and snorted into her catalogue. "Ssh," she hissed. Then after a pause, "Why?"

"Her, uh, official protector unexpectedly appeared and would have been most displeased to discover that Lola was augmenting her income."

Chase might not be well versed in the family relationships of the *ton*, but he certainly knew all about their unsanctified activities. She couldn't recall when, if ever, she'd been so diverted.

She was still sedentary, trying to summon the energy to eat, when a knock at the door had her plodding downstairs.

"Who's there?" she asked nervously.

"Chase."

She opened the door to admit the most delicious aroma, followed by two liveried footmen staggering under the weight of covered trays. The marquis brought up the rear bearing a wine bottle and a winning smile.

"Dinner," he said.

Juliana's rumbling stomach and quivering nose quelled the instinct to protest.

"Upstairs?" he asked.

She nodded.

"Upstairs," he directed the footmen.

"Right yer are, guv," replied one, who looked about fifteen years old. The other, even younger, had his coat misbuttoned and his wig slightly askew. In fact both lacked the orderly appearance usual in such retainers.

Chase indicated with a nimble bow that she should precede him in their wake.

"Why?" was all she could say.

"I'm accustomed to feeding working women at the end of a long day. Admittedly most of my friends are actresses, but I don't suppose booksellers are very different."

Juliana could just imagine what usually happened *after* he provided a meal. She repressed her misgivings, ignored an involuntary tremor of anticipation, and followed the smell of food.

Cain fully expected Mrs. Merton to protest with some nonsense about her reputation. He was ready to tempt her with delicious dishes from his cook but his best wheedling wasn't called for. She cleared some books off the table in a room that he guessed was more than half the total size of the flat. After looking around for a clean surface, she heaped them on the seat of the only comfortable chair. While Tom unloaded the dishes of food, she led Peter into another room to fetch plates and cutlery.

They were willing boys, his footmen, if on the unrefined side. He wondered what she'd think if he told her they were the sons of a whore from Mrs. Rafferty's. Their mother, Bet, along with Mel, had rescued him after he'd been robbed and beaten his second day in London. She'd been his first woman. That was in the old innocent days when the brothel had seemed like heaven on earth to a randy youth, and all its inhabitants angels of the most deliciously fallen variety. Later he'd discovered the dismal and dangerous reality of bordello life. Bet was dead, of the pox, and he mourned her still. When his fortunes changed he'd given her boys a home. Mel had cared for them until they became old enough to work.

The apartment was shabby and redolent of that same dusty leather odor that he now associated with old books. Not surprising, since the room was full of them, far more than could be shelved in the bookcase that occupied one full wall. A small gateleg table, two plain wooden chairs, a console table, and a desk with a glass-fronted cupboard above completed the furnishings. He noted that beneath the teetering towers of volumes the furniture was of decent quality, as were the china and glasses Peter carried in from the other room. The only decorative object was a watercolor portrait of a young woman with dark hair arranged in the style of the last century.

"It's chilly," he called out. "Shall I have one of my servants start a fire?"

Mrs. Merton came back into the room carrying knives and forks. "Please," she said. "I couldn't summon the strength to do it myself. But since I am to be treated to a meal we might as well enjoy it in comfort. You do intend to remain and share it, my lord?"

"Of course. Book collectors get hungry too."

"I'm glad to hear you call yourself a book collector."

"I'd like to talk about buying some more, but first sit down and eat. Let me pour you some wine."

"I rarely drink, my lord," she said, taking her place at the table and eyeing the chicken fricassee, York ham, buttered cauliflower, and stewed mushrooms the boys had uncovered.

He pulled a chair up across from her and filled both glasses. "Since we're breaking bread together I think we should drop the formalities. My friends call me Cain."

"An unusual name."

"As a matter of fact, fratricide is one sin I've never committed."

Her lips pursed into the little smile that made her look young and enchantingly pretty, despite the ugly cap. "Do you even have a brother?"

"Not that I know of. Cain isn't my Christian name. Before I inherited the marquisate I was known as the Earl of Cainfield."

"Does no one use your Christian name?"

"Never."

"What about your father and mother?"

"My mother called me Cainfield. My father called me Amnon." Now why the hell had he said that? In a room full of actresses it wouldn't matter, but Mrs. Merton was a woman of education.

Apparently she didn't pick up the reference. Her face showed nothing but polite interest melting into sympathy. "And both your parents have died, my lord? I am sorry."

"Cain," he insisted, ignoring the question. He never talked about his family. "What about you? Any embarrassing childhood names I can use?"

"My name is Juliana."

"Juliana as in J. C. Merton?"

"It so happened that my husband and I had the same initials. He was Joseph Charles."

So her middle name began with C. Was it Cassandra? The mystery he had sensed connected with the owner of Tarleton's *Romeo and Juliet* popped into his mind.

The coals in the tiny fireplace began to warm the room. Juliana let her voluminous shawl slide from her shoulders, and some of her fatigue seemed to go with it. A gulp of wine diminished the exhausted pallor of her face.

Unfortunately the gown beneath the shawl remained as hideous and unflattering as ever. But assessing her appearance was no more than Cain's reflexive reaction to a woman. Seduction was not what he had in mind for the evening.

He had come here to learn everything she knew about Sir Thomas Tarleton. Then, purely for his own amusement, he'd discover where Cassandra Fitterbourne came into the picture. There was no rush. He liked Juliana Merton, and making her comfortable gave him pleasure. He looked forward to an evening of companionship and conversation.

The footmen kept bumping into each other in the cramped quarters. "Wait for me downstairs, lads," Cain said. "We can look after ourselves."

Even without those improbable servants, the room seemed very small, Juliana thought, smaller than usual when filled with Chase's potent presence. Agreeing to dine *à deux* in her own home with a gazetted rake was hardly wise, but Juliana hadn't been able to refuse. She'd been so pleased to see him, as though she'd opened her workaday door to admit exotic splendor into her dreary surroundings.

And the food! Not since her guardian's death had anyone served her a meal in her own home, and Chase's cook far surpassed the one at Fernley Court. She followed a mouthful of tender ham with a second gulp of claret and allowed herself to relax into a delicious sense of warmth and well-being.

"Tell me, Juliana, how do those bookseller's codes work?"

Her companion sat across the table, with his engagingly open grin. Her stomach gave a little flip. But since, for once, his voice and manner bore no hint of the flirtatious, she allowed herself to simply enjoy looking at him.

"It's quite simple. You choose a ten-letter word with

no repeated letters and assign a digit to each. Or some people use a nine-letter word and X for the naught."

"Do you use a code? What word?"

"I do, my lord"—he raised an admonitory eyebrow— "Cain, but I am certainly not going to tell you what it is."

"Why not?"

"Because I don't choose to let you know how much I've paid for the books in my shop."

"Are your profits so shocking?"

"I sell books for what they are worth, regardless of their cost to me. And I don't believe a man who spends five pounds on a poor copy of Herrick would care what I charge."

"Tarquin Compton said I got a bargain because the book is complete, and in good condition aside from the binding."

Juliana was impressed. "I congratulate you."

"Beginner's luck, no doubt."

"Perhaps you will be a lucky collector. Some are like that. The best books somehow magically land in their hands."

"Was Tarleton lucky?"

"He didn't leave things to fortune. He made his own luck."

"What do you mean?" Cain asked.

"He wasn't always scrupulous in his dealings."

"You intrigue me. You said something the other day about the Shakespeare folios."

"He stole those folios," she said darkly. "Not literally but morally. A certain collector had tracked them down, and the owner agreed to sell to him. They would have been the crown jewels of his collection. But Tarleton was on the same trail. He persuaded the seller to break his word."

"Persuaded? Did he offer a better price?"

"I don't believe that was the case. Not in the opinion of the disappointed collector. He believed Tarleton threatened the seller with disclosure of something embarrassing or scandalous."

"Blackmail!"

"Yes. And that's not the only such story I've heard." It felt good to tell the truth about Tarleton to an appreciative audience.

"You say the folios were 'tracked down.' How would one do that?" Cain asked.

"Most important books are recorded at some point in their history. So you find the last known owner and follow the trail."

"I understand the Burgundy manuscript was lost for centuries. Do you have any idea how Tarleton would have found it?"

"I've never researched its history. But I can do so if you wish."

"Thank you. If I'm to buy it I suppose I should know everything about it."

"If you don't mind my asking, why do you want it?"

Cain shrugged. "Just a whim. And it's beautiful. Let's talk about some other books I'd like to buy."

Juliana was delighted, though anxious to divert him from thoughts of Shakespeare. "What did you think of the Aretino?" To her irritation she couldn't manage the question without blushing.

"You know, Juliana, I'm not really interested in erotic literature."

"I'm sorry . . ."

The reappearance of his grin cut off her apology. "I prefer the real thing."

Her blush deepened. To disguise her embarrassment she picked up her glass.

"I have decided to collect plays," he said.

She drained her wine and tried to sound business-like. "Any titles in particular?" *Please, not the quartos.*

He put down his knife and fork and refilled both their glasses. Then he reached back to the side table for the Tarleton catalogue.

"I noted some that sound better than the usual fare at Drury Lane," he said, flipping through the volume. "*She Ventures and She Wins.* Good for her. *The Nice Wanton.* What other kind is there?"

His farcical list, and the quizzical play of his mobile face, had her giggling.

"*Win Her and Take Her.* Thank you, I will. *The Town Fop*? Perhaps not. But *The Woman Turn'd Bully* I simply must have."

Juliana had read every word of the Tarleton catalogue without the absurdity of the titles striking her. Generally more interested in the rarity of books than their content, she wondered what these plays were about.

"I suppose you intend to *read* what you buy," she groused.

"Certainly I do." He turned another page. "Here's a good one. *The Rampant Alderman.* How could I resist?

It arouses certain ideas that the Lord Chamberlain might object to seeing portrayed on stage."

He threw her a wayward look, as though expecting her to faint at the vision he conjured. But wine had made her bold.

"May I ask you a question, Cain?" she asked, her laughter subsiding as she examined his face intently.

"Why not?

"Why are you so anxious to shock people?"

"Do I shock you?"

"A little. But I find you amusing. And I think you do it deliberately, not because you mean what you say."

"I behave the way people expect me to." He spoke flippantly and continued to smile, but the light left his eyes to be replaced by a harder expression.

"So you do it to please?"

"I didn't say that." His voice, always low, dropped a notch in both volume and pitch.

"And why do people expect you to shock them?"

"Because, and you are likely the only person in London who doesn't know it, my dear innocent book-worm, I am steeped in vice, a being so depraved that I was cast out of my ancestral home at the tender age of sixteen."

"What could you possibly have done at that age that was so terrible?"

"Acts too depraved for your ears."

"Really?" She was fascinated.

"My long slide into iniquity began at the tender age of twelve when I leered at one of the maids during evening prayers."

"Surely your father didn't send you away for that?"

"No, he merely beat me. The maid he sent away, without a reference. The first recorded instance of my getting a woman into trouble. The sin that caused my exile was far, far worse." He continued to speak in a light, humorous tone but Juliana detected an underlying bitterness and defiance.

"What did you do?"

Cain misinterpreted her question, deliberately she was sure. "I left," he said. "My father had me delivered to the nearest coaching stop with a hundred pounds in my pocket, and told me never to darken the doors of Markley Chase again."

And she knew he wasn't going to tell her why.

"What of your mother? Didn't she object?"

"My father was a saint—"

"I don't find it saintly to cast out a boy of sixteen," she said indignantly.

"My father never did anything wrong in the eyes of his wife, or indeed of the world. So I found my way to London and proceeded to live up to his opinion of me."

"So young to be alone! How did you manage?"

"I went to live in a brothel. I liked that." The amused light was back in his eyes.

"Good Lord!"

"And then I developed a close relationship with the theater. Or rather a succession of ladies who adorned the stage."

"You don't make a secret of it, I notice."

"What would be the point? I am, I believe, notorious. Five years later my father died. Sadly for him, it wasn't in his power to disinherit me."

"Did you return home?"

"Just for the funeral. A despicable act of hypocrisy on my part. My mother remains there. She is no more anxious for my company than my sire was. I live a life of blissful self-indulgence and ease in the family's London mansion, and she keeps Markley Chase as her province."

He didn't ask for her compassion but he had it. Juliana knew the pain and loneliness of being exiled from the only home she'd ever known.

"So you haven't been home in how many years?"

"Three."

"You are only twenty-four years old then, just a year more than me. I thought you older." Not that Cain's dissipations had marred his looks, but there was a world-weariness, a certain cynicism in his face when in repose that communicated a wealth of hard experience.

"Thank you for the compliment. My debauchery must be affecting my features. I shall have to speak to my valet about a skin tonic."

She suspected something in his tale affected him far more deeply than he liked to reveal, that his habitual glibness disguised a sorrow she felt the urge to comfort.

Then his expression shuttered for a brief but perceptible instant and he regarded her with a careless grin, the blue eyes as mocking and dangerously suggestive as ever. He'd erected a barrier against trespassers.

Cain had been enjoying himself, especially the early part of the conversation when he'd learned of Sir Thomas Tarleton's propensity for extortion. That might explain why his father had relinquished the Burgundy Hours, though he couldn't imagine what scandal threatened the Saintly Marquis.

Then he'd started talking about himself, far more than was his habit. Juliana's indignation on his behalf would be more gratifying if she knew the whole truth. When he sensed her sympathy turn to pity his mood changed. He loathed pity, resented it.

"Enough of my wretched life. Let's get back to books. If I'm going to collect plays, naturally I should buy Shakespeares."

"Naturally."

"Nothing but the best for me."

"They'll go high," she said weakly.

"I believe I've made clear that my fortune is adequate."

"You should buy the folios," she said firmly.

He let her wax lyrical for a few minutes about the beauty, condition, and brilliant provenance of the four volumes.

"I rather fancy those neat little quartos," he cut in abruptly.

Juliana dropped her knife with a clatter. She stood up. "Please excuse me for a few minutes."

Cain had intended to rattle her, not drive her from the room. But he took advantage of her absence to check a hunch. He'd already spotted a plain-looking Bible on one of the shelves; not, he thought, a collector's item. He snatched it up and checked the signature on the flyleaf before replacing it. *Juliana Cassandra Wayborn.*

She stumbled into the tiny water closet in something of a panic. Wine had dulled her brain. How could she stop him from buying *her* books without revealing the truth about herself?

The thought of simply asking him not to bid on the quartos occurred to her, only to be dismissed. In her experience men didn't respond well to straightforward expressions of either her desires or her opinions. Her guardian had never welcomed her assessment of a book when it conflicted with his own, preferring to willfully ignore the occasions when she had been proven right and he wrong. Her respect for all he had taught her let her accept his attitude, but when Joseph displayed the same outlook she'd resented it. And developed tactics for making him accede to her judgment. The male animal had to be made to think it was *his* idea.

She hadn't taken the Marquis of Chase's measure enough to know how to manipulate him to her will. Never mind the uneasy thought that she might never be able to outwit his quicksilver personality. For the moment she would return to her previous strategy of distraction. An idea buzzed into her head to join the second glass of claret. Did she dare? Last time she'd offered him an erotic book. And he'd made it quite clear he preferred the real thing.

Not that she had any intention of actually seducing him. A small flirtation should be enough. There was an attractive man in the next room, and the prospect of engaging him—just a little—on those terms appealed to her.

There was, of course, the problem that she had little experience in flirtation. But the man was a rake. How hard could it be? There was nothing she could do about her unappealing garb, but she had one asset men had always admired. She'd start with that, then improvise. Her heart racing, unsteady fingers untied the strings of her cap.

When Juliana returned, Cain was sitting innocently at his place, toying with his wineglass. He guessed she had withdrawn to think up a new ploy to distract him from the vexed subject of Shakespeare quartos, and looked forward to discovering it. And then he'd find out her connection to the lovely Cassandra Fitterbourne. His earlier irritation had melted away. He found the diminutive bookseller and her secrets entertaining.

Well, this was a surprise.

Right from the beginning he'd known Mrs. Merton was pretty under those gruesome widow's weeds. He hadn't suspected she had the most magnificent hair he'd ever seen. Tumbling from her head scarcely restrained by pins, shining curls caught the flickering candlelight in shades of honey, caramel, and pure gold. She was beautiful, a perfect pocket Venus. For the first time he felt a genuine urge to delve into more than the mystery of her background.

She swayed a little as she approached the table. "I decided to remove my cap. I hope you don't object to the informality."

She patted at her head with a self-conscious air, and a shower of hairpins tinkled on the floorboards. The shining masses flopped over her shoulders to her breasts.

"Not in the least," he said, eyes riveted.

Her brow, milky white beneath the gold, creased in annoyance. "I'm not very good at hairdressing."

"Dear me, Juliana. There seem to be a number of things you aren't very good at. Cooking, hairdressing. What else, I wonder." He leaned back in his chair and folded his arms, awaiting her response.

"I'd rather talk about the things I am good at," she said softly.

By God, he did believe she was flirting with him.

"I am all ears."

She struck a pose and her figure curved nicely, despite its unpromising casing of bombazine, then her eyes met his with an expression both come-hither and uncertain.

Definitely flirting, but not very good at it. Did she know what she was starting? He couldn't believe her goal was to bed him, but she played a dangerous game with a master of the sport. He could have her naked beneath him in minutes, and there'd be no turning back. She wouldn't *want* to turn back.

She cleared her throat. "I can enter a library and pick out the best books within five minutes."

That was an unusual beginning to a seduction scene. Resisting the urge to laugh, he merely cocked an inquisitive eyebrow.

"Even from among several thousand volumes. I have an unerring intuition for quality."

"Intuition should always be followed," he said encouragingly.

"I know a volume from the cradle of printing by its scent, as well as the incised impression of deep black ink on heavy paper, so crisp it might have been made yesterday."

Better. While he hadn't yet found the smell of a book arousing, he was always ready for a new experience.

"Show me any book binding and even blindfolded I can tell you what it's made of."

"Tell me more."

"Just a stroke of the fingertips is enough." She moved over to the bookcase. "Close your eyes."

In the dark he heard her make a selection of books and detected her faint clean scent, violet soap. Then she took his hand in her small one and brushed his fingers over the smooth cover of a volume.

"Feel this one. Glossy with a hint of roughness. Polished calf."

She might not be an experienced flirt but her instincts were superior.

"The finest vellum," she said, offering another. "Slippery as silk yet hard."

The warmth of the room, her proximity, her soft hand manipulating his over the cool surface of the book affected him. The book wasn't the only thing that was hard.

"And now for a more robust texture." He sensed firmness with a slight grain. "The virile strength of morocco."

She leaned over him, her breath caressing his cheek. With an effortless move he grasped the book, laid it on the table, and snatched her by her slender waist. She landed on his lap, a snug armful of enticing heat.

Keeping his lids hooded, he settled her against his chest, and his hands set forth on a slow voyage of exploration of flesh and bones beneath stiff fabric: slender shoulders; the bumpy ridge of her back (a different, more practical part of his brain registered that her garments must fasten at the front); the pronounced curve from waist to hips; breasts well-rounded, firm, and begging to be freed from the confines of cloth and corset.

He sensed an acceleration in her breathing and opened his eyes. At close quarters, by lamplight, hers glowed a deeper green. They gazed at him soft and vulnerable. Notions of self-restraint trickled away as her lips parted in invitation.

He kissed her, and any doubts he might have had about the widow Merton's limited sexual experience were put to rest. When he ran his tongue around the sensitive entrance to her mouth, then all the way in, there was an unquestionable frisson of shock, a stiffening of her muscles beneath his caress. But scarcely a second later she relaxed, sweet and receptive. Her hands, which had been trapped against his chest, fought free to cradle his jaw. The movement of her lips answered his own and her tongue emerged shyly, then with increasing boldness, to meet his.

He deepened the kiss, inhaling her breath. She was every bit as delicious as he'd suspected, tasting both honeyed and spicy.

And of his best Bordeaux.

He never seduced intoxicated women. It was one of his rules.

His mouth stilled, though his hands continued to caress her back and hips. Unwillingly he made his mind overcome his senses, engulfed by the warmth and fragrance of Juliana's body. He recalled her second glass of wine, the sway of her body as she'd returned to the room with her hair a glorious golden cloud. And the fact that she was behaving in a manner surely foreign to her better judgment.

And his own too. This hadn't been his plan for the evening. Avoiding middle-class women was another of his rules. They were too much trouble and tended to come with relatives. He'd once fallen afoul of a father with an evangelical bent and well-aged hams for fists. Only his skill for dodging trouble had kept him from serious injury.

Though he had to admit avoidance of the bourgeoisie was more of a recommendation than a rule. And Juliana appeared blessedly free of protectors. Perhaps . . .

But never drunk women. It was unsporting.

He lifted her off his lap and, with reluctant precision, set her on her feet.

Juliana tottered backward and somehow regained her own chair, her head in a daze. Cain's kisses made her feel rather as though she'd landed in the middle of an explosion of fireworks. She regretted they had ended, and felt bereft.

Lingering bedazzlement gave way to a wave of humiliation. She'd thrown herself at him and he had rejected her. She stared at the table, feeling small, powerless, and unattractive.

And drunk, but no longer in the light effervescing way that had melted her inhibitions. Her head felt fuzzy and slightly sick.

Cain broke an uneasy silence. "I apologize, Juliana." He spoke gently in that foggy voice. "It's probably better if we keep our acquaintance on a business footing."

Why was he apologizing? She was the one who'd made the first advance. And he, a rake, a man who reputedly would bed any woman that moved, had found her wanting. She wanted to die from the shame.

"But I hope we can be friends," he added. "I enjoy your company and your conversation and I value your knowledge."

Feeling marginally better, she ventured a glance upward. His blue gaze was on her. Those beautiful eyes that got her into this predicament. She fixed her attention on the half inch of claret in the bottom of her wineglass.

"May I ask you a question?" he said.

She nodded mutely.

"Who was—or is—Cassandra Fitterbourne?"

"Who?" she said weakly.

"The previous owner of the *Romeo and Juliet* quarto. Your middle name is Cassandra. I thought she might be a relation."

She looked up again and came to an abrupt and rash decision.

"She was my mother."

She'd said it. The truth known only by herself. The

fact that must never be mentioned. She had no idea why she'd broken a lifetime of silence to confide in this particular man.

"Did she die?"

"When I was an infant. My father too."

"Who brought you up? Was it George Fitterbourne by any chance?"

"Yes, my grandfather." The words emerged with strength and pride. She felt a surge of pleasure at finally claiming her guardian, the human she'd always revered above all others, as her own kin. For once she could imagine herself a young woman of good family instead of a nameless orphan of mysterious parentage.

She realized why she'd told Cain the truth. She might not be a beautiful actress, worthy of his attentions, but at least he'd know she wasn't a nobody.

"So that's how you learned about books?" His question contained nothing but friendly curiosity. Cain had no idea of the enormity of her confession.

"He was a great collector, with brilliant knowledge and taste. He taught me all he knew."

"Why did you choose to become a bookseller, instead of following in his footsteps as a collector?"

"Tarleton," she said bitterly.

"What did he have to do with it?"

"Tarleton was our neighbor, and my grandfather's rival. He always had more money. And greater luck. Without possessing one tenth of Mr. Fitterbourne's knowledge he beat him over and over again to the best books."

"The folios?"

"Yes. And others. By any means. Hatred of Tarleton ate away at my grandfather's soul, and I believe it killed him. He died with Tarleton's name on his lips."

"Why, then, did you sell the quartos to Tarleton?"

"It wasn't my idea, I can assure you. My grandfather's heir made the sale. The entire library in one underpriced lot to that man. He wouldn't listen to me, wouldn't even let me have Cassandra's favorite book."

"You were not, then, your grandfather's heir."

"The estate went to a cousin and the books had to be sold to pay my grandfather's debts. I had only a small legacy."

"Why didn't you remain with your cousin?"

"I preferred to leave," she said. Obviously she wasn't going to repeat Frederick Fitterbourne's assertion that her presence in the house would mar the reputation of his own family. "The books were gone. I married Joseph and we used my fortune to move to London and open our shop."

"You lost your home. I'm sorry," he said softly. His sympathy warmed her, and she felt their kinship. Like her he had been forced from his home. Even though he hadn't been deprived of his fortune he was, in a way, an exile. What she hadn't told him was that she too was an outcast.

"You want your grandfather's Shakespeares, don't you? Especially your mother's."

She felt a complete fool. All her stratagems had been exposed.

"You could have just told me, you know? I wouldn't buy something you want for yourself."

"I don't know that I can afford them," she said miserably, hoping she wouldn't succumb to the ultimate humiliation of tears. She wanted to present herself as a coolheaded professional, not a sentimental lachrymose female.

"Let's make an agreement. You can have first choice of any books you want. I will only bid on them if the prices are beyond your purse. Is that fair?"

"Thank you," she said with real gratitude. Her rakish client was apparently a gentleman after all.

He grinned and his blue eyes danced, far from innocently. "Not that I regret your efforts to distract me. The Aretino is a *most* interesting book. And I wouldn't have wished to miss this evening's lesson in bookmanship."

Chapter 6

During eight years in London, three of them as a marquis in full possession of his inheritance, Cain had never entered that bastion of aristocratic privilege, White's Club. Mounting the steps in full view of the famous bow window overlooking St. James's Street, he scorned to give fashionable London's most influential men a hint of his emotions.

"Chase," he said curtly to the porter who relieved him of hat and coat in the hall. "To meet Mr. Compton and Mr. Iverley."

His quiet words drew the attention of a gentleman in a Guards' uniform emerging from one of the rooms. They stared at each other, then the other averted his eyes.

"Bardsley," Cain said. "I haven't seen you since Eton." He allowed himself a slight smile. His own school career was cut short after the maid-ogling incident, his father having decided his son's lecherous urges were fed by the immoral company of his youthful peers. An early sign of his sire's developing irrationality, since most of his contemporaries, Bardsley included, had been as undersized, spotty, and naïve as Cain himself. He'd never have recognized the strapping officer from those days.

"But now I recall," he went on, "that we met on one occasion since."

Bardsley's throat convulsed. He'd never been an articulate boy. And they hadn't exchanged a word when Bardsley's father, a viscount, had brought his younger son to Mrs. Rafferty's to lose his virginity. Surprising really that his former schoolmate was embarrassed now. At that meeting he had been a customer while Cain was helping out the bullyboys keeping order at the bordello. Yet Bardsley now looked as if he'd been caught buggering a sheep.

Even though he'd got the better of this first encounter, Cain still felt, as he followed a flunky up the main staircase, he was entering a lions' den.

A dozen pairs of eyes lifted at his entrance into a spacious room, redolent of leather, spirits, and cigar smoke. No woman ever set foot in this haven of self-confident masculine comfort, nor ever would. This place had nothing in common with Mrs. Rafferty's brothel save some of the customers. Cain gained a glimpse into a world to which he belonged by birth, the milieu from which his sire had banished him.

No one arose and denounced him for unspeakable depravity. Not even the ghost of his father, who had, of course, been a member.

His hosts welcomed him from a pair of deep leather armchairs. "Let's go straight into dinner," Compton said. "We have an engagement later."

Of course, Cain thought, they wouldn't wish to

spend the whole evening with him. Compton and Iverley probably regretted the invitation.

The food was indifferent, the wine excellent, and the conversation entirely of books. Cain's companions spoke with knowledge and approval of the plays he'd purchased in the past few days. Iverley, especially, displayed a deep knowledge of every aspect of book collecting that arose in conversation.

"Wise of you to hold off the Aphra Behns," he said. "The condition of the volumes was not as it should be and the prices much too high."

"I can't take credit for my restraint. Mrs. Merton told me the same thing and dissuaded me from bidding."

That was a mild way of describing her refusal to buy them for him, an argument conducted in furious whispers in the middle of a crowded auction room. Cain hadn't cared that much about the books in question. He continued the dispute when he saw Mrs. Merton's indignation dispel her lingering mortification. The first time they'd met after their tipsy dinner she had scarcely been able to look him in the eye. His teasing had her right back on her high horse.

"Can't think why anyone would want them, anyway," Iverley added. "A female playwright can't be any good."

"Your prejudices are absurd, Sebastian," Tarquin Compton said. "I don't know about Mrs. Behn, but Uncle Hugo thinks very highly of Mrs. Merton."

Iverley grunted derisively but Cain silently agreed. The grounding Juliana had given Cain in only a few days, including that amusing impromptu overview of the materials of book bindings, enabled him to hold his own with this pair of seasoned collectors. As he became immersed in book lore he lost the feeling that a large sign hung over his head, inscribed with the word *debaucher.*

From time to time other diners nodded at them as they passed the table.

"There goes that idiot Bardsley." Compton broke into Iverley's description of an armorial binding he'd lately acquired. "I drew his cork at Jackson's yesterday and would have knocked his brains out if he had any."

"Always astonishes me, Tarquin, you can beat a hulk like that when you look like a male milliner," Iverley observed.

"I can assure you that were I a milliner the ladies of London wouldn't sport such hideous headwear." He turned to Cain. "Do you box?"

"I can fight but I don't care for it."

Compton gave him an assessing look. "You would strip well, I think. You must come to Jackson's one day and put on the gloves. All in sport of course."

Sensing no hidden aggression in the offer, Cain accepted. He'd have to study the rules of gentlemanly fighting.

Compton's shoulders shrugged beneath his impeccable tailoring. "We'll talk about it later, since Sebastian refuses to take an interest in any sporting pursuit. You'll come with us to the Berrys, Chase? The company is always entertaining, and even our friend here forgives them for being female."

Cain knew of Misses Mary and Agnes Berry, who

had entertained luminaries of society, politics, and the arts for decades at their North Audley Street house.

"Why not?" he said.

Apparently tonight's new experiences weren't over yet. Cain had never attended a bluestocking salon. He had a disturbing, but not disagreeable, sense of being drawn into a new world of masculine friendship and reputable female company.

"Isn't that the Tarleton heir Gilbert's dining with?" Iverley said. Compton followed the other's gaze to a table in a far corner occupied by two men. One of them Cain recognized as the man Juliana had spoken with at the auction room, just before her Aretino fiasco.

"Who is the darker man?" Cain asked.

"Gilbert. Excellent bookman. Wonderful taste. I've bought from him for years," Iverley said.

"Interesting," said Compton. "Do you think Tarleton's after the Burgundy Hours?"

"How deep are his pockets?" Iverley asked. "I'm thinking of bidding myself and I'd like an idea of what I'm up against."

"That depends on the state of his personal fortune."

As his hosts talked, Cain examined the man under discussion. From a distance all he could see was a head of fair hair.

"Rather a mysterious fellow, Sir Henry Tarleton," Compton continued. "Hasn't been in London long. He grew up in some outlandish place like the West Indies."

"Jamaica, I believe," Iverley said. "Very prosperous plantations there. Tarquin thinks anywhere ten miles outside London might as well be the American wilderness."

Compton shuddered. "Ten! Even five. I went to Kensington once. It was distressingly rural. Anyway," he continued, "rumor has it Henry Tarleton's father, the book collector's brother, married a Creole heiress."

Iverley looked skeptical. "If you believe rumor, every person in the colonies has made a fortune."

"Why does he have to buy anything at the auction?" Cain asked. "Doesn't it all belong to him?"

"Old Tarleton died in debt, virtually penniless. Aside from a fortune in books of course."

Cain began to see that Lord Hugo's warnings about the perils of bibliophilia weren't so far-fetched. First Fitterbourne, Juliana's grandfather, and then his rival Tarleton had been driven to the brink of ruin by their passion for books.

"He never changed his will after his son died. If Uncle Hugo is correct," Compton went on, "and he usually is, Tarleton left everything to his son and his son's children. Since the son never married there shouldn't have been a problem. But some old relation or retainer claimed the son had been secretly wed. There was enough credibility to make the executors investigate the claim."

"A missing heir?" Cain said. "How dramatic."

"Henry Tarleton arrived in London and announced he intended to follow in his uncle's footsteps, carry on the great Tarleton tradition, and generally behaved like a jumped-up parvenu." Compton glanced across the dining room with distaste. "He looked a bit of a fool when the will was questioned. The court ordered the sale to satisfy the creditors."

"Poor sod," Iverley said, with more sympathy than Cain had yet heard him express for a fellow human. "You're such a stickler, Tarquin. If I'd been in the fellow's situation I'd have wanted the books. I would not be happy to see them sold from under my nose."

"Why are you interested in the Burgundy manuscript?" Cain asked Iverley.

"The binding. I collect royal bindings. That book was bound as a gift from Francis I of France to Henry VIII."

Compton laughed. "You see, Chase. Sebastian always judges a book by its cover."

How right she'd been to see her presence at the Tarleton sale as an opportunity. Juliana would never have been invited to one of the Berry evenings had she not encountered Miss Agnes at the auction. The sisters had been occasional customers, some of the few females she'd seen either in her shop or in the salerooms. But she was fairly sure she had the Marquis of Chase's growing number of purchases to thank for the invitation.

She was happy to spend an evening away from her rooms. Twice more she'd awoken with a sense that something was moving down below in the shop. She convinced herself she was suffering from nerves, but those restless nights made her uncomfortable in her own home.

Among the crowd in the rapidly filling room at the

Berry house, she recognized several people, including Lord Spencer. How splendid it would be to meet him at last! She was grateful for her new gown, which she considered very elegant, though the low-cut bodice made her a little self-conscious.

She wondered what Cain would think of it. She'd dreaded seeing him for the first time after she'd made a fool of herself, but her embarrassment slipped away in the face of his own lack of concern. It was as though that evening had never happened. Instead he'd been his usual cheerful self and bought several books, enough to earn her a tidy commission and justify the purchase of the dress. They had an entirely satisfactory relationship based on business and she ought not to care what he thought of her appearance.

Anyway, the matter was irrelevant. She couldn't imagine him attending such a gathering.

One of her hostesses had presented her to several people on her arrival, but the group had drifted apart, and now she was in danger of being driven behind a piano, the disadvantage of her small stature. She hoped she wouldn't have to resort to the unseemly exercise of elbows to escape.

Socially she was inexperienced, sensing by instinct rather than actual knowledge that this gathering was not one of high *ton*. Judging by their attire, other guests mixed the modish and the merely respectable. Wondering how to gain further introductions, she was pleased to come across Matthew Gilbert.

How fortunate. The gentleman bookseller might be able to present her to some potential customers in the room. He was accompanied by a man of striking appearance, probably in his early thirties. No more than middling height, he boasted a broad chest and shoulders under his blue evening coat. Bright golden hair, cropped short, was in odd contrast to dark skin that Juliana guessed resulted from prolonged exposure to the sun. The man must have traveled abroad.

He also seemed familiar.

"Mrs. Merton," Mr. Gilbert said. "Allow me to present Sir Henry Tarleton."

Juliana was curious to meet Tarleton's heir, having heard much speculation about him among other booksellers. He smiled at her, revealing even white teeth that contrasted attractively with his tanned complexion. "I asked Gilbert to introduce us since we come, in a way, from the same part of the world."

"I understand, Sir Henry, that you have lived most of your life in the Indies. Did you visit England often?"

Perhaps she'd seen him during a visit to her Wiltshire neighborhood, but she didn't believe so. The two men exchanged glances, then Gilbert excused himself, leaving her alone with Tarleton.

"My mother and I spent a period of years here in my youth," Sir Henry explained. "My father had died, but she thought that as Sir Thomas's heir, I should receive an English education. We made several visits to Wiltshire and I knew of Mr. Fitterbourne. I regret never making his acquaintance."

"Your uncle and my guardian were not on visiting terms."

"I commend your restraint, madam," he said with a rueful smile. "I am well acquainted with my late uncle's reputation. He had a knack for making enemies."

Juliana found Sir Henry's openness appealing. "He and Mr. Fitterbourne often clashed over their collections."

"People jest about bibliomania, but I'm afraid with my uncle it was a true affliction, making him view his fellow collectors only as competitors."

Mr. Fitterbourne hadn't been very different, Juliana thought, remembering the long years of her childhood when she never met anyone from outside Fernley Court save the occasional visiting bookseller. Little surprise that she'd ended up married to one. There had been no one else.

"Just because Mr. Fitterbourne and my uncle were rivals, it doesn't mean, I hope, that we cannot be friends," Sir Henry continued. "We have many interests in common."

"Are you a collector yourself?"

"In my small way, yes. It grieves me to see my uncle's books go under the hammer. But I hope to acquire some volumes myself."

"I can appreciate your sentiments. I felt the same way when my guardian's library was sold." She bit her lip. Despite Sir Henry's frank disclosures, it was perhaps impolite to express dissatisfaction over the sale.

She needn't have worried. "I know my uncle purchased Mr. Fitterbourne's library," he said. "That must have been hard for you. Perhaps there are some volumes you wish to acquire for sentimental reasons."

Brought up to hate the very name Tarleton, she was astonished to find this man understood her feelings. Perhaps she should enlist his help. Cain, after all, had willingly agreed not to bid against her.

"The Shakespeare quartos were my favorite part of the collection," she said. "Particularly the *Romeo and Juliet*."

"A fine copy. I shall defer to you and refrain from bidding on it myself."

She flushed with pleasure and surprise. Frankness about her wishes had eliminated another competitor. "Thank you, Sir Henry. It belonged to Mr. Fitterbourne's daughter and I always liked it."

Sir Henry gave a little bow. "I look forward to calling on you," he said, taking his leave. "I hear you have an interesting stock."

Juliana looked after him, wondering where she had seen him before. Though she couldn't be certain, she thought it was in her shop. Why hadn't he mentioned it?

Mr. Gilbert returned to her side.

"Thank you for introducing me to Sir Henry," Juliana said. "I have every hope he will become a customer. Are you representing him at the sale?"

"He has asked me to, but I find myself in something of a quandary. I have several clients with competing demands. You might be able to help me. Would you be prepared to take over his bidding? Naturally you would receive the full commission."

"That's very good of you but I have been engaged by the Marquis of Chase. He has first call on my services."

"Is Chase serious then? I assumed most of your purchases have been on your own behalf."

Juliana was flattered that Gilbert had such an inflated estimate of the size of her purse. She murmured something noncommittal.

"You might want to consider withdrawing from your agreement with the marquis. In the long run Tarleton would likely prove a more valuable connection. From all I've heard Chase is . . . how can I put it . . . unreliable."

She was tempted. Not just because Gilbert echoed her own doubts about Cain's fortitude as a collector. There was something irresistible about the notion of making money from the Tarleton fortune.

"I will think about it," she said.

"Please do. And let me know. Shall I call on you tomorrow? I could look at those books we spoke about."

"I'd welcome that," she replied, happy to have the chance to offload some of her most unappealing stock.

"I'll come early before the auction begins, if that is convenient."

"If the door isn't open, ring the bell and I'll come down."

"I greatly look forward to furthering our association."

Gilbert leaned forward, making Juliana acutely aware of her décolletage. Yet his gaze was fixed on her face. Associating with Chase had scrambled her brain. Mr. Gilbert, unlike the marquis, was a most respectable man. Not one to be distracted by her transformed appearance.

"May I say, Mrs. Merton, what a pleasure it is to meet a lady with an interest in books." And now his pale eyes held a certain gleam.

"Thank you, sir. There aren't many of us."

"And I am sure none of them boasts your level of knowledge or taste."

"Why, Mr. Gilbert," she responded with a smile, "I do believe you flatter me."

"Oh no!" he said, "I never flatter."

"What, never? When a customer proudly shows you a treasure he 'managed to pick up' in some out-of-the-way country bookshop, do you inform him that it's a poor copy of a common book and he overpaid for it?"

Gilbert responded with a grave look. "I must admit that I am not always so frank. Are we not allowed our little sins of omission?"

"Does that mean that I can always assume you speak the truth, just not the whole truth?"

"As we become better acquainted I trust we can dispense even with that reservation."

Juliana was hard put to keep her expression demure and ladylike. What a splendid evening! Not only had she gained the prospect of an important new client. But a gentleman, an important, knowledgeable, serious bookman, was showing unmistakable signs of a personal interest in her.

She lowered her eyes and peered up at Matthew Gilbert's unremarkable and pleasant features. He might lack flashing eyes and a slashing grin. His presence might not fill her with new, dangerous, physical yearnings. But this was a man worthy of her respect.

Warm breath tickled her neck and a voice like a cello caressed her ear.

"My dear Juliana. What have you done to yourself?"

The infuriating man had crept up on cat's feet. She spun around to meet, just inches from her face, the blue eyes and laughing mouth of the Marquis of Chase.

At first Cain found the bluestocking party not so very different from any other gathering. The guests weren't as well dressed as those at one of Harriette Wilson's soirées. One couldn't expect the same level of peacocking at an event whose aim was intellectual enlightenment rather than a bed partner for the night. Yet the twinkle in Miss Berry's eye when Tarquin Compton introduced his companion indicated that she, at least, might have found a gathering of courtesans intriguing. Clearly regarding him as a new zoological specimen for her menagerie, she presented him to a group that included a poet, a politician, a painter, and a lady novelist known for her gothic fantasies.

They were discussing servants.

Cain had enjoyed better conversations with his own household staff. He could have contributed some interesting tales about his own hiring practices, but he was determined to be on his best behavior tonight and not offend the conventions.

Then he glimpsed her in a far corner of the room through a gap in the crowd. He'd already been treated to the glory of her hair, else he might not have recognized the little beauty in black, a soft velvet gown clinging to every delicious curve of her full breasts and shapely behind. A narrow black ribbon at the neck was her sole adornment and served to emphasize the expanse of bare white skin beneath it. The golden curls were carelessly tucked into a black velvet bandeau and set off the barely freckled fragility of flawless pale skin.

His little bookseller had shed her shroud and she was every bit as lovely as he had predicted. Judging by her expression she enjoyed her transformation, and he was gratified at her pleasure.

Until he saw the object of her smile. Not a smile, he amended, a simper. It was directed at a man who gazed at her with undisguised admiration. The bookseller Gilbert.

Cain's pleasure dissipated. He'd detected the gem concealed by monstrous bombazine. Now the treasure was revealed for all to see, including that stiff-rumped fellow.

Juliana Merton belonged to *him*. His hunter's instincts aroused, he excused himself and headed across the room.

He hoped she hadn't been drinking tonight.

"My dear Juliana. What have you done to yourself?"

"My lord." She spun round, her voice a little breathless. "I am surprised to see you."

"I hope you are happy to see me. And," he added, lifting her hand toward his mouth, "you are supposed to call me Cain."

"My lord," she repeated, her face guarded. Her fingers stiffened in her glove. "I am, of course, always happy to see a customer."

"Is that all I am?" He brushed his lips over her knuckles.

She glanced back at Gilbert with an expression of alarm and retrieved her hand rather abruptly. The other man regarded him with unvarnished disfavor.

"Allow me to present Mr. Gilbert," she said.

He and Gilbert assessed each other like a pair of fighting cocks preparing for the fray. Cain felt confident he could defeat the man, physically or otherwise. Judging by his demeanor, Gilbert's wit was as rigid as his back.

"Lord Chase." Gilbert nodded. "Mrs. Merton and I have been discussing books. We have so much in common in that area."

And there, Cain admitted, Gilbert had him. He couldn't compete with the bookseller when it came to Juliana's greatest passion.

But that could change: his own knowledge, her passion. Or perhaps both.

"I understand you have decided to become a book collector?" Cain didn't imagine the scorn in Gilbert's words. He was used to being on the receiving end of barely disguised insults.

He nodded. "Mrs. Merton is advising me."

"And you couldn't find a better counselor," Gilbert said with false heartiness. His features pinched. "I had the privilege of selling several volumes to your revered father. And Lady Chase continues to honor me with her custom. As doubtless you are aware, she has added many volumes to your family library."

Of course he wasn't aware. And Gilbert knew it too.

"What does Lady Chase collect?" Juliana asked.

"Ask Gilbert. He's the bookseller."

"Markley Chase boasts one of the best collections of devotional works in the country, in keeping with the Godfrey family tradition."

Cain folded his arms and cocked his head in a relaxed pose. And it was just that: a pose. His mother never left the Abbey, hadn't set foot in London in years, though doubtless she prayed for the souls of the inhabitants of the modern Gomorrah. *No one* knew his mother. But apparently this man did.

What had she said to Gilbert about him? The one thing Cain feared was an encounter with someone who knew the real reason for his exile.

Cain was upset, Juliana could tell. He stood casually enough, his lips twitched into a mocking smile, but she sensed a tension in his stillness. The mention of his mother and his home had distressed him and she couldn't blame him.

"Lord Chase shows great promise as a collector," she said. "He has natural taste."

"Natural?" Gilbert asked, a wealth of scorn in the syllables.

Apparently she'd chosen the wrong word. Cain's arms fell to his sides and his fists clenched.

"Yes indeed," she said hastily, searching for words that would defuse the encounter. She didn't want to affront Gilbert and lose his approval, but she felt she had to defend Cain. Because he was her customer, if for no other reason.

"I have bought some excellent volumes at his suggestion," she said.

"Really?" Gilbert asked. "I'm interested. Is he following his family tradition?"

Juliana's mind went blank. Almost. The only title that came to mind was *The Rampant Alderman*.

"I prefer to keep my counsel about my customer's preferences," she managed to murmur.

For a moment Cain's smile held real humor. "Thank you, my dear. I do prefer discretion in my ladies."

And now she wanted to hit him. She settled for a quelling glare.

"Lord Chase likes to provoke," she explained to Gilbert.

"Another natural talent."

"On the contrary," Cain drawled. "I've worked very hard at it."

"So I've heard," Mr. Gilbert said. "And at other activities."

Juliana didn't know which man exasperated her more. To her relief, the appearance of Tarquin Compton put an end to the exchange before fists began to fly.

"Good evening, Gilbert," he said. "I believe Lord Spencer is looking for you."

Gilbert collected himself and took his leave. Juliana would have too, had England's most prestigious book collector called.

"Did Spencer really want him," Cain asked, "or were you merely riding to the rescue on a white horse?"

Mr. Compton raised an eyebrow. "Whose rescue would that be?"

Mine, Juliana thought.

"I'm afraid Mr. Gilbert doesn't like me," Cain mocked, but Juliana fancied an undertone of tension.

"That was apparent from ten feet away. It looked as if you were getting ready to take a swing. Do you always hit men who don't like you?"

"If necessary."

"I couldn't allow a brawl in the Misses Berry's drawing room."

"Because you'd be embarrassed for bringing me here?"

Mr. Compton was an unusually tall man and he stared down at Cain, every bit the social leader. "Because I am fond of our hostesses and they wouldn't appreciate it." Then his attitude shifted. "Pity, because *I* might have enjoyed seeing Gilbert go down."

Juliana felt Cain relax and both men grinned.

"Matthew Gilbert is a bit of a stick," Mr. Compton said.

"I wouldn't phrase it as politely," Cain replied.

"He's a very intelligent and interesting man," Juliana said, unaccountably annoyed by the sudden masculine solidarity.

Mr. Compton remembered his manners and bowed to her. "I apologize, Mrs. Merton. I haven't said good evening to you."

She curtsied. "It's always a pleasure to see you, Mr. Compton. Is Lord Hugo well?"

"A little tired. Hence his absence tonight, though he always enjoys these North Audley Street gatherings. But you, Mrs. Merton, are obviously in the pink of health. May I commend your remarkably elegant gown? Black is unusual for evening dress, for ladies, that is." His own clothes were of almost unrelieved ebony. "But you can carry it off. You have the right coloring."

"Thank you, sir."

"May I find you some refreshment? A glass of wine, perhaps?"

"No thank you."

He left her with Cain, who was rocking back on his heels and looking at her with something unreadable in his eyes.

"You provoked Mr. Gilbert," she began, then, before he could object, "but he was every bit as bad. I'm sorry he brought up your parents. It must have been painful."

"I've suffered worse."

"He was very civil to me. He can be helpful." She wasn't about to admit that Gilbert had suggested she drop Cain as a client.

"He admires you."

Juliana made a self-deprecating noise.

Cain leaned in. His scent, warm and slightly musky, tickled her nostrils. His voice fell to a murmur. "That's why I don't like him."

He was flirting with her again. Truly, she was having more fun tonight than she had in years, perhaps ever.

"I'm having the most marvelous time, Cain. I met Sir Henry Tarleton and he wants to look at my stock."

"Thomas Tarleton's heir?" Cain asked, not much interested. A lemony curl had escaped the black velvet bandeau and drew attention to the sweet indentation of Juliana's collarbone, inviting him to taste the soft white skin.

"Yes. He's very upset that his uncle's books are being sold."

If Cain were a better man he'd go after the new baronet and find out what he knew about the Burgundy Hours. But Tarleton could wait. He had other plans for tonight.

"My dear girl," he said. "If you are happy, so am I. And I'm very happy to see you looking so fine. Every woman in London will wish to scratch your eyes out when they hear what Compton had to say. Did you know the ladies of the *ton* and the demimonde die to win a compliment from him?"

"How absurd. Why?"

"Because his taste is reputed to be flawless."

Juliana gave a low chuckle that warmed his heart. He loved to make her laugh, he realized. She took life much too seriously.

"Needless to say I've never received a comment on my dress from him before. Black bombazine does not apparently meet his approbation."

"But black velvet does. Why still black?"

"It's easier to remain in mourning. Fortunately I discovered this gown at a secondhand clothing shop in Conduit Street."

"Mrs. Timms. I know many actresses who patronize her."

"Actresses?" Juliana said. "Do you mean my gown might have belonged to an actress?"

"I doubt it."

"Thank goodness."

"More likely a courtesan."

She gasped delightfully. "Why do you think so?"

"Did you wonder, my dear innocent, how Mrs. Timms came to have such an unusual garment?"

"No, but she was quite pleased to sell it to me, at a reasonable price."

"I suspect it was cast off by Bella Starr. Her protector, Sir Mordred Morton, always insists on dressing his mistresses in black."

Her little freckled nose wrinkled. "How very morbid."

"Morton would be happy to hear you say so. He prides himself on his morbidity. Black liveries for his servants, black carriages inside and out. His upholstery and curtains are all black and he only allows himself to be served black food."

"That must limit his diet."

"Invitations to dine with Morton are not highly sought after."

"I can only think of grapes."

"Caviar."

"Blackberries," she said, getting into the spirit of the conceit. "In season."

"Olives."

"Chocolate."

"Plums."

"Burned meat?"

"Burned toast too," he said. "That's why he recently left for Bavaria. So that he can eat black bread without the charcoal."

"And black pudding."

"Precisely. He told me Germans are famous for their morbidity."

"Did he leave his mistress behind?"

"Yes. And she wasted no time banishing black from her wardrobe."

"Well I'm glad, since I got such a bargain. This gown had scarcely been worn."

"And I'm glad she did too," he said, suddenly serious. He looked at her intently and her laughter drained away, leaving her with lips slightly parted and naked awareness in her eyes as they met his.

Then she dropped her gaze, clearly flustered. "I should meet some more people," she said.

Not ready yet. She wasn't going to drop into his hand like a ripe plum at Sir Mordred's dinner table.

Good. He might not have inherited any part of his father's character, but his title was apt. Cain loved the chase.

Chapter 7

On a chilly and damp March night the red chariot was warm. The marquis's servants might not look the part but they knew how to make their master comfortable. Juliana settled back on the luxurious upholstery and let the hood of her black cloak fall to her shoulders.

"Thank you for your assistance tonight," she said. "I made some useful connections through your help."

She sensed his shrug beside her on the seat. "I merely asked Tarquin Compton to present you to Spencer."

"And others too. And they all seemed truly interested in my books."

"Are you sure they weren't just admiring your figure in your new gown? I know I was."

"Certainly not. Besides, some of them were female."

"So?"

"Stop trying to shock me. Seriously, thanks to you I met more possible customers tonight than have set foot in my shop in the last month."

"You are always so practical," he complained. "I'd

rather talk about something else." His voice was a raspy whisper. In the dark cabin, lit by a single lantern, she could barely make out his features. Instead the confined space enhanced her sense of his presence. His thigh brushed against hers.

"What then?" she asked. Perhaps he would tell her more amusing anecdotes of the demimonde.

"About kissing you."

She gasped, or rather, she feared, squeaked.

"Actually I don't want to *talk* about anything."

She could no longer fool herself that this was a simple ride home, an alternative to a cold and dirty hackney.

He framed her head between his hands and shifted to allow the light to fall on her face. The lantern light shone through his own locks revealing red tints in his brown hair and giving him an incongruously angelic halo. He examined her with absolute concentration.

"You are very beautiful."

"I have freckles," she replied nervously.

"Only six." He dropped as many gentle kisses on her nose and cheeks. "I missed one." And kissed her again, his lips lingering on the delicate skin beneath one eye.

Now was the moment to draw back but she didn't want to. She remembered his previous kiss through a haze of wine. Tonight she hadn't drunk so much as a glass of water and she couldn't wait to find out what it was like to kiss him when sober. Remaining still, neither retreating nor advancing, she waited for his next move.

He released her and leaned back into his corner. "Your gown matches my seats."

"That's why I chose it, of course," she replied, disguising her disappointment with an attempt at humor.

"The effect is extraordinary. In this light everything fades away except your head. All gold and white like a disembodied angel."

"Oh," she breathed. Compliments on her looks had been rare in her life.

"But you aren't an angel, are you? At least I sincerely hope not."

Those wonderful creases appeared to frame his mouth and he advanced again, without a hint of mockery in his smile or gaze.

"Juliana," he whispered, and he took her into his arms and kissed her with parted lips, mingling his breath with hers.

This time she needed no prompting to open to him, to meet his tongue with her own. His arms tightened as she slid her own over his shoulders and threaded her fingers through his soft hair, pulling him closer to deepen the kiss. His throat emitted guttural sounds of appreciation.

As the black horses clopped through the quiet late-night streets, Juliana discovered the joy of kissing, an area in which her experience had been sadly lacking. She allowed her late husband a fleeting thought. Poor Joseph.

Then the world contracted to a velvet-lined box and Cain's lips on hers. And on her cheeks and nose and temples and neck and even, deliciously, in her ear. But mostly on her mouth, licking, sucking, nuzzling, creating the most delightful sensations that flooded her entire body. By the time they approached the end of their journey she was aching for something more. Yet he didn't touch her anywhere else. She was locked in his embrace but his hands remained immobile on her back.

Touch me . . . somewhere, she begged silently. She couldn't bring herself to ask out loud.

The carriage drew to a halt and he released her. Groping in her reticule, she found her key and made no protest when he removed it from her limp hand, then helped her out onto the pavement. He unlocked her door and nudged her across the threshold with a nod over his shoulder to his coachman. As the door closed she heard the jingle of harness and the renewed clop of hooves.

Then the sound from the street faded behind the stout wooden barrier and she was in the dark entry at the foot of the stairs. Alone with Cain.

Now was the moment to thank him politely and send him home. But she didn't want to be alone, imagining prowlers downstairs. Perhaps even now a thief awaited her above.

At least that's what she told herself.

Cain would have preferred to take her to his own house, but he doubted she would agree. His honed instincts for the workings of a woman's mind told him she might still bolt. Juliana was eager, yes. Her response was as passionate as he'd hoped. Yet her brain had not yet fully accepted what would happen.

He wanted her to ache with longing until she lost any desire to retreat.

He'd had to exercise every morsel of control he possessed not to lift her skirts in the carriage. Had a few weeks' abstinence brought him to such a pass? Lovemaking might be his favorite occupation, but he hadn't been this desperate for a woman in years.

The art of seduction required taking things slowly and their first time together was not going to be a quick tumble, however comfortable his coach.

Keeping a hand on the small of her back, he followed her upstairs and waited while she fumbled with a candle. The disordered room appeared mean and shabby in the flickering light and the atmosphere was damp and chilly. She deserved better quarters.

"Would you like some tea?" she asked. "It's cold."

He placed his hands on her shoulders and nuzzled the soft nape of her neck, relishing her warm, clean female scent.

"We'd be warmer in bed," he whispered.

He felt her muscles stiffen and prepared to use all his powers of persuasion. Then the tension melted and she leaned back against him, relaxing into his embrace. For the first time he allowed his hands to wander, untying the strings of her cloak, palming her velvet-covered breasts, and pressing in to discover the slender waist and sweet swell of hips beneath the soft fabric. Soon, very soon, he'd be touching skin.

Then she pulled away.

"I need a few minutes to get ready."

"Let me help." He held on to her arm, afraid to let her out of his sight lest she come to her senses. Besides, undressing was part of the pleasure. "You'll need me to undo the buttons."

"How do you suppose I managed to do them up? I don't have a maid tucked away here."

Dragging him with her she pushed open the door of her bedroom. "Give me a few minutes," she said again, whisked herself inside, and closed the door in his face.

"Don't attempt those buttons without me," he called.

Sure that she'd talk herself into sense when freed of his presence, Cain was apprehensive, his usual self-assurance lacking. Putting his ear to the bedroom door, he tried to guess what she was up to. He heard none of the rustling of cloth and slamming of drawers denoting a hurried attempt to clear up. He'd known women who hated to reveal an untidy room. For himself, he enjoyed the sight of feminine clutter: stockings draped over a chair, discarded gowns piled on the bed, bottles of perfume and cosmetics unstoppered on a dressing table and lending their mingled scents to the ambience. Not that he suspected Juliana possessed an abundance of feminine fripperies: that was something he'd love to change.

He heard a low thud, a muttered "damn," and rushed into the room.

"Are you all right?"

She sat on the floor, legs apart, skirts askew. Her calves, clad in sensible black stockings that did nothing to disguise their shapeliness, were revealed to both knees.

"I'm fine," she said shortly.

He might have joined her but there wasn't room. In keeping with the rest of the flat the bedroom was tiny, most of it taken up by a chest of drawers and a none-too-large bed. That would have to change too.

He reached out a hand to pull her up.

"What happened?"

She looked thoroughly embarrassed. "Nothing," she muttered. "I lost my balance."

To his relief she made no objection to his presence. "Now for those buttons," he said. "Turn."

Obediently she turned her back to him. He loved this bit, like unwrapping a package.

"Beautiful," he murmured, caressing the contours of her upper back. "Your skin is soft as silk and not a freckle in sight. Like pure cream."

She flexed her shoulders with a purr of appreciation. Drawing aside the black velvet, he let it drop to the floor and ran his hands over her torso, sensing the curves beneath her no-nonsense linen undergarments.

Another thing he'd like to change.

"I knew there was something wonderful hidden beneath that black armor." She was perfectly proportioned for her diminutive stature, with just enough flesh in just the right places. Arching her back, she pushed her behind against his burgeoning erection.

The promise of enormous pleasure swelled to certainty.

Her petticoat was the next to go, followed by shoes, garters, and stockings. He knelt to remove her footwear and stole a kiss on the sweet spot behind one knee.

"Behold me at your feet," he said, drawing a chuckle, though otherwise she'd accepted his ministrations in silence.

He stood up and faced her, running his hands down her naked arms. "You have gooseflesh. I'd prefer to believe I have made you shiver with desire, but I'm afraid it's the temperature." And he drew back the covers on the bed, picked her up, now clad only in her shift, and deposited her there. She huddled under the blankets, staring at him with wide eyes.

He tugged at his neck cloth. "I want to reassure you about one thing. I shall make sure you are safe from any . . . unfortunate consequences."

She blushed. "I've already taken measures to prevent conception," she said primly.

Cain was impressed. Accustomed to taking precautions, there wasn't much he hadn't learned from his friends about the prevention of pregnancy and disease. With Juliana he wasn't concerned about the latter and, of course, she'd been married but had no children.

"Do you use a sponge?" he asked.

Her blush deepened as she nodded.

"Splendid." Far preferable to condoms or withdrawal as far as he was concerned. He grinned at her. "Did you fall over while inserting it?"

She nodded. He decided not to mention that he could have helped. He doubted she was ready for that kind of game.

Juliana's discomfort faded at Cain's matter-of-fact acceptance, a marked contrast to Joseph's cringing embarrassment when faced with intimate personal affairs. On their wedding night, he had produced the sponges and a bottle of brandy and explained their use. He had been resolved, and she had agreed, that they couldn't afford children. They'd never mentioned the matter again. She was particularly grateful now. She would never place herself at risk of bearing a child out of wedlock.

Going to bed with Cain might be the most reckless thing she'd ever done but she was going to enjoy it.

Now he stood in her tiny bedroom, laughing quietly as he unwound his neck cloth, his blue gaze fixed on her with a heat at variance with his careless stance. She sucked in her breath as he tossed the linen aside and unbuttoned his shirt, revealing etched collarbones and a glimpse of light brown hair on a muscled chest. He was truly a beautiful man.

And for tonight, perhaps only for tonight, he was hers.

She watched him remove his clothes. All of them. She'd never seen a naked man. She and Joseph had both worn decorous nightgowns to bed and despite their cramped quarters had respected each other's privacy, each leaving the room while the other performed his toilet. Cain seemed to lack even a shred of modesty so she stared, eyes increasingly wide, as he shed his garments.

My goodness. Had it not been for that wicked book she'd have had no idea how that thing looked in the flesh. The word *rampant* came inexorably to mind.

She didn't know whether to be glad or sorry when the exhibition came to an end and he joined her in bed, embracing her under the blankets.

"Warm me up," he murmured in that well-deep voice, and started kissing again.

Not that he needed it. His body was hot as a paving stone in the sun and almost as hard. As he gathered her closer she felt solid, beautifully formed muscle under smooth, pliant skin, flesh to flesh exciting every nerve at each point of contact. One strong leg curved around her own, slightly coarse hair complementing the smoothness of her own limbs.

And his kiss. Now she realized he'd been holding back in the carriage, keeping something in reserve. He took possession, devouring her, exploring and exciting every cranny of her mouth with his clever tongue. And since she was a quick learner she met him thrust for thrust, reveling in the taste and texture of him until she was as hot as he.

As for his hands, they certainly weren't still. At last her breasts, taut and aching, received the attention they craved. He stroked them with firm yet gentle touch and thumbed her small nipples until they tingled. She heard herself moan.

"More?" he asked, releasing her mouth, but didn't wait for an answer, fortunate since she was likely incapable of coherent speech.

Somehow he managed to divest her of her shift and—oh bliss—took one of the stiffening peaks into his mouth and sucked. Who would have thought that would be so delicious? And while he worked her breasts his hands wandered south, warming her flat belly, her hips, the tender skin between her thighs.

She lay passive, not sure what to do, reveling in Cain's skillful ministrations.

"Touch me," he whispered.

Of course. Yet could she possibly give him as much pleasure? Her relative ignorance of lovemaking nagged at her, but gathering her courage she tentatively ran her hands down his back and felt muscles jump at her touch.

"Yes," he urged. Encouraged, she applied her caresses with greater confidence, reaching everywhere she could, even to his buttocks, firm and shapely under her seeking fingers. His erection pressed against her pelvis and hardened even more.

She felt a surge of power and issued a little moue of complaint when he pulled back from her, until his fingers slipped between her lower curls and started to caress her *there*.

She'd never felt anything like it in her life. She could feel herself warm and wet as he stroked with unerring precision, finding a place that aroused the most extraordinary tension. She settled onto her back to give him easier access and maintained her own attentions to his shoulders and arms. With a corner of her mind she knew she wasn't giving him equal measure, but every fiber of her being was concentrated on the sensations he generated at her very core. Just when she thought she couldn't stand it another moment, would burst, go mad if something—she didn't know what— didn't happen, he removed his hand, came on top of her, and entered her.

He was long and hard and she felt stretched to the breaking point. Yet when he began to pump she found she was wet enough to accommodate him without discomfort. Curling her legs about his thighs she shifted herself up to meet him. Somehow, though she enjoyed the feeling of being filled, it wasn't quite the same as when he'd used his hand. That bursting sensation returned but with less intensity and she felt further from that nameless conclusion.

Cain had raised himself onto his elbows as he thrust and continued to kiss her and murmur encouragement. He worked in her a long time and there were moments when that feeling crested again, then retreated.

Suddenly he withdrew and lay beside her, continuing to hold her close.

"It's not going to work, is it?" he said softly.

"No," she said, feeling a wave of inadequacy, though not sure exactly how she was lacking.

"We'll do it this way."

It took minutes, perhaps only seconds. His fingers found that spot again and she tumbled into bliss, waves of heat emanating from her core up through her torso and down every limb to the tips of her fingers and toes.

She cried out, probably senselessly.

"That's it," he said and came into her again with a few hard, accelerating thrusts. He collapsed with a hoarse shout as she felt his seed gush inside her.

She was boneless, didn't believe she could ever move again. The waves of heat subsided to a hum, and as the humming sensation abated a delicious well-being continued to pervade her mind and body. She thought she'd happily remain buried in the warm cocoon of her bed, in Cain's arms, forever.

"Hey," Cain said, his voice teasing and amazingly

strong. "It's rude to go to sleep afterward." He rolled off her, sat up, and started arranging the pillows, including the one beneath her head, which he pulled out despite her muttered grumble.

By that standard Joseph must have been the rudest man in England. He always went straight to sleep.

Cain hauled her up beside him and settled them back against the pillows, tugging the blankets up under their chins. She protested a little but let him tuck her in his arm, her head nestled in his shoulder.

"This mattress has a lump in it," he complained.

"That's why I sleep on this side."

"Don't you think you should let a guest have the comfortable side?"

"I'm not much in the habit of entertaining." Her wits were returning, just.

"I'm honored to receive your hospitality. I enjoyed myself immensely." The caress in his deep voice was followed by a lingering closemouthed kiss. She felt herself melting back into a state of semi-somnolence.

Cain had other ideas. "Tell me how you learned about books."

"Do you want to talk? Now?"

"It's the best bit. Well, perhaps not the best, but I've had some excellent conversations after lovemaking. And it fills the time till we can do it again."

"Again?"

"Give me a few minutes."

"A few minutes?" She seemed to have turned into an echo, but the concepts of postcoital conversation and a repeat of the main event were new to her. But not unwelcome, she found. It was rather cozy tucked up in bed with Cain's lovely warm body. Her sleepiness faded away.

"How did *you* learn the difference between calf and vellum?" he asked.

"I was six years old when my g— grandfather showed me my first rare book. It was a first edition of Montaigne's *Essays*."

"Advanced reading for such a little thing."

"It wasn't meant to be read." She rolled her eyes and punched him in the chest playfully. "As a matter of fact he showed it to me because I told him about the book I *was* reading. Perrault's *Fairy Tales*. He'd never shown much interest in me before that. My nurse would take me to his library for ten minutes every evening and I remember it was always awkward. After he discovered I liked books, things changed. He taught me a game. I had to identify the kind of leather in a book binding and when I got it right he gave me a peppermint drop."

"I can see your childhood was one dissipation after another."

"I enjoyed it."

"Actually I envy you. I never did anything half as amusing with my parents. Did you go on reading fairy tales?"

"I did," Juliana said softly. She'd read them so often the volume fell apart like a pack of cards. She was sorry for it. The Perrault had belonged to Cassandra.

"Did you dream one of those princes would ride up on a white horse and carry you away?"

"I got over that." She didn't tell him her real dream

was that her mother, of whose identity she was then unaware, would come and rescue her from the loneliness of Fernley Court.

"Very wise," he said. "Men are never princes."

Juliana didn't want to talk about her disappointed dreams. "As I grew older," she said, "I had to guess the age of the binding as well."

"Let me try one," he said. A pile of books tottered on the small table that filled the space between the bed and the wall. "What about that big one?"

He had to reach across her to get to the volume but stopped halfway. He tugged the blankets down to expose one of her breasts.

"Smooth," he murmured, stroking it with the tips of his fingers. The breast tingled happily. "Soft as silk." He closed his eyes with a look of deep concentration. "Some kind of skin is my guess."

"Idiot," she said. "All leather is some kind of skin."

To her regret he removed his hand and pulled up the cover again. "Thanks, Juliana, for spoiling that moment. Before I start associating breasts with old boots, hand over that book."

"It's heavy. Can't you feel it from where you are?"

As she hoped, Cain almost rolled on top of her. His lovely firm chest rubbed against her, setting up a renewed tingling and an enhanced appreciation of the concept of "doing it again."

"Interesting texture," he said, stroking the worn cover. "A male beast, I believe, but not entirely virile. A rather shy badger? Am I right? Is it badger skin?"

"No."

"A bashful beaver? No?"

He rested his head on her chest, which was heaving with laughter, and appeared to be lost in deep thought.

"I'm on the wrong track," he mused. "I know! It's a smaller animal but a strong one. A stout stoat? A rapacious rat? A very vigorous vole?"

She couldn't speak, only shake her head.

"Give me a hint. Is it a small animal? No? A big one then?" She nodded. "An elephant? I don't believe you. Another hint, please."

The sound disintegrated into giggles but Cain managed to recognize a "mooo."

"A cow!" he cried in disgust, rolling off her and sitting up. "All the time the creature was a female. How could I have got it wrong? I may have to retire to a monastery."

"The book is bound in calf," she said. "The sex of the animal is not specified."

"What is it? A rare tome, I suppose, too precious to be sullied by a common eye."

"Actually it's not very valuable and extremely dull. A collection of documents and newspaper extracts relating to the recent history of the Church of England."

"And how do you come to possess such a fascinating miscellany?"

"I wish I knew. It was one of the last things my husband bought before his murder. The whole lot was rubbish."

"Your husband was murdered?" Cain appeared

shocked. It hadn't occurred to her he didn't know. "My God! Did it happen here?"

"Not here." She shuddered. "At an inn in Salisbury."

"Did they catch the murderer?"

"No. The magistrate said it was a common robbery and the killer escaped."

Cain put an arm around her and gathered her close. "I'm sorry. You must miss him very much?"

"Yes," she answered baldly. As usual she felt guilty for not missing her husband more.

"Are you lonely living all by yourself here?"

"Sometimes," she confided. "And lately I think it's made me a little mad. I hear noises in the night, downstairs."

"What kind of noises?"

"I don't know. It's more of a feeling really. A couple of times I've woken with the sense there's someone in the shop. It happened last night. But nothing seems to be missing, or even disturbed."

"Under the circumstances I'm not surprised you're afraid of robbery."

His tightening embrace comforted her. "I think I must be imagining things. Perhaps I am upset by the approaching anniversary of Joseph's death."

It seemed wrong to be discussing her late husband while she lay in bed with another man. Perhaps Cain felt the same restraint.

"I admire you for continuing your business alone," he said finally.

"What else could I do? Besides, it's what I wanted.

I can't imagine a life without books. And thanks to you, my lord, I am about to become more successful. It was a very lucky occurrence that brought you to my shop."

"I think so too." He squeezed her breast. "Happy to be of service, but I have the feeling you would have managed to meet a few people tonight without me. Mr. Gilbert, I am sure, would have been glad to oblige."

There was an edge in his voice. "Perhaps he'd like to buy that volume. My mother would probably find it fascinating. Ironic really, that we should both have become book collectors. At least I can be sure we won't be rivals for the same things. Our tastes could hardly be more different."

She tried to turn aside his bitterness with a joke. "I'm not so sure about that. You must be aware that the Book of Hours is a prayer book."

"Yes," he said shortly.

"By the way, I looked into the history of the Burgundy manuscript. It was a gift from the King of France to Henry VIII. Then it disappeared from the royal inventory without any record of its disposal. Most unusual for such a treasure. One history surmises that the king gave it to someone, a favorite perhaps."

She was about to add that she had another source to pursue when Cain interrupted.

"He did. My many-times-great-grandmother."

"You know! And you had me spend hours looking. Wait a minute. Did it belong to your family? Is that why you want it?"

"You'd be forgiven for doubting I had much familial reverence." His voice was at its most derisive, yet Juliana had the feeling he'd confided something important.

"I don't understand why no one knew where the manuscript was," she said. "Your family is famous."

"That's the point. Famous for its piety. But the original Godfrey title was granted because the recipient's wife was Henry's mistress. None of my reverend forebears wished it to be known they owe their fortune to a woman sharing the bed of a king. My father showed me the manuscript and told me the dark family secret when I was eleven years old and about to leave for Eton. He made me swear I'd never reveal to anyone outside the family that my ancestress was a whore.

"Whores are some of my favorite people. I would have liked that grandmother," he said with a smile, but Juliana noticed the humor didn't reach his eyes. Cain was up to his usual trick of saying something shocking to deflect criticism or questions. She refused to be distracted.

"You kept the family secret."

"I don't know why. You are the first person I've ever told."

"I won't tell a soul."

Cain relapsed into uncharacteristic silence. All his insouciance had fled while they spoke of his family. She had no idea how to console him.

"It's more important than ever not to let anyone know you want the manuscript," she said briskly, retreating to her own area of comfort. "The other bidders will run you up to the heavens."

"Perhaps I should just let it go. Iverley wants it."

"For the binding I suppose. What an idiot to want a Limbourg masterpiece and only care about the cover."

She'd love to defeat the woman-hating bibliophile in the auction room. Not to mention that she wanted the commission from buying such an expensive treasure.

"Iverley's reason might be better than mine." He worried his lower lip with his teeth. "God only knows why I should care about a family tradition."

"Or you could buy it and reveal the truth to the world. Secrets can be unhealthy."

She spoke from her own experience. And had far greater reason than he to hide the truth about her past. An ancestor's three-hundred-year-old indiscretion, especially one involving royalty, was almost something to boast about.

"You mustn't let such a masterpiece go," she said firmly. "And your information about Iverley is very useful. By the time it sells we'll make it our business to know every interested bidder."

The prospect of an auction room fight failed to revive Cain's enthusiasm. He slumped back against the pillow looking depressed. She feared the conversation about his parents had dampened his fervor in other areas.

Well, she might not know much about bed sports, but she had been married and knew a sure way to cheer up a despondent male.

"Are you hungry?" she asked. "For once I have food in the house."

Chapter 8

❧～∞～❧

C ain loved morning sex.

Of course he loved sex at just about any time: languorous afternoons in a boudoir; a hasty stolen coupling in an anteroom at a ball or a hidden garden alley; a way to break the tedium of a long carriage journey; long energetic nights in bed.

But nothing said "good morning" like a sleeping woman, just waiting to be awoken and aroused to desire.

Juliana's glorious hair spread over her pillow, catching the gray morning light from the small window and brightening the room. Her head rested on one curved arm and she slept deeply.

How extraordinary that their conversation— perhaps the thought of his mother—had effectively killed his lust for the evening. A simple but oddly fulfilling impromptu meal of crusty bread, butter, and honey washed down with milk had nourished his spirit but failed otherwise to revive him. Instead it brought back memories of innocent days in his nursery. Afterward they'd fallen asleep, curled up together like babes in the wood.

He'd found her attempt to raise his mood with food touching. He was sorry it hadn't raised anything else—if indeed that was her desired effect. It was hard to know. Unaccustomed as he was to sexual novices, Juliana's inexperienced enthusiasm in bed, her astonished awakening to pleasure, was utterly satisfying. Why, then, had he not been ready to repeat the performance the night before?

He was most certainly ready to repeat it now.

He detected a warm hip, sweetly curved under his caressing hand. Small but perfectly shaped and like silk to his touch. She shifted onto her back and parted her thighs. Still asleep, she knew by instinct what she wanted, and he was most willing to oblige. Tracing the shapely lines of her legs, the petal-soft skin between her thighs, he felt his morning erection swell.

"Good morning," he murmured against her lips, which issued a responsive murmur of approval. Her eyes remained closed but he could sense her ascent from the arms of Morpheus, her relaxed pleasure at his touch.

He ventured a kiss, his tongue running over the seam of her lips requesting entry, an invitation accepted with a sigh. She still tasted of honey.

Beautiful. This was not a moment to hurry. They had all morning. Perhaps all afternoon too. He had energy to spare and was prepared to lavish every care developing her sensuality. With practice his little bookseller promised to be a mistress of more than usual reward. Who would have thought it?

Propped on one elbow he gazed at his sleeping

beauty. Her lips curved a little. He knew just how to turn that faint smile into cries of delight. His fingers parted soft curls to discover wet warmth. He'd take it slowly, ensure her complete readiness, suppress his own urge to mount without delay. A wriggle of her hips communicated her enjoyment.

Playing with her gently, with enormous care, he postponed the moment when his thumb found that certain sweet spot. He could feel her becoming warmer and wetter. Her body was coming to life and his own tightened with anticipation.

Suddenly she bolted upright.

"What time is it?" she demanded, looking around in bewilderment and clutching the covers to her chin.

"Time to enjoy ourselves. It's early. We have hours."

He tried to embrace her but she shook him off.

"Oh Lord!" she wailed.

This was not going as planned.

She thrust both hands through her hair. "I must know what time it is. Do you have a watch?"

Hoping it was still early, he leaned over, found his waistcoat on the floor, and groped for the timepiece in the fob pocket.

"Only half past eight." Very early for him.

She slid off the bed, dragging the blankets with her and leaving him chilled, in more ways than one.

"You have to leave. At once."

"Why?"

"I have an appointment, in the shop."

Accustomed as he was to the company of working women—he'd kept a succession of actresses and opera singers since gaining his inheritance—he'd never spent the night with one whose profession entailed early rising. It was most inconvenient.

"I'll wait up here until you're finished," he said, not giving up hope of his morning sport. The bed wasn't that uncomfortable and he could take the unlumpy side.

She turned from the chest of drawers where she'd been searching through her linens. "No," she said, snatching his clothing from the floor and throwing it in his direction. "No one must suspect you've been here. I can't risk it."

"Who are you expecting that is so important?"

She managed to look self-conscious while attempting to step into a pair of drawers. "Mr. Gilbert. He wished to come before the auction today."

Gilbert. That prig.

She pleaded with him as she tugged on her shift and worked on her front-fastening stays. "Please leave quickly. And be discreet about it. I hate to think what it would do to my reputation if you were seen leaving here."

"It may take me some time to find a hackney. Or I could send a linkboy for my carriage but I might have to wait half an hour or more."

"Could you hide around the corner?" she asked.

"I suppose I could do that," he said with a pout. "If it isn't too chilly. Or raining."

He swung his legs over and sat naked on the edge of the bed. "Do you expect me to dress myself?"

"Oh for God's sake! I'll help you." She gave the laces on her corset a hasty tug, found his shirt and stockings, and flung them at him. "Can you at least manage these by yourself?"

Her panic was changing to exasperation and he decided he'd tormented her enough. "Relax, my dear. I'm teasing you. Of course I'll walk home. No one will find it odd to see me wandering around London in broad daylight wearing evening dress. And I don't need your help getting dressed."

He could have told her he didn't even employ a valet. He clothed himself, and Mel had found some "ladies" who knew how to keep a man's wardrobe in good repair.

"Fine," she snapped.

"Will I see you later?"

"There's nothing at the auction today that either of us wants."

"You wound me. I don't just love you for your books."

"Very well," she said with a harassed look. "Come at the end of the day, when I'm closing up."

The rap at the street door sounded barely ten minutes after Cain's departure. Mr. Gilbert, it seemed, was a punctual man. Juliana opened the door to greet not Matthew Gilbert's pleasantly refined face but Arthur Nutley's fleshy one.

"Arthur!" she exclaimed. She let him in out of the light drizzle, but grudgingly. His portly figure quivered as he wiped his feet on the doormat. She couldn't help contrasting his appearance with Cain's elegance. And wishing he'd leave. The presence of a respectable but undoubtedly common tradesman would hardly assist the image of refined scholarship she wished to project to Mr. Gilbert.

"Good day, Juliana."

"What brings you here on such a dreary morning?" She suppressed her irritation and felt some compunction at her uncharitable thoughts. "Is all well?"

"I am in good health, thank you. It is about you that I wish to speak."

There was something portentous in his tone. She hoped she wasn't going to have to deal with a marriage proposal.

"It's kind of you to call. Won't you come into the shop. I expect an important customer but I can give you a few minutes. If the matter isn't urgent I'd rather wait."

"Chase?" The word came out in a hiss. "Is it Chase you expect?"

Thank God! Cain must have got away from the neighborhood in time.

"Are you seeing him again so soon after last night?"

Juliana leaned against a bookcase, frozen with shock. Could Arthur possibly know?

"That's what I've come to talk about," Arthur continued. "I know you came home in his carriage. Such intimacy can only damage your reputation."

She relaxed slightly. If Arthur knew exactly how far her "intimacy" with the marquis had progressed, he would surely have opened with that accusation. "Lord Chase was kind enough to offer his escort home from an evening party," she said cautiously.

Arthur's frown deepened. "It would have been

wiser not to accept. Word reached me early this morning that his carriage was seen at your door at an advanced hour."

One of her neighbors, likely the butcher's busybody wife, must have seen it. It wouldn't take long for the news to travel a few hundred yards to the Strand.

"Really, Arthur," she said, annoyance gaining the upper hand over fear. "I don't know who has taken it upon themselves to report my private affairs, but I'd prefer they minded their own. I can assure you," she added with a straight face, "Lord Chase behaved like a perfect gentleman."

"I know you better than to suspect you would allow otherwise. But it is not the first time His Lordship has called in the evening. Word will spread."

Unfortunately he spoke the truth. The community of merchants in the West End of London was every bit as tight-knit and gossipy as a small village, or the world of their upper-class patrons.

Arthur hadn't finished, of course. "The morals of successful tradesmen are not those of the aristocracy. I am aware that you were born to better things but you have chosen to make your life among us. Close relations with a nobleman of ill repute are unacceptable."

Juliana detected a threat in the statement. Arthur was hinting that should her reputation suffer from her association with Cain, he would no longer want to know her, let alone wed her. Well, there was one positive effect, she thought dryly.

"It's only business," she said, attempting to mollify him, if only for the sake of her reputation in the neighborhood. "And most advantageous. I don't intend any indiscretion."

Arthur accepted her statement as a sign of remorse and, unfortunately, took her hand in his own pudgy one. "As a woman, you are liable to make errors, and I am happy to be able to enlighten you. Delicacy has prevented me from retelling all of the marquis's sins but perhaps it is better you should know. It pains me to inform you that the man resided for a while in a brothel." The last word was uttered in a whisper.

"My understanding is that he was very young."

"And since then he has maintained a string of mistresses," Arthur added, clearly taken aback at her calm reaction to his revelation.

"Shocking, I am sure, but surely common among young noblemen."

"Worst of all, he comes from one of the great families famous for piety and moral rectitude. I am not privy to the details but I have heard his late father, who was revered by all, dismissed him from his house for unspeakable acts of moral turpitude."

If by "unspeakable acts" he meant pleasuring a woman in bed, Juliana was in favor of them. But she couldn't dismiss the warnings out of hand. As Arthur had pointed out, she had chosen to make her life among his kind and needed to live by their standards. The trouble was she couldn't summon up the requisite indignation about Cain's immorality. If she truly belonged to the merchant class she would think like a member of it. Which meant perhaps that she didn't belong.

She'd never really belonged anywhere.

* * *

Matthew Gilbert entered the back room and added three more volumes to the already substantial pile of purchases.

"May I offer you tea?" Juliana asked. "I took the opportunity of a quiet moment to run upstairs and boil a kettle."

Mr. Gilbert sank into a chair. "Thank you," he said gratefully. "Your establishment is busy. Visitors require so much attention. It's why I don't maintain a shop but prefer to see people privately."

Juliana poured them both tea without mentioning that the morning's half-dozen customers, all of whom she'd met the night before, were a delightful surprise. "Sugar?"

"Please." He took the offered cup and smiled with distinct approval. Juliana knew she looked her best today. For whatever reason she'd decided to forgo the unflattering bonnet-style cap. Instead she wore a delicate lacy affair that merely perched on top of the head, her Sunday best from the days when Joseph was alive. She'd inserted enough pins that her hair had survived the morning without descending from its simple knot.

"I'd like to show you my collection, but of course you can't call at my house alone. My lady visitors are always chaperoned." Gilbert disdained words such as *stock* and *customer*. A gentleman bookseller was as much an aberration as a female one.

"How did you find yourself in our profession?" she asked, upgrading it from a mere trade.

"After I came down from Cambridge I was em-

ployed as secretary to Sir Humphrey Warburton."
She nodded. Warburton was an important collector as
well as a prominent Member of Parliament. "I found
myself spending most of my time in the library, and
in the end he took on another man to do his parlia-
mentary work. I found book collecting much more
engaging than politics. I discovered a certain talent
for bibliophilia and as time went by I acted for some
of Sir Humphrey's fellow collectors, particularly after
the Duke of Roxburghe's sale."

"That must have been thrilling. I wish I had
been there. The Tarleton sale promises to be just as
remarkable."

"I recall many happy hours in Sir Humphrey's
library, talking about books with his friends. I have
tried to emulate the atmosphere in my own house. I
hope you will join one of my gatherings. When other
ladies are present of course."

"I'd enjoy that. I have my own memories of such
conversations, with my guardian Mr. Fitterbourne
and Mr. Birch."

"Mr. Birch of Salisbury? An excellent bookman. I
was sorry to hear of his passing. I understand your
late husband was employed as his assistant."

"When Mr. Birch's nephew elected to take over the
business Joseph decided to set up his own establishment." She didn't add that he couldn't have done it
without her fortune.

Gilbert held out his cup to be refilled and regarded
her earnestly. "I would like to assist you now that you
are alone in the world. Sir Henry Tarleton feels the
same way."

Juliana looked down and made a play of stirring her tea. Surely she didn't imagine that he was looking at her with more than impersonal sympathy. "I can't imagine why," she said. "You must be aware of the former rivalry, indeed enmity, between my guardian and Sir Thomas Tarleton."

"I believe Sir Henry wishes to make recompense for his uncle's past behavior. In fact it was he who suggested you might take on his representation. Have you given it any further thought?"

"I would be honored. But I feel my first commitment is to Lord Chase."

Gilbert appeared displeased.

"But I will speak to Sir Henry and see how far his requirements conflict with Lord Chase's," she added quickly.

"As I said before, it would be very much to your advantage. He will be a contender for some important items." He lowered his voice. "Including the Burgundy Hours."

"Really, how remarkable," she said blandly.

"So you see, my dear Mrs. Merton, you stand to do much better with Tarleton than buying a few plays with indelicate titles for the marquis." He'd apparently been paying more attention to her purchases than he'd previously admitted. "And let me be frank. Further association with Chase can only damage your standing, perhaps even your reputation. I know well of what I speak. A lady on her own cannot be too careful."

Gilbert was sending her the same message as Arthur had done: leave Chase alone or suffer the consequences. And Gilbert's warning carried far more weight. He was at the peak of her chosen profession.

She couldn't help but be flattered, of course. If she read him correctly, the gentleman bookseller was cautiously expressing interest in a closer relationship. Who would have thought that two men would be interested in marrying Joseph Merton's humble widow?

Inwardly she sighed, and wondered whether the princes in fairy tales had been so inclined to dominate their princesses. Not that Arthur was prince material. Neither could she imagine the staid Mr. Gilbert riding around on a white charger and fighting dragons.

Cain looked the part. But he'd pretty much admitted he was no prince. For a start, he had no interest in matrimony. On the other hand he didn't insist on telling a woman what to do. And he made her feel awfully good.

As he drove around town, Cain pondered his unprecedented shortage of lust the previous night. Never, as far as he could recall, had he not been ready for a second, indeed a third, helping. In his distant youth, let loose in a brothel that seemed like heaven to a sixteen-year-old lad, he'd been up for six or seven. And the friendly whores, like angels to his innocent eyes, had been willing to oblige. Once he learned the ugly truth about their lives his amours had been conducted in more decorous circumstances, though with equal enthusiasm.

It wasn't as though he didn't want Juliana. He wanted her very much. Thankfully this morning's exchange, though frustrating, had relieved his anxiety that he had been struck with premature senility.

Dwelling on his family threatened his unabashed pursuit of pleasure. Perhaps he should abandon this notion of finding a way to change his mother's mind. His childhood had been joyless enough. Why would he want it back?

It wasn't as though he was making much progress. Yes, he'd discovered Tarleton was a blackmailer. The collector must have learned, or at least suspected, that the famous lost manuscript belonged to the Godfrey family. He must have come to the Abbey and used some threatened scandal to make the late marquis sell him, or give him, the Burgundy Hours. The event might even have hastened Cain's father's descent into insanity.

But Cain had no clue what knowledge Tarleton possessed to hold over the late Lord Chase's head. And not a single idea how to find it.

As for Esther, she was better off at home. Life at Markley Chase might not be enjoyable, but his sister was safe and well cared for. Their mother had always loved her daughter best.

Meanwhile Cain had a brand-new mistress who was in crying need of better living quarters, a new wardrobe, and his own intimate attention.

Not certain how Juliana defined "the end of day," Cain settled on four o'clock. He'd meant to wait till five but hadn't the patience. Thankfully she was alone. She came to meet him in the front room, looking good enough to eat, despite the resumption of her widow's weeds.

He couldn't wait to get beneath them again.

The new cap was an improvement. If this evidence of a relaxed sartorial standard could be laid at his door, he looked forward to extending his influence.

He found her averted eyes endearing. Shyness the day after wasn't the normal reaction of his bedmates. Most of them had been professional, or at least bold.

"Not here." She dodged his attempt at an embrace. "The butcher's wife across the road is always spying on me."

He glanced over his shoulder at the grimy windows and turned back with a quizzical look. "She won't be able to see a thing."

"I think she can see through stone walls."

Placing his hand on the small of her back he nudged her toward the back room, and she allowed herself to be guided. He turned her to face him and caressed her shoulders and collarbones, sensing the delicate bone structure beneath the unforgiving black cloth. He watched as her mossy green eyes, which had been wary, even troubled, grew soft under his gaze. Her lips parted.

"I missed you today," he whispered against her mouth. And felt her tongue emerge like a timid fawn to taste him.

Invitation enough. Drawing her close he accepted her summons to a deep, satisfying kiss. Any lingering fear of impotence was dispersed by his own reaction.

"Let's go upstairs," he murmured.

She pulled back, eyes wide. "At this hour?"

As far as he was concerned the hour had nothing to do with it. Juliana still had a lot to learn.

"Yes, now. You were beautiful last night and a repetition can't come too soon for me."

"Someone could come in at any moment. I've had lots of customers today." She didn't move from his embrace but he sensed her mental withdrawal.

"Very well, later," he said. "When we return."

"Are we going somewhere?"

"I have a surprise for you."

Her face lit up. "Is there a book you want me to see?"

Juliana's mind tended to run in a certain direction. Right now it traveled a whole different road from his own.

"That wasn't what I had in mind," he whispered, his lips against her ear. "Are you sure we can't go upstairs?" His breath and tongue followed the words, delivered with the sensual urgency that had seduced scores of women.

She pulled away from his contact, though an increase in her rate of breathing told him she wasn't unaffected. "Customers," she said wildly. "Paying customers."

Definitely not unaffected.

"When can we leave?" he asked.

"Why don't you tell me where you want to take me?"

"Not very far. You'll be able to walk there in ten minutes. I found the ideal place—convenient for you."

"What are you talking about?"

"Since you don't want to wait for your surprise, I'll tell you. I've found you a house."

"A house? What for?" She sounded bewildered.

"To live in of course."

"But I live here."

"I'm offering you something much better. Wouldn't you like to live in a warm, spacious, comfortable house?"

Juliana appeared to be speechless. With delight, he hoped.

"And with servants to look after you," he continued. "You shouldn't have to cook and clean for yourself."

She didn't seem delighted. "I do very well as I am."

"But your rooms are horrid. You can't wish to live in such a pokey little place."

"I'm sorry they don't please you but they are all I can afford," she said stiffly.

"Of course I would settle all the bills. You don't need to work at all unless you want to. Put on your bonnet and let's go."

One of the things he liked about Juliana Merton was her adult and collected approach to life. Accustomed to thespians who couldn't seem to avoid letting drama spill off the stage and into real life, he hadn't realized how much he'd valued the bookseller's calm good sense until she lost it and became as agitated as a soprano in a death scene.

The explosion came slowly. Her skin turned impossibly white, the few freckles standing out in vivid ocher contrast. The little rosebud of a mouth dropped open. Small but capable fingers clenched handfuls of her skirt. Her eyes, glinting greener with emotion, stared at him.

Then, in a flash, she turned and grabbed something

from the table behind her and bashed him over the head. "I am not your mistress," she cried.

She'd hit him with a book. It didn't hurt much. It was a small volume, and from her height she couldn't summon enough leverage to inflict real pain. This was not, however, the usual reaction when he offered a woman a comfortable home in a good part of town.

He laughed. "Darling," he said. "What do you think we were doing upstairs last night?"

"That," she said, every muscle of her small body bristling, "was a mistake."

"No, no," he said, trying to suppress his mirth at the sight of this tiny woman in a towering rage. She was shaking with such agitation that her cap fell off and her glorious golden locks tumbled down. In her passion she appeared infinitely desirable and he hastened to make up lost ground. "I'm sorry I laughed, sweetheart. Surely you didn't think I'd want you for only one night? I want many more. And I hope you do too."

He moved to embrace her, hoping his touch would rekindle her passion. She held him off with the flat of her hand.

"I am not any man's mistress," she said flatly.

"Mistress, lover. What do words matter? The important thing is that we want each other."

"They matter a lot to other people and *mistress* is the word they would use. My association with you has already caused me damage, but I ignored the warnings of friends. What do you think my business would be if I lived under your protection? Would respectable book collectors patronize the mistress of a rake?"

She spat out the last word and inwardly he cringed. He was only too aware how the world viewed him and for once he couldn't shrug it off. Not when his years of dissipation might deprive him of what he wanted, something that had never happened since he achieved his inheritance.

"And what of me, my lord?" she continued, her voice gathering pace and volume. "What of me when your fancy wanes and you are tired of me?"

"I'd never be tired of you—"

"Please don't insult me with such nonsense. I'd be left with no means of livelihood, my reputation in tatters."

"I am not in the habit of leaving my friends, or my former mistresses, in the gutter," he said.

"So you would keep me as your pensioner for the remainder of my life? I am obliged to you, my lord."

The my-lording irritated him. She hadn't been so formal trembling in his arms. His temper rose, a thing that never happened with him.

"If you are so bloody respectable, Madam Bookseller, what did you mean by allowing me into your home and your bed last night? For your information, *respectable* women don't entertain *rakes* late at night."

She'd been glaring at him, meeting him eye to eye, and now the soft green seemed to emit golden sparks.

"If I hadn't been afraid to be alone I would *never* have done anything so foolish," she yelled. "It wasn't just a mistake. It was the worst mistake of my life!"

The fact that she was very likely correct only fueled his anger. "I was under the impression you quite enjoyed our little encounter but apparently I was mistaken. Well then, you don't have to worry about your future because you have what it takes to succeed in another profession. A prime skill of the courtesan is the ability to feign pleasure in bed."

Pushing past him she strode through the shop and opened the street door. "Get out," she said.

"Wait!" How had he let this scene get away from him?

"Out!" she repeated, low and deadly serious.

Cain knew better than to argue with a woman in a rage. The door slammed hard against his back.

Chapter 9

❧

Juliana would have slammed the door in Cain's face when he turned up at the shop the next day, looking for all the world as though their exchange of words had never occurred. But she was arrested by the sight of his companion, a . . . Creature, dragged behind him on a leash.

"What's that?" she asked.

"This," he said, "is Quarto."

"No, it's not." The Creature was knee-high to Cain, rather taller to her, and its wrinkled face managed to combine misery and pugnacity in equal measure. "It's a dog. Isn't it?"

"Yes it's a dog. His name is Quarto. It remains to be seen whether he's a good Quarto or a bad Quarto. So far his behavior has tended toward the latter, but his former owner assures me he's good-natured."

Cain remained in the doorway, as though uncertain of his welcome. The Creature pushed past him and strained to sniff at her. She stepped back hastily.

"I don't know much about dogs. What kind is it?"

"A poodle."

"I see."

He looked at her incredulously. "Of course it's not a poodle. Can't you recognize a bulldog?"

"My guardian didn't allow animals in the house. They're bad for books." She looked at the Creature nervously, expecting any moment that it would leap up at a bookshelf and start eating a volume. Or do something worse.

"Since I named this boy for a book, I expect him to treat them with respect. Won't you, Quarto." He leaned down to pat the brindled head, and the Creature growled. "He doesn't like me much but that doesn't matter. He's yours. You see, he likes *you*. Perhaps he only likes women, sensible fellow. He wants to lick your hand."

Juliana drew back from the animal's tongue. It made her think of a wet slice of ham. "I don't want him. Why would you think I want him?"

He raised his eyes to the ceiling. "Isn't it obvious? He's a watchdog. And he'll be company for you."

That took the wind out of her sails.

"That's very thoughtful of you, my lord. But it isn't necessary. I'm certain my fears are irrational."

"Better to be safe. I insist. I'll leave you now. Here." He handed her the end of the leash and, before she could say another word, left the shop.

"Wait!" She rushed to the door. "Come back," she cried at his retreating back. Her voice grew shrill with panic. "Don't leave me with him. I don't know what to do. What does he eat . . . ?"

He disappeared around the corner and she turned back to confront her new companion, who sat on his haunches, panting and *smiling* at her, drool dripping from that hamlike tongue. Ugh. She might never eat the stuff again.

"What am I going to do with you?"

Quarto collapsed to the ground, front paws forward like a sphinx, his expression just as inscrutable.

"Company! You're not much of a conversationalist, are you? I'd rather have your late master for company and to keep watch at night."

She clapped her hands over her mouth, unable to believe she'd thought such a thing, let alone uttered it aloud, even to a dog.

"And don't think you're sleeping on my bed."

Don't think about beds. She swatted her unruly mind into submission. The wretched man, however attractive, had made it clear he regarded her as little better than the whores who were his usual companions. It galled her greatly that Arthur and Mr. Gilbert had been right about him.

"So what do you eat?"

The dog pricked up his ears and lumbered to his feet. Apparently *eat* was a word he recognized. He followed her upstairs into the kitchen. Rummaging in the cupboard she found the heel of a loaf and a morsel of cheese. He wolfed down the latter quite happily, not caring about its thin coating of mold, but surveyed the bread dubiously.

"It does look dry, doesn't it," she said, and spread some honey on it.

The dog liked the honey. "Good boy. Good Quarto." The name made her smile. The Marquis of Chase might be a louse but he was a witty louse.

"You know, Quarto, I may be crazy talking to a

dog, but I suppose it's no worse than imaginary discussions with book collectors."

It occurred to her she hadn't had one of those dialogues since Cain had come into her life. She'd enjoyed having someone real who talked back.

An ominous sound emerged from Quarto's throat, followed by a neat pile of vomit.

"Quarto! If you're going to live here, we're going to have some rules."

The shop bell rang and Juliana set aside the book she was collating.

"Behave yourself," she said sternly to Quarto, who looked longingly at the volume. After a couple of unfortunate incidents she'd managed to persuade him that a book was neither a meal nor a toy. He showed a particular penchant for morocco. A dog with expensive tastes. She intended to call at the binder's and look for an inexpensive piece of leather on which he could slobber without ill effect.

Her visitor wasn't Cain which was a relief. Just as it had been a relief every time the bell had rung in the last two days. She hadn't seen hide nor hair of him since he'd deposited Quarto at her feet. Which, really, was a relief.

Instead of the marquis's graceful figure and flashing blue eyes, Sir Henry Tarleton awaited her. And he was a fine-looking man. Very fine.

"Mrs. Merton, what a pleasure to see you," he said with a low bow over her hand, not at all the salutation she was accustomed to receive from customers.

"How do you do, Sir Henry. Welcome to J. C.

Merton. Is there anything in particular I can show you?"

"I would like to examine your shelves later," he said, "but first let us attend to another matter. I believe Gilbert spoke to you about representing me at my uncle's sale."

"And I would be honored to assist you, sir, as long as it doesn't conflict with my other commitments." She hoped she gave the impression of juggling the interests of a string of gentlemen, when in fact she wasn't certain she had even one client.

"That is Gilbert's quandary. Perhaps you aren't as busy as he."

Of course she wasn't. Mr. Gilbert acted as adviser to the cream of English bibliophiles, and Sir Henry must know it.

"Do you intend to make extensive purchases?"

"Before going into details, let me explain my situation. I know I can rely on your discretion."

She nodded and he continued. "I don't need to tell you that Sir Thomas was an eccentric man. He never changed his will after the death of his son, and since he spent a fortune on books, he died in debt and his creditors demanded immediate satisfaction. Once the legal questions are settled, I shall inherit what remains of the proceeds, which I expect to be substantial. I was unable to persuade the courts to let me take the pick of the collection so I must compete for them like anyone else. And the pick of the collection is what I want. I must be careful how I apportion my resources, which are not, alas, unlimited."

In other words, like any other collector, he needed a

strategy to make sure he got what he wanted most.

"I understand that you won't want to tell me exactly what you are pursuing until we come to an agreement, but could you give me some slight indication?"

Sir Henry rattled off the names of a dozen books, all rare and precious volumes but none of them items that interested Cain. "Some of the Shakespeares, of course. But what I want most, what I must win, is the greatest treasure of my uncle's library. The Burgundy Hours." He sighed reverently. "I fear the price will be very high. Who could resist such a magnificent work of art?"

Although not altogether a surprise, since Mr. Gilbert had mentioned Sir Henry's interest in the Hours, Juliana was disappointed. She'd been calculating the commission on the books Tarleton had mentioned and come up with a truly glorious sum of money. Yet if it was the single thing both Cain and Sir Henry wanted most, she couldn't act for both of them.

"How did Sir Thomas come to acquire the manuscript?" she temporized, unwilling to say *adieu* to such a wonderful client. "Its provenance is a mystery."

"I wish I knew. Once I have full access to my uncle's papers I hope to discover the source."

Chase's family had guarded its secret well. She wondered how Sir Thomas Tarleton had persuaded the late marquis to part with the manuscript. Given what she knew of Tarleton's ruthlessness, she wouldn't be astonished to find something underhand.

"Well, Mrs. Merton. What do you say? Will you act for me?"

Juliana bit her lip. If she was wise she'd say yes and

forget all about the Marquis of Chase. She didn't even know that she retained his custom and, as Gilbert had argued so starkly, Sir Henry was a much better bet as a future customer. Yet she knew how much Cain wanted the manuscript, and why. Aside from any ethical question, it didn't sit well with her to be involved in depriving him of it.

She was still wondering if she could have it both ways when Quarto emerged from the back room, no doubt ready for another meal.

"Goodness, who's this?" Sir Henry asked. "What a handsome beast."

Juliana couldn't agree. She'd reached an accommodation of sorts with the animal, was even grateful for his presence. But truly the creature was ugly as sin.

"I am fond of bulldogs," Sir Henry said, holding out his hand to be sniffed. The dog examined the visitor and seemed to approve. Quarto might not like Cain but his scorn didn't extend to the entire male sex.

"I recently acquired him as a watchdog."

"A wise decision for a lady living alone."

"Since you seem to know about the breed, perhaps you can tell me what to feed him. He likes bread and cheese. And honey. But it doesn't seem quite right."

He looked amused. "Dogs are generally fond of a bone to gnaw."

Juliana slapped her forehead. "Bones! Of course." Then frowned. "Just bones? That doesn't seem very filling."

"And meat. Dogs love meat. It doesn't have to be an expensive cut."

"Does the meat need to be cooked?"

"A strong animal like that will eat raw meat, but he might prefer it stewed and it will keep better. You don't have to concern yourself with the seasoning." The humor in his eye belied his serious tone.

Juliana wished she could accept Sir Henry's commission. Unfortunately the entrance of that dratted dog reminded her that Cain had treated her kindly. She couldn't betray him.

"I thank you for your advice, Sir Henry, and I wish I could reciprocate with my own, but on careful consideration I believe I will have to decline your offer. My other commitments would make it impossible to serve you as you deserve."

"I can't tell you how sorry I am to hear that." For a moment she fancied he looked more angry than regretful. "I am sorry not only because I will be losing the services of a very knowledgeable lady. I had hoped I might assist the ward of Mr. Fitterbourne."

Sir Henry's repeated wish to help her for this reason struck Juliana as odd. It wasn't as though *he* were responsible for any offenses of his uncle. As far as most people knew, Juliana's connection to the Fitterbournes was a distant one. She wondered if, somehow, he'd learned the truth about her birth.

Three days passed and Juliana was worried. She'd turned down Sir Henry, yet she hadn't heard a word from the Marquis of Chase, about buying books or any other subject. Three days of Tarleton books had gone under the hammer and she had no reason to attend the auction, let alone buy anything.

An hour spent going over her accounts did nothing for her mood. The improved state of her balances wouldn't last long without a client to represent.

She looked up eagerly when the door opened, but it was only the binder's delivery boy with a package.

"Wait, please. I'm not expecting anything."

She recognized the volume, bound in opulent red morocco, the spine lavishly gilt and the covers emblazoned with a coat of arms. She didn't need to open it to recognize Herrick's poetry.

"There's been a mistake. This should go to the Marquis of Chase in Berkeley Square." About to rewrap and return the book, she changed her mind. "Never mind. I'll deliver it to Lord Chase myself."

Truth to tell, she was glad of an excuse to seek out Cain. Yes, his offer to set her up as his mistress was insulting, but on reflection she realized he hadn't intended it as such. It was simply his way of dealing with women. And his final riposte had been in response to her own jeers. However much he might try to disguise it, Juliana knew he was sensitive about his poor reputation.

She recalled the evening at the Misses Berry's house when he'd made it his business to introduce her to so many people. At the time she wasn't sure how he did it. He didn't hover at her side but stayed in the background. But as soon as a conversation lagged he was at her elbow, steering her in the direction of the next meeting and not incidentally sending shivers up her arm each time he touched the bare skin between the sleeve of her gown and her glove.

She had noticed that his own reception by their fellow guests was less enthusiastic than her own. Not that anyone was overtly rude. Just that he was avoided by many and treated with reserve by most.

Further intimacy was impossible for her own reputation and peace of mind. But Lord Chase was a man who needed friendship, and that she could offer.

And she needed a client.

And Quarto needed a walk.

Though deliveries sometimes took her into the more rarefied areas of London, most of Juliana's life was spent in streets where commerce dominated. By the time she had threaded her way through the traffic-clogged lanes surrounding the building of the new Regent Street and into the quieter quarters of Mayfair, she was beginning to doubt the wisdom of the expedition.

First of all there was the behavior of her dog. Predictably he'd set eyes on Cain's volume of Herrick and decided it was dinner.

"Stop it, Quarto," she said. "The binding will not be improved by tooth marks." It had become unnervingly natural to converse with the creature.

Once dissuaded from trying to snatch the parcel away, Quarto turned his attention to the horse droppings that littered the streets, regarding them as delicious perfume that would immeasurably enhance his appeal. Juliana told him sharply that he was ugly enough already, an opinion shared by a pair of elegant lady shoppers on Bond Street. He tried to sniff them in embarrassing portions of their anatomy, and it took all Juliana's strength to drag him away.

She felt hot, bothered, out-of-place, and nervous

about how Cain would react to her bearding him in his own house. Would he sneer at her presumption or take it as an invitation to repeat his overtures?

When they entered elegant Berkeley Square a crossing sweeper directed her to Chase's address on the west side, an imposing gray brick house, six windows wide, with a stuccoed porch. For the first time Juliana appreciated that Cain, so casual in his manners, was truly a member of the aristocracy and every bit as rich as he had claimed.

She could just imagine the kind of butler who presided over this mansion.

Juliana gathered her courage. She had a legitimate reason for her visit. The worst that could happen was for a toplofty servant to refuse her entry, in which case she'd leave the book and depart.

Then a young woman emerged from the area steps. Juliana had lived in London long enough to recognize the tawdry costume and rouged cheeks of a streetwalker. The girl passed them, a satisfied look on her face. She glanced at a few coins in her open palm, and smiled.

Juliana felt a complete fool. She'd been warned about the Marquis of Chase and she should have listened.

"Let's go home, Quarto," she said.

Chapter 10

Cain returned to Berkeley Square some time after noon in a very bad mood, having endured a morning of utter tedium. In former days—how long ago two weeks seemed—his time had been agreeably occupied, swiving by night, sleeping all morning, calling on a few ladies (in the broadest definition of the word), then attending a theater, usually to view the onstage performance of his current paramour. Now he felt this ridiculous urge to belong to a gentlemen's club and spend the morning reading the *Times* and chewing over the news and gossip of the day with his peers.

Since that option wasn't open to him, he'd wandered over to Sotheby's. None of the historical works being sold that week appealed to him and he missed Juliana. The auction wasn't as much fun without her to tell him what not to buy, or to disturb their neighbors with smothered giggles at his tales of the demimonde. The room was filled with men and not a sign of a shapely little lady in black.

"Any messages?" Perhaps she had written to him.

"The usual." Mel had bustled out to the hall when

she heard him come in. She was worried about him, he knew. "Your post is in the library. Another girl turned up, sent by one of Rafferty's girls. Silly little chit. Came to London with the usual foolish notions. Found her senses before too much harm was done. She said she's clean and not in the family way and her kin'll take her back."

"Good," Cain said, only half listening.

"I gave her money for coach fare back to Lancashire and some decent clothes. Hope she buys something warm. Bloody freezing up there." Mel had never left London in her life and was convinced the Arctic began north of Watford.

Cain stamped off in the direction of the library. "Not now, Mel," he said when she followed him. He wasn't in the mood for her brand of salty wisdom.

"What happened to get your breeches in the wringer?"

Mel wasn't easily put off so he had to give her something. "Lady Moberley passed me in her barouche as I came in."

"The snotty cow!" Mel put her hands on her hips and shook her head. "Your own mother's sister, living just across the square, and never a word in three years. Don't let it get to you, Cain. The old bitch ain't worth it." Her loyal indignation gathered force. "I've a good mind to march over there and give her what for."

"Please don't trouble yourself."

"Don't worry. That stiff-arsed butler wouldn't let me in. Thinks he's the bloody Prince Regent."

"Last week he was the Tsar of Russia."

"And next week he'll be Napoleon."

"Forget it, Mel. And bring brandy."

Mel gave him a troubled look, but for once didn't argue. Cain settled into his favorite leather armchair and systematically worked his way through half a bottle of Cognac's best. His well-laid plans should be ready to come to fruition, but he felt the strangest reluctance to deliver the *coup de grâce*.

Once his temper at her rejection had subsided he'd pondered his next step. Juliana Merton would be his mistress whether she liked it or not. And of course she would like it. He knew she wanted him. He'd merely handled her in the wrong way, an unusual misstep for him who could read women's minds like a book. Her background was different from his other *chères amies* and he'd failed to take it into account in his approach.

The gift of the dog was the start of the campaign, although it wasn't an entirely cynical gift. He was genuinely concerned for her. Unlikely as it was that anyone would rob a shop so devoid of easily fenced merchandise, her husband's fate made her terror reasonable. And by presenting her with a companion and guard he'd given her something she needed. Women loved that.

A few days of neglect and she should be ready to reopen negotiations.

God, he hoped so. Celibacy was straining his temper. If he had any sense he'd take himself off to Drury Lane or Covent Garden and find a willing actress, reimmerse himself in the theatrical milieu that had been his principal haunt for several years.

The idea had no appeal. He wanted to chat with Juliana about books and make her laugh at his stories. He wanted to burrow under the bombazine and reveal the buried treasure of her exquisite little body. And bury himself in her and teach her that not all knowledge could be found between the covers of books, even those by Aretino. The very thought . . . agitated him.

So what was he waiting for? Why wasn't he even now on his way to St. Martin's Lane with hothouse roses in hand and diamonds in his pocket?

Because he had the lowering suspicion that Mrs. Juliana Merton deserved better. He admired the way she fought to make her own way in a difficult world. He respected her knowledge, gained through hard work, intelligence, and determination. In comparison he led an idle and useless life. Her example gave him an urge to take up his own responsibilities and attend to his substantial estates.

Yet there seemed little point when he couldn't even visit them, thanks to the promise his mother had wrung from him.

So he admired and respected Juliana and feared that he was very bad for her.

And that thought put him in a very bad mood.

His hand on the decanter was stayed by a commotion in the hall. Probably the footmen playing again. Perhaps he'd join them, as he sometimes did for a few minutes before Mel arrived to chase them away. But his momentary interest in indoor cricket faded and he continued to fill his glass.

"I must see His Lordship." A female voice. His ear pricked up.

"You can't. You should've come in the servants' door. Mel will see to yer." That was Peter.

"I don't want Mel, whoever he is. I want to see Lord Chase."

" 'E don't see the likes of you. I'll take you downstairs."

He slumped back into his chair. He never saw the prostitutes who came looking for help. Mel made sure only those with merit received assistance. Cain had a well-deserved reputation as a soft touch.

There was a scuffle, followed by a curse from Tom.

"She hit me with 'er umbrella, Pete!"

A whore with an umbrella? How singular.

When he entered the hall, his first impression was that this particular bit of muslin hadn't been long in her business. Dressed in brown, she looked like a country servant. Not long off the stagecoach, he guessed.

"Do you need help, boys?" he asked.

The girl—he could see that she was young, fifteen or sixteen years old at a guess—shook off Tom's grasp on her arm and looked at him.

"John?" she said. "Oh, John!"

Only one person in his whole life had called him by his Christian name.

It couldn't be. She was just a child. But that had been eight years ago.

"Esther?"

She ran to him and threw her arms about him.

"Esther. My little Esty." His voice was strangled, choked with tears, as he returned his sister's embrace.

Chapter 11

"**Y**ou smell of wine, John."

Wonderful! The first time she'd seen him in eight years and he was half seas under.

"Can I have some?" she asked.

Was he drunker than he thought? He might not know a great deal about well-bred young ladies, but he was fairly sure they didn't drink alcohol. Especially not one raised by the Saintly Marquis and his spouse. On the other hand he could easily imagine life with his mother driving her to the bottle.

"Certainly not. I'll ask Mel to bring us some tea. Or perhaps lemonade. Are you hungry?"

Esther nodded. Cain ordered Tom, who was rubbing his arm and regarding Esther resentfully, to go downstairs and fetch a light repast to serve in the morning room. He wasn't having his sister anywhere near the decanter.

"Do you usually drink wine?" he asked, guiding her toward the rarely used room.

"Never," she replied. "But I'd like to try it. I'd like to try lots of things." Apparently his sister had some things in common with him.

He took her cloak and bonnet and absorbed the sight of her. She was plainly attired in the kind of garments worn by the maids at Markley Chase, but still showed promise that, to his partial eye at least, she would grow into a beauty. Like him, her height was no more than average, her hair a little darker than his own and draped over her shoulders in untidy curls. Her figure was slender and as yet barely formed. She had his blue eyes.

"How did you get here?" he asked.

"On the stage."

"*Why* are you here?"

"Didn't you understand my message?" she said reproachfully. "Mother reads my letters so I couldn't say more, but I know how clever you are. I thought you'd understand."

"I'm sorry, my dear. I didn't believe it could be anything serious. I take it I was wrong."

"Well, it was. It is."

"Why don't you tell me about it."

"Mother wants me to marry Mr. Ditchfield."

"What?"

Since their last meeting Cain had many resentful thoughts about his surviving parent but he'd never questioned her sanity. His eyes narrowed. The Reverend Josiah Ditchfield had been present at their last interview following his father's funeral. Forty-five if he was a day, the man had rubbed his hands together in a particularly egregious fashion as his mother recited her husband's version of Cain's sins, with a few apposite biblical quotations. He hadn't bothered to persuade Cain to renounce his wicked ways. As far as Ditchfield was concerned, nothing could save his former pupil from hellfire.

"You don't have to marry anyone you don't want," he assured Esther.

"Mother talked and talked at me. She told me I was a wicked girl to turn down such a worthy and godly gentleman who was good enough to wish to wed me. Even though I am frequently defiant and don't show sufficient respect for the Lord's will."

Good enough! Cain had no doubt that Esther's fortune of fifty thousand pounds was the incentive, greater even than her youthful flesh. The thought of the Reverend Josiah getting those greasy hands on his little sister made him want to retch. What on earth could his mother be thinking?

He considered for a moment. "Old Staveley won't allow it. Does he know? I'll write to him."

Esther's lower lip quivered. "Lord Staveley is dead."

That showed the depth of the family estrangement, that he'd never heard his mother's cousin, who was joined with her in Esther's guardianship, had died.

"And I didn't think I could refuse Mother," Esther continued. "She locked me in my room and said I would have only bread and water until I agreed."

"How did you escape?"

"I climbed down the ivy." She rolled back her sleeves to display fading scratches on her lower arms.

"Well done, you little minx." He was delighted that a lifetime in that gloomy mansion hadn't broken her spirit. "Where did you get those dreadful clothes?"

"Mother made me wear them. She said I showed an excess of vanity and must wear homespun and dark colors until I amended my attitude."

Lady Chase had outfoxed herself there. Esther would have found her escape on a public coach much harder had she been dressed according to her rank.

"I'll have to let her know where you are."

"Oh no! Please, John. She'll make me go back and marry him."

"I don't approve of her plans," he said gently, "but she is your mother and she'll be worried. I won't let anything happen to you."

He only hoped that was true. The first thing he needed to do was consult a barrister, a good one. His face hardened. He was going to find the best damn lawyer in London.

Mel bustled in with a tray. He was surprised it had taken her this long.

"So who's this, Cain?" she asked, arranging the food on a small table. "Tom said it was your sister. 'And I'm the Queen of France,' I says. 'I've heard that one before.'" She turned and subjected Esther to a sharp-eyed examination. "But since she's the dead image of you it might be true."

"Mel, this is Lady Esther Godfrey. And you are quite correct. She is my sister. My dear, allow me to present my housekeeper, Mrs. Duchamp."

"That's all right, love. Call me Mel. We ain't formal here. Come and sit yourself down and have something to eat."

Esther stared at Mel with huge eyes. Cain doubted she'd ever heard an endearment from a housekeeper.

Or seen one so oddly dressed. Oblivious to Esther's astonishment, Mel chattered on, pressing the girl to try the cold meats, salad, and fruit. Only when she took herself back below stairs did Esther, who had tackled her food with youth's healthy appetite, speak again.

"Your housekeeper is quite unusual, John."

"Yes, but perfectly capable. Is the meal to your satisfaction?"

"But she's wearing a pink gown."

"Tell me about your journey," Cain said hastily.

Esther gave him a look suggesting she'd like to stick with the original subject, but good manners prevailed. She was happy enough to describe the journey from Gloucestershire, the characters she'd encountered on the stage, the novelty of spending a night in an inn at Hungerford.

"I told the landlord I was a lady's maid traveling to a new situation and he believed me," she said proudly. "And when I reached London I didn't know how to find your house and a lady came up to me and said she'd take me in a carriage."

Cain froze.

"But then," Esther continued blithely, "a kind man told me he'd take me in his hackney and the lady needn't trouble herself." She paused. "He was a little bit rude to her, I think. She said a word I'd never heard before and went away."

Having been merely grateful that Esther had made her way on the public stage without mishap, Cain offered fervent silent thanks to the unknown driver for deflecting the marauding abbess. He was only too familiar with tales of such despicable creatures who met the coaches, trolling for country flesh to fill the brothels. Hazardous as Esther's journey had been, it was nothing to the dangers she'd face as a young female alone in the metropolis.

"Listen, my dear. You're in London now and you must never go out alone."

"I won't need to," she said. "You'll take me about. Will you take me shopping? I've spent almost all my pin money but you'll give me some more, won't you?"

"As soon as I've determined your situation. I'm not your guardian, remember."

Cain fully expected that Lady Chase, or her emissaries, would be hard on Esther's heels to recover her from her wicked brother. Until he'd examined his legal options he intended to keep his sister indoors and well guarded. And little as he was accustomed to trouble himself with matters of propriety, things were different when it came to Esther. In the general run of things there was nothing exceptional about a girl being escorted by her brother. Except when the brother was Cain, one of London's most scandalous denizens.

"You won't make me go back, will you, John? Please let me stay with you."

"There's nothing I'd like better and I'll do everything I can."

"Why don't you ever come home?" She rose from her chair and came around the table to stand in front of him, her face creased in distress. Suddenly she seemed eight years old again. "Even when you returned after Papa died, you didn't come and see *me*. Why? *Why?* I missed you so much."

He couldn't explain why his mother refused to let him spend even a single night under the same roof as them.

"It's complicated."

She began to weep. "You've been gone so long."

He took her in his arms and hugged her, as he had the day his father dismissed him from the house. Just as he had then, he murmured comforting words, rubbed her back, and dried her tears.

Then he recalled what happened next. He drew back and handed her the handkerchief. "The day I left. Why did you cry?" His father had interrupted them before she could tell him. "Do you still remember?"

"I remember," she said with a gulp. "But I shouldn't say."

"Esty! This is your brother, John. You can tell me anything."

She paused and sniffed again. "I went into Mother's sitting room."

"Yes?"

"Papa was there. He whipped her, with a switch."

The bastard. The hypocritical bastard. His chest burned with impotent anger.

"Did he ever hit you?" If his father were still alive he'd ride to Markley Chase and tear him apart with his bare hands.

"No. Mother spanked me when I was naughty."

He hoped "spank" didn't equate with the severe whippings he'd suffered at his father's hands.

"And our mother? Did he beat *her* again?"

She looked away.

"Esther?"

"Yes. Mother explained to me he only did it when she misbehaved. I don't know why. Mother is always good."

Guilt fastened like a vise on his gut. His life hadn't always been easy, it was true. But he'd left his mother and sister in the hands of a violent monster.

Chapter 12

❧❧

"Good afternoon, Juliana."

Cain entered the shop as though he'd just dropped by to take her to the auction.

"My lord," she said coldly. How dare he? He was a conscienceless whoremonger. And he hadn't been near her in days.

"You're very formal."

"I think it best under the circumstances."

"That's right. We quarreled. It seems like a long time ago." He sighed.

Quarto emerged from the back room, his peaceful afternoon nap on a large pillow disturbed by the doorbell.

"The dog!" Cain said, as though he'd forgotten the creature's existence. "No more disturbances in the night, I trust?"

"None, thank you, my lord."

Quarto growled.

"Splendid. I hope he greets everyone that way."

"As a matter of fact you seem to be the only person he dislikes. For every other man he rolls over and presents his stomach." She didn't mention the dog's unfortunate sniffing habits when it came to females.

She expected a ribald observation but Cain seemed distracted.

"What can I do to help you? Have you come about a book? Something you need at the auction?"

"Oh, that. No. Not today." Instead of looking at her, he rocked back and forth on his heels and stared at the floor. If she didn't know better she'd have thought him nervous.

"Can we go upstairs?" he asked abruptly. "There is a private matter I need to discuss."

"I don't believe, my lord, there is anything we need to say to each other that cannot be discussed here."

Her prim refusal at least drew a smile, though a pale shadow of his usual slashing grin.

"Don't worry. I'm not about to make you another indecent proposition. I'm rather afraid my indecent proposal days may be coming to an end. I might as well go about the business properly."

He went down on one knee before her and she stared, noting that he executed the maneuver with rare elegance. He looked absurdly romantic down there, perfectly fitting knitted pantaloons hugging his thighs and his fine wool topcoat spread around him.

Quite princely, really.

Looking up at her, his fathomless azure eyes expressed uncertainty, pleading even. He must be about to apologize. She kept her expression carefully blank. She might forgive him, and really she shouldn't.

He cleared his throat. "Mrs. Merton. Will you

do me the great honor of granting me your hand in marriage?"

She almost joined him on the floor in a graceless heap. A fleeting moment of joy was driven away by the knowledge that he'd employed a whore within the past two days.

"Why?" she asked, once she found her voice.

"Not quite the response I expected. I'd have preferred something along the lines of 'Thank you, Cain. I would be delighted to be Marchioness of Chase.'"

A marchioness! She was being offered such an exalted position. It was ridiculous.

"I don't understand," she said. "Are you telling me you've fallen madly in love with me?"

"Would that help?"

"Not unless you meant it. And even then . . ."

"Yes, I do understand. Why would you wish to marry a wastrel like me? Even if I did love you."

"Which is to say you don't."

"I have too much respect for you to lie."

"Then answer my original question, please. Why?"

"The short answer is, because I need to reform my life." He sounded so mournful about it Juliana almost laughed. "The complete story will take longer. Are you sure we can't go upstairs?" He stood up and raised a protesting hand with a laugh that sounded more like the old Cain. "I promise not to leap on you and I could use some . . . tea."

"My goodness, you are intent on reform."

"If I have to swallow tea to prove it, I will."

* * *

Seated at her table, Cain told her about Esther's appearance in London. By the end of his recital Juliana was left in no doubt that he greatly loved his sister. The very knowledge of her existence completed the picture of his lost family life, and perhaps explained the mystery she'd sensed behind the matter-of-fact narration of his exile.

What she didn't understand was why the girl's arrival had precipitated Cain's proposal.

"I can't let my mother take Esther back." He spoke quietly and his voice was deeper than ever in his determination. "I've just come from Lincoln's Inn where I've been learning about the law. Luckily my father insisted she have a male guardian as well as my mother. Since one of her guardians has died and she's more than fourteen years old, the law allows her to name the replacement herself."

"So she can chose you?"

"Yes, but the court must approve her choice and I've given my mother many reasons to oppose it."

"Where do I come in?"

"The barrister I consulted—and my solicitor says he's the best—gave his opinion that my marriage to a woman of good reputation would help convince the court that I was a suitable guardian for a young woman, despite my past transgressions. You are the only woman I know that I could stand to be married to."

Juliana couldn't help a rush of pleasure at his words, until he spoiled the compliment.

"Besides," he said, "you are the only woman I know with a good reputation."

"I think you must be mad," she said acerbically, "if you think *I* am suitable. I make my living through trade. Not exactly the usual avocation of a future marchioness. Naturally I'm very flattered by your offer."

"You don't sound it." He smiled wanly. "You are a lady and had a lady's upbringing. Your grandfather was a gentleman. He may have been a little eccentric but it's not him I plan to marry."

"And now I run a bookshop."

"For God's sake, Juliana. You need to win the approval of a gang of doddering old men who run the courts, not the Patronesses of Almack's. There's nothing about you anyone could conceivably object to. And if it comes to that, I wager those tiresome biddies would come around too."

"No."

"Yes. Please." He reached around the teacups and took her hand. "Please, Juliana. We'll have fun. We'll buy books together. You can buy every book in London if you wish, and even Sebastian Iverley will have to respect you."

Oh, he was good. He knew just how to appeal to her baser nature.

"We'll have a wonderful time." His voice dropped again. "You know you'll enjoy yourself in bed. And I will too."

It was lucky he reminded her of that. Enjoy himself in bed with her, and how many others? She'd already experienced one marriage of friendship. While Cain was correct that his intimate attentions were preferable, infinitely so, to Joseph's, she wasn't sure she wanted another marriage of convenience. It suddenly occurred to her that if she was to relinquish her independence and put herself in the power of another man, she'd like it to involve a warmer sentiment.

At least with Joseph she'd never doubted his fidelity.

"I don't wish to marry a rake."

Cain's nod of agreement was disarming. "I don't blame you. But I am going to be a reformed rake. I'm sure you will be a wonderfully good reformer. I need you, Juliana. I can talk to you. And I can give you everything you want. Jewels, clothes, servants. You won't ever have to cook again. And you'll love my sister. She's a darling."

She'd have been inhuman not to be tempted. Very tempted. For a moment she envisioned herself as Cain's wife: wealthy, powerful—and well pleasured. But all other reservations aside, there remained the unalterable truth.

"It's impossible," she said.

"But why? Why won't you say yes?"

She owed him the real explanation. "I will not serve your purpose."

Cain leaned back in his chair and folded his arms, ready to swat away any argument like a tiresome fly. "Go on. Bring up your objection." He needed to be married and Juliana was the only wife he could contemplate.

She stood and took a deep breath. "My birth is illegitimate."

Whatever Cain had expected, it wasn't this. Juliana looked ready to spit blood. The admission had cost her dearly.

"Then your mother, Cassandra—"

"I don't even know for certain she was my mother." Her eyes glistened. "No, I am sure. But no one had ever admitted it to me. And I haven't an inkling who my father was."

"Tell me about it," he said softly.

"I was brought to Mr. Fitterbourne's house as an infant and grew up in the nursery at Fernley Court. My nurse had been nurse to my guardian's only child, Cassandra. I grew up on tales of Miss Cassandra, played with her toys and read her books. When we had gooseberry tart Nurse told me Miss Cassandra loved it so it became my favorite too. I never saw any other children and I imagined Miss Cassandra lived in the nursery with me and she became my friend."

She'd been circling the room during her recitation. Now she stopped in front of the watercolor he'd noticed on his first visit. "Then one day Nurse showed me her portrait and I realized my friend was grown-up. So I decided Miss Cassandra was my mother."

Poor child, Cain reflected. His own childhood had been on the bleak side but at least he *had* a mother, though she hadn't much time for him, worn down as she was by a succession of fruitless pregnancies and obsessed with piety. He ached for the lonely girl and wondered if her parentage was as imaginary as her little friend.

"I asked Nurse if it was so, if Cassandra was my

mother." Juliana closed her eyes as though picturing the moment. "She said no, but I knew she was lying. I could tell. She said Miss Cassandra was dead and had never been married."

"Didn't anyone ever tell you who your parents were?"

"When I grew better acquainted with my guardian, I asked him. He said I was the daughter of distant cousins. But," she added, "he would never talk about them."

"Perhaps he spoke the truth."

"Do you know what my name was?" she asked with a harsh little laugh. "Wayborn. Everyone knows that is a name given to bastards. And my second name is Cassandra. Why else would I be so named if I wasn't his daughter's child, born out of wedlock?"

Cain could think of reasons. That Cassandra was a family name, for instance.

"He was ashamed to admit I was his granddaughter. Why else was I never permitted to leave Fernley, except to go to church? I grew up knowing no one save servants, my governess, and a few booksellers who came to visit him. He was ashamed of me."

"How could anyone be ashamed of you?" Cain asked.

She was not to be distracted from her tale, which was growing in pace and now tinged with anger. Taking her seat once more, she leaned across the table and glared.

"Do you know what happened when my guardian died? His cousin"—she positively spat out the word—"Frederick Fitterbourne inherited the estate and told me I wasn't welcome to live in the same house as his wife and children."

"He tossed you out without a penny?"

"Oh no. He reminded me that I had the inestimable good fortune to possess a thousand pounds left me by Mr. Fitterbourne. Safely invested in the three percents, the income would be entirely adequate to the needs of one such as me. But he wouldn't tell me who I was. He said if my guardian had wished me to know, he would have informed me himself."

What kind of man would abandon a young woman to her own devices? It was good to know that his own father was not the only bastard in the world, though that was hardly the right word under the circumstances. Mr. Frederick Fitterbourne was clearly of the same ilk.

"You were only . . . how old?"

"Nineteen."

"And he wouldn't look after you, even though you were a member of his family?" His doubts about Juliana's interpretation of the tale must have shown in his voice.

"You don't believe me, do you? You think I'm imagining that Cassandra was my mother."

She rose again and removed the portrait from the wall.

"Look!" she said, standing behind him, one hand on his shoulder, the other holding the picture of the young woman in front of him. "This is Cassandra. I look like her. I have her eyes."

He twisted around to look at her face and back at the image. True, the girl in the amateurish watercolor had greenish eyes and could, if one looked hard, be said to bear a resemblance to Juliana, despite her dark hair. He turned back to the woman standing beside him and his expression dissatisfied her. Snatching the little picture to her breast she stepped back and began to cry, quietly but as though her heart would break.

"Oh, love," he said, leaping to his feet. "Hush. Don't cry." He pulled her hands away from her body and carefully loosened her fingers from the frame. "It's all right," he said, placing the portrait on the table with the care that befitted her greatest treasure. "I believe you. You look just like her."

And maybe she did. Juliana might very well be correct in her assumptions, and he decided to take her at her word.

He knew what it was like not to be believed.

He took the sobbing woman into his arms, enveloped her body for protection, held her fast for comfort, murmured words of consolation.

He wanted to tell her he didn't care if she'd been born to a Gypsy girl in a ditch. That what she'd become, the clever, witty, fiercely independent woman she'd made herself, was far more important than who she was. He wanted to make things right for Juliana, chase away her past, ensure she never felt another moment's disquiet.

And if he married her, an idea that suddenly seemed much more acceptable than the life sentence he'd arrived dreading, he could do so.

But, damn it all, she was right about that. He could imagine the arguments of his mother's counsel if he presented a tradeswoman with a dubious background as his bride. He'd never persuade anyone that he and Juliana were proper candidates for the care of the gently raised, well-endowed daughter of the Saintly Marquis.

He was taking enough of a risk himself, allowing his mother to repeat her husband's foul accusations for the world to judge.

Chapter 13

"**W**hy can't I have a purple dress?" Esther's eyes followed Mel as the housekeeper left the room. Mel's ensemble for the day featured a cotton twill dyed a particularly virulent shade of deep violet, startlingly trimmed with burnt orange ribbons.

"Because you are sixteen and sixteen-year-olds don't wear gowns like that. Eat your breakfast. Will you pour me some tea?"

If anyone had told Cain he'd ever be preaching propriety to an unfledged girl, he'd have laughed his head off. That was before he found himself in charge of a sister who had discovered bright colors. He hardly knew how to tell Esther that Mel's fashion choices were unsuitable for a *lady* of any age, let alone why. Fortunately the resourceful Mrs. Timms had produced a few garments in a more appropriate style, castoffs from a ladybird whose former protector fancied his women dressed as schoolgirls. Mrs. Timms had been very happy to sell them to Mel, so Esther was unexceptionally clad in demure white muslin.

Esther pouted a little but carefully performed her allotted task with the teapot.

"At least we'll be going out today," she said, her face brightening. Esther had been sequestered in the house for several days and she was restive.

"Will we?"

"Of course. What time is church?"

Cain hadn't even noticed it was Sunday. "I think you can miss it this once."

"But John!" Esther's mouth pursed in a shocked O. "It's *Easter*."

"Wouldn't you like me to teach you piquet?"

"Yes, I would. Very much. But we must go to church for Easter."

Cain frowned. Though his sister showed every sign of making a speedy recovery from years of gloom at Markley Chase, he understood that her religious upbringing made it inconceivable to miss worship on such a day. Yet he couldn't take her himself. Certainly not to join the fashionable throng at St. George's or even the slightly less *tonnish* parishioners of St. James's. Her presence remained a secret. Especially since her residence in his disreputable household could do nothing to enhance her reputation. It went without saying that none of his servants was a suitable escort for her.

Some words chimed in his memory, Juliana's claim that she left her childhood home only to attend church. He'd wager she maintained the habit. He scribbled a note and summoned one his footmen.

"Deliver this to Mrs. Merton. And take the old carriage."

* * *

He hadn't set foot in a church in eight years and didn't need to today. But once Juliana had taken Esther up in the nondescript blue town coach, he'd found himself following them on foot.

The church of St. Martin-in-the-Fields was full this Easter morning, every seat in the lower pews and galleries taken. Cain slipped in and placed himself with others standing in the side aisle, halfway back.

Churchgoing had been frequent and compulsory in his childhood: the Royal Progress of the family and upper servants to the dark medieval parish church; the twice-daily household prayers in the gloomy, unadorned chapel his ancestors had carved from one of the older parts of the mansion. Cain couldn't recall when the irony first struck him that the Godfreys, priding themselves on their godliness, drew their fortune from lands seized from a monastery and lived in a house resurrected from the ruins of an abbey.

There was nothing remotely gloomy about the congregation at St. Martin that day. Light poured in from the huge window at the rear of the chancel, illuminating the soaring barrel-vaulted ceiling supported by slender white columns. The congregation was as cheerfully dressed as the huge flower arrangements surrounding the pulpit and altar. Hundreds of voices joined lustily in the Easter hymn.

Cain surveyed the crowd, searching for a lady in black. He found her near the center, her black bonnet contrasting with his sister's straw chip hat. Even at a distance, something in their mien told him that Juliana and Esther had become friendly during their surreptitious journey. The latter had been in a state of high excitement at being smuggled out through the mews to meet the carriage at the corner of Charles Street. Doubtless she'd regaled Juliana with the tale of her adventure. Now and then their eyes met over their shared hymnal. Esther's expression could only be described as one of unholy glee, returned with equal warmth. Their mouths moved in unison, heads tilted back, both faces carefree, relishing the sheer pleasure of song.

Regarding them, Cain caught something of their spirits, not caring exactly what inspired them. He felt a moment of pure happiness, so unusual as to startle, at being alive on a beautiful spring morning in the presence of the two people in the world who were, he realized, most dear to him. He wanted to squeeze through the crowd, stand between them with an arm around each, and share this moment with them. Then he'd take them both home and celebrate the day.

Abruptly he turned toward the exit. His buoyant mood slipped away as he left the church. Keeping both Juliana and Esther was impossible and his newly found sense of responsibility made the necessary choice easy, if not painless. The course that had been nagging him could no longer be avoided.

He was going to beard the dragon in her den.

It was perhaps two hundred yards through the central garden to the other side of Berkeley Square. To Cain it felt like two hundred miles, while paradoxically the five-minute walk seemed to take five seconds.

The house was deceptively modest given the influence wielded by its inhabitants. Lady Moberley, through a combination of her husband's political career and her own forceful personality, had achieved a power in the *ton* equaled or exceeded by only a handful of other ladies. Cain had spoken to her just once in the years he'd lived in London. Taking a deep breath, he grasped the door knocker and gave it a sharp rap.

Mel's monarch of the week opened the door. Too short for the tsar, too tall for Napoleon, and too thin to be either Prinny or Louis XVIII. Cain favored the servant with a slightly derisive grin.

"Is Her Ladyship at home?"

The butler's nose was high enough for all these monarchs rolled into a single master of the universe. "May I say who is calling?"

Cain stared him down. "I believe you are aware of my identity."

The servant didn't argue. "I shall inquire if Her Ladyship is receiving," he said with a mere excuse for a bow, and left Cain alone in the hall, uncertain whether his aunt would admit him into her majestic presence.

A painting caught his eye, a portrait of two young girls in white dresses by George Romney: Lady Moberley, his Aunt Augusta, and her younger sister, Maria. His mother.

His parent had never, in his recollection, looked as carefree as the girl playing with a small fluffy dog. In his experience her companion had always been devotional not canine, a prayer book or volume of sermons ever at hand. She'd been pretty then. He fancied he saw something of Esther in her. Yet the artist had captured a certain weakness in her expression, especially when compared to the haughtier features of her elder sister. Augusta looked as though she couldn't wait for Mr. Romney to put down his brush so she could snatch away their pet. Though not well acquainted with his aunt, who had visited Markley Chase but rarely, Cain recognized the middle-aged dragon in her youthful likeness.

Poor Mother. She'd escaped an overbearing sister into the keeping of a dominating and cruel husband. Cain wondered, as he still occasionally did, if there was any point trying to reason with her. Probably not, he thought with a shudder. Not after their last bitter meeting.

The King of the World returned and indicated in a voice rich with disapproval that Her Ladyship would, in fact, see him. Cain followed him up the stairs with a puddle of dread in the pit of his stomach. It felt almost like going home.

"So, nephew. You have decided to call on me at last."

Lady Moberley didn't rise at his entrance. She remained enthroned on a straight-backed chair, her considerable height enhanced by a turban in deep red velvet over crisp salt-and-pepper curls. She bade him approach with a wave of the hand and a sharp nod.

Cain gave her his best bow. "You'll forgive me, madam, for my neglect, but the last time I was in this house you told me you didn't wish to see me again."

"Why would I wish to see a debauched wastrel?"

The customary defensive irritation roiled through him. "I make no apology for my life."

"Well you should," she replied harshly. "For eight years you have consorted with the lowest company and for the past three you have filled my sister's house with servants I will only describe as irregular. I have too much discretion to name the occupation of the women who visit you, day and night."

"I would never have suspected you were so interested in my affairs. Do you spend your time looking out of your window across the square?"

"There's no need. Your associations are a scandal throughout London."

"What an unvaried and narrow view you hold of the bounds of our capital, madam. I assure you there are many in this town who find my behavior quite unexceptional."

The nostrils of Lady Moberley's prominent nose stretched as though to exude fire. A sharp "hah!" said what she thought of those particular opinions.

"My friends accept me as I am and I return their tolerance." He felt his temper rise. This woman had spurned him when he came to her, alone and frightened, and aged only sixteen. "Had I been welcomed elsewhere perhaps I would have different friends."

"I said you could come back when you reformed your ways," she sniffed.

He stepped back a few paces and tried to calm down. He hadn't come here to quarrel with her. For Esther's sake he needed to control his resentment.

"Well have you?" she barked. "Reformed?"

"Not yet, but I hope to. That is why I have come to call on my aunt."

"Why?"

Cain looked at her in silence for a few moments, not sure he could trust her. Yet if he didn't, why was he here?

"Esther is in London."

"Alone? Is my sister here?"

Cain shook his head.

"I thought not." He detected a note of satisfaction in her voice and perhaps a softening in her attitude as she spoke. "Sit down. You'd better tell me the whole story."

She listened intently, interrupting to demand refinement of a detail here and there. When she heard of Lady Chase's plan to wed her daughter to Mr. Ditchfield, those large nostrils widened again. This time Cain took comfort from Her Ladyship's dangerous expression. She nodded approvingly when he reached his plan to win Esther's guardianship.

"I always suspected Maria was unbalanced," she pronounced at the end of his recitation. "Now I am certain of it. You know, Chase"—for the first time she addressed him by name—"Maria was the prettier of the two of us. She made a better match, to a wealthier man of higher rank, but I never envied her."

Something told Cain she spoke only part of the truth. There was a sisterly conflict he didn't understand. Children tended to be oblivious to currents of strain between their elders. Certainly he'd never understood his own parents' bond.

His aunt shook off the moment of introspection,

rose to her feet, and made her way to the bellpull with a good deal of energy. "There's no time to be lost. We must get started."

Cain followed and stayed her hand. "Started with what?"

"Why, your rehabilitation of course. I need Kentish."

"I assume Kentish is your butler. Before you summon him, or any other servant, I'd like to hear what you propose."

Lady Moberley gave an impatient snort, then began to speak briskly. "First, we must remove my niece from under your roof. You say no one knows she's there? Good. She must stay here until we've cleaned out that Augean stable you inhabit."

"I assure you my house is very clean. You insult my servants."

"Don't be absurd. No servant of decent character will share quarters with those you already have."

Unfortunately Cain knew she was correct. However much he valued his assorted band of reformed rogues, the *ton* would never see it his way.

"I shall begin my preparations for bringing Esther out next year. I'll have the clothing bills sent to you, of course. Then I shall make some calls. You may expect invitations to start arriving immediately and I expect you to accept them. With the season just beginning it couldn't be better. You'll have your choice of the latest crop of eligible young ladies."

"Eligible young ladies? Are you so sure their families will find me acceptable?"

"A rich marquis is always acceptable." She flicked

away his objection with a sweep of an amethyst-embellished hand.

Cain wished he felt her confidence. "Do you know why my father dismissed me from his house?" Fear gripped his stomach. He'd spent eight years dreading to hear the charge put into words.

"My sister has told me of the rantings of that madman she married."

He felt a glimmer of hope. "Do you think my father was mad? I thought everyone respected him."

"I was never fond of Lord Chase. By the end of his life his pious gibbering had gone beyond the bounds of acceptability. I wasn't alone in thinking him unreasonable in his treatment of you. If you seduced a maid or two you wouldn't be the first, or the last."

"As it happens I never laid a finger on any woman, maid or otherwise." He smiled, probably not a wise thing to do, but he couldn't help it. The relief overwhelmed him. His aunt didn't know.

"From all accounts you've more than made up for it since," she said tartly. "But if you mend your ways people will dismiss it as youthful indiscretion.

"Then why, when I came to you a few weeks after I arrived in London, did you refuse to help me? 'Debauched beyond the hope of rescue' were, I believe, your words."

"My dear boy! You were living in a brothel! And it is only with the greatest reluctance that I bring myself to utter that word."

Bardsley and his father must have spread the tale. As far as he knew they were the only people who had recognized him during his three-week sojourn at Mrs.

Rafferty's. Of course the whores had thought it a fine joke to have a lord in their midst, and later the gossip had seeped upward via their customers. He hadn't realized his aunt had known so soon.

"I left soon afterward," he said.

"Yes, to become an actress's kept plaything. A fine situation for one of your station."

As it happened, the small allowance Robinson, his man of business, had wrested from his father had meant he never took money from Lucinda Lambert, his first mistress. But essentially his aunt was correct: Lucinda paid all the expenses of the house they shared for a year.

"There is no need for us to further visit the past," Lady Moberley said. "There is too much to do. I shall speak to Kentish at once about engaging you some decent servants. And you may address me as Aunt Augusta."

Cain feared that pleasing Aunt Augusta would carry a heavy cost. Yet as an ally in his campaign to keep Esther, his aunt was invaluable. And his mother hadn't even confided in her, her own sister.

Lady Moberley had no idea that the late marquis had accused his son of incest, a transgression that would place him beyond the bounds of any decent society. Even a hint of such an abomination would condemn him. She didn't know Lady Chase had threatened to tell the world if Cain went anywhere near his sister. If she didn't know, perhaps no one did.

Chapter 14

❧∽◯◯∽❧

Cain had given up everything that made life worth living. And that, he thought morosely as he concluded an endless meeting with old Robinson, was only a slight exaggeration.

His aunt had him dancing attendance at every breakfast, ball, rout, or musicale the fashionable world could cram into two weeks. He'd long since lost count of how many.

When he finally had a moment to himself, he couldn't go to Sotheby's and buy books because there was a two-week break in the auction. His home was no refuge. The Berkeley Square house was occupied by two rival camps of servants whose fragile truce threatened daily to erupt into violence. King Kentish and his minions had swept into Cain's house and established what Lady Moberley pleased to call order. Cain refused to dismiss any of his staff until they had somewhere to go. And Robinson was taking an age to complete the purchase of the house he'd found for his former servants.

He had to listen to Robinson grumbling about the cost. Of establishing a fund so that, through Mel, he could continue to aid her former sisters in frailty. Of paying the lawyers preparing Esther's guardianship petition. And of settling his sister's clothing bills. Finally he ordered the old bleater to sell out of the funds if necessary and do as he was told.

The worst of it was, he didn't even see much of Esther. Aunt Moberley had her niece as busy with dress fittings, dancing, and deportment lessons as Cain was with *ton* events.

He'd rebelled the previous day and told his aunt he'd be tied up with business all day. Finally he was free to indulge himself. As his carriage left the City and entered the Strand, he directed his coachman to a small bookshop in St. Martin's Lane.

Juliana came from the back of the shop to greet him, Quarto at her heels. The dog wasn't pleased to see him. He indicated his displeasure by biting the tassel off Cain's Hessian boot. Cain wasn't bothered. Attending to the repair would give his new valet something to do.

Juliana, on the other hand, seemed delighted, almost as happy as he was to see her. Her Cupid's bow smile matched the narrow strip of sunlight filtering through the window, revealing swirling dust motes that danced and echoed his new mood. Cain had met, conversed, and danced with numerous ladies in the past week, all of them gowned, jeweled, and coiffed as finely as Bond Street could provide. None of them held a candle to Juliana Cassandra Merton in her widow's weeds. She was, quite simply, the loveliest woman he knew. And alone in the shop. Apart from the dog.

No! He beat back his unruly thoughts and fixed his eye on the baleful canine flopped at his feet.

"Since the creature is a monster of ingratitude toward the man who saved him from a life hunting rats in the East End, I hope he is at least performing his allotted task and disturbing any intruders."

She laughed. "I haven't heard anything amiss downstairs since he came. But he's certainly disturbed *me*." The look she gave the bulldog was indignant yet affectionate.

"What happened?" Cain found himself hungry for news of even her trivial activities.

"Last night I was awoken by a weight on top of me. I wondered what it was." To his pleasure she blushed absolutely scarlet.

"I felt warm breath in my ear."

"Do tell more."

"Then a huge wet tongue all over my face." She shot a look of mock irritation at his laugh. "He just wouldn't go away until I paid attention."

"We males can be like that."

"I lit my candle and discovered the wretched animal had been chewing a book. I thought I'd trained him to understand that books are not toys, but he relapsed. So I dragged him into the kitchen and shut the door."

"The animal is supposed to guard the shop. That's where he should have been."

"But it's cold down there at night."

Cain rolled his eyes. She was hopeless. The supposedly hardened tradeswoman brought down by a hideous beast. "To punish him you shut him in a room with food?"

"There wasn't any food."

Of course not. By God, the woman needed a keeper. He raised both hands and eyebrows in exasperation.

"Then," she continued, "just as I was going back to sleep, he started barking and scratching at the door. I let him howl for a while."

"Your neighbors must have enjoyed that."

"I read somewhere that it's good to let infants cry until it's time to feed them, to teach them a routine. I thought maybe it would work the same way with dogs." She seemed quite serious.

"And did it?"

"No. Finally I couldn't bear it and let him out of the kitchen. And do you know what?" she asked indignantly. "He wanted to go for a walk. At three o'clock in the morning!"

"Uh, Juliana. I've never owned a dog but I do know they need to go outside from time to time. To take care of things."

"Oh no. It wasn't *that* kind of noise. I know that one. This was his 'walkies' noise."

"And I suppose you took him out in the London streets in the middle of the night, despite the fact the animal is clearly incompetent when it comes to protection."

"No, I was firm with him."

"Oh, well done."

She looked sheepish. "He ended up sleeping on my bed, but," she concluded, "I didn't let him lick me again."

Cain stopped trying to suppress his mirth and she gave up any pretense of annoyance. They joined in a bout of laughter and he felt better than he'd done in days. He'd have liked to embrace her, not lustfully—at least not entirely—but to show his affection.

Not a good idea. He was supposed to be finding himself a bride and that bride couldn't be Juliana.

"The Tarleton sale starts again tomorrow. Is there anything you want to buy this week?" That was Juliana, single-minded when it came to books.

"I looked for the catalogue yesterday but my new servants seem to have hidden it."

"Never mind, I'll fetch mine." She hurried into the back room with the bounce that bibliographic enthusiasm always added to her step. "There's some very fine poetry coming up this week," she called. "Better than the Herrick. Beautiful copies of some true rarities. How do you feel about Spenser? Or do you prefer Milton?"

Cain was fairly sure he didn't have any feelings about Spenser, one way or the other. Milton he quite liked. He found the character of Satan interesting.

She returned with the catalogue in one hand and a package in the other. "The binder delivered the Herrick to me by mistake last week."

He tore off the paper and surveyed the red morocco volume with satisfaction.

"You're the only man in London with a library to match your carriage."

"So it does. I don't know how much I will be adding to it. I've been busy trying to get married."

The words were jaunty but his enjoyment dissipated. Judging by Juliana's expression she felt the same way. He wondered if her displeasure went beyond anxiety about how matrimony would influence his book-purchasing habits.

"And how are you going about that?" she asked.

"I've attended balls and danced with young ladies."

Aunt Augusta had been correct. The mamas of these pretty creatures were only too happy to welcome a reformed marquis to their collective bosom and offer him his choice of nubile lovelies as his marchioness.

Not that he had anything against them, mamas or daughters. Cain rarely encountered a woman he didn't like.

"Do you enjoy that?" He didn't imagine the strain in her voice.

"The girls are sweet, well drilled in polite conversation, and ready to be charmed by me."

"I'm sure you are very charming." She sounded quite cross.

"I do my best, but it isn't really important. My Aunt Augusta, who has undertaken the restoration of my character, assures me my wealth and title are enough to ensure forgiveness of any past transgressions."

"I see. Have you made your choice?"

"They all seem so young. I've never fancied extreme youth." Which was ironic under the circumstances, and perfectly true. His first mistress, Lucinda, had been twenty-eight to his sixteen. "But I suppose one of them would make a good sister for Esther."

"How is Lady Esther?"

"Staying with my aunt, Lady Moberley, until the court hears her petition. And buying a lot of clothes."

"She'll enjoy that. Will your aunt allow her to have a purple gown?"

"Told you about that, did she? I'm thankful to say my aunt took over Esther's wardrobe choices before I gave in and indulged her craving for unsuitable colors. I did just settle the account for an evening cloak in claret ruched velvet, lined in white satin and trimmed with ermine."

"My goodness, that seems hardly suitable for a girl of sixteen."

"No, I recognize my aunt's taste. She's exacting her pound of flesh for helping me by replacing her entire wardrobe at my expense. If she continues at her current pace I shan't be able to afford so much as a pamphlet, let alone the Burgundy Hours."

"Cain . . ." She approached him and put a hand on his arm. But whatever she meant to say was interrupted by the entrance of a customer.

Juliana drew back hastily. "The poetry we spoke of is on that shelf, my lord," she said indicating a section of books in the alcove formed by two bookcases emerging at right angles from the wall. "May I suggest you examine them while I attend to Mr. Penderleith?"

The look she gave him he interpreted as *Do not leave.*

He plucked a volume from the shelf, half listening to her conversation with Penderleith, an elderly quiz in a periwig and a moth-eaten moleskin waistcoat liberally stained with snuff. He wondered what Juliana wanted to say to him. He wasn't, at this particular moment, feeling terribly reformed. If she were to make the first move and invite him upstairs, he feared for the fate of his good resolutions.

Not finding anything remotely interesting in an edition of Cowper's works, he tried to replace it. It wouldn't go in all the way. Something was wedged at the back of the shelf. Removing several neighboring volumes, he reached in and removed a slender square book in a green leather binding. He recognized it at once.

What the hell was Cassandra Fitterbourne's *Romeo and Juliet* quarto doing in Juliana Merton's shop, instead of awaiting sale at Sotheby's, along with the rest of Sir Thomas Tarleton's library?

Juliana closed the door firmly and with relief behind the foxy old collector. A customer since she and Joseph had opened their shop, Mr. Penderleith no longer had credit with any bookseller in London. She'd promised to set aside Grose's *Antiquities of England and Wales* for him, but the book wouldn't leave her premises until his account was settled.

At least Cain hadn't left. She'd told herself she was merely anxious about his intentions vis-à-vis the auction. The intense pleasure she felt upon his appearance this morning threatened that particular illusion. She'd missed him terribly.

"Thank goodness he's gone," she said as she closed the door behind Penderleith and came back around the corner into the main aisle of the shop.

Cain stood with a book in his hand. There was no need to ask what he held. She knew that volume as well as her own face in the mirror. Better perhaps.

"My God," she whispered. "Where did that come from?"

"I found it behind the books on this shelf."

Juliana felt sick. A book she desperately coveted had been found in her shop. And it was stolen property.

"I didn't put it there," she said.

"I didn't believe for a moment that you had." The certainty in his voice reassured her. "I've been thinking. Someone was meant to find the *Romeo and Juliet*. That volume of Cowper was thrust forward a little so I pulled it off the shelf. When I couldn't put it back properly I investigated the obstacle."

"I might have been the first to find it."

"You don't sound confident."

"I'm not. That corner is a little dark so unless I had reason to look for a particular book there I wouldn't have noticed."

"When did you last examine the poetry section?"

"At least a week ago," she said after some thought. "A customer asked me for Pope's *Satires*." Her mind reeled as she grasped that any number of visitors to the shop could have recognized the *Romeo and Juliet*. She had narrowly avoided being taken for a thief.

"And has anyone else been in that area of the shop since then?"

"Not that I recall."

"The dog, last night," Cain said. "He barked because he heard something."

"He didn't want a walk, he wanted to stop an intruder!"

Cain looked grim. "It appears I've wronged the animal, but I'm damn glad you didn't give in and take him downstairs. Someone has the ability to break into your premises at will, and whoever it is may be dangerous."

"But why? Why would anyone want to get me into trouble?"

"Perhaps the question we should ask first is, who knew this book was special to you?"

"A number of the booksellers know of my connection to Mr. Fitterbourne. My upbringing was never a secret, merely my birth. I mentioned it to Sir Henry Tarleton. And to Mr. Gilbert. And to a couple of other dealers in the last week."

Cain stared at the volume, his face creased in a frown, then opened it, peering at the rear paste-down endpaper.

He gave a little grunt.

"What?"

"Look at this. I think someone had done something to the binding inside the back cover."

Juliana knew the book well enough to detect a slit in the paper along the hinge, and faint traces of glue that looked fresh.

"You are right," she said in wonder, running a finger over the repair. "Something could have been removed from the binding." She turned to the front. "The same thing has happened here."

"May I have another look?"

She relinquished it willingly. Even holding it for a few seconds frightened her.

Cain started to go through the volume, page by page. "Why are there so many blank leaves in the book?" he asked.

"It's only a single play, so the binder added blanks to make the volume thicker and have enough room to put the title on the spine. What are you looking for?"

"I don't know." He continued turning the leaves, even when he got to the end of the play.

"Have you ever looked at these blanks?" His voice sounded odd.

"No, why should I?"

"There's something written here, covering part of a page."

"What?" Juliana tried to peer over his shoulder, an impossibility due to his superior height.

"Here, stop jumping up and down." He held it so she could see.

"My mother wrote that." She recognized Cassandra's handwriting at once. Unfortunately she could make nothing of it. It was gibberish, an apparently random collection of letters without spaces or punctuation. She peered at it desperately, trying to discern meaning. She yearned for a message, a thought, even something as mundane as a household receipt.

"It's nonsense," she said sadly.

"Do you notice that the same letters are used over and over again? Tell me again how those price codes work."

"Of course!" Immediately she knew Cain had the answer. "I never knew Cassandra's code but there are Js, Es, Ts and Xs here, just like in the price at the front of the book."

She repeated her explanation of how collectors disguised their prices. "You take a ten-letter word and assign the digits to each letter." Seizing the volume she turned back to the front. "Xx/je/t. The Xs are probably naughts so we are looking for a nine-letter word or phrase made up from the other letters on this page."

Without another word they both hurried back to the library table where Juliana, hands trembling with excitement, found pens and paper and wrote a list of the letters in Cassandra's mysterious message. There were indeed a total of nine in addition to the X. The two of them sat side-by-side and furiously scribbled, trying to find the anagram that was the key to the code.

"It's impossible!" Juliana moaned. "I can't make anything work with the J."

"No, wait. Look." Cain pointed at his sheet of paper. "JULIET. The letters of the name Juliet are here."

"What's left?"

"A. P. C. PAC. CAP. Cap! JULIET CAP! This was her favorite book, wasn't it? She probably loved the play before she even bought the book and used Juliet Capulet as her code."

"You solved it!" She flung her arms around Cain's neck out of sheer gratitude. "Thank you, thank you!"

Juliana had spent years trying to guess the code, but there were only a handful of books that had belonged to Cassandra. It was such a little thing, but she somehow felt closer to the woman she thought of as her mother. Cain held her close, pressing his lips into her hair. Relaxing in his arms, she was happy he was there to share this precious moment with her. She tucked her head under his chin, feeling crisp starched linen under her cheek and inhaling his now familiar scent. She sighed with deep satisfaction.

"Juliana," he murmured after a minute or two. "I'm glad you are happy, and I'm even happier this discovery has brought us, er, into such an intimate connection. But what exactly have we solved?"

"Now I know what Miss Cassandra paid for the book." She thought for a second, counting the words off on her fingers. "J equals 1, E equals 5, T equals 6. Fifteen shillings and sixpence. That was a good price," she said approvingly.

"Wonderful as it may be that your mother got such a bargain, it still leaves us with nothing but a lot of numbers."

"Oh!" She pulled out of Cain's embrace. "Let's 'translate' the page."

Loath as she was to admit it, he was right. When they made the "translation," substituting digits for letters, they were no closer to a comprehensible message.

"It must mean something, it must," she said, now frantic to know what Cassandra had written.

"There has to be a second step to the translation," Cain said, staring at the sheet of numbers she'd transcribed. For a short while he was silent, nodding his head back and forth, his full lower lip curled over the upper in a thoughtful pout. Then he looked up. "Do you notice there are a great many 1s?"

"So there are. So what?"

"Suppose the numbers need to be turned back into letters. The simplest thing would be to make 1 equal A, 2 equal B and so forth. 13 could be either AC or M, the thirteenth letter."

"Let's try."

It took about an hour and much trial and error before they coaxed the full meaning from the sheet of digits. The breakthrough came when they realized some of the numbers should remain numbers. The solution contained a date. All their work boiled down to one short sentence.

"On the 27th of March, 1795, Cassandra and her beloved Julian became one."

"Julian," she breathed in wonder. "My father."

"When were you born?"

"The 3rd of January, 1796."

"The timing is right. It sounds to me, Mrs. Merton, as though your parents were lawfully wed."

"Perhaps not." Juliana could hardly bear to hope. "Perhaps it's just the date they . . . you know."

Cain smiled. "That too. The date is definitely right for 'you know.'"

He drew her to her feet and tipped her face upward with two fingers on her chin. She saw a hint of humor or mischief in his eyes, and something else too, that she'd never perceived before. He lowered his head and kissed her lips softly.

"I think," he said, "we should find out if they were married. Because if they were, there's no reason we shouldn't be too."

Chapter 15

‗‗‗‗‗‗‗‗‗‗‗‗‗‗‗‗

The auction viewing room was crowded with men looking over the new selection of books, brought out after the two-week hiatus. Cain wandered casually over to the section of the room where the greatest treasures were kept, the ones that wouldn't be sold until the last day: things like the Burgundy Hours, and the Shakespeares.

A small card inscribed in a neat italic was pinned to one of the shelves: "Lot number 9324 is unavailable for viewing."

Lot 9324 was, in fact, tucked into the capacious inner pocket of Cain's greatcoat.

Juliana had been reluctant to let the *Romeo and Juliet* go, but anxious to get it off her premises. "Maybe I should tear out the page with the inscription? It's only a blank so would it count as theft?"

Having listened to her argue back and forth at least six times, Cain had lost patience, though not sympathy.

"We know what Cassandra wrote and that's the important thing. The inscription doesn't actually prove anything." He removed the book from her slackening grip. "You'll have the book eventually. If you don't buy it yourself, I'll buy it for you. In the meantime I'd like to try and get this back where it belongs before anyone misses it. "Don't go out," he ordered, before she could summon further argument, "and keep the dog close."

Quarto growled at him. "Good boy," Cain said. "That's the way to treat visitors."

Cain was beginning to recognize some of the auction regulars, among them Iverley and Compton, who stood against a wall. The latter called to him. "Chase! Last time I saw you, at the Duchess of Amesbury's ball, you looked as though you'd swallowed a hedgehog."

"I'd sooner swallow a hedgehog than attend a ball," contributed Iverley. He shifted in irritation. "I wonder how long we'll have to wait for a place at a table."

Compton raised a quizzical eyebrow at Cain. "Rumor has you a reformed man."

"That's what my aunt tells me."

"I make it a point never to believe what aunts have to say. Yet the presence of the Marquis of Chase, dancing with the lovely young maidens, was the talk of the card room."

"Do you think you could bring yourselves to call me Cain? I've heard nothing but Chase the last week and it makes me think of my father."

"As you wish. Call me Tarquin. I take it, Cain, the Saintly Marquis doesn't arouse fond memories. My own sire died years ago. Perhaps I should be grateful."

Iverley grunted something that sounded like "mine

fell out of a window." Cain would have liked to pursue this fascinating piece of information. Another time.

"Do you know what happened to lot 9324?" he asked.

"The *Romeo* quarto?" said Tarquin. "Did you hear anything, Sebastian?"

"Some idiot probably put it away in the wrong place. They'll find it eventually."

Indeed they would, once Cain chose where, among the laden shelves and tables, that "wrong place" would be. Leaning against the wall with folded arms, he surveyed the room for a likely spot.

"Where's Mrs. Merton today?" Tarquin asked. "I was thinking of going over to St. Martin's Lane later. I hear she's acquired a damn fine collection of English poetry."

The blunt rustle of turning pages and the buzz of a dozen bibliographic conversations faded from Cain's consciousness. "Where did you hear that?" he asked in a rasp.

"Newman. I think it was Newman who told me."

"Where would I find this Newman? Is he here?"

Tarquin looked around the room and shook his head. "The best place to find him is in the taproom of the Red Lion. Better catch him soon or he'll be senseless."

"Always is." Iverley had, contrary to appearances, been attending to the conversation. "The man's a sot and you can't credit a word he says. Highly unlikely that a female would acquire a collection of the caliber he mentioned."

Cain was torn between defending Juliana's abil-

ity to stock good books and a fervent desire to keep
everyone away from her poetry section. His instinct
was to take carriage to St. Martin's Lane without a moment's delay and search her shop for further incrimi-
nating surprises. Whoever had planted the quarto, he
thought with rising anger, wasn't playing games. It
was sheer luck that Juliana hadn't already been accused of theft.

"Mrs. Merton said nothing to me about any new acquisitions," he said. "And we were discussing poetry
only this afternoon. I fear the rumor is unfounded."

"Sadly, rumors so often are," Tarquin said.

"But," Cain continued, "I would like to know how
this tale began. It seems someone is playing a little
joke on Mrs. Merton, and I do not believe that is kind
to an unprotected lady."

He glared at Iverley. Not that he suspected him,
but he suddenly resented the scruffy collector's every
disparagement of Juliana.

His rage seemed to penetrate Iverley's habitual ab-
straction. "I may not have much time for women, Cain,
but I don't go round playing 'little jokes' on them."

"Do you suppose the inebriated Mr. Newman in-
vented the tale himself?"

Iverley thought for a moment. "No. Someone else
must have told him."

"Would he tell me who?" Cain was quite prepared
to throttle the truth out of Mr. Newman if necessary.

"If he knows. Newman never forgets a book and
never remembers a name or a face."

Cain would stop at the Red Lion before he returned
to St. Martin's Lane. First he had a task to perform.

His heavy coat brushed a tower of books on the end of one of the long tables where Matthew Gilbert was seated.

"I do beg your pardon," he said to the visibly irritated man, steadying the tottering pile by picking up several volumes and rearranging them so they lined up nice and straight.

Childish, yes, but Cain hoped the pompous bookseller would be just a little embarrassed when the missing quarto turned up among them.

"I've had two people come in and ask for poetry in the last hour!" Juliana almost dragged Cain into the shop and relocked the door.

"I'm surprised it's not more," he said.

She felt chilled when he told her what he'd discovered. The excitement of deciphering Cassandra's code had driven the question of how the book got into her shop to the back of her mind. But as first one and then a second customer asked for poetry, she'd begun to panic, closed the shop, and started an organized search through her shelves. Books she hadn't touched in months were dusted off to see what mysteries might lurk behind them.

"Someone wants to get me into trouble," she said. "But who?"

"I couldn't get anything out of this Newman fellow. Sebastian Iverley was right. Newman had no idea who told him the story about you."

"Who? What about *why*? What have I ever done to anyone? I cannot think of a single person who has even the smallest reason for a grudge against me."

Juliana actually found this fact depressing. There were no booksellers envious of her superior success, no disgruntled collectors whom she'd beaten out for an important purchase. The sad truth was, she'd done nothing even to ruffle a feather or two, let alone inspire spite and retaliation.

"I've been thinking about it," Cain said. "Whoever placed the book here knew it meant something special to you."

"I agree."

"And he seems to have been looking for something in the volume."

"Yes."

"We have no way of knowing if he found anything, but *we* certainly did. And that is too much of a coincidence for me. I refuse to believe that what the thief sought and what we discovered are unrelated to each other."

"Do you suppose the thief found the inscription too?"

"My guess is not, or if he did he couldn't decipher it. If my idea is correct, he would never let you get near the volume if he knew what it said."

Finally Juliana understood where Cain's argument was leading. "You mean this person wouldn't want me to know about my parents, about Cassandra and Julian."

"Exactly. I think he was looking for proof of their marriage. Perhaps he found something hidden in the binding, perhaps not. Either way, he then decided to get you into trouble by planting the book, a book that many people know you wanted, in your shop."

Juliana's head reeled. Since she had spent her entire life believing herself baseborn, the possibility of discovering her father's identity and her parents' marriage was enough to take in for one day. Add a conspiracy to have her branded a thief and Cain's theory of how the facts were connected, and she felt her composure unravel.

"It's all nonsense, Cain. You're making this up to suit your own goals. You want to marry me to save you the trouble of finding a young woman of your own station. Who else would even care whether my parents were married or not? No one, that's who. No one!"

She stared at the ground, avoiding meeting his eyes. Something cold and wet nudged her hand. She sank to her knees and buried her face in the bulldog's brindled neck. Quarto was a safe source of consolation.

"Juliana?" Her name was a caress close to her ear. Looking up she found Cain squatting beside her, his blue eyes deep and kind. To her relief he made no attempt to touch her. She didn't want to find herself weeping in his arms again. She didn't want to rely on Cain for her peace of mind.

"Juliana, my dear, you are upset. Hardly astonishing under the circumstances. What has happened today is not about me and my wishes. You are the center of this story. At the very least there is a mystery to solve concerning your birth, and it seems only too likely that someone else is interested in the truth as well."

His words comforted and calmed her. She took a deep breath, and the chance of succumbing to a fit of the vapors subsided. "There's no sense to it. It's not as though my legitimacy would make me heiress to a fortune."

"Are you sure about that?"

Her abating distress was accompanied by a commensurate awareness of Cain's proximity: the sleek planes of his face with a hint of afternoon shadow on chin and jaw; the faint, clean masculine scent; muscled thighs brushing her skirts where she knelt on the dusty wooden floor; his intent gaze fixed upon her face.

She stood up and stepped back. "I told you. My grandfather . . . My God, he really was my grandfather! My grandfather died in debt."

"But the estate that went to your cousin? Would your mother have inherited it?"

Juliana shook her head. "I don't know. I don't believe so. There was never a question of my having it, so I never asked. I do know Frederick complained bitterly about having to find a thousand pounds in the estate for me. It was one of the excuses he gave for not letting me keep any of the books."

"Did you ask him for the *Romeo and Juliet*?"

"Many times. He said I didn't deserve another penny."

"So Frederick Fitterbourne knew the book was significant?"

"Yes," she replied. "He did."

"I think a conversation with Cousin Frederick is in order."

"He's in Wiltshire," she said stupidly.

"I shall leave tomorrow."

"*You'll* leave tomorrow?"

"No! I'm not leaving you here. We'll go together."

"What has it to do with you?"

"Listen to me," he said. He caught her shoulder and turned her, then took her face in his two hands, forcing her to look at him. What she saw there was new to her, an expression of deep concern and gravity. There was no trace of the cynicism, defiance, or even the humor that usually dressed Cain's features.

"Listen, Juliana. My supposition about what is going on may be completely mistaken. But you are in trouble, perhaps in danger. And I am not going to leave you to face this alone. I take care of my friends."

Chapter 16

His final argument persuaded Juliana. "I need a place for some of my servants to stay for a few days," he said, couching it as a favor to him. "They can guard the shop and feed the dog."

She said yes, thank God. Cain wasn't prepared to leave her in London without him, not even with half a regiment for protection. He could scarcely bear to leave her for the night. He sent for Tom and Peter, his youthful footmen, to set up camp downstairs, but he would have felt better—in a number of ways—if he shared her bed.

Together they planned a discreet departure from London. Cain's personal traveling carriage, he assured Juliana without cracking a smile, was a very ordinary-looking equipage, a chaise painted a sober black. With the use of hired horses and postilions from the very beginning of the journey, no one would penetrate his disguise. Lord Chase would disappear to make way for Mr. John Johnson, a merchant of awful propriety and a most suitable second husband for a widowed bookseller.

The next morning found him waiting at Charing Cross. Following the principle of hiding in plain sight, he'd agreed to meet Juliana at one of London's busiest corners. The furtive nature of their departure for Salisbury was as much to protect Cain's reputation as Juliana's. Now was not the time for him to be jaunting around the countryside in company with a female. None of the citizens going about their affairs paid the least attention to him, clad as he was like a man of little consequence.

She was late. Mel was supposed to have arrived at St. Martin's Lane with the carriage an hour ago. Cain pulled his topcoat closer and huddled his shoulders against a stiff breeze. He wouldn't have expected the efficient Juliana to keep him waiting, but Mel, once she got started, could talk the hind legs off a donkey. He occupied the time imagining the discourse between that unlikely pair. And fighting the urge to run the few hundred yards to the bookshop to fight off murderous book collectors armed with . . . whatever murderous book collectors wielded.

Frederick Fitterbourne might be the obvious candidate for their villain but he was in Wiltshire. Whoever broke into the shop and hid the book was in London.

At last he recognized his traveling carriage passing the King's Mews, making slow progress due to the frequent stops of other vehicles in the busy commercial thoroughfare. Tired of delay, he crossed the street and met it as it reached the corner of the Strand.

"You're late," he said, slamming the door.

He settled into the front-facing seat, next to Juliana, and felt his chest expand with relief and anticipation.

It felt good to get out of London. Esther was safe at their aunt's, and the law proceeded at its customary treacle pace. So he'd exhumed the garments he'd worn before he inherited his fortune, told his aunt and household he had business at one of his estates, and disappeared.

His spirits soared at the adventure ahead of him. And his company on the quest.

"I had to show Mrs. Duchamp everything," Juliana explained. "And change my clothes."

"Are you warm enough? Why don't you take off your pelisse? I'd like to see the gown."

He'd sent Mel around to the ever-obliging Mrs. Timms for garments suited to a widowed tradeswoman traveling to visit relations, accompanied by her affianced husband. He'd absolutely insisted that his "betrothed" not be dressed in black.

"I like the color," he said, with a slight frown. "And the cut too. It suits you, but it's still too sober." The revealed traveling dress in blue wool was distressingly decent. "I wonder if Mrs. Timms is changing her clientele."

Juliana liked her new dress and loved the compliment. Her blush was caused by the knowledge that it fastened behind, as did her new stays. She wasn't sure she could manage them alone.

She'd worry about that later.

Meanwhile, she decided, she'd have her adventure.

Though she didn't share Cain's optimism about the outcome, she could at least enjoy the opportunity to travel out of London for the first time in four years. And in such comfort.

"By the way, Cain."

"Yes?"

"You told me your carriage was quite undistinguished."

"It's black, plain and unmarked."

"And quite roomy."

"I had it specially made." His lips widened the merest twitch and his eyes began to twinkle. "According to a Russian design. I've never seen why one should travel in discomfort."

"The upholstery is velvet again."

"What other kind is there?"

"I've never seen red velvet seats."

"I like all my carriages to match my book bindings." He reached forward and tugged on a handle under the seat in front of them. A panel opened up to reveal a hidden compartment. "May I offer you a bite to eat? Or a glass of brandy, if it isn't too early."

By the time they reached Andover the evening was well advanced. They might have spent the night at Basingstoke, where they'd stopped to dine, but Cain appeared as eager as she to press on. They'd spent hours of the journey discussing recent events and the light Frederick Fitterbourne might be able to cast on them. Between the two of them there were plenty of theories, but their speculations only left them in desperate need of more information. The sooner they reached Salisbury the better.

Juliana had barely considered that she was about to spend the night with Cain in an obscure inn, chosen because it didn't cater to the gentry.

"A room for myself and my wife. The name is John Johnson."

Unable to disagree with the statement without causing a scandal, Juliana simmered her way upstairs in the landlord's wake.

When planning the journey they'd agreed to present Cain to Frederick Fitterbourne as her betrothed, though not under his true name. It was far more likely that Frederick would agree to reveal the truth to her future husband than to Juliana herself. Cain hadn't broken the news of their changed marital status on the road.

Once alone with him in a small but clean room, Juliana folded her arms and glared. "Why didn't you tell me you were going to tell the landlord we're married?"

"I thought you'd object."

"Wrong question," she said through gritted teeth. "*Why* did you say we're married?"

"You need help with your buttons. Probably your stays too." Trust him to have noticed that.

"I can call for a chambermaid," she said frostily.

Yet a nagging voice in her mind asked what she was making such a fuss about. It wasn't as though she hadn't already shared a bed with Cain, and enjoyed it.

The slightly shabby coat and breeches he wore detracted not one whit from his appeal. He looked just as good as he did in fashionable pantaloons and figure-fitting tailoring. He still held himself like a great, sleek cat: slender, strong, and flexible as a whip. She knew with what pleasure that body could affect her own.

She'd thought him in one of his teasing moods, the blue eyes dancing with laughter. Then his gaze darkened. It wasn't the color that altered, but the mood.

"We may have been followed," he said. "I thought you were safe out of London but I'm not taking any chances. You can argue all you like but you are not staying alone in this room."

She began to speak.

"I'll sleep on the floor," he interrupted, "and that's my best offer."

She'd been about to give in, to agree to sleep with him. But that was not, apparently, what he wanted. He hadn't even asked. She felt a little foolish. She'd believed he'd come up with an elaborate excuse to get her back into bed, but apparently he was only concerned for her safety.

Which was gratifying.

Highly gratifying.

Of course, being a man he'd probably lie with her if she offered. But regardless of what had happened, no matter that she was hugely grateful for his assistance, all the arguments that made her refuse to be his mistress still applied. As for his continuing whim about marrying her? The notion wasn't worth serious consideration.

It was a very good thing he wasn't really interested.

* * *

What a fool he was! He could have had her.

He could now be drifting into sleep, pleasurably tired. Juliana could be curled up in his arms, her sighs of satisfaction fading to the deeper breath of slumber.

She was enjoying slumber all right. And he was miserable, his body wound up after a day in the carriage, longing for movement and exercise.

He didn't understand his restraint where Juliana was concerned. Why the hell didn't he just seduce her, as he had countless women? He knew he could and he knew she'd enjoy it. She already had. Even now he could slide into bed beside her, caress her to wakefulness, and arouse her to passion.

He cursed his own scruples and tried to find a soft spot on the rough wooden floor. A pillow, a single blanket, his topcoat, and Juliana's cloak were not enough to make an acceptable bed. The room wasn't warm either. Damn it, unselfishness went only so far. If he had to control himself, let him at least do it in comfort.

She murmured but didn't awaken when he joined her in the bed and pulled the covers up to his chin. He lay on his back for a while, staring at nothing in the dark room, Juliana's warmth and light violet scent tickling his senses.

A rustle of bedclothes, movement, then the warmth

was no longer two feet away but tucked against his body. It was just as well he was clothed. He turned onto his side and gathered the sleeping woman close, nestling her head under his chin.

Cain smiled to himself ruefully. One of London's most noted libertines in bed with a beautiful woman, and letting her sleep. He hugged her a little tighter.

Strangely enough, he felt quite content.

Chapter 17

The following afternoon Cain visited the village of Fernley. Since Juliana would be recognized by the local people, Cain went alone to discover what he could about Frederick Fitterbourne's current circumstances before they called on him.

It didn't take many minutes in the public house to learn that George Fitterbourne hadn't been highly regarded among his neighbors and tenants. The application of Cain's purse to the beer supply turned polite but reserved conversation into freely expressed opinion.

The landlord and a couple of elderly rustics, who formed the afternoon population of the taproom, regarded the late Mr. Fitterbourne as at best quite mad, at worst criminal.

"Spent everything on books, he did," said one old fellow, whose perfectly bald pate contrasted comically with a bushy white beard.

All three of them shook their heads in disbelief.

"Not a penny piece went to the land or the cottages," said the other customer, mumbling through the one remaining tooth that could be seen in the front of his mouth. "Those were bad times in Fernley."

"What of his family? His wife?" Cain asked. "Did he not have a daughter?"

"His lady died when the girl was but a child," said the landlord. "Miss Cassandra, a pretty young lady. She died too, must be she was twenty-two, twenty-three years old."

"Did she marry?"

The landlord avoided meeting Cain's eye. "No," he said without elaboration.

"So Mr. Fitterbourne lost his family. That's hard on a man."

Cain's companions were unimpressed. "Made no difference, far as I could see," said One Tooth. "He were no better before."

"There was the girl," contributed the bearded bald one.

The other two looked embarrassed. "We don't talk about that," the landlord said. But White Beard merely drained his tankard and gave Cain an expectant look. Cain nodded, and not a man refused his refill.

"The girl?" he asked.

"Aye. Came to live at the Court." A significant pause.

"Who was she?"

"That's what we don't rightly know." The man winked, waggling an eyebrow as bushy as his beard. "Came just after *Miss Cassandra* died. Only a babe she were. Never saw her much save on Sundays at St. Peter's."

"Kept her out of sight of decent people," the landlord said, "except in church. Don't know why the vicar allowed it."

Cain swore there and then he would apologize to Juliana for ever doubting her. There was no question the local people of Fernley had the same interpretation of her parentage as she. He also felt like hitting the publican. He'd better move on to the real reason for his inquiries, before he lost his temper at the cruelty of men who would despise a helpless child for the accident of her birth.

"What of the new Mr. Fitterbourne? What manner of man is he?"

His informant snorted, sending flecks of beer into his beard. "Turned the little bastard out of the house right away. Powerful proper gentleman, he be."

Cain gritted his teeth and kept his hands at his side. "Is he a good landlord?"

The three of them, after some discussion, allowed that Mr. Frederick Fitterbourne was an improvement on his predecessor. After three years the Fernley estate showed signs of renewed prosperity.

"A close man with a shilling, but fair." The publican's final comment expressed the unanimous opinion.

He was also, Cain established, now in residence, along with his wife and family of five promising children.

It was odd to be in Salisbury again, a scant five miles from where she'd passed most of her life. Not that Juliana knew the city well. It hadn't been her own choice, but she'd grown up as much of a recluse as her grandfather.

Yet there was something in the air of the cathedral town that was familiar and homelike. And her husband had lived here for several years before they married and moved to London. Joseph's family came from the North of England, otherwise he wouldn't have been staying in an inn when he made that last visit.

She and Cain occupied a comfortable suite of rooms at the White Hart, close to the cathedral. Cain had left her behind under strict orders to stay in the room and lock the door.

He was slightly irrational on the subject. If someone wanted to cause her physical harm there had been numerous opportunities, even since she acquired the dubious protection of the bulldog Quarto. Hiding the stolen book in her shop, then spreading a rumor to send eager book collectors to find it, was the work of a subtle schemer, not the kind of man to attack her in the street. Besides, all that had happened in London and she was in Salisbury.

So she decided to go out.

The soaring spire was a constant presence even before she reached the close and was treated to the full effect of the great cathedral. She'd been confirmed there; even Mr. Fitterbourne's eccentricity didn't extend to ignoring the forms of religious observance.

Passing through the medieval High Street Gate, she spared a glance at Mr. Birch's bookshop. Her old friend was dead and his sister's son now ran the business. Joseph had had ambitions to take over when his em-ployer retired, but the nephew wanted it. That's why Joseph had married her and her thousand pounds.

The High Street was lined with shops, including a drapery she remembered as a treasure trove of wonders. She'd had a governess for a few years. As she approached womanhood Miss Beeston attempted to teach her some of the more conventional skills of young ladies, such as how to dress attractively. The bolts of silk and muslin, spools of ribbon in every conceivable color, marvelous buttons in silver, ivory, and pearl, fascinated the fourteen-year-old Juliana and, for a time, replaced her passion for printed pages. For a very short time.

When Mr. Fitterbourne discovered how much these fripperies cost he'd remonstrated with her. Surely, he demanded, she'd rather have a first edition of Locke than a new gown? Meekly she agreed and won back her guardian's approval. Miss Beeston departed, and that was the end of Juliana's formal education and her brief flirtation with vanity.

The trouble was, it occurred to her now, she never got the first edition of Locke. Like every book on which her grandfather had lavished his fortune, it was sold to Tarleton.

The medieval Poultry Cross lay ahead of her. Beyond it stood a largish building, its half timbers and irregular construction proclaiming its vintage. The Haunch of Venison was Salisbury's most venerable hostelry, perhaps as old as the cathedral itself. Without consciously knowing it, Juliana had decided to visit the spot where her husband met his demise, exactly one year ago from tomorrow.

The landlord, Mr. Phillips, greeted her with deference, sympathy, and a touch of defensiveness. She supposed he'd sooner forget the anniversary of an ugly crime on his premises. Since it was currently unoccupied, he agreed to show her the room.

The narrow stairs and corridors of the ancient building wound up to the third floor. Mr. Phillips used a key and opened a door to reveal an attic room with a narrow dormer window overlooking the market square. Not much of a place to end your time on earth, but Joseph had always been frugal and would have taken one of the cheapest rooms available.

"It must have been hard carrying all those books upstairs," she mused.

"Didn't have to," Phillips replied. "Miss Combe's servant carried them in for him. I remember because she died the same day. Or maybe the next. I don't rightly recall. She was an old lady, and ailing."

So the old woman hadn't even lived to enjoy the proceeds of selling her wretched books.

Juliana tried to imagine her husband's last hours. She didn't know when he'd been killed, only that it was nighttime and he'd been found in the morning.

"Was it market day?" she asked.

"Aye."

"It would have been noisy."

"That it was," agreed the landlord. "We're always busy on market days."

"Did my husband dine in the tavern that evening? But perhaps you don't remember."

"Well, normally I wouldn't, but I had to answer a whole lot of questions the next day. So I can tell you we served a nice steak and kidney pudding, and Mr. Merton enjoyed a good meal."

"I'm glad. That was his favorite dinner." Joseph wasn't particularly interested in food but sometimes, to celebrate a particularly profitable sale, they dined at a chophouse in Leicester Square. That was the dish he always ordered.

"Did he linger in the taproom after dinner?" She asked.

"Not late. He told me he wanted to catch the early mail coach to London, asked me how early he could break his fast. That's how I came to find him. I went to his room the next morning. Reckoned he'd slept longer than he meant and I'd better give him a call."

"That was good of you."

"Well," said the landlord gruffly, "we take care of our customers." He seemed to be struggling with a long-held resentment. "The magistrate, he wanted to know how I'd let a villain in to do murder. How am I supposed to know every soul that comes in with the inn full to bursting? Not to mention them that come in just to wet their whistles. Twenty-five years I've run this inn, and my father before me just as long. And we've never had such a thing happen. A bit of a brawl or fisticuffs in the taproom, that's one thing. But murder and robbery? Never! There was blood all over the room."

Juliana felt sick. Her own feelings threatened to overset her composure. Extracting herself from the landlord's indignation at the insult to his house, she fled back onto the street.

She'd never properly mourned Joseph. Shock at his death had been rapidly superseded by the necessity of working for her own survival. And when she'd discovered how hard it was to make a living on her own, her resentment toward the world had extended to her late husband. She'd always felt he hadn't appreciated her own knowledge and talent but married her for her money. Finding that most of the book world she wished to inhabit regarded her as of little account without him only increased her anger.

Anger. Yes, she realized, as she strode along at the fastest pace her annoyingly short legs would carry her. She'd been angry with Joseph.

Yet their two years of marriage hadn't been all bad. They'd endlessly talked about books, their mutual passion. They'd shared triumphs and failures. They'd lived together. They'd shared a bed.

He hadn't loved her and she hadn't loved him, but Joseph Merton and she had been partners and friends. Like any human being he deserved to have his passing mourned.

So Juliana walked through the streets of Salisbury with her eyes blinded by tears. She wept for Joseph's short life, for the waste of his youth and knowledge and ambition, for his sordid, painful death in a cheap, noisy room.

She cried until there were no more tears to fall, and it seemed entirely fitting that, as she approached the White Hart Inn, the heavens themselves opened. She stopped and loosened her bonnet strings, pushing the headgear back and ignoring those who looked at her askance as they rushed to reach shelter. She raised her face to the sky and let the cool rain rinse away her grief.

Cain was still angry when he returned to Salisbury and the rooms at the White Hart taken by "Mr. and Mrs. Johnson." Little wonder that Juliana could be a little prickly at times. Beyond taking care not to add to their number, Cain had never given a great deal of thought to the lives of those born out of wedlock. The scorn shown by a trio of rustics toward a young child, just because her parents hadn't been married, shocked him. Living as he had among the demimonde and those sunk even lower, he thought he'd seen meaningless hardship and brutality. But the cruelties of life in London's rougher areas had, at least, the excuse of poverty and desperation.

Juliana had grown up the ward and unacknowledged granddaughter of a man of property. Cain had failed to appreciate just how much her shadowy birth placed her outside of the range of society's tolerance.

She'd understood of course. She'd lived with it. And seen at once why she couldn't marry him.

Cain should know better than anyone that noble birth and great wealth didn't guarantee happiness. His own family history was stark proof of that. He had, he supposed, thought it peculiar, imagined that every other prosperous, wellborn family was a happy one. But when it came down to it, his own grievances were nothing compared to Juliana's, for he had the hope and possibility of redress. Nothing could correct the stigma of illegitimacy. Except proving her birth otherwise.

Cain swore there and then he'd leave no stone unturned, no parish register unscrutinized. If Cassandra Fitterbourne had married her beloved Julian, Cain would find the proof.

And he'd take personal pleasure in forcing it down the throat of every inhabitant of the village of Fernley in Wiltshire, starting with Mr. Frederick Fitterbourne.

The sitting room of their suite of rooms was empty. Juliana must be taking a nap. He knocked softly on the door of the bedchamber.

No answer.

He knocked louder.

She couldn't be sleeping that deeply at four in the afternoon. He banged on the door.

My God, he thought. Her husband had been murdered in the room of an inn in Salisbury. Not the same inn, but still. He should never have left her alone.

Abandoning niceties, he wrenched open the door. Their portmanteaux stood undisturbed on the floor. Of Juliana herself there was no sign. Gripped by panic, Cain rushed into the dressing room, empty save for a washstand and a small bed.

Why had she gone out? He should never have left her alone when some murderous villain, perhaps the same one who'd killed Joseph Merton, was at large. He was trying to think calmly about where to begin a search, when he heard someone enter the bedchamber.

Her pelisse exuded the scent of damp wool. She'd removed her bonnet, which she now dropped onto the floor, and her tawny golden hair hung in damp hanks about her shoulders. Her face shone with water.

She looked better than a five-course meal to a starving man.

"Where have you been?" he shouted, grabbing her shoulders and shaking her.

"I went for a walk."

"Are you mad? When there may be an assassin out there waiting to attack you?"

"Nothing happened." Her voice was quite without expression. She sounded almost dazed.

"For God's sake, let's get you out of that coat before you take a chill and die."

She said nothing, merely staring at him with a look of wonder in her face, as though she'd never truly seen him before.

His fingers trembled as he worked the buttons of the pelisse and ended up ripping one clean out of the fabric before he was able to throw the garment to the floor.

"Your shoes and stockings are soaked," he scolded. "Off with them." Down on one knee he unbuttoned her half boots, tugged them off, and threw them over his shoulder. Her hosiery suffered the same fate. He didn't ask himself why her exposure to a simple rain shower urged him to such frenzied action. As a lifelong resident of England she'd survived many such wettings. Instead he snatched a towel from the washstand in the corner and used it to give her head a vigorous rub. And all the time she merely stood, acquiescent, watching him, not uttering a single word.

Then, easing off his attention to her wet hair, he stared back into her face and noticed something for the first time.

"You've been crying." The hitch in his voice matched a jog in his heartbeat. He examined her face intently, running his thumbs gently over the soft, slightly swollen skin beneath her eyes. "Did someone frighten you?"

She parted her lips, and his gaze was captivated by the perfectly formed raspberry pink bow. Instead of answering him with words the mouth parted further. Her eyes changed from cool green moss to smoldering golden embers. She reached up, grasped his head between small, capable hands, and pulled it down to kiss.

All thoughts of murder, injustice, or the dangers posed by a head cold fled his mind.

He tasted cool rain and warm honey on lips that clung to his with a force echoing the strength of his own desire.

At last. He'd been waiting for this forever.

Mouths and tongues clashed in voracious kisses. His arms enclosed her slight body; hands clasped her behind through her skirts and tugged her against him. The evidence of his desire had reached rigidity with a speed that recalled, but didn't surpass, his most desperate adolescent fantasies.

Only a few feet behind them was a bed, a large, tall, and comfortable bed. To Cain's great joy he had no need to push Juliana in that direction. He was pulled. Her hands dropped to his shoulders and, without releasing him from their kiss, she stepped backward, taking him with her, until she hit the mattress.

Acting by instinct he grasped her hips and lifted her to sit on the edge. Cain was sure he'd never needed anyone or anything as much as he needed Juliana at this moment. Miraculously her fervor seemed to match his own. Even as her mouth and tongue clashed and melded with his, her hands shoved at his coat, fruitlessly since his arms were firmly around her, his expert fingers unhooking the back of her gown. She gave up and clasped his head instead as though she'd never let him go, never stop kissing him.

Her legs parted and, as much as was possible when covered with slightly damp skirts and petticoats, wrapped themselves around his hips. She rubbed herself against him in a frenzy of desire he was only too eager to satisfy.

"To hell with it," he growled, abandoning his bedroom manners and forgetting all about undressing or foreplay. Instead he wrenched at her skirts in a manner that made up in force what it lacked in finesse.

She encouraged him with noises from the back of her throat, perhaps some coherent words that he was too excited to make out, and by shifting her weight to assist him in lifting her gown and pulling off her drawers. And as she perched on the edge of the mattress, her sex in its nest of golden curls sweetly exposed to him, her fingers plucked at the buttons of his breeches.

"Hey," he managed to say, half desperate with lust, half laughing at her impatience. "Are you sure you don't want to take just a little time about this?"

"No," she said, and undid the last button. His breeches fell and she reached for his cock.

Grasping her firmly by the bottom, he entered her in one smooth thrust.

With the force of their union, they fell backward onto the bed, and the soft feather tick fluffed up on either side of them. Their legs still hung over the side. To prevent their sliding off he grabbed hold of her hands and stretched them up over her head, then seized her lips in a fervent kiss, thrusting tongue echoing the movement of his loins. She groaned her pleasure, sucking on his tongue and folding her legs about him so he felt the cool skin of her calves against his buttocks, even through the fine linen of his drawers.

They were both almost fully dressed. Aside from their hands and mouths, only their groins actually touched flesh to flesh. The muting of every other point of contact by the presence of garments enhanced the sensations where they joined.

She felt so good, so hot and tight. It had been far too long since their night together in St. Martin's Lane.

But he knew it wasn't just a couple of weeks' celibacy that made this joining especially good. It was Juliana herself. Through the blissful slaking of his body's urges and the familiar crescendo of pleasure in the act of sex, he recognized something important. This wasn't just any woman to share his pleasure, and God knew there had been enough of them in eight years.

This was *the* woman.

As he pumped into her, relishing the clasp of her tender passage about his cock, he had a strange feeling that he was home at last and there wouldn't ever be another.

Surely nothing could be better than Juliana's gasps of pleasure, the way she gloved him in wet heat with increased force as his pace quickened. He sensed his bollocks ache and his own imminent explosion. Never, since he'd learned to become a lover who always pleased his bedmate, had he experienced such difficulty holding off the end. Yet in this, the most important coupling of his life, his easy confidence vanished. He feared the ultimate humiliation of leaving his lover unsatisfied.

With a supreme effort he adjusted the angle of his thrusts to increase the rhythm and pressure against the places that would give her the greatest pleasure. Her accelerating breath was music of the heavens to his ears, matching the thud of his own heart.

"Come, come with me," he rasped against her lips, with no idea whether he'd actually managed to articulate the words.

Hear them or not, she appeared to respond. Suddenly her entire body became rigid. Her head tilted back into the mattress and her mouth opened to emit a strangled scream. Her inner muscles clamped around his shaft with a power that shattered his control. With a few last thrusts he joined her climax and emptied himself into her quivering womb. The joy of release seared every nerve and he felt his senses scatter to the four winds as he collapsed on top of her.

So he lay, mindless, for some time, he had no idea how long, his head resting on her chest. They were still joined.

It was her heartbeat he noticed first, slowing to a steady pace beneath the wool cloth of her gown. Gradually Cain regained a sense of time and place. He raised his head from her bosom and met Juliana's eyes just inches from his own. Their expression was wary, guarded. He might have experienced an epiphany in their lovemaking, but he had no idea what was in Juliana's head. She had initiated the encounter but he didn't know why.

Did he dare ask or should he accept the gift without question?

Chapter 18

❧〜∞〜❧

Cain's head rested on her bosom when Juliana returned to her senses.

Well, almost to her senses. Every limb still buzzed with a vigor that made her feel more alive than ever before. At the same time, by some odd contradiction, she was certain she would never move again. These remarkable sensations emanated from her private parts, which seemed to be literally humming with subdued bliss. And which were, good Lord, still occupied by Cain's.

She found herself torn between conflicting urges: ask him to do it again, or disengage herself and hide in the nearest closet. The latter plan seemed like a good one when she recalled that she'd virtually forced him to make love to her.

It wasn't as though he'd shown any eagerness the previous night. When she awoke and found herself curled up next to his warm, hard, sleeping body, she'd felt humiliated. He'd been interested only in a comfortable berth and not in the least overcome by her charms. Clearly he hadn't wanted to make love to her or he would have done something about it.

And now she'd thrown herself at him and given him precious little choice.

He stirred and raised his head from her breast. She looked at him warily and he stared back, his blue eyes steady and without a hint of laughter or mockery.

"Juliana," he began. The rumble of his voice, so close to her breasts, sent shivers through them and she felt them tighten. "Perhaps I shouldn't ask. That was, after all, one of the more delicious . . . periods of time . . . I've ever spent. But why?"

Cain was a kind man with much better manners than he'd ever own up to. But surely he wouldn't have used the word *delicious* if he didn't mean it at least a little bit. She decided to trust him with the truth, or attempt it.

"You see," she said, "I went to the Haunch of Venison, the inn where Joseph was killed."

Instantly she felt a chill as the lovely warm blanket of Cain's body was removed, leaving her covered by a slightly damp gown above the waist and nothing at all below.

"What?" he shouted. He was on his feet, looking most unfairly elegant, considering his coat and neck cloth were rumpled and his breeches halfway to his knees. "What the hell were you thinking?"

"I wanted to see where he died."

She felt slightly resentful. How did he manage to rebutton his breeches gracefully? Give him a minute or two and he'd be neat as a pin. She struggled to sit upright, no easy matter when flat on her back on a soft bed, her legs dangling helplessly over the edge. She tugged at her gown, much of which had bunched up under her. When her private parts, at least, were covered, she held out a hand.

"Will you help me up, please."

Once she was on her feet Cain completely disarmed her by taking her into his arms, laying her head against his chest, and stroking her hair.

"Don't do that again," he said hoarsely. She heard the steady thump of his heart. "Don't go out alone. You might have been killed."

She gave a little humorless laugh. "Not likely. The Haunch is a reputable hostelry. The landlord was most apologetic, and indignant. He insists nothing like Joseph's murder has happened there in the last fifty years."

"You were crying. I thought someone had scared you, perhaps attacked you."

"Nothing like that."

He was silent for a moment. She sensed a stiffening in his stance. "Of course," he said. "You went to see where your husband died. You were weeping for him."

"Yes."

"Very understandable." He took her chin in one hand and raised her head so he could study her face. "Why then? Why this afternoon?" He jerked his own head toward the bed.

How could she explain why mourning her late husband should entail making passionate love to another man? She wasn't sure she understood it herself. She'd walked into the bedroom, seen Cain standing there looking alive and strong and more gorgeous than anything she'd seen in her life, and she'd had to have him. Immediately.

"When Joseph died," she began tentatively. "When Joseph died I was . . . shocked."

"I imagine you might have been," he said dryly. She winced at the sarcasm in his tone, drawing a murmured apology and a kiss on her brow. "Go on," he said gently, and rested her head back against his chest.

She played with a button on his waistcoat, twisting the brass circle this way and that. She found it easier to continue her story without looking at him. "I was shocked and then life became . . . difficult." She sighed. "We were supposed to be partners but he was sometimes secretive about things. I found the business in worse case than I'd expected. He left debts that had to be met."

"That must have been distressing."

"As I've told you before, things got worse because so many of our customers didn't care to do business with a woman alone."

"You were angry," he said.

"Yes. Angry at them, and very angry at Joseph. I blamed him. Both for dying and for leaving me in such straits."

"And now I suppose you feel remorse for blaming him?"

Cain understood, she realized. She'd never met another soul so adept at comprehending her feelings.

"Exactly," she said. "I did. Terrible remorse."

"Did?"

"Did," she agreed. "No longer. Today I saw the

shabby little room where he died and I wept for him. I realized I had never truly done so before. And now I've cried for him, given him the mourning he deserved, I no longer feel ashamed."

She stopped fiddling with the button and gave the waistcoat an absentminded pat.

"And then I came back here." She stopped. She simply didn't know how to account for irrepressible lust. And certainly not how to explain it in words, out loud, to the object of that lust.

And then he said it for her. "You felt you had to thrust aside death by celebrating life. And what better celebration of life is there than lovemaking?"

"That's right!" she said. "How did you know?"

"I've heard of such response to death before." He turned her to face him and cupped her face in both his hands. "May I say that I am honored to have been your chosen partner in the festivity?" He gave her closed lips a light but lingering kiss. "Of course, I did happen to be the only candidate at hand. Unless you asked the hall porter and he turned you down."

She gasped when she realized he was jesting. And saw that this was a splendid moment for a joke. A laugh emerged from her lower vocal register, full-bodied and in its way as satisfying as her earlier tears. Cain joined her and for several minutes they clung together, shaking with mirth.

"What now?" she asked after a while.

"Well, Mrs. Johnson. I think we should investigate the dining room and cellar of this excellent inn."

Suddenly ravenously hungry, Juliana could find no fault with this plan.

"I shall acquaint you with the particulars of what I learned this afternoon."

"At Fernley!" she cried. His visit to her childhood home had completely slipped her mind.

"And after dinner, Mrs. Johnson—"

Somehow Juliana suspected it was no accident that Cain kept addressing her by the name he'd bestowed upon her as his supposed wife. She turned out to be correct.

"And then, Mrs. Johnson, I propose we continue our celebration of life."

If she had any sense she'd object. It meant she was truly becoming the Marquis of Chase's mistress and likely opening herself up to a wealth of future grief. But somehow she could no longer summon the strength to resist him.

The first thing Juliana noticed on entering the book room of Fernley Court was the Persian carpet near the hearth. How many hours she'd spent sitting on that rug, reading, collating a volume, or merely listening to her guardian talk.

Only when she took in the rest of the room as it was now, under the occupation of Mr. Frederick Fitterbourne, did it strike Juliana how much her own living quarters, on a much smaller scale, resembled the big room in her grandfather's day: books everywhere and a lack of concern for the presence of dust. Nowadays the place was spotlessly clean, every surface sporting a beeswax shine. The smell of furniture polish had driven out the odor of old leather and book dust. There were still books, several neat shelves of volumes, arranged according to size and binding as though they were decorative objects. But some shelves actually displayed ornaments: vases, Dresden shepherdesses, a few china animals, and a handsome clock.

Along one whole wall a pair of giant breakfront bookcases with gilt trellis doors had disappeared. She wondered if Tarleton had bought them, along with the books they'd housed. She couldn't count the times she'd heard collectors remark that it was so much easier to acquire books than bookshelves, a complaint that passed as grand wit in bookish circles.

She wished she could share the thought with Cain, who would appreciate just how odd bookmen were to find this feeble jest so intensely humorous. She realized with some surprise that in her head she aligned herself with Cain in mild derision against the biblio-philes, her own people.

Not so odd perhaps, given how much she'd enjoyed the previous night: a superior dinner followed by two more bouts of excellent lovemaking and a good night's sleep. She could grow to adore the White Hart Inn's feather bed.

The butler announced them to Frederick, who rose from a familiar wing chair beside the fire. The worn brown leather had been replaced with upholstery in a tasteful maroon, just as Frederick had replaced her grandfather.

"Mrs. Merton." He bowed stiffly. "I understand this gentleman is to be your next husband."

"John Johnson at your service, sir," Cain said, re-turning Fitterbourne's courtesy. "I do indeed have that ineffable joy." Juliana could tell by the gleam in his eye and a slightly curling lip that Cain was enjoying himself.

She hoped he could maintain the guise of a highly reputable and slightly dull gentleman, the kind of man Frederick would feel able to confide in without concern.

"It is good of you to receive us," Cain went on. "I have wanted to see the house where my dear Juliana grew up. She has spoken so much of her happy years at Fernley."

Frederick looked a trifle uncomfortable, as well he might since he'd ejected her from her childhood home.

"How few books there are now," she remarked. "One could scarcely call this a library anymore." Her sense of injury was rising to the surface.

Their host leveled a reproving look at her. "You know, Mrs. Merton, why my late uncle's collection had to be sold. There's no point revisiting ancient history."

"For goodness' sake, Frederick, stop calling me Mrs. Merton. We've known each other for twenty years." She pointed scornfully at the shelves of curios. "There's a china cat in the natural history section! Your uncle would turn over in his grave to see what his book room has been reduced to."

"Nothing to what his insane lust for books reduced his estate."

"But to sell them to Tarleton! His worst enemy."

"I did what was necessary. There can't have been a bookseller in England to whom he didn't owe money. There were legacies to the servants to pay. And let's not forget your thousand pounds, Juliana. I was happy to receive an offer to raise enough money, and quickly, to meet obligations and begin to put the estate back onto a profitable footing."

She felt a touch on her arm. "You must forgive Juliana, Mr. Fitterbourne," Cain said. "Returning to the scene of so many happy memories has quite overset her."

His condescending words were intended to lull Frederick into seeing Cain as a man of reason, in contrast to the foolish and sentimental female he called his betrothed. A squeeze of his hand reassured her it wasn't his own opinion.

Yet rationally she could see she *was* behaving like a foolish and sentimental woman. Somehow, since coming to Salisbury, her feelings had been spilling over, out of control.

Juliana tucked her emotions in her breast as she retrieved a handkerchief from her pocket. She dabbed at an illusory tear. It was time to return to the text of the play she and Cain had constructed.

"I'm sorry, Frederick," she said, leaning on Cain's arm as though overcome with sensibility. "It's just that I am so distressed about the *Romeo and Juliet* quarto."

She peered at him through her lashes but could see no reaction but bafflement. "The Shakespeare quarto that belonged to Cassandra," she prompted.

"I remember now. That was one of the books you wanted." Frederick paced back and forth a few steps. "Perhaps I should have let you have it," he said gruffly. "I had received an offer from Tarleton for the whole collection and I wasn't in a position to negotiate. But I daresay I could have excepted that one volume."

"It wouldn't matter," Cain interposed. "I'd buy it for Juliana as a wedding present."

"Well that's all right, then," Frederick said, brightening up.

"But it disappeared from Sotheby's auction rooms. It appears that someone has stolen it from the Tarleton collection."

Cain could read nothing but polite surprise in Fitterbourne's reaction. Either Frederick was an excellent actor, or he knew nothing about the adventures of *Romeo and Juliet*.

There hadn't been much hope in Cain's mind that he did. He already knew from his questions at the Pen and Pheasant that the master of Fernley hadn't left home in months. Of course he could have employed an agent. Cain wasn't yet prepared to absolve Frederick of all guilt. But he was prepared to keep his feelings to himself in the interests of acquiring information. Juliana, he thought fondly, was having a little difficulty in that direction. If he splashed her with water now she'd hiss steam.

"Might I ask the reason for your call?" Fitterbourne inquired.

"Mrs. Merton is anxious to discover all there is to know about her parentage. It seems to be no secret that Juliana's mother was Cassandra Fitterbourne."

Fitterbourne's lips narrowed in distaste. "Unfortunately our family disgrace was widely suspected, no matter how much we tried to keep it secret. My cousin bore a child out of wedlock."

"Do you know who the father was?" Cain could

feel the muscles of Juliana's arm tense. He placed her hand in the crook of his elbow and covered it with his own.

Fitterbourne shook his head. "I never knew the name of her seducer."

"Perhaps you could tell me the whole story, as you know it."

"I know only what my uncle revealed to me. It's quite simple really. Cassandra was enamored of an unsuitable man and her father forbade her to see him. I don't know precisely why, but I infer that he may have been of inferior birth, or perhaps married. She absconded with her lover, and that was the last her father heard of her for many months."

"When was this?" Juliana burst in.

Fitterbourne raised a hand for silence. "I was staying in the house at the time so I can attest to this. A communication came express from a clergyman near Bristol. Cassandra was in his care and gravely ill. My uncle left at once and found her dying, having given birth to a daughter."

"Me," Juliana said softly.

"It seems that Cassandra had been abandoned by her seducer and was traveling home to her father's house when she was brought to bed. The good vicar took her in and summoned her father. Alas, she died a few days after his arrival. The child"— he looked at Juliana for the first time since he began the tale— "you, Juliana, came home with him and he brought you up as his ward."

"Why did he never tell me I was his grandchild?"

Fitterbourne looked astonished at the question.

"Your very existence was a disgrace to the name of Fitterbourne. I strongly advised him to find a suitable family to care for Cassandra's child. But my uncle insisted on keeping you. At least he had the sense to give you a different name and put out the tale that you were the child of distant cousins."

"No one believed him," Juliana said bitterly.

"Of course not. But the forms were respected."

"Where was this place that Juliana was born and her mother died?" Cain looked down at her and gave her hand a comforting pat. "I fancy, my dear, that you would like to visit your mother's grave."

Juliana shook him off. "Why wouldn't you tell *me* all this when I asked, Frederick?"

"My uncle never thought it proper to acquaint you with the full story, and naturally I respected his example. But as your intended husband, it is of course Mr. Johnson's right to know the whole story."

Cain was prepared to prevent Juliana from leaping at Fitterbourne's throat, when her cousin's next words drew a gasp from her.

"I told Merton the whole story."

"Joseph knew? He never told me!"

"Of course he didn't tell you. He never went home again, poor fellow. In fact it was the very day of his unfortunate death that he came here asking for information."

"Joseph came here that day?" Juliana repeated.

"Yes, he had some odd notion that Cassandra had been married and you were of legitimate birth."

"Do you know why he thought such a thing?" Cain asked.

"He didn't explain."

"We have reason to believe he may have been right."

Fitterbourne frowned and shook his head. "Why would Cassandra have kept her marriage a secret? No, she must have been abandoned unwed."

"If her parents had been wed, would Juliana have inherited the estate?" Cain asked.

"No. The estate is entailed to the male line."

So much for that idea.

"But of course under that circumstance Juliana would have come into her mother's fortune."

"Cassandra had her own money?"

"Ten thousand pounds, from her mother. Settled on the children of the marriage. Since Cassandra died unmarried and intestate, her father inherited it."

"I thought," Cain said carefully, "that the late Mr. Fitterbourne died penniless, aside from his collection."

"He did. Didn't I already say he squandered everything on books?"

Someone, Cain thought, had a good motive to suppress the fact of Cassandra's marriage. Too bad that he was already dead.

And what exactly had Joseph Merton known, or suspected?

Someone very much alive had killed Merton. And Cain would wager the same person was responsible for Juliana's present troubles.

Chapter 19

"**I**f Cassandra was married, my grandfather didn't know it." Juliana had steadily, during two hours of travel, refused to even contemplate the possibility of such perfidy on the part of the late Mr. Fitterbourne. She was prepared to discuss theories about Joseph Merton's investigation into her parentage. But not a suspicion of her grandfather's motives would she entertain.

"He loved me," she insisted. "As far back as I remember, even as a tiny child, I came down to the library to visit him every day."

"Your later relationship has no bearing," Cain pointed out logically. "If he made the decision to suppress Cassandra's marriage, you would have been a newborn infant at the time."

"You heard what Frederick said. He insisted on keeping me instead of finding me a home elsewhere. And made up a name and a story so I wouldn't have to live with the stain of illegitimacy."

"I can't believe you are defending him now! From everything I've heard of the man, he was obsessed with books to the exclusion of all else. And your mother's ten thousand pounds must have bought him a lot of books."

"We bought them together," she insisted. "He taught me all he knew and we became companions and partners. When he received offers from booksellers I would read them aloud to him and give him my opinion. And I wrote all the letters back. I unpacked the books when they arrived by carrier and collated them to make sure they were complete. He couldn't have managed without me."

Cain barely restrained himself from saying it sounded more like slavery than partnership. Juliana couldn't see that the old man had been a selfish monster, not the loving grandfather of her memory. Even if Cassandra hadn't been married, Fitterbourne had still spent all his daughter's money and made almost no effort to ensure the future of his granddaughter.

"He was my grandfather and he loved me."

Juliana kept saying those words, like an anthem, as though repetition made them true. As though, poor deluded woman, the fact of kinship inevitably led to affection.

They sat side-by-side on the plush red seat, but as they argued during the journey from Salisbury she retreated from his proximity. He reached across that distance, only a couple of feet. Her hand felt cold in his, her delicate fingers cool, tense, and unresponsive to his grasp.

He murmured her name. She snatched away her hand.

"The ties of blood mean nothing, nothing at all," he said bitterly. "I haven't the least doubt my own father would have declared me a bastard had he the power. He would have loved to see his titles and estate pass to my cousin, a godly member of my wonderfully godly family."

She swung around and faced him, her face contorted with fury. "Your father rejected you because you were a dissolute rake and everything you've done since has proven him correct. You have no notion of the behavior of a gentleman. My grandfather was a gentleman and he would *never* have stolen from anyone."

Something shriveled inside Cain. He'd heard such charges from scores of others and tossed them off with a laugh. But, fool that he was, he'd believed Juliana saw him differently, that she'd looked behind the mask of defiance he'd presented to the world for eight years and seen the real man.

The previous night had been one of the sweetest he'd ever spent. He and Juliana had dined together, laughed together, made love and slept together. And though no words of any great gravity were spoken, he'd believed that he was more to her than he had been to scores of other women. More than merely an amusing companion, a satisfactory lover, and a deep pocket.

He was a fool. Because his own feelings were exceptional in all his experience, he'd made the mistake of thinking hers were too.

As they passed Bath, Cain stared out of the window at the mellow stones of the famous city. He barely registered the architectural beauties, any more than he could have described the glories of the Wiltshire

and Somerset countryside on this fine spring day. For
every second of an hour or more he was aware only
of Juliana, squashed into the opposite corner of the
carriage, as far from him as the confines of the vehicle
would allow. Each time he looked in her direction she
was gazing out of her own window. He wondered if
she saw as little as he did.

In all that time neither one of them uttered a single
word, until they entered the village of Greatfield, a
misnamed punctuation mark on the main road from
Bath to Bristol. According to Frederick Fitterbourne,
this scattering of houses surrounding a shabby public
house and a small undistinguished church had witnessed Juliana's entrance into the world, and Cassandra Fitterbourne's departure.

It was the first record in the parish register for the
year 1796. "Jany 5th. Cassandra Fitterbourne, of Fernley, Wilts. was buried."

The next line read, "Jany 5th. Juliana Cassandra,
born Jany 3rd, daughter of Cassandra Fitterbourne,
was baptized."

"It's not much, is it?" Cain said.

She gazed at the neatly written inscription, the final
confirmation that she was *filia nullius*, the daughter of
no one, in the eyes of the law. Her unmarried mother
didn't count as a person when it came to providing
a name and social position for her offspring. Juliana
hadn't expected, but she'd still hoped, quite desperately, to discover the identity of her father.

"I don't usually record the child's birth date," said
Mr. Howard, the clergyman who had led them to the

vestry of the church and found the volume containing the records of baptisms, marriages, and burials for the last decade of the last century. "But I remember the occasion. I pitied the child with her mother dead and no father. I thought if I didn't record her birthday perhaps she'd never know it. Especially since she was born in my house."

"I was?" Juliana asked, dragging her eyes away from the words that demolished her slender hope.

He peered at her curiously, his faded eyes compassionate and without judgment. "You were that infant?"

"Yes. I'd be very grateful, sir, if you could tell me how I came to be born here."

"Would you like to sit down?" He indicated a plain wooden bench.

Cain remained standing, sideways to them. He continued to stare at the parish register where it lay open on a table. Despite his sober dress, he was a vibrant presence in the small room with its whitewashed walls and arched stone windows. Juliana was intensely aware of the warmth and restless energy of his body, of the questing mind she'd learned was uncommonly incisive in its perceptions. At the same time she'd never felt more distant from him.

Waking this morning in his arms she'd felt a harmony of mind she'd never experienced with another soul. His support in getting her through the difficult interview with Frederick Fitterbourne had deepened the sense of intimacy and left her in danger of losing her heart.

Then he'd ruined it all with his cruel and unfounded

suspicions about the only person Juliana had ever loved. She glared at him from her seat next to the vicar. As though sensing her regard he looked up. For barely a second their glances held and the fathoms-deep blue of his gaze caused the familiar skip in her heartbeat. But she still burned with rage at the way Cain had accused her grandfather of betraying her. His eyes returned to the parish register as the parson spoke.

"The stage from Bristol drives straight through Greatfield, but that January day it stopped to let out a female passenger, a lady whose time had come. The Kings Arms is only a tavern, without an inn's accommodations, so the landlord summoned me and I took the lady to the parsonage and summoned the midwife. Poor soul, her labor was long and hard. But finally a daughter was born. The midwife said she was very weak and seemed distraught with grief."

Although she had a thousand questions, Juliana couldn't speak. Her heart ached at the tale and at the knowledge of what would come next. For though death in childbed was common, it dismayed her to hear in stark terms that her birth had killed her mother.

"The midwife said the lady lacked the will to live, and when the fever came upon her she had no strength to throw it off. I went to her bedside and tried to encourage her, but she was barely sensible. All she could do was cry out for 'Julian.'"

"My father," Juliana whispered.

"So I inferred. Once it became obvious she was dying I tried to prepare her for the end. The truth must have penetrated her tormented mind. She managed to let me know the name and direction of her father and begged me to summon him."

By this time Juliana was choked by tears. The kindly clergyman patted her hand.

"Mr. Fitterbourne came the next day. I believe the distance was not great. He arrived and sat at his daughter's bedside for the last hours of her life. When she passed away he arranged for her burial and for the baptism of the child. For your baptism, Mrs. Merton."

"Did he choose my name?" she managed to ask through her tears.

Mr. Howard frowned. "No. He wished to name you for your mother, but she had told me she wished to call you Juliana. Mr. Fitterbourne was unhappy about it, but he acceded to my suggestion that his daughter's last wish be respected. I particularly remember this because his next revelation was such a shock."

A pit opened up in Juliana's stomach.

"It came as a complete surprise to me when Mr. Fitterbourne informed me his daughter was unmarried, that the father of her child was an unscrupulous seducer. She wore a wedding ring and had given the midwife her name. We both had the impression she was a widow."

Juliana could scarcely breathe. "What name?"

Mr. Howard thought for several seconds, then shook his head. "I don't remember. It's been a long time, and once her father told me the sad truth the name no longer seemed important."

"Would the midwife remember?" Cain asked. "Can we question her?"

"Mrs. Smith died five years ago."

"What of your own household?"

"I am unmarried and keep few servants. Like Mrs. Smith, my housekeeper from those days is no longer with us."

Cain uttered a word under his breath that was probably unsuitable for their location and company. Whether Mr. Howard heard it or not, he must have caught their frustration.

"I am sorry, madam," he said. "I had no reason to disbelieve Mr. Fitterbourne, who appeared a proper gentleman. And why would he proclaim his own daughter unchaste if it were not true?"

Chapter 20

Juliana sat in the vestry awaiting Cain's return. Mr. Howard had been called away, but had invited her to remain there as long as she needed to recover after his tragic tale. Cain had walked to the tavern where the postilions were taking refreshment.

He'd said nothing of what they'd discovered. "If we leave now we can cover a good part of the distance back to London tonight," he said. "I'll return with the carriage."

One side of her shied from a continuation of their previous argument. Mr. Howard's narrative gave Cain ammunition in his fight to proclaim George Fitterbourne a villain. And much as she didn't wish to think ill of him, Juliana now had to accept that if she was, indeed, of legitimate birth, her revered grandfather had almost certainly lied about it. And robbed her of her rightful inheritance along with her name.

On the other hand, having been given an intimation that she might not be a nameless bastard, she found herself reluctant to relinquish that hope, however faint.

Her feelings about Cain were equally contradictory. If her legitimacy was proved, it would mean George Fitterbourne had treated her villainously and how could she bear it? How could she forgive Cain for being right?

She stood up and shook her head in irritation. Ever since the *Romeo and Juliet* had appeared in her shop and they had deciphered Cassandra's code, her emotions had been in turmoil. She hardly knew the tearful and irrational woman she seemed to have become. She needed to rediscover her grounding. Looking around the room she fastened on an object that had, unfailingly, provided the anchor in her life. A book.

It was a Bible, bound plainly in black morocco. A late seventeenth-century edition, she guessed as she opened it. Not a valuable edition but a clean, fresh copy of a nicely printed book with good wide margins. She turned a few pages, the sight of crisp black type on creamy paper exercising a calming effect. Then a word caught her eye. A name, Amnon.

Who was Amnon and why was the name familiar?

The evening Cain had brought her dinner came back to her, the first time they'd eaten together. She'd drunk too much and her memory of much of the conversation was fuzzy, but a fragment of speech floated through her mind.

My father called me Amnon.

It sounded like a biblical name, in keeping with the late marquis's well-known enthusiasm. Later she'd learned from Esther that Cain's Christian name was

John and she'd been surprised. Now she realized why. But who was Amnon?

She read the page of the Book of Samuel that had caught her eye. Amnon, a son of David, had fallen in love with Tamar, his own sister.

"Howbeit he would not hearken unto her voice: but, being stronger than she, forced her, and lay with her."

Amnon had raped Tamar. Cain's father called him Amnon.

She could hardly believe the words. Yet she'd always had the impression Cain hadn't told her the whole story of his family estrangement, that a deeper conflict with his father lay beyond vague charges of debauching maids. Esther had been eight years old when Cain had left. Her mind reeled with the horror of the accusation.

Not for a moment did Juliana credit him capable of such an outrage. She had no doubt that brother and sister were sincerely attached to each other, but definitely not in *that* way. During the time she had spent with Esther, the girl had expressed nothing but artless sisterly affection for her older brother. Her delight at their reunion was, Juliana would swear, uncomplicated by any shadow of evil.

True, Cain was no saint. But she had faith in his ultimate goodness. His nature was fundamentally kind. She'd always suspected much of his attitude was snapping his fingers at the world. Now she understood why. Her own anger at him dissolved in the face of indignation that his father had accused him so cruelly, and a profound sympathy for what he must have suffered.

She was ashamed of herself. Cain had problems and responsibilities of his own, yet he'd dropped everything to set off with her on this voyage to unearth her past. He'd been nothing but a rock of support every step of the way, and his care of her was wholly unselfish.

Now Juliana could only wonder why she had become so irate at his speculations about her grandfather. Speculations that were, she had to admit, reasonable. They might or might not be true, but either way Cain hardly deserved the level of wrath he'd invoked. And she'd said cruel things to him.

Your father rejected you because you were a dissolute rake and everything you've done since has proven him correct.

How those words must have hurt. She looked at the door and wished he'd return so she could apologize. She wanted to tell him she had been wrong, dreadfully wrong. That he was a wonderful man and worthy of her love.

She could no longer deny the truth. She did love Cain.

And, she thought sadly, she was, in more than one way, unworthy of his. Though he still claimed to wish to marry her it was becoming less and less likely that she would be proven of suitable birth for a match with a marquis. In fact it was absurd.

Cain needed a bride of impeccable standing to fight for Esther's guardianship. And he would have no difficulty finding one. Setting aside the obvious advantages of his fortune and position, no woman would be able to resist his looks; his charm; his intelligence, wit, and kindness; his beautiful blue eyes; his skill as a lover . . .

Then the door opened and Cain appeared. Juliana's heart leaped at the sight of him. He lacked his usual unperturbed grace. His stance was tense and his expression cautious, as though expecting a resumption of their quarrel.

She walked straight to him, reached up to place her arms around his neck, and rested her head on his chest, rubbing her cheek against the rough cloth of his greatcoat. She felt his arms surround her and heaved a sigh of content.

"I'm sorry about your mother, my dear," he said.

"I'm sorry I said such things to you," she murmured into his chest. "I didn't mean them."

"It's all right. You were upset."

"I was unfair to you. Whatever my mother, father, or grandfather did, it isn't your fault."

He maneuvered under the brim of her bonnet to kiss her forehead. "Don't give it another thought. Now we need to find out where your parents were married."

For a short time, perhaps just for an hour or two, she decided, she'd give in to the luxury of sharing his optimism and believing they might have a future together.

They'd passed back through Bath and almost reached Chippenham when it occurred to Cain that Juliana had scarcely uttered a word in over an hour.

He'd passed the time wondering how one went about searching for evidence of a wedding, knowing only the bride's name and a date when the ceremony might have occurred. Anywhere in England or Wales. Or Scotland, for God's sake. That's where most runaway marriages were performed, though Cassandra had been of age and not needed her father's consent. Still, it wouldn't do to overlook the obvious. Cain made a mental note to send someone to Gretna Green. And there was Ireland too.

On the outward journey from London Juliana had been full of theories about her parentage, eager and willing to discuss any possibility. Then her desire to defend her grandfather had entered the arena and she'd had plenty to say about that. He hesitated to raise the subject and spoil their rediscovered amity. If life was to offer only a short time more in Juliana's company, he didn't wish to waste it with a quarrel.

Yet her lack of response to his occasional uncontentious suggestions was unlike her. Juliana seemed distracted, as though thinking of something quite different.

Finally she cleared her throat, interrupting his mental instructions to Robinson about the marriage search.

She'd removed her bonnet, revealing her tawny gold hair in all its disheveled glory. Ecstatic as he was to see her discard those hideous caps, he could appreciate their practicality for a woman as incompetent at hairdressing as Juliana. The fact that her coiffure looked ready to descend with any sudden movement did nothing to detract from her beauty. Sitting across from him she was ravishing as a Titian goddess, though rather more clothed.

The dove gray of her traveling dress contrasted with the red seats. She'd look good in red.

After a few moments' hesitation she spoke. "While I was waiting for you, I looked at Mr. Howard's Bible."

"A very proper thing to do," he answered gravely. "Of course, you don't *read* books, do you. Was it a good edition?"

Normally this mild provocation would be enough to start her off on a lengthy discussion of the bibliographic history of the Authorized Version, until she realized she was being teased.

"As it happens I did read part of it," she said. "The Book of Samuel. About David's son Amnon."

He felt he'd been punched in the gut. "Now that story," he managed to answer, "is not, I believe, very proper. Not a suitable tale for a gently reared lady."

"No. I'd never read it before. But I'd heard the name. You told me your father called you Amnon."

"Was I drunk?" he asked with studied nonchalance.

"No, I was."

"Oh yes. I remember the occasion. Are you sure *you* do? Perhaps it never happened. You were somewhat the worse for wine."

His feeble attempt at deflection had no effect. "Cain, is that why you left home? Is that why you weren't made Esther's guardian once you came of age?"

He didn't want to answer the question. He'd never

minded owning up to any other sin. Indeed he positively reveled in his reputation. But the one charge he feared was the last one leveled by his father, the offense too terrible to name, or even contemplate. He'd lived much of his life in terror that someone knew of it. And now someone did. The person whose opinion meant the most to him had heard the worst.

"I didn't do it," he almost whispered. "I'd never hurt my sister."

Her eyes widened. "Of course not! It's utter nonsense. You would never, never do such a thing!"

Until the constriction in his throat loosened he hadn't known he could scarcely breathe. "You believe me? Just like that?

"Of course I do. I don't wish to pry, but would you like to tell me what happened?"

"Why not? No one has ever heard the whole story." He leaned back on the bench seat and folded his arms, staring at nothing.

"Looking back, I can see that the last year or two I spent at home my father was becoming less and less rational. By the end I think he was quite insane. He was obsessed with sin, specifically sins of the flesh. He decided I was guilty of them in every form. He even removed me from Eton, claiming I was learning debauchery from my fellow pupils. Such nonsense. Schoolboys talk about a lot more than they actually experience. I was an innocent then. I more than made up for it later. Became as wicked as he'd always said I was."

"Stop, Cain. You aren't wicked, but when you say things like that people believe you."

"I always thought I might as well have the pleasure of living up to my reputation."

"I have no doubt you've committed some deeds not strictly sanctioned by the church. But nothing like what your father accused you of."

"No, not that. That day I came in from riding. That was part of my regime; His Lordship had a notion that exercise calmed the demons of lust. I climbed the main staircase. Very impressive the main staircase at Markley Chase Abbey. You must see it one day."

He was procrastinating. He feared he was going to weep. He forced himself to continue.

"I made for the family wing. I had my own rooms there from the age of ten when I removed from the nursery. I entered the long passage and met Esther coming out from my mother's sitting room. She was only eight then, and the sweetest little thing. I didn't see her as often as I would like since she was still in the nursery and our lessons were completely separate. She was crying and she called my name. I crouched down and caught her in my arms, asked her what had upset her. She was sobbing so hard she couldn't speak but I could tell she was terrified."

Closing his eyes, Cain relived that moment for the thousandth time, trying to make sense of it. "Then I heard my father's voice, coming from my mother's rooms. 'Daughter,' he cried. His voice was angry. All I could think of was that I must hide Esther from him. I picked her up and ran to the end of the corridor into my room."

He breathed heavily, as though he'd been running,

but Cain found himself growing calmer as he neared the end of the story.

"My father must have heard the door slam. He followed us. Esther was still in my arms, clinging like a mad thing. He bellowed at me, like an incensed bull, grabbed me by the collar and pulled me away from her, dragged me downstairs to his study."

He relived the moment in his head, the certainty that his father's temper had slipped its moorings and that he was about to endure the worst beating of his life.

"I begged him to tell me what I'd done." The memory of his abject supplication left a bitter taste in his mouth even now. His father had been a large man with a strong right arm when wielding a cane or a switch, depending on the perceived severity of his son's offense. The sixteen-year-old Cain had been terrified. "He gave me no reason for his anger until he'd finished with the whip."

"He beat you?" Juliana asked, horror in her voice.

"He whipped me. Not for the first time. But it was the last, and the worst."

Even now he remembered how much the lashes on his back and rear had hurt. "In the end I tried to defy him. I told him, through my pathetic snivels, that he was a bully and a lunatic. A stupid thing to say to a large man with a whip. I was lucky he didn't start again. Perhaps his arm was tired. Instead he went to his desk, quite calmly, and opened a drawer. He walked over to me and threw a purse on the carpet. He didn't touch me again. Just ordered me to leave the house and never return."

"But what did he say?"

"Let me see if I can recall the words." Of course he recalled them. They were branded on his memory. "'You are guilty of the sin of Amnon and I cast you out of my house. From this day you are no longer my son.'"

"Did you understand what he meant?"

"I had no idea at the time. My studies, believe me, especially with the Reverend Josiah Ditchfield, included plenty of Bible reading. I thought I'd found every spicy story the Good Book contains. Somehow I missed that one. I probably would have found it amusing."

He drew his lips into a ghastly semblance of a grin. Instinctively he wanted to climb out of the emotional trough he'd dug and return to his habitual state of cavalier insolence.

"Cain, please." Her soft protest told him she wasn't fooled. "What did you do next?"

"I left, with the hundred pounds he'd given me. It seemed a fortune." He shook his head in wonder at his own naïveté. "I packed a few things, walked five miles to the nearest mail stop, and took the coach to London. I was happy to escape."

"When did you realize?"

"About Amnon? On the coach. One of the passengers had a Bible and I borrowed it." All trace of humor, feigned or otherwise, vanished. He couldn't begin to express his revulsion. "I thought I was going to be sick when I found it.

"The worst of it was I knew I would likely never see Esther as long as my father lived. How could I even write to her without appearing to confirm his accusation?"

"And after his death?"

"I returned to Markley Chase for the funeral. I thought it was all over. That I could go back and live at home. I even looked forward to seeing my mother again." He gave a short, humorless laugh. "She wouldn't even let me *see* Esther. Repeated my father's accusation and forbade me to go near my own sister. I could have made her leave the house. My father had no power to disinherit me. But the one thing he could withhold from me was my sister. If my mother left, so would she. And I couldn't punish Esther by making her an exile from her home. I knew what that was like. For three years my mother and I maintained an uneasy truce. I left her in possession of my house and my sister. She refrained from publishing my sins to the world."

"Until Esther ran away."

"Until then," he agreed. "I will fight for her in the courts, but I take the risk that my mother will openly accuse me of incestuous rape of my eight-year-old sister."

Juliana blanched at the words in all their ugliness. "Surely no one would believe anything so vile?"

"God knows I've done enough damage to my own reputation."

Little did Cain expect so bitterly to regret his years of merry dissipation. "You don't know the worst," he said.

"The worst!" Juliana exclaimed.

"I learned why Esther was crying that day. It was because she had found my father beating my mother. And I left them. I left my mother and sister behind while I went off and enjoyed myself. I escaped and left them in his hands."

Chapter 21

The black chariot with its red appointments had become home for the past three days. How many hours had she and Cain spent in this small velvet cave, a space too small to be comfortably shared for any length of time save by lovers?

By some strange contradiction, she'd learned, two people so confined could feel either powerfully close or leagues apart.

Now as she sat across from him, knees almost touching, she could sense a deep shame that he had, in his own estimation, abandoned his mother and sister.

"You didn't fail them," she said.

He slouched on the bench seat, thumbs tucked into the pocket of his waistcoat, his chin resting on the linen ties of his neck cloth. Unfocused blue eyes stared at nothing. The sensual mouth appeared pinched and unhappy.

"I should have known," he said. "He must have been beating her for years."

"You can't be certain of that. And if it's true I'm sure

he was careful to keep you from the knowledge."

"I never spent much time with her. For most of my life she was increasing and kept to her rooms and her endless prayers. I was cared for by servants."

"Yet there are only two of you," Juliana whispered, appalled by the thought of what violence might have wrought on a pregnant woman.

"Only Esther and I lived. She must have lost half a dozen children, at least, some at birth, some earlier. I wonder if he punished her for it. I should have known and I should have done something."

"You were a child, Cain, still only a boy when you left. How could you have stopped him?"

"I grew older. At least I could have tried to protect her. Esther says he went on beating her until he died. Had he lived longer he might have started on Esther too. And I had no idea. I resented my father's treatment. But it was nothing to how he treated my mother. I enjoyed a life of happy dissipation while she was living in hell." He raised his head and sat up straight to look at Juliana full-on. "I am as bad as my father."

"Stop! If there is one thing I know about you it's that you would never hurt a woman. You have too much esteem for them." The words emerged unconsidered but she knew them for the truth.

"I have spent most of my life in the company of men," she continued slowly, "and none of them has shown me as much respect and consideration as you have. You never treat me as an ignorant fool, just because of my sex."

"I'd be an ignorant fool myself, to do so. If there's one thing I've learned in my misspent life, it's that women are just as clever as men, and a lot nicer."

"I don't know very many women," Juliana said. "If by 'nice' you mean honest and honorable, then many men of my acquaintance qualify for the word."

"Lucky you. I can't say I share in your good fortune."

"But, despite their virtues, men, in my experience, expect women to bend to their will. And there isn't much we can do about it."

"The law sanctions it, encourages it even," Cain said. "My mother had no redress against my father. She and Esther were completely in his power."

She leaned forward. "Look at me," she said, willing him to meet her eye-to-eye. "You are nothing like your father. Any woman who, thanks to the law, found herself under your authority, would be safe and well cared for. I know what you have done for so many of them."

"What do you know?"

"Your housekeeper, Mrs. Duchamp, told me the other morning while I was getting dressed."

This drew a fleeting grimace. "Mel has a big mouth."

"You are giving a considerable portion of your fortune to make sure your former servants and others like them have a sanctuary."

"I don't wish to discuss it and I'd appreciate it if you wouldn't either."

"Why would you keep such acts of generosity to yourself? Besides, I've seen one of your . . . objects of charity myself. I came to your house one day to deliver a book."

"Did you, by God? Was I out?"

"No. When I saw this young *person* leaving I decided not to call after all."

A shadow of amusement crossed his features. "Clearly you leaped to the same conclusion all my neighbors have done for three years. They believe me a man of Herculean vigor."

"It's sad they are so wrong about you," she murmured.

"That, my dear, is an ambiguous statement," he drawled. "I hope you don't mean it the way it sounds. I would be very sorry to have disappointed you."

A wave of heat went through her and she blushed. She realized how much she enjoyed Cain's wicked innuendos. "I see you've returned to your usual outrageous self," she said, maintaining a straight face.

"I'm sorry. I can't help myself. Years of habit, making fun of everything."

"Don't apologize. There's nothing wrong with enjoying yourself. I like that in you. I like your jokes, and your . . . irreverence."

"Truly?"

"You sound surprised. Don't you understand? It makes you . . ." She waved a hand, searching for the right words. "I have fun when I'm with you."

"You mean I'm a comic figure, a clown?"

"Never that." She shook her head. "It makes you wonderful company. I've never enjoyed myself as much as when I'm with you. I scarcely recall my grandfather or Joseph laughing."

"No jokes? Perhaps they had more important things to think about."

"I'm beginning to think nothing is so important it can't be improved by a little levity."

"That's a challenge I can't resist." He relaxed back into his seat, surveying her through half-hooded eyelids. "Let me see. There's one thing you always treat with the utmost gravity. Suppose I were to buy one of those books printed by Caxton. Since I can't read it, I could take it apart leaf by leaf and use it to wallpaper my library."

Her grandfather would have been shocked. To him a great book was a sacred object. As for Joseph, he just wouldn't have understood the jest.

A bubble of laughter formed inside her. "Why stop at one?" she asked. "Buy two copies and paste the pages on the wall in order. Then you could use them for decoration *and* read the book."

"What would I do with the bindings?"

"Fifteenth-century leather makes excellent kindling."

"I suppose you know this from personal experience."

"It burns beautifully. Though when it comes to starting fires there's nothing like the classics."

"Any particular works?" he asked.

"I've always found an Aldine edition of Horace or Virgil works best."

"I would have thought Catullus or Ovid would generate more heat."

Although she'd actually read very little classical literature, her knowledge of Latin going little beyond the ability to decipher a title page, Juliana grasped Cain's allusion to the most amorous of Roman poets.

"I've never tried them," she said. "But I'd like to."

"Now you've shocked *me*," Cain rejoined. "Remind me not to let you into my library on a cold day."

"Not even if I asked nicely?"

"Particularly not if you asked *nicely*." The words, delivered in Cain's most gravelly tones, caressed like the velvet of the carriage seats.

"Just like a man. Always ready to command a woman but never listens to her carefully framed suggestions."

"I'm different, remember? I wouldn't dream of ordering you about. But don't bother with careful phrasing. Just come straight out and tell me what you want."

He continued to lounge against the red backrest, but his eyes were wide open and the intent blue gaze had its customary effect. Every nerve in her body buzzed with sensual anticipation. There was no question what he offered.

She had only to ask.

Really, she told herself piously, Cain had just gone through a disturbing confession. It would be a kindness on her part to cheer him up and turn his thoughts to happier activities. She choked back a sputter of laughter at her marvelously selfless justification.

A vision of their first encounter at the White Hart came to mind. While making love with Cain had been pleasurable every time, there had been something particularly satisfying about that quick, artless coupling.

The one she had initiated.

She ran her gaze up the lean, well-sculpted length

of his body and he watched her examine him. When her inspection reached his face she met a look of smoldering heat.

"Whatever you want," he said softly, "if it's in my power I shall be happy to provide it."

"You'll do as I wish?"

"Exactly."

"Even if it means I am in charge?"

"I should enjoy that. Tell me what to do."

"I want you to do nothing. Don't even move. Leave it all to me."

Cain held up his hands in a gesture of surrender. "I'm all yours."

He was all hers, this magnificent male specimen. What, she wondered, was she going to do with him?

Chapter 22

⁓◦◦⁓

This sudden boldness on Juliana's part fascinated Cain. Not that she wasn't a brave woman, but her audacity hadn't shown itself in the bedroom. With her obviously limited experience he was curious about her ability to improvise. He relaxed against the soft yet firm seat cushions in a state of happy anticipation. While by no means the first seduction advanced in this carriage, it was the most eagerly awaited.

Their knees brushed in the narrow space between the seats, communicating her tension. Her eyes like smoky emeralds sent him an unmistakable invitation, one he yearned to accept. To reach across the divide and take her. His fingers flexed in an involuntary move.

She frowned. "Keep those hands still." And held up her own.

"Yes, madam."

Like his, her hands were bare. Both had discarded their gloves earlier. Though it was late in the day, the weather was warm for April and the atmosphere in the carriage comfortable, rising to torrid. He trusted her plans for those delicate little fingers involved touching. His skin tingled at the notion. Soon, he sincerely hoped, she would be removing some of her clothing, and his.

She bent to unfasten her sensible half boots. Her head nudging his knee threatened the stability of her hairstyle, but to his disappointment the pins held. She kicked off the shoes and rose to her feet. Just then a rough spot in the road shook the carriage, despite its excellent springs. To restore her balance she placed her hands on his shoulders. The posture seemed to give her an idea. She climbed onto his seat, straddling his knees with her own.

His cock, already stirring, reacted firmly when she lowered herself onto his lap, clasping his hips between her knees. It was immediately aware of its preferred destination only inches away, notwithstanding the barrier of several layers of cloth.

With a clumsiness he found endearing, she settled herself into a secure position, then enclosed his face in her hands and kissed him with barely open mouth, probing the flesh inside his lips with her delicately questing tongue.

There was something about her that made even a simple kiss infinitely exciting. An emotional side to their connection set it apart from the countless couplings he'd enjoyed with dozens of women, even though he'd liked all those others and been very fond of a few of them. Juliana's thoughts and desires were at least as important to him as her actions.

Which wasn't to say he wasn't exceedingly interested in what she was *doing*, right now.

"Am I allowed to kiss you back?" he murmured against her lips.

Her brow creased a little as she drew back and gave his question solemn consideration, looking so delectable he wanted to hug her to him and gobble her up. Keeping his hands to himself wasn't the plain sailing he'd expected.

"Yes," she said, and kissed him again.

What was the question?

In a moment he remembered and returned the kiss, gently forcing her to widen to him and engaging his own tongue, exploring the hot cavern of her mouth, tasting her distinct flavor and sharing the sweet air of her breath. She raised herself so her face was slightly above his, wresting back the control he'd threatened to take. Pushing his head against the backrest with the force of her kiss, she freed her hands to work at the knot of his neck cloth. Without thinking he tried to help and she rested back on his knees again.

"Naughty," she said. And pressed each of his hands against the seat with her palms.

"I crave my lady's pardon. May we continue as we were?"

"First this needs to come off." With a look of intense concentration and the tip of her tongue provocatively protruding, she unwound the crisp linen cravat and cast it aside. Carefully she undid the buttons of his shirt to reveal his neck, which she scrutinized with hands, nose, and mouth, caressing, sniffing, nuzzling. She seemed fascinated by his Adam's apple; he had no idea why. He didn't believe it was overly prominent, but perhaps her husband's had been particularly small. He wondered idly if the size of the laryngeal bump was related to sexual prowess, until she stopped examining it with her fingers, placed her mouth on the prominence, and sucked. At which point he ceased to ponder obscure physical hypotheses and thought about all the other parts of his anatomy he'd like to feel her lips on.

"I need your help," she said after a few minutes' groping behind her own neck. "I can't undo my gown."

At last he was going to get his hands on her. Not that he wasn't enjoying himself. But some slight assistance on his part would speed them toward the really interesting bits. He unbuttoned the gown with practiced speed and, for good measure, unlaced her stays. She rose, small enough to stand in the carriage without bending, and shrugged the gown to the floor.

Cain leaned back in his seat and enjoyed the show. Juliana placed her feet firmly and slightly apart and adjusted her balance to the rocking of the carriage. Next to go was the corset, tossed onto the seat behind her. At last, to his great pleasure, she located and removed enough hairpins to send her glorious mane down over her shoulders. She bent her head and gave it a little shake, then looked up, her tumbling locks a fiery aura in the light of the swaying carriage lantern.

She looked like an angel, but not, thank God, in a saintly way.

Her simple linen shift, all too decent at the neck-line, stopped well above the knee, to reveal a narrow expanse of creamy skin between its hem and the tops of her gartered stockings. Cain felt his mouth go dry at those tantalizing inches of flesh, a coy yet mesmer-izing hint of the delights that lay higher, hidden by the no-nonsense undergarment. He actually consid-ered sitting on his hands to stop them reaching out to touch, to feel . . . to climb those slender limbs.

Patience, he adjured himself.

She was contemplating her next move, surveying him lazily from head to Hessian boot. His breeches were much too tight and seemed more so when she fixed her eyes on the evident bulge.

Undo them, please, he urged silently.

Instead, in one smooth motion, she whipped the shift over her head and dropped it. Naked from the knees up, she was Venus, perfection itself, the white and gold epitome of feminine beauty.

Cain was quite prepared to get down on his knees and worship, should his goddess demand it.

Venus had other ideas.

It was, Juliana thought, unbearably arousing to stand before him, almost naked and wholly exposed to Cain's burning, desirous eyes. She climbed back on top of him and started kissing him again. Her bare breasts rubbing against his wool clothes were swol-len and aching. Her nipples tingled with pleasurable pain when they caught the cold resistance of brass buttons. And straddling him, her now naked sex touched the bulge of his still confined erection. With a little moan she thrust her hips forward and ground against him.

"For God's sake," he groaned. "Undo my trousers. Please."

Immediately she disengaged herself. "Silence!" she ordered. "You may not speak, move, or touch."

Juliana returned to her own seat and received a practical demonstration of the sensuous effect of velvet upholstery. As she wriggled, enjoying the soft texture against buttocks and thighs, she caught him staring at her, his mouth slightly agape. After a moment's hesitation she leaned back and placed her stockinged feet against the opposite seat, on either side of him. His expression at the sight offered between her slightly bent knees was worth the courage she'd drawn on to display it.

Hot, naked need. But being Cain there was something else too. An undercurrent of amusement mixed with the desire in his azure eyes. He appreciated the drama as much as she enjoyed performing it. Her heart gave a little flip, separate from the physical passion that enveloped her.

"You're overdressed," she said. His eyes gleamed his agreement. "Take off your coat."

The dark blue garment joined her gown on the floor with remarkable speed.

"And your waistcoat."

He moved more slowly this time, one by one slipping the shiny brass buttons from their slits, teasing her with the gradual revelation of white linen beneath. As he shrugged the garment off his shoulders, the plackets of his shirt parted, offering a glimpse of muscles and hair beneath.

Hmmm. There was no reason to keep *herself* waiting.

"You may as well remove your shirt while you're about it." She issued the command with a smile, and his answering grin was every bit as wicked as hers felt.

Oh yes oh yes oh yes. Bare to the waist, he sprawled back. She noted the nice contrast of skin against the scarlet background. Whether to keep them from wandering, or because he knew he appeared to advantage thus, he hooked his hands behind his head. The resulting enhancement of chest muscles made *her* hands itch to wander.

Her eyes traveled lower, to the waistband of his breeches. And stopped.

She could take them off and skip to the conclusion. She wanted it, badly. Every inch of her skin yearned for the touch of his. Between her legs she was hot, wet, and aching for fulfillment.

Yet she hesitated, not because she wasn't ready, but because she wasn't ready for it to end. It might be a game, it *was* only a game. Yet she found the illusion of total power and control immensely enjoyable. She wished to prolong it.

An image from *that book*, the French version of Aretino she'd looked at with Cain, shot into her head. *Kiss the winged God Priapus.* She examined the concept and found it somewhat bizarre, quite embarrassing, and very exciting.

Did she dare?

Why not? Somehow she didn't think he would have any objection.

Her arms too short to reach the buttons from where she sat, she had to kneel on the floor. An upward glance showed his eyes as blue and wide as a sunlit sky staring down at her. She gave him a pouty little smile, then turned all her attention to the task at hand.

She stroked his member through the soft cloth. It was hard and twitched at her touch. Cain's throat emitted a strangled sound, though she couldn't accuse him of uttering an actual coherent word. Clearly he expressed his dissatisfaction at her progress, so she teased him, releasing each button with agonizing deliberation, enjoying his obvious frustration. As the ninth and last gave way, the "God Priapus" burst forth, knocking away the fall of the breeches and making a linen tent of his white drawers.

In about a minute she'd pulled off Cain's boots, breeches, and undergarments, rendering him even more naked than she. From her vantage point on the floor she admired the completed picture: the incised contours of shoulders and chest, the gradual taper to slim, firm waist and hips, the intriguing ridges where hard stomach gave way to muscular thighs.

And *it*. Bolt upright against his torso.

She grasped it gingerly, pulled it forward a few inches, and released it. It jerked right back.

It seemed very large. It couldn't possibly fit, not all the way. Perhaps, she imagined wildly, Frenchwomen had bigger mouths. Or Italians. Aretino was Italian, wasn't he?

One small Englishwoman was going to have to manage with what she had. Resting her elbows on Cain's knees, she considered the problem. Then wrapped a hand around the shaft. A quick glance at his face showed no objection so she tightened her grip and moved her fist up and down, working smooth skin over rock-hard muscle. Downward movement uncovered a ridged bulbous head and, after several repetitions, a bead of liquid formed there. Greatly daring, she licked it off with a single stroke of her tongue. It tasted salty, not disagreeable.

Taking a deep breath, she leaned over and closed her mouth over the head. Combining the use of hands, mouth, and tongue, she tried to establish a rhythm akin to that of intercourse. After a while she ventured to raise her eyes and meet Cain's, which were fixed on her head and hands. The look of bliss on his face boosted her courage. She felt a surge of exhilaration at her power to give him pleasure, and an answering arousal in her own sexual parts. There was something exciting about being the one to set the pace and control the progress of the encounter. Yet she wasn't sure whether she could bring him to climax.

As though aware of her unspoken doubt, Cain disobeyed orders. "Suck." She could feel the growled word reverberate through his body.

With that extra stimulation she heard his breathing increase to a steady pant. His shaft began to thrust and she had to tighten her grip to maintain her position and rhythm. It was like a battle, but one in which they were both equally antagonists and allies. As she sensed him primed for completion, he tried to pull away but she refused to release her grip. She'd started this and, by God, she'd see it to its conclusion.

She was still there when he released with a hoarse, ecstatic shout and a salty torrent.

The shudders that racked his body subsided. Cain was wrung out, worn out, wholly depleted. But his mind, blissfully humming, was filled with the woman who had just given him the greatest pleasure of his life. For such a tiny little thing she certainly wielded a punch, figuratively speaking. Without a moment's further consideration of her "rules," he pulled her up onto his lap and wrapped her slender body with his own. Using his neck cloth he tenderly wiped her cunning mouth, then kissed those rosy lips. Her avid response and the heat of her skin against him reminded him of unfinished business. While he was more sated than he could ever recall feeling, she wasn't even halfway there.

"Darling," he whispered, tonguing the warm porcelain whorls of her ear. "I'm afraid it'll be some time before I can rise again. You've quite worn me out. But I should be more than delighted to reciprocate your generosity."

He pictured her supine on the cushions, open to the ministrations of his tongue. The very idea had things stirring down below.

"I can wait," she said, twisting in his arms to face him. "Today I'm in charge. I'm not ready to give that up."

He understood at once. The events of the past days had been a journey into her past dominated by men who hadn't always treated her well. Who had, at the very best, dominated her. George and Frederick Fitterbourne. Joseph Merton. Each of these men had put his own needs and ambitions before hers and she'd had no right to gainsay them, to exert her own wishes.

It was the way of the world, most men, even most women, would say. A few lone voices of dissent, like Mary Wollstonecraft, who'd written a book on the subject, could do nothing to defeat the overwhelming weight of law and custom that put men "in charge." Cain realized he came down firmly on the side of the revolutionaries. From his own mother and sister to the meanest whore in the London stews, he'd known too many women oppressed or destroyed by the rule of men.

It was a discussion he'd have with Juliana another day, one he'd look forward to. Meanwhile, he must ensure she got the gratification she deserved in the way she wanted.

"Whatever is your pleasure," he said. "Might I humbly request that my lady withdraw her prohibition on touching?"

Tucked against Cain's chest, Juliana nodded. While she rejected a purely passive role, her every nerve was taut with yearning for her own climax, but she wanted it to be a shared one.

"Yes," she said, "touch me." And rubbed her cheek on the rough hair of his chest, breathing in the earthy scent of male sweat.

"Touch me," she repeated, finding the tight nub of his nipple and flicking it back and forth with her tongue.

"Oh yes!" She gave a little cry, more than a gasp, less than a shriek, when he reached between them and found her entrance, slipping a finger through curls and soft folds toward the hot, damp, aching core.

She feared she might explode before he was ready to join her. "Too soon," she whispered, and, understanding, he withdrew. Instead he turned his attention to her breasts, stomach, and the tender skin of her inner thighs, his caresses driving her to the edge of ecstasy yet keeping the fires banked. Fingers and palms, mouth and lips, teeth and tongue, all were applied with consummate skill and accompanied by sweet words of praise for her loveliness.

Without knowing how, she was on her back against the velvet, relishing the friction of her torso and limbs against the skin, hair, and hard muscle of his. Before long, one particular hard muscle was back in business, demanding entrance.

She gave him a shove. "I want to be on top." She'd never done it that way.

"Of course you do," he said with a snort of amusement, and rolled over.

Clinging to each other with shrieks of mirth, they landed on the floor of the carriage, wedged between the seats, their fall broken by the piles of clothing accumulated there. The amazed thought flashed through her head that lovemaking could be hilarious as well as blissful.

She struggled to rise but the carriage floor was narrow and they were laughing too hard to sort out their limbs sensibly.

"I can't get up," she moaned.

"You're in command." Cain stopped moving and she sensed all his muscles relax. Most of his body, save an entangled limb or two, lay limp beneath her.

Except for one part that, far from limp, nudged her stomach. She thought about it but there really wasn't room on the floor. She couldn't see where she'd put her knees.

With some effort she managed to get back onto the seat. She knelt on the bench and leaned over to look at him. Lying on his back with a giant erection, laughing his head off, Cain looked so delectable she almost went back to join him. But there still wasn't enough room down there.

"Come on up," she said.

With easy grace he pulled himself upright and knelt on the seat, facing her. And she knew what she wanted, what to do.

Once again she straddled his knees. When he placed his arms around her waist she made no objection.

"That's it," he whispered, sitting back. "Face to face and equal." Without being told, he understood her. Neither of them would play a passive role.

Her restrained desire would no longer be denied. All mental lucidity vanished as her hands found and steadied his shaft and she impaled herself on the hot, thick length of him. With a sigh of relief she began to ride.

Mouth to mouth, chest to chest, their arms surrounding each other, they moved in perfect rhythm. The mutual friction of skin, the taste of his mouth, the spicy perfume of sex and sweat, the slight chill of air against her buttocks, her lover's pleasurable groans. Every sense enhanced the spiraling ecstasy where Cain filled and stretched her. Their movements—his, hers, both—roused her to a peak of tension. Control shattered at last as every muscle reacted without her volition. Her arms and legs convulsively gripped him and her inner passage clenched around his cock. She felt his climax shake him and a hot gush flood her core, just as her own release spilled over in wave after wave of joyful fulfillment.

Chapter 23

❧

Juliana couldn't sleep.

She lay on her side in a perfectly comfortable inn bed, huddled against "Mr. Johnson's" chest. One arm curved around her, one hand cupped her breast, one leg, careless and possessive, was flung over hers.

Despite a long, eventful day they'd made love again, slow and lazy. Afterward Cain had fallen asleep at once. Juliana, though equally exhausted, could not. She lay in the dark and reveled in his physical closeness. The texture of his skin, the rough kiss of his chest rising almost imperceptibly under her cheek. The heat of his body. His scent.

Her wakefulness wasn't just the consequence of her busy thoughts. She didn't want to miss a moment of this night with Cain. The last night she'd ever spend in his arms.

Cain, Juliana suspected, hadn't quite faced the fact they had no future together. Until they reached London, neither would she.

She indulged in a little fantasy in which he was, indeed, Mr. Johnson, as the Chippenham innkeeper had been told. She'd happily spend the rest of life as Mrs. Johnson, the wife of a man of no great material wealth or worldly distinction, but rich in intelligence, spirit, and compassion.

She forgot the fact that he was a marquis, one of England's most important men by reason of his inheritance. And one who could live up to his rank now that he was ready to accept his responsibilities and return to the world of his birthright.

She forgot everything except that she lay in his arms and she loved him.

Such happiness was fleeting and she refused to waste a minute in sleep.

Since they'd elected to make the journey in a single day, it was well past dusk by the time the chaise passed through Hammersmith.

Juliana had slept much of the journey. Her size was a great advantage in a traveling companion confined in a small carriage. He would happily have shared one seat with her all the way, but once he discovered she could stretch full length on the opposite side, he'd tucked her under a blanket and watched her succumb to deep slumber. He liked taking care of her.

"Cain," she said. She'd been sitting upright for the past hour or so. They'd exchanged desultory comments on the progress of the journey. What they'd do when they reached the city hadn't been mentioned.

"Yes."

"I want to thank you."

"What for?"

"For this journey. For helping me. Even though we

didn't really find anything, I shall always be glad I tried, thanks to you. What the world says about you is completely unfair and unfounded."

"*Everything* the world says? You wound me." Unaccustomed to praise of his character, he deflected the compliment with flippant words and a suggestive leer.

"In the future," she continued, "if anyone ever says a word against you in my presence, I shall tell them you are a true gentleman and worthy of respect."

"You speak as though we are going to part," he objected.

"We *are* going to part. You know what you need to do, what kind of woman you need to marry."

He moved over to sit beside her and cradled her face in his hands. "You are the kind of woman I need to marry," he said, and kissed her.

For a few moments her lips clung to his, then she drew back and shifted to the opposite seat, where he'd been a minute before.

"No, I'm not. Get it into your head. I am a bastard. Under any circumstances I would be an improbable wife for a marquis. For you I am impossible."

"I'm not giving up," he said, crossing the carriage in pursuit. "Tomorrow I shall set old Robinson to track down Cassandra's marriage." He laid his arm about her to put an end to the seat-swapping back-and-forth.

She relaxed against him with a sigh. "I've been thinking about it."

"Don't. Think about *our* marriage instead."

"I've been thinking about it and I can't see how the

marriage can have happened without my grandfather knowing it."

"Let's not start this argument again, just when we are getting along so well."

"I'm not going to quarrel with you. I understand why you might think he suppressed the marriage to inherit Cassandra's fortune. But you didn't know my grandfather. It doesn't suit his character. Such a deception would never occur to him. He simply didn't care about money."

"By all accounts he spent plenty of it."

"Yes, but he spent without thought. If he found a book he wanted, he bought it and worried about paying for it later. He had to have it, and he had to have it immediately. The only time he became truly angry was when he lost a book to another collector."

"Tarleton?"

"Especially Tarleton," she agreed. "But he didn't intend to ruin his estate. He just ended up doing so. And I'm certain he didn't intend to spend Cassandra's fortune. If he thought about it at all he probably meant to save it for me. My grandfather knew what was right, he just didn't always do it. If booksellers were dunning him and refusing him further credit, he'd take any money he could lay his hands on to pay them. Ten thousand pounds no doubt melted away without him noticing."

"Ten thousand pounds would buy a lot of books."

"He had a vast collection. Only a fraction the size of Tarleton's, but the library you saw yesterday was full to overflowing."

"From what I've seen, and I'll grant you I'm new to

this business, most books don't cost more than a few shillings, a few pounds at most."

"My grandfather pursued true rarities. And he never cared about price. Late in his life I often tried to argue that he was overpaying for a title and he would become annoyed. Some booksellers took advantage of him. They knew he wouldn't quibble if they had books he wanted."

Unfortunately Juliana's argument was too logical to be easily dismissed. He tried a new tack. "Perhaps Cassandra died without telling him she was wed."

"You are so stubborn. Can't you admit it's hopeless? I am a bastard and will remain so. You should be doing what is necessary to become your sister's guardian. Go to St. James's or Almack's or wherever your kind gathers, and find yourself a true lady."

Cain found the bitterness in her voice encouraging, because he didn't think it resulted only from her base birth. She wasn't relinquishing him without regret.

And he wasn't relinquishing her at all.

He'd made the mistake in the past of giving in too easily, of taking the easy road of mindless pleasure away from both his wishes and his responsibilities.

He should have at least tried to fight his father and that insane accusation. And he should have refused to let his mother prolong his exile because she remained dominated by her husband, even after his death.

He should have fought for her and for Esther. And he would. He wasn't giving up until he had everything he wanted.

And that included Juliana Merton, no matter what her birth, as his marchioness.

"I shall return to St. Martin's Lane and the life I have," Juliana said, a little wobble in her voice. "I am a good bookseller and I shall become a successful one."

Go right on thinking that, my lady. I have a better plan.

"What about the *Romeo and Juliet*?" he asked. "The fact remains, someone hid it in your shop and made sure it would be discovered."

She shrugged. "An unpleasant jest, perhaps." Her face darkened. "I'd suspect Mr. Iverley if I could fathom how he put it there, but he hasn't been in my shop in weeks."

Cain considered the idea. It was possible, he supposed.

He didn't believe it for a moment.

Chapter 24

C ain was unhappy to leave Juliana in St. Martin's Lane. Not alone, of course. Mel had departed for her new quarters but Tom and Peter remained.

"Until we get to the bottom of this," he'd told Juliana, "I want you to keep my footmen with you at all times, day and night. As well as that dog."

He hoped he could trust her to obey. He'd have preferred to stay with her himself, or better yet bring her to Berkeley Square. But his stratagems to protect both their reputations would be for nothing if they openly spent the night together in London. So far they'd been lucky, but he couldn't expect that to last.

Before returning home he walked up to Holborn. Mel had left a message requiring his presence, urgently. Some complaint about the renovations to the house that she should take to Robinson, he guessed. Still, if he couldn't spend the evening with Juliana it might as well be with Mel. Better her than his new servants.

The minute he arrived at the shabby house it became clear this was no housekeeping crisis. "There's someone you need to see," Mel told him the minute he walked into the hall. "A girl from Mrs. Tudor's in Pimlico."

"I don't believe I've heard of the place."

"It's a flogging house."

Cain knew what that meant. "How is she?" he asked, feeling nauseated.

"About what you'd expect after years as a receiver."

"My God!" He didn't need to tell Mel what to do. She'd call a doctor if the victim of a thousand flagellations needed one. If it would still do any good. "I don't understand why you sent for me."

"She says she'd have come before but she wouldn't come to Berkeley Square. Couldn't come to Lord Chase's house because he was a customer."

"Good Lord, Mel! You know me better than that."

"I think you'd better see her, Cain."

Mel led him into a room where a woman cowered in a chair. "This is Lucy," she said.

The woman raised a head of crudely dyed red hair to reveal a listless, gray-tinged face with dark rings around her eyes. She looked forty or more and was likely half that age.

Though it had never been to Cain's taste, he knew of half a dozen houses where a gentleman might submit himself to discipline if such were his inclination. Houses that catered to men who liked to hand out pain were less plentiful and far more squalid. The whores that serviced those establishments rarely lasted long.

"You ain't Lord Chase," she said, and a measure of

fear faded from the dull complexion, leaving indifference or despair.

"I am, Lucy," Cain said gently. "But don't be afraid, you are safe here."

She shook her head. "Chase was an old cully."

"Was?" Cain asked.

"He was my first. And a wicked hand with the switch."

In years of consorting with a variety of London's fallen sisterhood, Cain had never heard his father mentioned as a customer. The late Lord Chase had been well-known among London's whores, but only for his speeches in Parliament. He'd raged against vice, and his recommended remedy always included severe, usually physical, punishment for the female involved. Apparently he'd liked to attend to it personally.

"When was this?" he asked.

Through gentle questioning, with Mel's help, Cain tried to establish a chronology of his father's involvement with Mrs. Tudor's brothel. Lucy had little sense of time. Such episodes as the change of governments, the assassination of a prime minister, even the Battle of Waterloo, meant little or nothing to her. Luckily she remembered sporting events: wagering on boxing was a popular activity. The first Cribb-Molineaux prizefight happened not long after her arrival at Mrs. Tudor's.

Lucy, it turned out, had been at Mrs. Tudor's for about nine years. She knew she'd been a fourteen-year-old girl when Lord Chase, already a regular customer for some years, introduced her to the birch.

Cain had heard many tales of the miseries endured

by fallen women. Lucy's was as horrible as any. He was amazed she'd survived so long. Again he assured her Mel would make sure she was cared for and could find a healthier livelihood. He only hoped it wasn't too late.

"Did you ever hear of a man named Sir Thomas Tarleton?" he asked.

Lucy nodded. "Peephole cull. Ain't seen him for a while."

So Tarleton paid whorehouses for the privilege of watching his fellow men in action, doubtless furnishing him with ample blackmail material.

"And how long since you saw this Chase?" he asked.

"He ain't been round for years. But the girls all know about him. And 'ope he'll never come back. He only did me the once but I was the lucky one. He killed a girl not long after, beat her to death. Ma Tudor wouldn't let him back in."

Chapter 25

A t nine o'clock the next morning Juliana asked Tom to unlock the shop door. Tom's brother and fellow footman was upstairs clearing away the breakfast the two boys had prepared. Juliana enjoyed having servants again.

"Cor," Tom said. "'Ere comes that corpse Benson."

"Benson?"

"The guv's new footman."

A very correct liveried servant entered the premises and bowed his wigged head. "A note from His Lordship, madam."

"Thank you. Will you wait for an answer?"

"No need, madam. His Lordship left London at first light."

The servant departed, even as Juliana ripped the seal off the letter.

"My dear," she read. "I must go to Markley Chase Abbey for a few days. Don't do anything foolish. Keep the boys and the dog close and your doors locked. *This isn't over.* Cain."

What, she wondered, did the last, heavily underlined sentence mean? And why was Cain suddenly returning to his home? Had he decided to confront, perhaps to attempt reconciliation with his mother? For his sake she hoped it was true. Then he could truly take his place in the world.

And she must do the same thing for herself. With more than a hint of melancholy, she realized that, contrary to what Cain had written, it *was* over for them.

"I need to go out, Tom," she said. "Close the door behind me again. I shan't be open this morning."

"I'll come with you. I told the guv I wouldn't leave you alone."

A footman trailing behind her, even an undersized and underaged one, would be a hindrance on this morning's errand.

"I'll take Quarto. He'll be enough protection in broad daylight. You stay here and help Peter guard the shop."

In the end it took the best part of three days for Juliana to get what she needed. She visited every bookseller in London with whom she had anything approaching cordial relations. She called in favors dating back to Joseph's time. She offered prize items of stock at tempting prices. She questioned, she cajoled, she gossiped.

And she learned. She learned a great deal about what was going on in London book-collecting circles. She heard numerous predictions for the last day of the Tarleton sale and made her own deductions.

And she enjoyed herself. She found these bookmen— and they were all men—quite human. Most of them,

once they discovered she simply wished to engage in
the kind of talk and transaction they'd have with any
other of their kind, seemed to forget she was a mere
woman. The suspicion and reserve that had been her
normal lot since Joseph's death didn't disappear. Yet
she began to see that she might, despite her sex, find a
place in this world. Which was a good thing, since she
had no other prospects and had better be prepared to
spend many years as a bookseller.

She refused to entertain the slightest hope of a
future with Cain.

By the morning of the fourth day she was ready.
She suppressed her scruples about what she was
about to do and hoped it wouldn't end up damaging
her reputation and the career that was so important
to her future.

Sir Henry Tarleton lived in a small house north of
Oxford Street, a genteel but not fashionable neighborhood. The prices at the Tarleton auction continued to
exceed expectations and common sense, so the heir
to the estate would receive a very large sum from the
proceeds. In the meantime the mean nature of his
abode confirmed that Sir Henry was short of ready
money.

Calling on an unmarried man was not proper for
a lady. But it wasn't a social call and she didn't see
why she had to be governed by restraints her male
colleagues didn't suffer. She could have written and
requested he call at the shop, but she didn't wish
Cain's servants to hear her conversation with Tarleton. She gave Quarto a fond scratch behind the ears
as she waited at the door. The bulldog would double

as protector and chaperone. His discretion she could
certainly count on.

Sir Henry received her with obvious curiosity. "I
haven't seen you at Sotheby's lately."

"I was in Salisbury for a few days."

· "Was this a book-buying trip or were you visiting
family?"

"A little of both," she said, not knowing why he
was interested.

She discreetly examined her surroundings, and the
room confirmed what she'd heard about Henry Tarleton. Whatever his aspirations, he wasn't much of a collector yet. Perhaps his library was stored in a different
part of the house, but Juliana had yet to meet a book
collector whose enthusiasm wasn't obvious in every
room. Tarleton had received her in a sitting room that
contained not one single volume.

"To what do I owe the honor of this visit?" he
asked.

"I wonder if you are still seeking advice and representation at your uncle's auction."

"Have you changed your mind about Lord Chase
then?"

"Lord Chase is no longer in the market for books."

"As I suspected, his interest was whimsical." Sir
Henry spoke with satisfaction, but without rushing
to request her services again. "You would have been
wise, Mrs. Merton, not to give too much credence to
such a notoriously unreliable man. And so you find
yourself without a customer."

Very well, she thought, *he wants to be asked*. "You

were good enough, a few weeks ago, to ask for my assistance."

"Let me be blunt, Mrs. Merton. I explained to you before that my resources are limited. Why should I pay you a commission instead of bidding myself?"

"Let me be blunt, Sir Henry. How much gossip do you hear? Do you know what other collectors are planning?"

Sir Henry's eyes gleamed. "Do you know, Mrs. Merton?"

One of the things Juliana had ascertained in her researches was that Sir Henry was something of an outsider. Sir Thomas Tarleton had been disliked but respected. His heir, perhaps unfairly, had inherited the aversion but not the admiration. He wasn't likely to have been the recipient of many confidences.

"I know a great deal. I can make a very fair guess as to who will be bidding on the best books in the collection. And how much they are prepared to pay."

"Such as?"

Juliana reeled off the names of a dozen books she knew Tarleton wanted.

"I am interested."

"And, of course, the Burgundy Hours."

"Mrs. Merton. I do believe we shall be able to come to terms."

Henry Tarleton, it was rumored, had been engaged in trade of a questionable nature in his native West Indies. An hour later Juliana could well believe it. The man drove a hard bargain. The "usual commission" had been beaten down and he wanted every last Shakespeare, folios and quartos. He ignored or forgot his promise not to compete for the *Romeo and Juliet*.

Juliana had a customer for the finale of the Tarleton sale. She hoped she hadn't made a contract with the devil.

Chapter 26

Cain had forgotten what a beautiful house it was. Abbey was a misnomer. When the first Godfrey had been granted his barony for services rendered to the crown by his future wife, the title of Lord Cainfield had been accompanied by a substantial portion of monastic land. His relatively modest manor, converted from the original priory, had been transformed into a mansion to celebrate the receipt of an earldom from Queen Elizabeth. Markley Chase Abbey was a masterpiece of Cotswold stone and glass set in rolling green hills.

Cain entered the great hall, which retained the original Elizabethan oak paneling and tapestries. His memory of the room, of the whole house, was of darkness and gloom. Now it struck him how light it was, the vast chamber illuminated by sunlight pouring in from the tall windows.

The butler hurried to greet him, doubtless alerted to the unlooked-for arrival of the master of the house. "My lord!" he said, with barely concealed astonishment.

"How are you, Stratton?" The man had presided

over the household for at least twenty years, yet Cain couldn't remember much about him. The late marquis had never permitted hobnobbing with the servants, even the male ones.

"Is Her Ladyship expecting you, my lord?" he asked.

Cain handed the man his outer garments. "I believe I can enter my own house without prior notice," he said. "Where is Her Ladyship?"

Was that a ghost of a smile on Stratton's face, or did Cain imagine it? "In the saloon, my lord. I believe Mr. Ditchfield is with her."

"Don't bother to announce me. I know the way."

He climbed the grand staircase to the main floor, remodeled some eighty years earlier. The first marquis spent a fortune celebrating his promotion, his taste influenced by a visit to Rome. The saloon was a lofty cavern of marble and gilt, embellished with huge canvases by Italian masters. Rather popish, Cain thought. Amazing really that his sire hadn't burned the lot of them.

Or got rid of them along with the Burgundy Hours, that other masterpiece of Roman Catholic art. Except that now Cain knew why his father had disposed of that particular piece of his family history.

Lady Chase sat in a straight-backed chair next to the massive Carrara marble fireplace. She held up an open leather-bound volume and appeared to be consulting her companion about a passage in the book. The Reverend Josiah Ditchfield stood next to her, his head cocked attentively.

The sight of the clergyman caused Cain a spurt

of rage. Setting aside the miseries he'd inflicted on Cain when acting as his tutor, the middle-aged bully aspired to wed a sixteen-year-old girl. Cain repressed the urge to seize Ditchfield by his overly long, slicked-back, greasy locks and rub his long, thin nose in the ashy hearth.

The reaction of the pair to Cain's entrance was almost comical.

"Cainfield!" boomed the old hypocrite, dark beady eyes bulging unattractively in his sallow face.

His mother closed her eyes, as though to avoid viewing an abomination. She slammed her book closed and clutched it to her breast for protection. Some work of piety, no doubt. "Cainfield," she said faintly.

Cain's bow was all that was correct. "I believe I may be properly addressed as Chase." He looked at Ditchfield. "You, sir, may address me as 'my lord.'"

Lady Chase opened her eyes. "I cannot bring myself to call you Chase. That was your father's name and one you don't deserve to bear." His mother's soft, die-away tones belied the severity of her words.

"I would be honored, madam, if you address me as John. And I would prefer to call you Mother."

He'd always addressed her formally, as he had his father. But he'd come to make peace. He intended to treat his mother kindly, if she would allow it.

She appeared not to know how to respond and looked down at her lap. Ditchfield suffered no such doubts.

"Have you come to restore Lady Esther to her rightful guardians?" he asked.

Bad mistake, Ditchy.

"Guardians?" Cain asked, walking over to the clergyman and deliberately crowding him. They were much of a height but Cain no longer found him remotely intimidating. *"Guardians?* Plural?"

Ditchfield stared back. "I have enjoyed Her Ladyship's confidence in the upbringing of Lady Esther. In the future I expect, with her mother's blessing, to establish a more formal dominion."

Cain leaned in and spoke softly, inches from Ditchfield's face. "If by those words you refer to your presumptuous, not to mention disgusting, notion that you should marry my sister, I recommend you put it out of your mind. I also suggest you leave this room. Now."

His mother made an exclamation of protest and half stood, dropping her book in her agitation. Cain retrieved it from the floor and looked at the title. *Selected Sermons of the Northern Bishops.*

"Is it good?" he asked derisively, before placing it on a nearby table. "Better than the sermons delivered by a certain clergyman who appears to be still here, although I asked him to leave?" He swung around to glare at the sputtering Ditchfield.

"I won't leave this room while Lady Chase demands my presence."

"Wrong, Ditchfield. You are forgetting something. This is my house and I am the master here. You can walk out now, I can throw you out, or I can summon servants to throw you out. The choice is yours."

Ditchfield turned to his patroness, who looked distressed but made no further argument. Not that it would do any good. His departure wasn't open to negotiation.

"You'll regret this, Cainfield," he said.

Cain raised an eyebrow. Part of him hoped Ditchfield would refuse to leave, giving Cain the very great pleasure of picking him up and tossing him through the door. Unfortunately Ditchfield read the message correctly and walked out of the saloon, trying to look dignified.

His mother didn't invite him to sit and Cain decided not to make an issue of it. He remained on his feet.

"Why are you here? Have you brought Esther back?" She couldn't possibly be as unemotional as she sounded.

"I am hoping we can come to an accommodation about my sister without an unpleasant battle in the law courts."

"I object to Esther's request to have you named guardian."

"So I am informed by my lawyer."

She looked around, as though waiting for someone else to reply. But Cain had dismissed her ally. She would have to speak, and think, for herself. "As though a girl her age would know how to select a guardian," she said.

"Yet the law allows it."

"I fear for her immortal soul, living in the cesspit you have made of your father's house."

"As you know, Mother, Esther is now under the roof of your sister, Lady Moberley. My aunt is ready to prepare Esther for her presentation next year. She'll find her a much more suitable husband than that middle-aged hypocrite you tried to foist on her."

"My sister, Augusta, is given over to worldly vanity. And Mr. Ditchfield is a good man, a gentleman of true virtue. He reminds me of your father."

"I'll never let Esther wed Ditchfield. It's a ludicrous match. What can you be thinking to approve a union so unequal in every conceivable way?"

"Oh no! Marriage to such a man is the only way to save Esther from the taint of bad blood. The bad blood she gets from me."

"I cannot believe this! If there's any bad blood in this family it comes from my father. By the time he died he was quite, quite mad."

Throughout the exchange, his mother had spoken in soft, matter-of-fact tones, suitable for incontrovertible truths about the current weather. She spoke of bad blood as though commenting on a shower of rain. Cain's words about her late husband roused her to something resembling animation.

"Don't speak of your father like that. He was a saint. He forgave me for my blood, he helped me overcome it. Esther must be chastised in order to be saved. Mr. Ditchfield will correct her, as my lord corrected me. As he tried to correct you until he discovered you were incorrigible."

"Mother, he beat you. That has nothing to do with saving you. He was a brute."

"I deserved it."

Cain got down on his knees next to her chair and took her hands. She tried to pull them away but he wouldn't let her.

"No woman deserves to be beaten. Don't you understand? My father was a bully, preying on you because he could. Because he was stronger than you. And because he enjoyed it."

"No! I deserved it. He was a saint." She pulled away from him and rose to her feet. A slight figure in subdued gray silk with a lace cap, she presented an odd contrast to the exuberant caryatids that held up the marble mantelpiece.

"How dare you," she said with as much ferocity as she could project. "How dare you impugn your father. When you are guilty of sins against God and nature."

So, after all, it had come down to this.

"Mother," he said, rising from his knees. "Unlike my father I have never pretended to be a saint. But I swear I never set an improper finger on Esther. How can you believe me, your own son, guilty of such a terrible crime?"

"Your father saw you."

"My father saw nothing because there was nothing to see."

"My lord never lied to me."

"Think for yourself, Mother. Did you ever see anything yourself, anything in my behavior toward Esther to arouse such a suspicion?" He was pleading with her now, desperate for some softening, an indication that she didn't believe him loathsome.

"He wouldn't lie. He was a saint." She kept repeating those words, which seemed ingrained in the fabric of her brain.

"If you truly believed me guilty of incest, why haven't you informed the world?"

She stared at him, as though the answer was obvious. "It would damage my lord's reputation to know he had such a son. Your depravity caused him endless pain. For his sake I wouldn't publish your sin."

"Even if I fight you for care of Esther?" he asked, holding his breath. Could it possibly be this easy?

"To save his daughter, I must betray him. I shall inform the judge why you should never be Esther's guardian."

No, it wasn't going to be easy.

"What if I can prove to you that my father was as much a sinner as any man?" He really hadn't wanted to do this. He knew what he had to relate would devastate her. He had never wished to hurt her. And yet it wasn't as though news of his father's proclivities should surprise her.

"What calumny is this?" she asked.

"My father . . ." Somehow it seemed less cruel to say "my father" rather than "your husband." "My father for some years patronized a certain house of ill repute in London." He hoped she understood the phrase. He'd prefer not to use a cruder term.

"It's not true," she whispered. "Adultery is a sin and my husband never sinned. For all my failures he would never have played me false."

"As to that, he may not have committed adultery in the strictest sense. I apologize, madam, for speaking to you of such matters. The house in question is patronized by those who like to wield the whip. The unfortunate women there are paid to accept beatings."

"Then they deserved it. They were vipers and serpents attempting to seduce my lord. He was helpless in the face of their wiles and temptations."

Cain wouldn't let her convince herself her husband had been a victim.

"Let me tell you what happened," he said, striving for a voice of reason. She allowed herself to be guided back to her seat. He moved a chair next to hers and would have taken her hand again, but both hers were clasped together in her lap.

"Do you remember when my father had the fever? Just after I started Eton."

"By the grace of God he was spared."

There'd been many times over the years when Cain had wondered whether the intervention that saved his father's life on that occasion had been divine, or the work of a more malevolent power. Before his illness the marquis had been domineering, bad-tempered, and overly pious. Afterward he had maintained all those qualities in greater force, mixed with an increasingly irrational rage.

"I believe it was then he started to have these violent urges. He went to London each year for Parliament but he no longer took you with him."

"In punishment for my transgressions, he put me from him."

"What transgressions?"

"After your sister I never increased again. God punished me for my sins by rendering me barren." His mother seemed unsure as to whom her imaginary sin had offended.

Cain ventured to touch her clenched knuckles and

she snatched her hands back and pressed them against her midriff.

"You had two children," he said.

'"In sorrow thou shalt bring forth children; and thy desire shall be to thy husband, and he shall rule over thee.'" As always, his mother had a Bible verse for every occasion, whether it made sense or not.

"He killed a woman," Cain said bluntly, his eyes fixed on her face. "He beat her to death. That was the same year he sent me away. Was that when he started beating you? Because even the London whipping houses wouldn't admit him anymore?"

"No." The word was almost whispered. "I deserved chastisement." His heart sank as he read the frozen expression on her face. He wasn't getting through to her. She wouldn't accept that her husband was capable of error.

"If you object to Esther's request to have me named guardian I shall reveal to the world what my father was."

"He was a saint."

"Do saints frequent whorehouses? Would a saint beat a whore to death? Do saints beat their wives? His peers would certainly sneer at just how *un*saintly the Saintly Marquis was."

"You would destroy his good name!"

"With the greatest of pleasure, madam. Just as he destroyed mine."

For a moment his anger against his father overcame the pity he felt for his mother. Then he looked at the ashen face of the woman who'd given birth to him.

She had suffered at the hands of the same madman. And she had never escaped.

"How can I allow his daughter to fall into your wicked hands?" she cried, her distress palpable as she buried her face in her hands.

"Mother," he said softly. "Look at me. I am your son. Remember? You've known me all my life. Think back, I beg you. Do you truly believe me capable of such evil?"

She raised her eyes, and for a moment he thought she looked at him as a mother would, as he remembered her from his childhood. Then her face hardened.

"I cannot believe my lord a liar," she said.

Even now, more than three years after his death, her husband's hold over her was absolute.

"I shall argue that my father belonged in an asylum," he said with brutal frankness. "I have plenty of evidence to make the case." He made the threat with every intention of carrying it through, and hoped he wouldn't have to.

He could almost see her mind at work. In her heart of hearts she knew her husband had been insane. She'd witnessed, indeed suffered, numerous demonstrations of the fact. Yet she couldn't bring herself to admit it.

"You are an ungrateful son but I cannot allow you to destroy the memory of your father." Her words were icy but he knew he'd won. "I shall withdraw my objection."

"You mustn't fear for Esther," he said, trying to comfort her now she'd given in. "I will never harm her, and you will still share her upbringing with me.

I am to be married. I look forward to presenting my bride to you. Why don't you come to London?"

Somewhat to his relief she refused. It was bad enough having to replace all his friends with servants of his aunt's choosing. Having his mother in residence at Berkeley Square would make life barely worth living.

"Excuse me, my lord," she said, rising from her chair. "I will withdraw to my rooms. Will you stay here long?"

"I must return to London tomorrow." He would have liked to show some gesture of affection, to kiss her hand or cheek. Instead he merely picked up her book and handed it to her. He recognized that surrender had been a bitter draught for her to swallow.

"You will see that you are doing the right thing," he said, bowing deferentially. "As my mother you have my respect and affection. I hope that one day you will be able to return them."

Perhaps she never would. Yet Cain wasn't without hope that he could change her opinion of him. Certainly he would continue to try.

Chapter 27

Juliana arrived early at the sale room. Knowing the last day of the Tarleton sale would attract every bookman in London, and more than a few from elsewhere, she'd arranged to meet Sir Henry in plenty of time to find good seats. In the center, only one row back from the horseshoe of tables surrounding the auctioneer, they'd be able to see as many bidders as possible.

The great room buzzed with greetings and gossip. "I see Spencer," Sir Henry whispered. "Are you sure he isn't after the Hours?"

Juliana kept her voice low, though there was little chance of being overheard in the surrounding din. "He may buy a few lesser books, and he wouldn't want to miss the spectacle, but he doesn't now have the resources to buy anything important. I have it on good authority he's in negotiation to buy Lord Blandford's collection."

"I still find it hard to believe Blandford is retrenching."

"After spending over two thousand pounds on one

book at the Roxburghe sale? And that's the least of his extravagances."

"He's the son of a duke."

"I imagine even dukes have their financial limits."

Tarleton's eyes constantly scanned the room as they talked. "Winchester is here. He would be interested in the Caxtons."

"He won't bid high."

"How do you know that, Mrs. Merton?"

Juliana blushed. "He has a new . . . lady friend. I gather she is very expensive."

"I am impressed by your knowledge. Is Lord Chase one of your informants by any chance?"

"I have many sources," she said coolly. And tried not to think of happy hours in Cain's carriage, listening to tales of the demimonde. When she wasn't herself behaving like a member of it.

A change in the pitch of the chatter, a general movement into seats, alerted her that eleven o'clock approached.

"So we are agreed," Juliana whispered. "High on the Caxtons and the Shakespeares."

"Agreed. But make sure I have enough left for the Burgundy Hours. I must have that manuscript."

"I assure you I have your priorities in mind."

A warning rap from the auctioneer's hammer silenced the gathering. Juliana sensed the tension in the room at the long-awaited climax of the Tarleton sale.

The early bidding was somewhat desultory although prices were healthy enough. Things livened up when the fine section of early English printing went under the hammer. Juliana, competing on Tarleton's behalf, won two Wynkyn de Wordes and paid five hundred and twenty pounds for one of the Caxtons against stiff opposition. They lost the other Caxtons to Matthew Gilbert, who was buying with steady determination for his various noble customers.

"More than I hoped to pay," Sir Henry muttered.

"A bargain at the price," she said. "I doubt you'll have to pay more for anything else. Except the Burgundy manuscript, of course."

Juliana found the information she'd garnered correct: there were more spectators than bidders in the rooms but those who did bid were there to buy. Prices on certain books were exorbitant enough to build an atmosphere of growing excitement and anticipation.

She watched the crowd, trying to guess who was bidding on his own behalf and which booksellers represented which collectors. Then the porter held up the next lot, a large folio in an armorial binding. With a silent start of recognition she looked in her catalogue to see what it was.

"A collection of original documents relating to the early history of the Church of England. Letters of Henry VIII, Edward VI, Queen Elizabeth, Cranmer, Hooker, etc.," she read.

A valuable group, she thought, unlike the contents of the volume sitting in her bedroom. But the binding was the same. How odd that Tarleton owned it. She scribbled a word in her catalogue and circled it. "Combe."

Cain discovered the ladies in the drawing room, Esther clad in demure white muslin, Lady Moberley in blue corded silk. Both garments looked new, and the dressmakers' bills no doubt reposed on his desk across the square. He hadn't been home yet.

"John," Esther cried, leaping up with obvious delight.

He kissed her cheek and bowed to his aunt.

"Chase," Lady Moberley said, with equally apparent disapproval. "I can't fathom what business should take you out of town for so long at this time. You've missed a dozen events."

"I've been to Markley Chase. It's all right," he responded to Esther's anxious look. "Our mother has agreed to my guardianship. You shall live with me, though I am sure you'll wish to visit her frequently."

"Mr. Ditchfield?" Esther asked.

"Need not concern you. I've seen to him."

"I should like to see Mother."

"Of course you would. We shall go together." Cain wasn't sure if his mother would ever welcome him, but he wouldn't give up hope. "Now, my dear, I should like to have a few words with Aunt Augusta, if you will excuse us."

"Well, nephew," Lady Moberly began, as soon as they were alone. "Are you going to tell me how my sister came to change her mind?"

"No. It's a matter between my mother and myself. I want to thank you for your assistance and I shan't impose on you for much longer. I doubt if it will be very long before my guardianship is approved by the court."

His aunt appeared put out. She wouldn't, of course, wish to lose her ability to send him her clothing bills.

"Yours is still a bachelor household. I do not feel it a suitable residence for Esther until you are wed."

"I agree, Aunt. I hope my marriage will take place soon."

"I hadn't thought things had progressed so far," she said. "Which young lady has caught your fancy?"

"Not anybody you know."

The feathers ornamenting her turban quivered. "If I don't know her she must not *be* anybody."

Cain gave a faint smile. "The lady in question might argue with your phrasing. I certainly do. But in essence you are correct. My bride-to-be is not a member of the *ton*, which is why I must, again, ask for your help."

"Are you intending to bestow my sister's title on one of your light-skirts?"

"I have a proposition for you. I shall continue to pay Esther's dressmaking bills without question. In return you will, just for a start, speak of my future wife with respect."

It was close to noon when Cain wearily entered his own house. After nearly two weeks of unremitting travel and a session of hard negotiation with Lady Moberley, he was ready for an hour or two in his library with his feet up. His new butler handed him a note from Juliana. He very much hoped the contents wouldn't require him to get back in his carriage and cross southern England again.

"My lord." The letter began formally. "Now that your responsibilities preclude you taking an interest in bibliophilia, I feel it is in both our interests to resign from representing you at the Tarleton auction."

What the devil? He skimmed the rest quickly, two carefully constructed pages in the same vein, with one clear meaning.

The foolish woman had taken him seriously when he'd complained about the expense of clothing Esther and his aunt and joked that he might not be able to afford the Burgundy manuscript. Dear girl, so clever in some ways and so naïve in others. She truly had no idea how rich a rich marquis could be.

Thrown over, by God. He'd see about that. It looked like he was going to have to get in a carriage after all, but at least the trip would be a brief one.

Then he noticed the postscript. "In case you remain interested, the Burgundy Hours should come up for sale at about four o'clock on Wednesday."

Cain yelled for his butler. "I want the catalogue of the Tarleton sale and I want it now, wherever you've hidden it. And summon the town coach."

The auction room was as crowded as a dockside brothel offering free samples. Forget any chance of finding a seat. Cain was lucky to be able to infiltrate the frenzied bibliomaniacs and find a spot against the wall at the side. He looked over the occupants of the seats, searching for one small woman.

"Cain!" Tarquin Compton's languid tones were threaded with excitement. "The Caxtons are exceeding the Roxburghe prices!" He and Iverley were also standing, separated from him by three or four other men.

Cain didn't give a damn about the Caxtons. "Can you see Mrs. Merton?" he asked, almost yelling.

"In the middle," Tarquin replied, pointing.

"She's bidding for Henry Tarleton," Iverley added.

And there she was, right in the center of the action. She raised her hand to buy a hideous book for that tanned Adonis.

There was no getting near her, without trampling over the heads and shoulders of a dozen men who filled the benches between Juliana and him. It might come to that, if he couldn't get her attention. He stared at her, willing her to turn in his direction. She was talking to Tarleton, exchanging congratulations on his purchase, no doubt. Really, he'd like to wring her neck.

Then he saw her startle, eyes popping. He followed the direction of her gaze and recognized the volume at once. Or rather the cover. A much shabbier version of the same binding resided on the table in Juliana's bedroom. His fingers almost ripped out the pages of the catalogue in his haste to find the description of the lot.

"Iverley," he called. "Do you know anything about that binding?"

"Combe arms. Family of the Earls of Melkbury."

Combe. The name of the woman who had sold a collection of books to Joseph Merton just before his death. And who had, conveniently, died the same day.

"Any idea where Tarleton acquired it?"

"Might have belonged to his wife. She was a Combe."

Oblivious to the outrage of the men he pummeled en route, Cain pushed his way to the side of his two friends.

"Tarquin, Sebastian," he said. "I need your help."

"If I'm longer than I expect," he said five minutes later as he prepared to fight his way out of the room, "don't allow Mrs. Merton to leave."

The Shakespeares came up next, first the four folios, sold as a set, then the quartos individually. For Juliana's plan to work, Sir Henry had to spend a lot of money on them, more than any of these books had ever fetched before. Then he'd have only a small sum left for the Burgundy Hours and Cain would be able to buy it.

As for her own interest in the Shakespeares, she'd sacrificed it, even her mother's *Romeo and Juliet*. The thought of losing the book brought a lump to her throat. She consoled herself with the thought that she'd likely not be able to afford it anyway. There was a lot of serious money pursuing the Bard of Avon today.

By contrast, for the Burgundy manuscript Tarleton and Cain were the only contenders whose desire was as deep as their pockets.

Cain was there. He'd returned to London in time. She'd caught a glimpse of him earlier, but lost him among the mob packed into the airless room. He would, after all, get to stick his hand in the air and buy it, just as he'd suggested at their first meeting.

The memory made Juliana want to weep.

The auctioneer called the lot number for the four Shakespeare folios. Seeing no reason to be coy, Juliana sought his eye at once and entered the bidding at the beginning. She announced to the assembly that she meant business. She never once looked away as the price ascended in rapid increments.

"Three hundred," the auctioneer said finally. The room was so quiet you could have heard a mouse cross it, assuming the mouse could find floor space. The hammer fell.

Sir Henry looked a little queasy. No one had ever paid more than a hundred for the First Folio, which generally sold for more than the other three put together.

"Worth every penny," Juliana said bracingly. "Did you see who was underbidding?"

"I'm not sure, but I think it may have been Tarquin Compton."

"We can beat him every time," she said. "He only has five thousand a year. Now for the quartos."

Except that something wasn't right. The prices for the quartos soared to unprecedented, ludicrous heights. Juliana bid bravely but Tarleton hadn't given her carte blanche. When the "bad" *Hamlet* reached fifty pounds, he told her to stop.

"Who is paying such ridiculous sums?" she hissed.

"Compton," Tarleton replied, definitely aggrieved. "You didn't tell me he was interested."

"I beg your pardon, I didn't know."

She guessed what was happening. Tarquin Compton was a friend of Cain's. Her conjecture hardened to certainty when Compton won the *Romeo and Juliet* for seventy-five pounds, one hundred times the sum Juliana's mother had paid all those years ago.

The idiot. The dear fool. He was spending a fortune

on the Shakespeares and she knew it was for her sake. She only hoped she'd misjudged Cain's resources, because Henry Tarleton was going to have lots of money left for the Burgundy Hours.

As the prices rose, shattering all precedent, the mood in the auction room approached hysteria. Undreamed-of sums were changing hands in the pursuit of bibliographic rarities.

The occasion was a triumphant endorsement of the tastes and collecting habits of Sir Thomas Tarleton, her grandfather's hated rival. No one but Juliana cared that much of his collection had been acquired from the Fitterbournes, at a bargain price. She watched as books her grandfather had bought and, at the time, overpaid for, sold for many times more.

The great Burgundy manuscript was the final offering, the climax of the day. A blanket of silence muffled the saleroom chatter as the number was called.

Lot 9382.

Nothing more, just the number. Everyone knew what it meant. And everyone was agog to see if the price would exceed the two thousand, two hundred, and sixty pounds paid at the Roxburghe sale for the famous Valdarfer edition of Boccaccio's *Decameron*. On that occasion Lord Blandford had defeated Lord Spencer in a famous auction duel. Neither man was buying today.

What two new knights would enter the lists?

Cain was nowhere to be seen. Surely he wouldn't miss seeing his family treasure sold? Even if Compton acted for him, Juliana regretted bitterly that it wasn't she. That she wasn't sitting with Cain, arguing with him about his bids and exchanging commentary on their neighbors. She glanced at her client, who looked about the room with an avidity Juliana found repellent. At that moment she almost hated Sir Henry.

A scattering of bids were placed. The price was still in the hundreds and everyone knew these were skirmishers, idlers without a hope of victory who wanted to boast they'd fought for the great book. Juliana remained motionless. She'd decided not to enter the bidding until the auctioneer called one thousand. She was preparing to raise a discreet hand when Sir Henry covered it with his own.

"I'll bid on this one myself," he said.

She was disappointed yet also relieved. If Cain had to lose the manuscript to Tarleton she'd prefer not to strike the killing blow.

Sir Henry raised his hand at one thousand and fifty, and someone else bid eleven hundred. Juliana strained her neck to see who. Iverley had made a symbolic attempt at seven hundred and fifty, then dropped out. Compton was quiescent. Sir Henry reached fifteen fifty before she spotted him.

The picture of nonchalant elegance, he leaned against the wall, one boot braced behind him. His eyes were half closed, and the casual observer might have thought him bored and detached from the proceedings. Juliana knew better. She knew the dazzling blue eyes glinted with mischief behind the hooded lids. The Marquis of Chase was experiencing enjoyment of no small order.

And yet he didn't engage the auctioneer's eye, neither did he raise an arm. Both hands were busy with a large snuffbox. Even at a distance she could tell it was a valuable piece, flashing gold and encrusted with glittering diamonds.

The bidding reached eighteen hundred, eighteen fifty, nineteen. Sir Henry stopped and thought. Juliana wasn't sure of his limit, but she guessed he could manage two thousand pounds. The attention of the room was divided between Sir Henry, to see if he had another bid in him, and a mad search for his opponent, whom no one had identified.

"One thousand, nine hundred pounds," intoned the auctioneer, giving Sir Henry an invitational look.

Tarleton nodded.

"One thousand, nine hundred, and fifty. Two thousand pounds." There was scarcely a pause between the bids but Juliana had been ready and looking. She'd seen the auctioneer aim the fleetest glance in Cain's direction.

Cain hadn't moved. He leaned against the wall, holding his snuffbox. He didn't need her, Juliana thought. He'd set up his signal with the auctioneer and was secretly bidding like a practiced collector. She was proud of him.

Tarleton nodded again. "Two thousand, one hundred pounds."

Could Cain afford to go higher?

"Two thousand, two hundred."

The room was dead silent. Juliana's fists clenched. She willed Sir Henry to stop. The baronet thought about it, seemingly for a lifetime. Then nodded again.

The bubble of tension burst as the Roxburghe record went down and the room erupted in applause. Each succeeding bid was greeted by howls of approval.

The manuscript was Tarleton's at twenty-nine hundred. Surely Cain would stop now. This was a far greater sum than they'd ever discussed. But he remained motionless.

The Marquis of Chase never took snuff.

"Three thousand pounds!" The auctioneer gave up his air of disinterested calm and cried out the incredible sum in a paroxysm of delight.

Sir Henry's shoulders slumped and he shook his head in defeat.

The hammer fell. "Three thousand pounds to Lord Chase!"

And that was the last Juliana saw of Cain as a mob surrounded him, until he was borne out of the room in triumph on the shoulders of a dozen cheering bibliophiles.

Chapter 28

C ain found himself the hero of the hour. He suffered congratulations and backslapping from scores of men, every one of them anxious to make the acquaintance of London's newest collector.

Not a few of them wanted to sell him books. Among the diverse offerings were a series of sixteenth-century French romances, two hundred and fifty English Puritan pamphlets, and a New Testament printed in Glagolitic characters, whatever they were. One enterprising gentlemen went so far as to offer Cain the hand of his daughter in marriage, or rather his choice of three young ladies, each one generously dowered with a selection of duplicate volumes from her father's collection.

Only one young lady interested Cain and he couldn't find her. Drat her for being so short. He'd quite lost her in the crowd. In the end he left the premises, expecting to catch her as she emerged. He didn't think she was in any peril inside the auction rooms, among so many people, but he couldn't risk missing her altogether.

The street was scarcely less crowded, as auction-goers swarmed out and milled about, awaiting their carriages or merely chewing over the events of the afternoon.

"Splendidly done, Cain," Sebastian Iverley called out. "I thought Tarleton would have an apoplexy. Pity he didn't." The lanky collector actually laughed.

Tarquin Compton nodded his approbation. "I'm glad you returned in time for the Hours. It was priceless to see the room go wild trying to find out who was bidding. Did you get what you wanted from Uncle Hugo?"

"I did, and thank you for suggesting I call on him," Cain said, his eyes glued to the door.

"The old boy is the fount of all knowledge when it comes to births, marriages, and deaths. In his next life he should be a copy of the *Morning Post*."

"Have you seen Mrs. Merton?"

"She got into a hackney, not five minutes ago," Tarquin said.

Cain swore. "I told you not to let her leave."

"I didn't know you meant after the auction was over."

"Was she with Tarleton?"

"I don't think Tarleton is best pleased with Mrs. Merton," Sebastian remarked. "He didn't get one half of the books he wanted today."

"That's hardly her fault," Tarquin said. "And at least he'll get all the money once the legal niceties have been concluded. Do you think—"

"For God's sake," Cain interrupted. "Was she with Tarleton?"

"She was alone. Are you going to tell us what this is about?" Tarquin's last question was directed at Cain's back as he ran across the street and jumped into his waiting carriage.

"St. Martin's Lane," he ordered his coachman. "Fast."

He caught her as she paid off her hackney and extracted the key to her door.

"Why in hell didn't you wait for me?" he demanded.

She turned in surprise. "Why would I? I expected you to be angry with me for accepting Sir Henry's offer and bidding against you."

"Oh that. I know why you did it. To make sure I got the Burgundy Hours."

"I thought you were short of money. Clearly I was wrong."

"Yes, my love. Even after today I'm nowhere even close to the poorhouse. But I am touched by your thoughtfulness. Thank you."

"It wasn't just for you," she said with a rueful smile. "Sir Henry would have been an excellent customer in the future. You ruined it by buying all the Shakespeares. Now he's furious with me."

"I thought you'd be happy I bought the quartos for you."

"Thank you," she said primly, "but it would be most improper for me to accept such a gift. And the prices were far too high for me to buy them from you, even my mother's *Romeo and Juliet*."

Cain's inclination was to take her in his arms and tell her not to be a goose. That she could spend whatever she wanted on any book she liked once they were married. But he'd made the mistake in the past of pre-judging Juliana's response to proposals, honorable or otherwise.

Besides, there had been a number of recent devel-opments about which she knew nothing.

"I have some important news for you. Let's go inside."

He dismissed his carriage without giving orders for its return. She unlocked the door leading to the stairs, but instead of taking him up to the flat, she led him through the connecting door into the shop.

Quarto, the canine version, lumbered out to greet her, licking her hand in an adoring fashion, then baring his teeth at Cain as though he were an early dinner.

"Good Quarto," Cain said. "Where are the boys?"

"I sent them to Holborn. They were anxious to see their new home."

"They were not supposed to leave you alone. I'm not happy you went out without them today."

"I came to no harm," she said dismissively, discard-ing her bonnet and flinging it onto the book table at the rear of the room. "What news? What happened with your mother?"

"I know who your father was."

The gloves she'd just removed fell to the floor.

Juliana gaped at him, unable to utter a word. What-ever she'd expected, it wasn't this. "Who? How?" she finally managed.

"I'll answer both questions. It's quite a tale." He in-dicated she take a seat.

She sat with elbows on the table, chin on her fists, watching Cain, who was pacing as much as the cramped space allowed.

"I returned from Markley Chase this morning to find your delightful letter." He flashed a wicked look at her and her stomach turned a somersault.

"The reason for my journey will have to keep. This is more important for the moment. When I received your note I naturally dashed hotfoot to the auction to see why my representative had resigned, without even the courtesy of giving me her reasons." She would have argued but he held up a hand for silence. "Then I noticed the volume of manuscripts and recognized the binding."

Once again Juliana was impressed by Cain's powers of observation. "I noticed too," she said. "It's the same as the one I have upstairs. But in much better condition."

"And what did you think?"

"I wondered who the binder was."

Not the right answer apparently, judging by Cain's expression of exasperated amusement.

"Didn't it occur to you, my dear little bookworm, to wonder why two similarly bound volumes of manuscripts, on the same subject, ended up in two different places?"

"Yes, I did think it odd."

"Iverley told me the coat of arms was that of the Combe family."

"That's what I thought. Perhaps Tarleton bought his volume from Miss Combe. It certainly had more valuable contents than mine."

"Tarleton's wife was a Combe."

"Oh?" This was all very interesting but Juliana didn't see the point.

"As soon as I heard that, everything fell into place. I just needed confirmation. So I went to see Lord Hugo Hartley."

He'd lost her. She threw up her hands in bewilderment.

"Don't you see?" he asked. *Romeo and Juliet* was the clue. The Capulets and the Montagues. Cassandra was Juliet. She fell in love with her enemy's son."

And finally Juliana understood.

"Tarleton," she whispered.

"Lord Hugo told me that Sir Thomas Tarleton's son was named Julian. I'd wager a large sum that he and Cassandra ran away to be married against the wishes of both fathers. You, my dear, are Juliana Cassandra Tarleton, the missing heiress to the Tarleton estate."

"And Sir Henry?"

"Sir Henry has a very good reason to make sure you never prove Julian and Cassandra married."

She fetched the volume of manuscripts and they sat together at the book table, going through each document and examining it minutely. Or rather Juliana did, at times using a magnifying glass to examine any fine print or microscopic script.

Cain kept busy finding the answers to Juliana's questions about his deductions.

"Miss Combe was Lady Tarleton's sister?"

"Lord Hugo wasn't certain, but it seems a fair inference."

"And she was the person who reported that Julian Tarleton had married, thus delaying Sir Henry's inheritance."

"That fact at least should be easy to confirm."

Juliana wrinkled her nose. "If she knew Julian had married, why didn't she tell Sir Thomas?"

"Perhaps she quarreled with him. Everyone else did. Or perhaps Sir Thomas knew but didn't care. Perhaps he hated Fitterbourne so much he preferred to deny the marriage. But I don't think so. Lord Hugo says he loved his son. And he never changed his will."

Cain didn't want to bring up Fitterbourne's attitude to the marriage, the cause of his worst quarrel with Juliana. Yet it lay between them, almost palpable, during a long moment of silence.

"My grandfather must have known," she said at last.

He said nothing, merely gave her shoulders a comforting squeeze.

"It makes sense now," she went on. "He wouldn't do it for money, but I can see him not wanting to share his grandchild with Tarleton. He hated him so much." Cain couldn't believe how dispassionate she sounded. Fitterbourne had deprived her of legitimate birth and two fortunes, and still she didn't condemn him.

"You know," she mused, "a child belongs to his father's family. My grandfather may have wanted to keep Cassandra's daughter for himself. Perhaps that's why he didn't tell anyone."

In Cain's opinion George Fitterbourne had been a selfish old bastard, and if he didn't change the subject he was going to tell her so. Instead, without going into details, he recounted his own discovery that Tarleton had blackmailed his father to gain the Burgundy Hours.

"You've discovered a charming new grandfather for me," Juliana said. Preferring to dwell on Tarleton's crimes rather than face Mr. Fitterbourne's, she was grateful to Cain for allowing her to excuse the latter's conduct.

"I spoke with my mother," Cain said. "She has withdrawn her objection to my being Esther's guardian."

"What? That's wonderful news! Are you reconciled with her?"

"Not entirely," he said. "It's complicated. I'll tell you the whole story another time. How are you getting on with those manuscripts?"

She turned back to the folio and gave a little huff.

"What's that? Did you find something?"

"Quite the opposite. There's something missing here." The individual documents had been mounted onto the blank leaves of the volume. Juliana showed Cain how one item had been removed, leaving only a stub.

"Is it the only one?"

A quick search revealed evidence of several similar removals. She leaned back in her chair and sighed deeply. "Supposing there was evidence of the marriage and it has been removed?"

Cain stood and rubbed her shoulders. She leaned against him gratefully. "You're tired," he said. "What you need is a drink. And food. I don't suppose there is anything in your kitchen? No, of course not. I'll go out and get something. Where is your key?"

"Take the key to the shop door." She showed him where it hung on a hook, just inside the entrance to the back room.

"I'll lock the door behind me. Don't let anyone else in. I won't be long."

He stepped over Quarto, who was lying on the floor in the aisle. "Look after your mistress, Quarto."

The bulldog opened one eye and growled.

"Good dog. That's the idea."

Juliana was tired of reading about tithes, benefices, and preferments. Whoever assembled this volume seemed to have no sense of organization and little discrimination. She couldn't see the rationale for collecting such a dreary miscellany. If this represented the history of the Church of England, she would have to say the Reformation had been a poor idea.

A glass of wine would be more than acceptable and her stomach rumbled at the prospect of dinner. She rubbed her itching eyes, wondering what time it was. Later than she'd realized. The shop was in darkness apart from the narrow pool of light cast by the reading lamp, an oil-fueled contraption designed to focus illumination on a small area. Only the dog's rhythmic breathing disturbed the silence.

There was no need to feel edgy. Accustomed to working in the evenings, she had never come to any harm. Previous break-ins had come in the middle of the night. The door was locked. She had a dog.

True, the dog was fast asleep. But he was a big animal and looked quite alarming when awake. And he lay on the floor in the middle of the passage that led from the front of the shop. Anyone who came in would have to go through Quarto to get to her.

She resisted the urge to huddle next to him on the floor. The comfort of another warm, strong body would be even better, and she wished Cain would hurry back.

Summoning her resolution, she returned to her discouraging task. Perhaps she could get to the end before he returned with dinner.

Her heart practically leaped from her chest at a noise from the direction of the door. Then she heard the key turn in the lock and turned weak with relief.

The doorway was hidden from view by the rows of bookshelves that jutted perpendicular to the wall, so she only heard Cain's stumble. Knowing from experience that the front of the shop would be in darkness, she rose and picked up the lamp.

"Hold on, I'll bring light."

She rounded the table and almost tripped over Quarto, who was awake and on four paws. He looked down the aisle and woofed a happy welcome.

That was odd. Quarto hated Cain.

"There's a good boy," said a familiar voice. "Now sit."

Quarto sat. Juliana stood frozen beside him.

"Such a welcome, my dear. First your delightful dog. And now you, bearing illumination."

Sir Henry Tarleton stepped into view, an unlit lamp in one hand, a key in the other. "Rather a surprise too," he said, approaching steadily. "I expected the place to be empty. The lamplight didn't penetrate to the street. He glanced briefly over his shoulder. "You need to clean your windows."

"Where did you get the key?" Juliana blurted.

"I've had it for months." He pocketed it with a jaunty flourish. "You keep yours in a foolishly accessible spot. It was easy to borrow it for long enough to make a wax impression. Luckily *I* didn't make an impression. You never remembered that I came into the shop once."

"I thought I knew you."

"Once openly, that is. I searched the premises thoroughly in the weeks after your husband died. I didn't know until recently that he'd bought more books from the Combe collection."

Juliana shook her head, trying to think what to do. At least Tarleton hadn't, as she'd initially feared, wrested the key from Cain.

"I have no idea why you are here," she said, praying Cain would return soon.

"Really, my dear? I suppose that's still possible. But I have confidence your clever little brain will soon work it out now you know of the connection between my uncle and Eleanor Combe. Don't bother to deny it. I saw you write in your catalogue this afternoon."

Juliana hadn't realized he'd noticed her reaction to the volume of manuscripts at the auction. He had, she thought ironically, an inflated opinion of her powers of deduction. Without Cain she'd never have seen the significance of the connection.

"Since you're here, I'd like to see any volumes from the Combe collection you have tucked away." Sir Henry's courteous tone, for all the world as though he were a customer making a perfectly regular request for a book, was contradicted by his hand's painful grip on her upper arm. "There must be some I haven't found during my previous . . . visits."

"Why?" she asked, trying not to look at the table where the Combe folio lay open in plain view.

"Eleanor Combe gave your husband the evidence of Julian Tarleton's marriage and I haven't found it so far." He smiled unpleasantly. "Believe me, I've looked."

"She gave Joseph the proof?"

"So she informed me, the crazy old witch."

"You killed her, didn't you?"

"Let's just say I may have hastened her death. She had a weak heart, and who's to say she wouldn't have died that night anyway?"

Juliana shuddered to think what Tarleton might have done to frighten an elderly lady. And he must, of course, have killed Joseph too.

With a knife.

She eyed his clothing, trying to detect a hidden weapon. She was terrified at the thought of facing a blade. With instinctive revulsion she tried to pull away from him and almost dropped the lamp.

"Careful there. You had better put that down. We wouldn't want to set fire to the place." She could see the thought enter his head as she placed the lamp on the table, carefully aiming the light away from the book. "Or perhaps we would. A fire would take care of several loose threads."

One of them being herself, she thought with a shudder. Being burned to death was even more appalling than stabbing. Quarto, alerted to his mistress's distress, actually roused himself from his posture of abject adoration and barked at Tarleton, who put his own unlit lamp down and reached for his pocket.

"Don't touch him," Juliana begged, imagining a blade plunged into the poor bulldog. She had no faith in Quarto's ability to defend himself, or her, against a knife.

"I thought your dog was just a puss," Tarleton said. "I think he'd better be shut away. Put him in the back room and close the door, otherwise at least one of you will be hurt."

She did as he asked, taking her time about it.

"I don't understand," she said, once Quarto was safe in her office. She needed to keep Tarleton talking until Cain returned.

"Come, come, Mrs. Merton. I have more respect for your intelligence than that. You aren't going to pretend you haven't guessed who your father was. My cousin Julian Tarleton and his little *Romeo and Juliet* romance!"

"*You* hid the quarto in my shop."

"When you told me that was your mother's favorite book, I saw the significance at once."

"You stole it and slit open the binding."

"Noticed that did you? I thought I'd mended it quite neatly. Hiding her marriage record in the book was the sort of romantic thing a runaway bride would do. There was nothing there. In this case I was wrong."

Except he hadn't been. He just hadn't found the record.

"Once I knew the book held no evidence, I had

to get rid of it. I decided a little legal trouble would keep you busy, perhaps even send you on a trip to the Antipodes. A midnight visit to the shop, a few words in the ear of that sot Newman, and the trap was laid. Unfortunately you found the book yourself." He shrugged. "Oh well, things don't always work out. I thought it a neat solution to the problem of how to get rid of you."

Visions of blades and flames assaulted her. "How did you even know my parents were married?" she asked desperately.

"I didn't. For most of my life I expected to inherit the baronetcy and the estate after my uncle's death. As soon as I heard the old scoundrel was dying I sold everything and shook the dust of Jamaica from my boots. Then Eleanor Combe fouled things up. Julian had told his aunt about his marriage but after his death she kept quiet."

"Why?" Juliana almost shouted. She was getting sick of hearing this.

"Julian and Cassandra were both dead and she wasn't on speaking terms with Sir Thomas. She never knew of your existence until she received a letter from your husband with the information that his wife had been George Fitterbourne's ward."

Of course. Joseph loved to boast about her connections.

"Miss Combe was an eccentric old recluse but she wasn't stupid. She put two and two together and wrote to the executors."

"That must have been upsetting for you," Juliana said dryly.

"Quite so. Luckily she didn't furnish all the details. As soon as I heard, I traveled to Salisbury and got the truth out of her. Including the fact that she'd summoned your husband from London and given him her record of the details of the marriage. Unfortunately she'd hidden it somewhere. I couldn't find it among the books he took from her, nor among those sent to you later. I've been searching for it ever since. It has, believe me, been an anxious business, expecting any day for you to find the proof yourself and come forward to claim the Tarleton estate."

"You killed Joseph!"

Sir Henry actually had the nerve to bow. And it really came home to her just how dangerous a man he was.

"Once your husband knew of your legitimate birth it could only be a matter of time before the trustees found evidence of the marriage. I'd hoped to avoid it, but you will have to go the same way." He gave her a nasty look. "I regret it less since your advice resulted in my losing the Burgundy manuscript. Is it possible you lied to me when you said Lord Chase wasn't buying? Were you acting in concert with him?"

As if on cue, Juliana heard a sound at the door. Having awaited it eagerly, she had the advantage over Tarleton. In the couple of seconds before he realized someone was entering the shop, she dodged around the table and grabbed hold of one of the chairs, with some mad idea of using it to hit Sir Henry over the head.

"Cain!" she shouted, tugging at the seat. The thing

was wedged between the table and the bookcase on the wall behind it. "Tarleton's here!"

Quick as a wink Sir Henry pulled out a wicked-looking knife and swung around to face the new arrival.

Juliana had seen illustrations of men wielding weapons. She recalled an engraving of Macbeth attempting to grasp the ghostly dagger floating above his head. Nothing had prepared her for the prosaic reality. Tarleton held the weapon in his fist so the blade stood upright, the business edge toward him. Juliana could imagine him plunging the point into her gut and lifting, slitting her open from belly to breast.

Thus, she thought, her stomach churning, must Joseph have died. Was she sending Cain to his death the same way?

Even before Juliana cried out her warning, Cain knew there was trouble when he found the door unlocked. Damn it! He shouldn't have left her alone.

Swiftly he assessed the situation. Tarleton would be out to kill them both: no other outcome would do once he learned of Cain's presence. He'd have to kill Cain first. Then finishing off Juliana would be easy.

Cain considered his options and looked for a weapon. Dropping the food he'd purchased from the bake house, he took hold of the wine bottle by its neck and advanced into the shop to find out what he faced. He was confident of his ability to fight off anything save a loaded pistol at close range. If Tarleton stayed true to form he'd use a knife, and Cain had fought off rougher customers than Sir Henry armed with blades. He only hoped Juliana would have the sense to stay out of the way.

The light was very dim, but in the near darkness he caught the flash of steel in his adversary's hand. With a measured application of force he cracked the bottle on the hard corner of a bookcase.

Even at a moment when all his concentration was focused on the struggle ahead, a corner of his mind registered amusement as Juliana shrieked, "My books!" Trust her to be worried about red wine stains. The dear girl simply couldn't help herself.

He'd done a nice job with the bottle. Not as good as a blade, but it had a sharp edge he could use to parry Tarleton's attack. And he had a few tricks learned in the alleys of London's less salubrious neighborhoods. But underestimating his adversary would be a mistake. Jamaica, he guessed, had a few insalubrious neighborhoods of its own.

He took up a fighting position, feet apart, knees slightly bent, his weight balanced and prepared for an attack. At the other end of the aisle he saw Tarleton settle himself into a similar stance. They waited, assessing the terrain and each other.

Tarleton had the advantage of the better weapon, but the light favored Cain. The lamp on the table, ineffective as it was, cast some illumination on Tarleton, while Cain stood in almost total shadow. Tarleton wouldn't be able to see his movements.

Then Juliana entered the picture, stepping into view with a chair brandished at the not-very-elevated height of her shoulder. She attempted to crash it down onto Tarleton's head, at the very moment Tarleton moved forward out of the light, avoiding the blow.

"Get back and stay back," Cain yelled. "Leave this to me." He couldn't spare her any more attention. Tarleton's concentration had been distracted for a bare second before he moved forward purposefully, his powerful knife pointed squarely at Cain's heart.

Hoping to seize the advantage of the first blow, Cain sprang forward, his left arm raised to ward off the attack, his broken bottle aimed for Tarleton's face. Tarleton parried it easily and the fight was joined in earnest, each seeking a chink in the other's guard.

The broken bottle wouldn't be enough to deal a winning blow. Cain had to disarm his opponent. He brought his legs into play, attempting to bring Tarleton down with a series of kicks to the knees. Finally he landed one, but though it upset Tarleton the kick also disturbed his own balance, and one of the knife thrusts penetrated his guard, striking a glancing blow to the inside of his right arm.

First blood to Tarleton, literally, as carmine stained Cain's sleeve.

But Tarleton was panting and his movements became labored. The kick had hurt. Scarcely feeling his own injury in the excitement of combat, Cain pressed his advantage with another kick. Tarleton continued his thrust and parry but Cain could sense him weakening. He kicked him in the thigh. Then again, higher and harder. Tarleton's knife arm became unsteady and the slashes of the blade less confident. Cain sharpened his focus, seeking the moment he could break through and knock the knife out of his opponent's hand.

And then he became aware of activity beyond Tarleton. Juliana was up to something. Heaven preserve him from women who thought they ought to get involved in fights.

Tarleton could sense it too. Cain read it in his eyes. The man's brain was working, looking for a way of using Juliana to his benefit. He was backing up. If he was allowed to get too close to her, Cain would lose the upper hand. He'd be restrained by the need to protect her from being harmed in the cut and thrust.

Pretending to be bothered by his injury, Cain let down his guard. The feint worked. Tarleton launched himself forward, his knife in gut-slitting position. Cain prepared to use his enemy's own weight to bring him down. What the outcome would have been, he would never know.

Books rained down on Tarleton's head. Cain stepped briskly back as, with a mighty crash, the bookcase at the head of the aisle hit the floor, taking Tarleton down with it.

"Goddamn it, woman!" Cain roared. "I told you to leave it to me."

Juliana stood at the other end of the fallen shelving, chest heaving.

"He had a knife!" she yelled back. "You needed help."

"I was fine. I had a bottle."

She rolled her eyes heavenward. "Don't remind me. You spilled wine all over the history section. The knife looked really dangerous."

"Don't ever, ever, ever interfere in a fight again." He was still shouting, dizzy with relief that it was over and Juliana was unhurt, and more furious than he'd ever been in his life. She looked small and frail. His blood ran cold at the thought that he might not have returned in time to protect her from Tarleton. That he might not have been there at all.

She placed her hands on her hips and jutted her chin forward. "Don't look at me like I *wanted* to be in a fight. I hope I never have to do it again. I hope I never have to see a fight again, or even hear of one. I never want to see a knife again as long I live. Even to cut up my food." Her voice broke and her face crumpled.

In an instant he leaped over the fallen bookcase, without giving a thought to Tarleton, and seized her in her arms.

"Never," he said, still shouting. "Never," he repeated, his voice moderating as she sobbed into his chest. "Never," finally he whispered, "am I going to leave you alone again. I am so sorry. I should have been there to protect you."

"But you were," she said, looking up at him, her eyes big and green and shining with tears. "You came when I needed you. He was going to kill me."

Her voice wobbled and Cain knew her composure hung by a thread. He held her closer and brought his lips against hers, kissing her with increasing fervor between murmured words of comfort and apology.

"It's all right, love. You're safe, love. I'm sorry, love."

As her sobs subsided he thought only of the woman in his arms and how he'd never let her go. But after a minute or two the very silence disturbed him. Although Tarleton hadn't made a sound since he fell, the villain was still there and Cain supposed he'd better see to him.

"We're not alone," he said, reluctantly releasing her. Tarleton's head, face down, protruded from the end of the toppled bookcase. A boot stuck out of the side at an odd angle. Cain felt for the pulse at the baronet's temple and detected nothing.

"Can you help me lift this?" he asked Juliana.

They'd only pivoted the bookcase a couple of feet back toward upright when he saw the pool of blood. Cain tried to recall Tarleton's position as Juliana had crashed down the shelving.

"I think he's dead. He fell on his own knife."

Chapter 29

After many hours of dealing with constables, magistrates, coroners, and lawyers, the seemingly endless list of men who were concerned with the death of Sir Henry Tarleton, Cain returned to St. Martin's Lane where he'd left Juliana that morning. Once she made her statement to the representatives of the Bow Street magistrate's court, she and Quarto had retired to get some sleep. Now, late in the afternoon, she came down in response to his knock.

Fatigued as he was, Cain's spirits rose at the sight of her. She was back in her blacks, minus the cap, God be praised, and her hair knot was its usual teetering disaster. As soon as the door closed he embraced her in the dark passage, happy just to hold her. While not exactly resisting his touch, her response seemed perfunctory and she drew back almost at once.

"You must be tired." She sounded flustered. "Come up and have some tea."

The sight of the cheerless little room fueled Cain's determination to get Juliana out of there at once, if not sooner. A snore in a corner alerted him to the presence of Quarto, who clearly hadn't had enough sleep. Cain knew just how he felt.

"These fellows certainly ask a lot of questions," he said, throwing himself into a chair. "But Tarleton's executors are ready to examine your claim to be Julian's daughter."

"Thank you for helping. I wouldn't have known how to start."

He waved aside her gratitude. "You don't have to thank me. Naturally there isn't anything I won't do for you. I left old Robinson to discuss the details. With the exact date there's a reasonable chance they'll discover the church where the marriage took place. But finding a record among Miss Combe's books would help."

"I haven't been able to bring myself to go down to the shop today and look, but I've been thinking," she said. "I think Miss Combe lost the proof, whatever it was. I think she lied to Sir Henry Tarleton when she said she gave it to Joseph. Why else would Joseph have gone to Fernley?"

Cain leaned back in his chair and considered the theory. "It makes sense," he said. "He would have no reason to ask Frederick Fitterbourne about Cassandra's marriage if Miss Combe had given him the information."

"Exactly. And that's why he bought all these dreadful books from her. Because she thought the document was lost among them somewhere. She was old and sick and couldn't remember where she'd put it."

"Did you sell any of them?"

"That is what I am trying to recall." Juliana sighed and looked discouraged. "Perhaps I did. Suppose I sold the book that contains the record of my parents' marriage?"

"I think people will accept the truth, even without it. Why else would Henry Tarleton have tried to kill you? At the very least they'll know you were Sir Thomas's granddaughter. The coded inscription in the *Romeo and Juliet* proves that. Legally legitimate or not, that's more acceptable than having an unknown father."

"But they won't accept me as the heiress."

"I don't give a damn about the money. We don't need the Tarleton fortune."

"You may not need it," she said. "I would find it quite useful."

"Juliana," he said softly. "You are being deliberately obtuse."

She stood and came around the table to stand next to him. "Don't be a fool, Cain. Even if I am Sir Thomas Tarleton's heir, I'm still not the right wife for you. I'm the widow of a bookseller, a tradesman, and I've lived by trade myself. It would be a ridiculously unequal match. Now that you've resolved your difference with your mother there's nothing to stop you from finding an aristocratic bride. You need someone who can stand next to you as you take your place in the polite world. Help you take your seat in Parliament and work for all the good things you believe in. Someone who can present Esther to society." Her hands clenched into fists at her side and her brow creased ferociously. "You don't need me," she concluded.

"You're quite right," he said. "I don't need you."

Juliana stared at him. He sprawled gracefully in his seat, regarding her with an unreadable expression on his face.

"I don't need you or any other bride. I don't give a damn about taking my place in the *ton*, which consists of a lot of not very interesting people giving not very interesting parties. The last time I looked there were no women in the House of Lords, so I don't think an aristocratic wife is going to be much use there. My aunt can bring out Esther and will be happy to do so as long as I foot the bills for her wardrobe. I don't need to marry at all. I can do exactly as I want."

"I see." She felt a fool. Here she was, making a grand renunciation, and he made it clear he had no intention of marrying her. Of course, the only reason he'd ever proposed was to help him become Esther's guardian.

"And what do you want?" She despised herself for asking.

With the grace she loved to watch, he got to his feet. She was going to miss him horribly. She bent her head to look at the floor. His hands enveloped her fists.

"Unclench them," he said, and his smoky voice had its typical effect on her abdomen. Her hands unfurled and his thumbs massaged her palms. "Look at me."

His eyes burned while his mouth curved in a

tender smile. Mesmerized, she stared at him, hope kindling in her heart.

"I'll tell you what I want," he said. "I want to live with you for the rest of my life. I want to make love to you and then lie in bed and make silly jokes. I want to sleep with you every night and wake up and make love to you again, especially in the morning. I want to buy books with you and argue over them and not listen to you when you tell me I'm paying too much. I want to dress you in laces and silks in gorgeous colors, then remove them one garment at a time until I can see every freckle. I want you to stop my sister from dressing in purple. I want you to stand at my side as I return to my home and try to make peace with my mother. I want you to be the new Marchioness of Chase and the mother of the next marquis."

Then, just as he'd done the first time he proposed, he dropped down onto one knee. "My dearest Juliana. Will you do me the great honor of being my bride? Not because I need a bride or you need a fortune, but because I want to marry you."

She opened her mouth without any confidence in her ability to articulate a word.

"Don't say anything until I finish. There is only one reason I will accept no as an answer. That is if you don't love me as I love you."

Somehow, despite the elation that threatened to paralyze her vocal cords, she managed to speak. "You fool, Cain. Of course I love you. How could I not?"

"I can think of dozens of reasons, but I'm certainly not going to tell you what they are. Is this a yes?"

She bent down to throw her arms around his neck and managed to tumble them both to the floor. "Yes, yes, yes. I will marry you."

A heated kiss that might have turned into something more was interrupted by Quarto, who objected to sharing the floor of the small room with two rolling human bodies.

"Am I supposed to house that dog for the rest of its life?" Cain demanded.

"You gave him to me," Juliana reminded him, climbing off her betrothed husband to escape a butting bulldog head.

Cain helped her to her feet. "Not only is he the most inept watchdog ever born, he has no idea of his proper place."

Quarto sat up on his haunches, panting, drool dripping from his huge pink tongue. "He's a big, beautiful boy, and wherever I go, he goes too," Juliana said fondly.

Quarto, possessing some sense of self-preservation, refrained for once from growling at Cain. He was also saved from being sold into canine slavery as a ratter when his mistress paid him no further attention. Instead Juliana happily complied when Cain returned to his chair and pulled her onto his lap.

"Let's be married tomorrow," he said, nuzzling her neck. "You don't want to stay here any longer than you have to."

"Very well," she said. She sounded a little distracted.

"I like it when you don't argue with my suggestions. I trust this is how it will always be."

"Don't count on it. I happen to be in an unusually agreeable mood today." She held his face between her hands and kissed him on the lips. His heart thumped. "I love you," she said.

"When did you know you loved me?" he asked, a few minutes later.

"In the vestry at Greatfield, when I found Amnon in the Bible and realized what a terrible injustice you'd suffered."

"It took you so long? I knew weeks earlier."

"Oh really?"

"When I saw you in black velvet in the Berrys' drawing room with that tiresome ass Gilbert looking down your dress. I wanted to tear him away, tell him, 'She's mine,' and throw him out of the window."

Juliana laughed. "That's almost what you did. Poor Mr. Gilbert. He was here earlier. The news spread around town in a matter of hours. He came to apologize for introducing me to Henry Tarleton."

"And so he should."

"I told Mr. Gilbert about the Combe books I had in my back room and he mentioned them to Sir Henry. That's why he started breaking into the shop again to search for the marriage proof. Mr. Gilbert feels terrible about exposing me to danger. And of course he was very excited to hear that I am the granddaughter of two such important book collectors." She lowered her chin and gave Cain a sly look through her lashes. "Mr. Gilbert is a single gentleman."

"And he can stay that way as far as you are concerned. I don't want him anywhere near you."

Cain sounded jealous. Surely he couldn't possibly believe that Juliana, or any other woman for that matter, could prefer Gilbert to him? And yet only a few weeks ago Gilbert had seemed a paragon of solidity, a bookman of discrimination and impeccable repute, a desirable contrast to the wild, unreliable, frivolous marquis. Beneath his confident manner, Cain wasn't an arrogant man; neither did he possess exaggerated notions of his own worth. Quite the contrary. It was cruel to tease him.

"I'm not interested in Matthew Gilbert. I just became betrothed to the best man I ever met."

"I could have sworn you agreed to marry *me*."

"Foolish! You *are* the best man." It wasn't easy for Juliana to articulate her feelings, but for Cain's sake she made herself find the words. Leaning back, she held his shoulders, engaged him eye to eye. "You are the kindest person I know," she said. "You protect women. You love your sister, your friends, even your mother. You possess uncommon intelligence and powers of perception. Without them I would never have found out about my parents. You are clever and witty and the best of companions. You have only to look at me with your beautiful eyes to make me want to make love to you."

During her recitation she saw a range of emotions in his face: uncertainty, turning into acceptance and gratitude, giving way to happiness, amusement, and a very Cain-like unholy glee.

"And, most importantly," she concluded, "you

show promise of becoming an exceptional judge of a book."

"I'm glad to pass the most important test, but could we go backward a step. I am looking at you now."

He was indeed. And her bones were melting. She climbed off his lap and took his hand.

"I have a bedroom," she said.

Chapter 30

Although eleven o'clock had long passed, Lord Chase found his wife in the library, surrounded by the crates that had been packed by his servants in St. Martin's Lane and carted around to Berkeley Square. She perched on the library steps, volumes piled on a large table in front of her. As usual she had a book in her hands. Also as usual her hair was falling down. Not as usual, she wore a clinging red silk evening gown that left a good portion of her upper anatomy uncovered and the remainder outlined in loving detail. His heart hitched at the sight. Dining with his fellow book collectors was enjoyable, but Cain hadn't changed so much that he no longer preferred the company of women. One woman in particular.

"Sorry I'm late," he said, bending to kiss away a smut of dust on her nose.

"What was decided?"

He removed the book from her grasp, set it aside, and drew her to her feet. "After some discussion it was agreed to call our association the Burgundy Club, to honor the outrageous sum I had to pay to buy back my own property."

"Sounds like a drinking club."

"I have no doubt the membership will crack a bottle or two on occasion."

Juliana gave a derisive snort. "What else?"

"Iverley wouldn't relent. The Burgundy Club will be for men only." He placed his hands on her shoulders and stroked her collarbone with his thumbs.

"Why am I not surprised?" Juliana appeared less upset than Cain expected at the news that the society of bibliophiles, founded to celebrate the Tarleton auction, would be an all-male affair. Perhaps because he was doing his best to soften the blow by kissing his way from her chin to her breast. She arched her neck to give him better access.

"I'll resign," he said, running his lips along the edge of the minuscule bodice, the pale skin softer than the adjacent silk cloth.

"Of course you mustn't," she said a little breathlessly. "If you want to dine once a month with a group of foolish men, I'm not going to object. I can assure you that Esther and I are capable of amusing ourselves. Oh!" The last word was a reaction to his tongue dipping beneath the cloth and finding a tightly peaked nipple.

"You are a prince among women and Iverley's a fool." The man had no idea how fine it was to have a wife. Of course Cain had the best wife in the world. He pitied all the men who weren't married to Juliana.

His right hand descended from the delicate sculpture of her shoulder over the warm swell of her breast and traced the arc of waist and hip. No other woman, he thought, was so perfectly formed.

He found the junction of her thighs and pressed suggestively, drawing a gasp of approval. No other woman was so perfectly responsive.

"Don't worry about me," she whispered as she pushed against his hand, "I'll take care of Iverley. I have a plan."

No other woman was so perfectly ruthless.

For a fleeting moment he wondered if he should ask what hideous revenge she had in store for Sebastian Iverley, who, for all his faults, had become a friend. Then she wriggled her hips and inserted her clever little hands under his brocade waistcoat. His stomach muscles tightened and he lost all interest in his fellow men.

Lifting her by the waist he perched her on the edge of the sturdy table of *pietro duro*, picked up in Italy by some Godfrey forebear. The marble surface was chilly but, he knew from recent experience, they'd soon warm it up. One reason she hadn't yet sorted through all the books was that he kept diverting her.

"New gown?" he asked.

"I bought it to match your carriage."

It slithered up her legs very easily, revealing silk stockings, matching red garters, and an agreeable absence of other undergarments. He liked the dress too.

"I stopped in Conduit Street."

"You know you don't have to buy your clothes from Mrs. Timms anymore." He slid a hand between her thighs and found her hot and ready.

"Her garments always have such an interesting provenance. I daresay you'll be able to tell me who likes to dress his mistresses in red."

"I'm a reformed man."

"It's only been a week," she pointed out. "Oh! That feels good."

She stopped asking questions, thank God, and started to work on his buttons. But she kept emitting little appreciative sounds at his caresses, her eyes closed, and she made a pitifully slow job of it.

He ignored her protest at the removal of his hand and concentrated on the fastening of his trousers. She fell backward till she lay on the table, next to a pile of books, propped on her elbows and giving him the come-hitherest look he'd ever seen. Only too ready to come hither with a vengeance, he'd never know why, at that particular moment, the title of a book should have distracted him.

In later years he'd say it proved he'd become infected with bibliomania. Presented with a choice between his semi-naked wife and two volumes bound in dark blue morocco, for just a fraction of a second Cain's attention fixed on the books. And that was enough.

"What?" Juliana sputtered, not at all happy to find herself abandoned.

Cain held a volume in each hand and frowned at the matching red spine labels. "Does this book always come in two volumes?" he asked.

Juliana struggled upright and slid to the floor.

"What have I created?" she cried. "When did you start caring about such things?"

He handed her a volume and opened the other. She looked at the spine. *Selected Sermons of the Northern Bishops*, Vol. II.

"What does it matter how many volumes of this incredibly dull book were published?" she asked, then realized. "Oh! This must be a Combe book. I don't ever remember seeing it. It must have been mis-shelved months ago. I've just been unpacking a crate full of English topography."

"My mother was reading this book."

"It looks very boring.

"Her copy was thin, and only one volume."

Juliana opened volume two and turned a few pages. "It's extra-illustrated," she said. Her heart began to race.

"What does that mean?"

"It's a fairly new fashion," she explained. "A collector assembles material relating to the subject of a work. Engravings, portraits, letters, and documents. Then a binder makes a special, unique copy of the book, inserting the extra items. It's very popular with titles like Southey's *Life of Nelson*. A lot of dreary bishops seem like unlikely candidates for such treatment. But Miss Combe did have this fascination with church history."

Cain needed no further elucidation. Each of them began to leaf through his respective volume of the sermons.

"There are documents here that must have been removed from the big folio volume," Juliana said.

"Here's a letter from the Bishop of Durham about the appointment of a deacon. Fascinating."

"A marriage license issued by the Bishop of St. Asaph!" At once Cain was at her shoulder. "No, it's not them. Some other couple. Keep looking."

She found it near the end of her volume: a record of the marriage of Julian Tarleton and Cassandra Fitterbourne on the 27th of March, 1795, at the Church of St. Cuthbert, Liverpool. The signature, attesting to the ceremony, was that of the performing minister, the Reverend Samuel Morland, who, according to a note added by Miss Combe, had the following year been appointed Bishop of Lancaster.

"They really were married," she said. Until this moment she hadn't truly believed it.

She looked at Cain, who regarded her with an expression of aching tenderness. His joy was all for her, for her happiness in discovering the final truth about her family. Wordless, he held out a hand for hers. Her heart swelled. Compared to her supreme good fortune in finding Cain the fact that she was no longer *filia nullius* seemed a relatively unimportant detail.

"You're as legitimate as I am," he said. "Not that I care, but I know what it means to you. Rich too." He grinned. "Not as rich as I am."

"It'll be better for Esther."

"Much better. You can bring her out next year and I can stop paying for Aunt Augusta's clothes."

"And better for our children." She and Cain hadn't discussed offspring since their marriage, but given the regular pursuit of certain activities, their appearance seemed likely. She gave him a smoldering look, then cast a longing sideways glance at the table.

Instead of taking the hint he kept hold of her hand and pulled her toward the door.

"Where are we going?"

"To bed."

"Why do we have to wait until we get upstairs?"

"Because, Lady Chase, you have just become entirely respectable. I've never made love to an entirely respectable woman, but I'm told it needs to be done in a bed."

"Always?" she groused.

He stopped and turned, framing her face in his hands, his irresistible smile slashing his cheeks. His eyes were oceans of humor and love, his voice a sensual fog that sent shivers through her.

"Don't worry, my love. I may be happily domesticated but I can safely promise I'll never be respectable."

Author's Note

I n 1809, Thomas Frognall Dibdin published *Bibliomania, or Book Madness*. Described as a bibliographical romance, the work is a semi-fictional conceit both celebrating and deploring the obsessive acquisition of books. I don't know of any collectors who committed the crimes of my deceased duo, Tarleton and Fitterbourne, but there were a few driven to financial ruin.

The Regency was a great era for book collecting. My Tarleton auction was inspired by the sale of the Duke of Roxburghe's library in 1812. Prices at the Roxburghe sale reached previously unheard of levels. The record price for the Boccaccio, for which the Marquis of Blandford outbid Earl Spencer, wasn't in reality broken until 1884. In fact Blandford, himself a sufferer from bibliomania, had to sell his library in 1819. Spencer won the Boccaccio this time, paying less than half the Roxburghe price. (To get Spencer out of the bidding at the Tarleton sale, I have him in negotiation to buy Blandford's books. For the record, the collection went to auction.)

I enjoyed choosing and inventing books for Sir

Thomas Tarleton's collection. The Burgundy Hours
are of course inspired by the famous manuscript, the
Très Riches Heures of the Duc de Berri. I found the plays
with suggestive titles listed in the Roxburghe catalogue. The Shakespeare editions mentioned all exist.
The division of Shakespeare quartos into "good" and
"bad" didn't happen until the early twentieth century,
but I couldn't resist the dog. So Juliana is ahead of her
time in judging these early texts. Aretino, I discovered, became almost a generic name for pornography
in the eighteenth century. A lot of dirty books published under his name bore little resemblance to the
Italian original. I took my quotation from one of his
French imitators.

The one-year anniversary of the duke's sale was
marked by the formation of the Roxburghe Club,
which remains, to this day, England's foremost society
of bibliophiles. My collectors form the Burgundy Club,
and in my next book Sebastian Iverley, who refuses to
admit female members, will get his comeuppance and
fall in love.

Lastly, I'd like to apologize to my erstwhile em-
ployer, Sotheby's, for suggesting that, back in 1819,
they might have had a security problem.

Miranda

Unforgettable, enthralling love stories,
sparkling with passion and adventure
from Romance's bestselling authors

A V O N

Thanks for the Memories

CECELIA AHERN

978-0-06-170624-0

kitchen chinese

978-0-06-177127-9

marian keyes

this charming man

978-0-06-112404-4

978-0-06-157826-7

Tainted

978-0-06-185337-1

A Second Helping

978-0-06-154781-2

At Avon Books, we know your passion for romance—once you finish one of our novels, you find yourself wanting more.

May we tempt you with . . .

- **Excerpts** from our upcoming releases.

- Entertaining **extras**, including authors' personal photo albums and book lists.

- Behind-the-scenes **scoop** on your favorite characters and series.

- **Sweepstakes** for the chance to win free books, romantic getaways, and other fun prizes.

- Writing **tips** from our authors and editors.

- **Blog** with our authors and find out why they love to write romance.

- **Exclusive content** that's not contained within the pages of our novels.

Join us at
www.avonbooks.com

AVON

An Imprint of HarperCollins*Publishers*
www.avonromance.com